THE BURNING GEM

A SOUL CATCHER NOVEL

DON SAWYER

CASTLE BRIDGE MEDIA
DENVER, COLORADO, USA

CASTLE BRIDGE MEDIA
Denver, Colorado

Cover photo by The Girl With the Red Hat/Unsplash,
Marek Piwnicki/Unsplash, Mafujur Rahman/Unsplash.
These photos have been modified.

This book is a work of fiction. Names, characters, business, events, and incidents are the products of the author's imaginations. Any resemblance to actual persons, living or dead or actual events is purely coincidental.

THE BURNING GEM
©2024 Don Sawyer

ISBN: 979-8-9895934-3-9

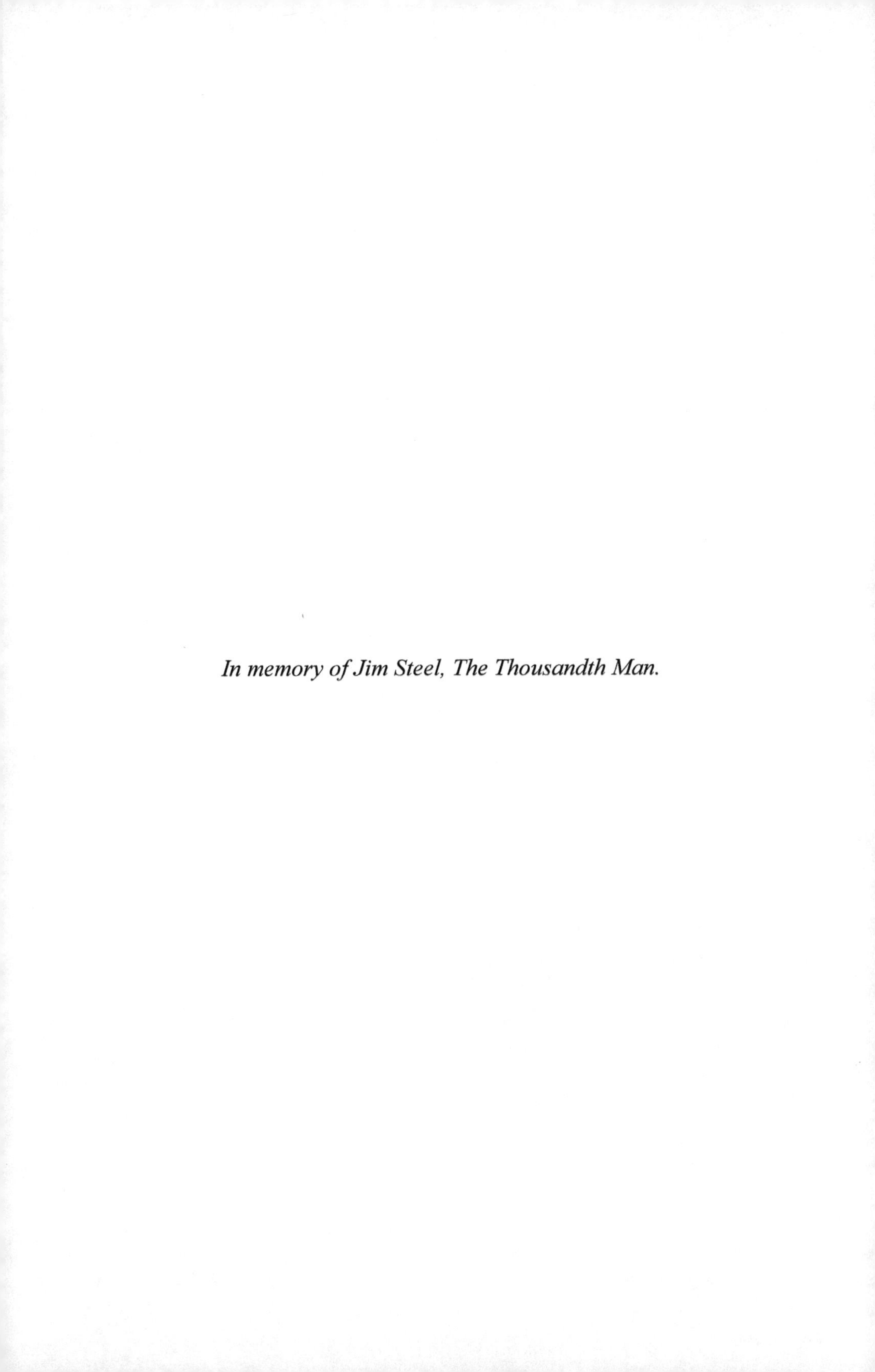

In memory of Jim Steel, The Thousandth Man.

Chapter 1

DEANGELO SIGHED AND EMERGED FROM under the cloth, still holding the shutter bulb in his hand. Souls could not be captured when clients wiggled like restless toddlers. If she would just sit still…

"Madam, we have been through this," he said, trying to temper his annoyance. "You are not having your picture taken. You are having your soul crystalized." He took a deep breath, the dark suspenders that ran over his shoulders stretching slightly across his chest, and shook his head slightly in frustration.

He checked his equipment again to give her a moment to compose herself and considered how it might appear to her. From a distance, the machine next to him looked like an early wood box camera, maybe a Scovill Adams, with a black accordion lens extension that folded up into a neat, oak case. But now, it was fully expanded, the brass lens housing protruding from the front wood panel and the whole unit sitting on a sturdy tripod. The shutter bulb cord ran from the lens back into his hand. Antiquated yes, but then so was he.

Looking at her again, he took her in, wondering what led her here—not that he particularly cared; they came and went. He did his job and moved on. There was nothing particularly striking about the woman, apart, perhaps, from her bright red hair, which tumbled in long, curling ringlets down her back. Her thin white face was rather plain except for light brown freckles on her small nose. Scarlet red lipstick—clearly chosen to imitate the color of her hair—emphasized full red lips.

And her eyes, which were a surprising emerald green.

"Please, madam," he continued, his voice betraying his exasperation. "You must hold perfectly still for a full thirty seconds!"

She shifted uncomfortably in her metal lawn chair, smoothed down the front of the long white dress she wore, and brushed her hair back. "I'm sorry," she apologized. "And please call me Barbara. But thirty seconds is a long time to stay perfectly still." She scrunched up her nose. "I've had lots of photos taken in studios. They never took this long. At least not the same pose."

He shook his head again, almost imperceptibly. It was not a portrait session—how many times must he explain? Despite his best efforts, sometimes his clients were so trying. Impatient, demanding, stupid. This woman was none of those, just fidgety, but he still found his own patience wearing thin. Perhaps he had been at this too long, catering to celebrities or nouveau riche looking for some sort of identity. Or CEOs of mid-range corporations, arrogant and brusque. But they had the money—who else would pay $50,000 for a gemstone the shape and color of their soul? —and somehow, they sent out the call.

He rubbed his left hand across his eyes. "This will be the fourth attempt. Barbara, yes? Please, try to hold still."

She settled reluctantly into her chair. "It's so hot! Don't you find it warm in those wool trousers?" She looked down at her dress, a lacy affair the man thought made her look like an extra from *Gone with the Wind*, and tugged at the high neckline that was choking her.

He walked to the front of the machine and ducked back under the hood, the bulb held waist high in his left hand. "Yes, Madam. It is warm indeed. Now, are we ready?"

The woman sat up straight and looked directly into the purple lens of the machine. "Barbara," she corrected. "This time I'll hold my breath."

"Good," he replied from under the black cloth. "Then this time we should have no trouble, yes?"

She did not reply.

"So. I will recalibrate the transformer, and when done, I will squeeze the bulb, yes?" Hearing nothing, he continued, "The lens will glow bright red for thirty seconds, and the beams will be projected through your eyes. During that brief period, I will monitor the intake to ensure your soul is fully and accurately encapsulated. And during that time, I cannot be disturbed, and you, you cannot move. And especially, do not blink your eyes. Yes?"

She nodded.

"Madam, do we understand each other?" he demanded from inside the hood. His growing exasperation gave an edge to his voice.

"Oh, sorry. Yes, yes," she said loudly. "I promise."

"Excellent." There was a brief pause. "All right, here we go. One, two, three." She stilled and held her breath.

A metallic click emanated from the machine as DeAngelo squeezed the bulb, and then the lens began to glow, brighter and brighter until a twin beam of red light shot outwards like a laser pointer, directly into the sitting woman's eyes. She started a bit then caught herself and managed to stare unblinking into the lens.

In the darkness under the hood, he peered at a screen that looked like a tiny 1950s TV with small buttons along the bottom of the screen. Signals flooded the screen. Grey strings of light, then black objects that seemed familiar but not, and then some yellow strands. A tiny pink flower bloomed and disappeared, followed by sharp white teeth, and then droplets like red blood that grew into a rose. He frantically turned the knobs, enhancing the yellow, turning down the greys, shunting the rose blossom to one corner, the teeth to another, pulling the black objects downward like they were being sucked off the screen by a vacuum. He pushed the small pink blossom to one side and left the screen a patchwork of black, grey, and red squares. Suddenly, there was another *click*, and the beams disappeared. The tiny screen froze. Then he squeezed the bulb again.

"Excellent!" he exclaimed, throwing the black cowl over the top of the wooden structure.

The woman let out her breath in a whoosh while DeAngelo dropped the bulb and turned his attention back to adjusting the bank of small knobs. The screen above the viewfinder hummed slightly; red, blue, and yellow lights blinked methodically along the bottom of the six-inch glass square. A small leather bag hung underneath the back of the machine where the old glass plates would have been. If the machine had been a camera.

He pulled a white handkerchief out of his shirt pocket, pushed his glasses up into a tangle of grey hair, and wiped beads of sweat from his forehead. He stood up straight, beaming at the woman. "Excellent!" he exclaimed. "Just a few more moments."

The whirring from the glass-walled compartment grew louder. He stepped from behind the hissing machine and peered at the leather bag attached to the underside.

The woman leaned forward, intrigued. "How long before—"

"Before your gem is created and delivered?" DeAngelo hitched up his wool pants with his thumbs and glanced at her. He smiled imperceptibly as her bright green eyes sparkled with anticipation and wonder. "It depends. Sometimes a few seconds, sometimes a few minutes."

"That's odd." She stared at the humming wood box. "Why wouldn't it be the same for everyone?"

He turned back to the machine, bending slightly to monitor the activity on the small screen. "I have no idea." He really did not. He had never been able to see a correlation between the time it took to create the gem and any relevant factor. Gender, age, nationality. No one ever explained it, and he had never cared enough to ask.

"No idea?" Barbara stood from the chair and walked cautiously toward the machine. She leaned forward, peering curiously at the whirring, blinking device. "Didn't you build it?"

DeAngelo turned back to the glowing glass screen. "No, madam. I acquired it under, shall we say unusual circumstances. It is not mine, actually."

She turned toward him, her forehead furrowed in surprise. "If it's not yours, then whose is it?" She unbuttoned the top snap of her dress and spread the collar in relief.

He stood and looked directly into her green eyes, impressed by her curiosity.

"It was leant to me. For a fee. Think of it as a piece of rented equipment, yes?" He could not, would not, begin to explain.

"Well, you certainly seem to know how to use it." She tugged idly at a tress of red hair as she bent further to get a better view of the camera. Suddenly, a brilliant light erupted from underneath the rear of the machine. She stood up in alarm. "What the hell... What was that?"

He stepped to the back of the device, now quiet and looking again like an antique camera. He reached underneath and removed the leather bag, pulling the drawstring tight as he drew it off a brass tube. Something round and about the size of a golf ball was in the bottom of the bag. He turned to the red- haired woman.

"This, madam, is your soul crystalized into a gem. Well, actually, just part of your soul." He paused. "There is no other exactly like it in the world. Would you like to see it?"

"Oh, yes!" she said eagerly.

"Then let us open the bag, yes?" He carried the soft leather pouch to a low patio table, also in white- painted cast iron. He set the bag gently on the table and pulled up a chair. He turned to her, motioning toward the chair. "Please, take a seat and open the pouch."

She sat, her eyes wide with expectation, and picked up the bag. Her hand shook slightly as she pulled open the top of the pouch. She glanced up uncertainly at him for a second, her right hand poised over the pouch. "Just reach in?"

He nodded. "And bring out what is inside."

Barbara slowly, hesitantly, reached into the bag. Inside was a small, smooth sphere, which she carefully pulled into the sunlight. She gasped.

It seemed to be made of clear glass, a perfect ball, like a small Christmas tree ornament. DeAngelo saw her catch her breath as Barbara peered through the outside shell and saw the deep, throbbing ruby red gem burning inside. The stone was flat on one side but perfectly round, with thousands of tiny, shimmering facets, a luminous glowing hemisphere. She turned the globe slowly, studying the stone inside silently from all sides. Though mainly red, a small, iridescent black pearl glowed from the stone's heart. A filigree of yellow and white filaments, like impossibly fine gold and platinum threads, circled the pearl. And at the center a tiny, glittering white diamond.

She stared at the stone for several seconds, maybe minutes. DeAngelo watched carefully. He had seen this scene hundreds of times. It was always moving, but this time something was different. Perhaps it was the stunning, tiny white diamond at the center of the gem, something he had only seen once before.

But it was more than that. The woman's eyes were fixed on the jewel, but her lips parted slightly, and wonder spread across her face.

She is quite beautiful. The thought was as unexpected as it was uncomfortable.

"It is lovely, yes?"

When he spoke, the spell seemed to break. She drew her gaze away from the globe and glanced up at him, shuddering slightly.

"Yes," she quavered. "More beautiful than any jewel I've ever seen." Her eyes returned to the jewel inside the clear ball. "Can I touch it?"

"Of course, madam." He hesitated. "Barbara, I believe?"

She nodded, still gazing at the jewel in front of her. "You don't much like being on a first name basis with your clients, do you? It scares you."

DeAngelo stood and took a step back. He realized his breathing had quickened.

"It is true," he said at last. "Madam, I am here to provide a service. The less you know of me the better. And vice versa."

Barbara glanced up briefly. "If you say so." She turned back to the gem. "Can we remove my gem from the glass now?"

"I will be delighted to remove the glass. But first, I'm afraid, you must pay me the balance of the fee we agreed upon. This you knew when we signed our contract, yes?"

She sat silently staring at her jewel inside its glass case. "Yes. I read the contract closely. This would come under Section 4, paragraph 5: 'Accessing the gem.'"

"Precisely, Madam. I am impressed."

"But it says nothing in the contract about bargaining."

"Madam?"

She sighed deeply. "My husband. He is a lawyer. Contract and real estate law." She hesitated. "He was furious when I told him I had signed a contract to buy a jewel sight unseen." She looked up at him. "To tell you the truth, I could hardly believe it myself. He said you were a charlatan and that

I'd been scammed. He demanded to see the contract. He threatened to freeze my bank account unless I bargained you down to $30,000."

DeAngelo hooked his thumbs through his suspenders and ran them up and down. His professionally cordial expression slipped. He'd been afraid of this. For most of his clients, the fee was of little significance. A small payment for an interesting bauble, like buying an expensive watch or necklace that caught a client's eye. But for some…

"Unfortunately, we are not permitted to bargain. The fee is set. You signed a contract for $50,000, and it would be most unfortunate if you did not pay the full amount."

"Unfortunate? And why would that be?"

"Unfortunate, because if you do not pay the remaining $40,000, I will have to destroy the gem. Section 9, paragraph 12: 'In the event of non-payment.'"

Barbara's gaze swung back to the glowing red stone. "Yes, I know," she said, her fixed on the gem. "I read it. But can you not extend me a discount?" she asked, raising her eyes to the man's face. "It would make it so much easier with David, my husband."

The man rolled his shoulders as if to loosen them. He closed his eyes, took a deep breath, and then opened them again. "This is very awkward," he said. "I am sorry your husband has objected. However, I am not authorized …no, more than that, I am not *allowed* to adjust the price under any circumstances." He thought of Welser, kicked to death in Buenos Aires. Whether it was true or not, he didn't know, but the rumor was he had been killed for trying to lower the price of a gem for a desperate client.

Barbara's green eyes clouded. DeAngelo saw doubt there, but also fear. "$10,000 then? Please?"

He looked directly into Barbara's eyes until she shifted uneasily in her chair. "Madam, would you negotiate with a taxi driver after taking a trip with the fare clearly displayed?"

"Well, I suppose not," she said. "But that is a few dollars. We are talking about thousands."

"Indeed. But back to the taxi driver. You would not bargain about the fare because you know he may not own the car, yes? And that the owner will know from the meter what he received in fares during a day and will expect her share. Is this not true?"

Barbara said nothing, watching him carefully.

"And if the driver does not have the money indicated on the meter, what will the owner do?"

"I don't know. Take what is missing from his share, I guess."

He smiled ever so slightly. "Exactly, madam." He paused. "As I have already explained, I do not own this machine."

The woman glanced by him to the wood and brass instrument behind him.

"The owner of my machine is not, I am afraid, a generous man." *That is an understatement of grand proportions,* DeAngelo thought grimly.

"And," he continued, "if I do not provide the fee the owner expects, which is exactly $50,000..." DeAngelo paused again and straightened the collar of his white shirt. "Let me just say my penalty will be significantly greater than that of our hypothetical taxi driver." His eyes lowered as he recalled pictures of Welser's bloodied face that had been sent to all of the agents. "Significantly," he repeated more softly.

Barbara stared at the odd man. She didn't even know his name, and it sounded like she wasn't going to find out. And it wasn't just because the man was shy. His evasiveness hid fear and sadness. She could feel it. She looked directly into his eyes and realized for the first time how dark they were. Almost black. Like looking into a deep well and not being able to see the bottom. They were as compelling as they were unsettling.

She shuffled her feet nervously. "Look, I hate negotiating with you, I really do." *More and more by the minute.* She felt a growing fascination for the man. But she also knew if she paid the asking price, there would be hell to pay at home. And escaping home was what brought her here in the first place. She had sensed from the day they met that this man and this jewel were somehow the key to her escape from the mistakes of her past and – was it possible? — a future free of the stultification and emptiness that was her life.

But to defy David so brazenly. What would be the price?

"I don't want to do this," she said. "But maybe I cannot have it." She turned back to the gem encased in glass glowing on the white iron table. "Maybe it's not worth it…" she whispered, recognizing the self- doubt that so haunted her.

The man sighed again. "That, madam, is also impossible. You either take the gem or it is smashed, shattered into tiny fragments." He walked over to a cloth satchel sitting by the machine and drew out a small hammer. It was about the size of a tack hammer. At one end was a perfectly round brass head.

The other end was sharpened into a blade. Though tiny, the man struggled to lift the hammer as if it was far heavier than it looked.

The gem maker walked back and held the hammer upright in his right hand. It was too small to be threatening, but for some reason she felt fear surge through her like an electric shock.

"It is impossible to break the gems," the man said. "Except with the sharp end of this hammer." He eyed the woman, his face a little softer. "But we will not require it, yes? Instead, we will use the other end to open the glass case and free the gem when the fee is paid."

Barbara looked at the gem maker defiantly. "You are pressuring me. Go ahead, break it. I don't care." Perhaps a little hardball would work in her favor. She truly wasn't trying to be difficult. He just had no idea what she would face when David got home. She would escape somehow, she had to, but provoking David's wrath now would just make it more difficult. And more dangerous.

But she also knew she could not afford to lose the gem. From the day two weeks ago when the gem maker showed up on her doorstep, saying he understood she was looking for a special piece of jewelry, she had known. The sparkling red hemisphere was more than a stunning gem; it was a passport, a portal.

The gem maker leaned closer toward her, until his face was just inches from hers. Now he spoke in a quiet voice, almost a whisper. "Perhaps not, although I do not believe you." He stared unblinking into her eyes. "But you *should* care. You see, madam, despite your husband's comment, I am not a charlatan, and this is not a joke." He waited for several seconds for this to sink in.

"A portion of your soul is now inside that gem glowing on the table."

He paused again. "When it is smashed, that part of your soul encrystalized is also smashed."

She stared into his black eyes, feeling her pulse quicken. Her left hand drifted slowly to her throat. *Smashed soul. Soul smashing. Soul shattered. Crashed. Crushed.* The words reverberated. *Wasn't that sort of how she felt now?* "And...and what happens then?" she murmured.

The man stood slowly, still looking at her steadily. "As I have told you, I do not fully understand the machine or how it works. I was only trained to operate it, yes? I do not know how it removes a sample of the soul and freezes it in stone. And I do not understand why dreadful things happen to the customer when his or her stone is broken." He was silent for a moment. "I only know that this is true."

Barbara dropped her hand onto the top of the table. "My husband said you would do this, try to frighten me into paying the full amount."

The man took off his glasses and slowly polished them with the handkerchief in his pocket. He spoke as he polished: "Yes, madam, you are quite right. I am trying to frighten you. But not because of what you think."

"David said you would make up dreadful stories about people who have not paid you in the past," she said, "and then use them to scare me into paying the entire fee."

The man sighed deeply and carefully positioned the crook of the temples of his glasses behind his ears. "Then there is no use for me to share the stories. You will only think I am lying, yes?"

"Yes...yes, that's right," she said, but her voice carried no conviction. *He is not lying. He is not a liar.* She knew this as certainly as she knew her husband's anger, as clearly as she knew she was trapped in a tower of bad choices to which she had lost the key.

He shrugged. "Then I won't waste anymore of your time. You have made up your mind, yes?" He picked up the small hammer from the table and held it at his side. He shrugged again. "I am sorry. I truly am."

She studied the man anxiously. His face had fallen; sadness seemed to fill his dark eyes. His shoulders slumped slightly. *He isn't lying. I can't let him go.* She lifted her hand from the table and held it open to him.

"Wait," she said softly. "There's no hurry." Her gaze darted from him to the glowing gem on the table to the hammer. "Maybe you could, uh, entertain me with one or two of your stories?"

DeAngelo shrugged once more. "As you wish. Perhaps we should sit down?" He pulled the chair out for her, and then drew another chair to the table for himself. Barbara sat, perched uneasily on the edge of her seat. She leaned forward slightly over the white patio table toward the gem maker, who sat directly across from her.

"I have been doing this work for..." DeAngelo hesitated. "For a very, very long time. I have created gems for royalty, for oligarchs, for movie stars..." His voice trailed off, as if remembering. "Hundreds of people. Not thousands, you understand. The process is too expensive, too...dubious." In front of him Barbara nodded slightly. "So, my customers have generally been committed. And wealthy, yes?"

She nodded again, now hanging onto each word.

"So. Non-payment has not been a common problem." He paused. "But not unheard of. Five..." He glanced upwards trying to remember. "No, perhaps six times the client has not paid his or her balance." He nodded. "Yes, six times I believe."

"Why, why didn't they pay?" Barbara stammered.

He nodded. "Yes. Different reasons, as I recall. One did not like his stone."

She glanced adoringly at the beautiful stone glowing just a few feet away. "Why? Was it ugly?"

"It was black, you see. A beautiful, deep shimmering black, but black it was."

The woman sat up slightly. "Oh, my. I'm glad mine was not black."

The gem maker smiled slightly. "No, madam. Yours could not be black. You see, the gem captures the color of the soul." He nodded toward the red gem. "Of your soul. Oh, I can make slight adjustments while the transmission is taking place." He raised his eyebrows slightly, a mischievous glint in his jet eyes. "After all, I do want my customers to be happy. So, I try to emphasize the best impulses, the deepest good." He held up both hands helplessly. "But there is only so much I can do. This man's soul was black."

Barbara's breathing was shallow. "What happened after you broke his gem?"

DeAngelo leaned back in his chair, his eyes opaque now, sooty. "It wasn't right away," he began. "I wish it had been. He committed suicide. Shot himself in the right temple, it seems."

Barbara gasped. "Oh, no!"

He nodded. "But not until he had killed so many others..."

There was an awkward silence as the gem maker stared blankly over Barbara's shoulder. Barbara felt the man's bleakness. "I am sorry," she said at last. "For you."

He shifted his gaze and looked back at her. "You said there were others as well..."

"Oh, yes." The man's eyes shifted to Barbara's pallid face and refocused. "I am afraid so..." His voice trailed off.

"Such as?" she prompted.

DeAngelo sighed. "There was one," he began. "So sad. So talented. Such a musician. And his jewel! One of the most magnificent I ever created. It was oval, deep amber, glowing, with yellow and orange flakes burning like miniature tongues of flame. But at its heart, oh, at its heart..." He paused.

"Yes?"

"At its heart was a cluster of tiny black, red and white jewels, so vibrant they almost seemed to sing from the stone." He sighed again. "So sad. Only 27."

Unconsciously, Barbara's grip tightened on the armrest of her chair. "What happened? Didn't he like his stone?"

The man's black eyes clouded. "Oh, yes. Yes. I believe he liked it very much."

"Then what happened?" she asked again.

"I think he just forgot."

"Forgot?" Barbara looked puzzled. "Forgot to pay? So why didn't you just, I don't know, mail him a reminder, or phone him, or something?"

"Oh, I did, I did. I assure you, I did. But he was in London, or Sweden, the Isle of Man. And then his 30 days ran out."

Barbara nodded. "Section 9, Paragraph 27: 'The client has 30 days after the gem's creation to pay in full.'"

The gem maker's eyes widened. "Madam," he said in admiration.

"But the contract says nothing about the consequences of non-payment. What happens if payment is not received within the 30 days?" she asked, her eyes darting to the glass-encased gem. "Do you destroy it? With the hammer?"

"No, madam. Would that it were so simple. I would be more lenient, yes? If it were up to me. But it is not."

"What do you mean? Who is it up to?"

The man's eyes dropped to his hands, lying palms up in his lap. "I do not know. All I know is that if I do not receive payment, and if I do not place a percentage in a very old bank account in Switzerland within 30 days, the gem implodes."

"Implodes?" she asked. "What do you mean?"

He shrugged. "I do not know how else to describe it. You see, if a client is not able to pay immediately, his or her gem is returned to the pouch." He motioned to the soft brown leather bag lying flat on the table. "I then tie the strings in a knot. Not just any knot. A very special knot. A knot only I can untie." His eyes returned to her face. "I then place the bagged gem in a safe." He stopped and leaned back in his chair.

"Go on."

"And I pray each day that the client will send me the money he or she owes."

"And if they don't?"

"Then at midnight of the 30th day after the gem's creation, the bag becomes...the bag is empty."

"Empty? How can that be?"

His lips twisted upwards slightly. "I do not know. All I know is that when I open the safe, the bag is empty. There are no glass shards inside. No shattered gem stone. Nothing. It is empty, yes?"

Barbara was quiet for a long moment. She rubbed the back of her neck with her right hand. "And this man. This man who did not pay. What happened to him?"

"He choked on his own vomit."

"Oh, no!"

The man's eyebrows arched. "Alcohol, barbiturates. They do not mix well, yes?"

"Yes," Barbara said distractedly. "I suppose they don't."

"Perhaps you have heard enough. Or would you like to hear one more story? A very strange one."

Barbara dropped her right hand into her lap. *He is not lying*, she thought once again. *He is telling me the truth.* She nodded for him to go on.

"Have you been to Australia, madam?"

"No."

"It is a fascinating country. A mix between the new and the very, very ancient. Often an uncomfortable fit. There are shades neither can see, just beyond their sight, their imagination. My client was a teacher. Oh, not a teacher such as you are thinking of. No. This man was the son of a duke, and he taught at a very exclusive school. More as a hobby, he told me, since he received a rather handsome remittance. I took him at his word.

"His stone was gorgeous in a drab sort of way. Greys, browns, some moss greens. It fit him, and he loved it instantly."

"So, what happened?"

The gem maker drew his collar farther apart with both hands as if to breathe better. "I warned him," he said, his black eyes now bright, almost angry. "I told him not to sign the contract if he had any doubt he could pay the full fee." He ran his hand through his wavy grey hair. "He seemed insulted that I would even raise the issue. Waved me off like a nattering schoolboy." DeAngelo shook his head. "You can only do so much, yes?"

The woman leaned forward. "But he couldn't pay?"

DeAngelo sighed deeply. "That is correct. He could not pay. I offered to keep the gem for 30 days, but he said it was impossible. He had lied about the remittance. He actually struggled by on his small teacher's salary. He had cashed in what little he had to make the down payment. And now...I think he thought it was something of a joke, something he could shrug off. Apologize and move on. "So," he pointed to the two-headed hammer on the table, "I had no choice, yes?"

Barbara's body trembled, as if she were chilled. But the sun was bright and warm in the clear sky. "Go on," she whispered.

"I heard about it several months later. It seems he took three boys on a hike not far from the school to a strange geological formation, a single hill that rose high above the eucalyptus trees and flat, hot plains. The rock had been part of the Wiradjuri dreamtime. For many thousands of years, young Wiradjuri men went there to complete their initiation into the tribe. The teacher told the headmaster they were going to look for artifacts — spear heads, pottery shards. They would be back for dinner." DeAngelo cocked his head slightly. "One boy turned his ankle and went back to the school." He paused. "The teacher and the other two boys never returned."

Barbara flinched. "Never returned? But what happened to them?"

The man sat back in his chair. "No one knows. They vanished."

"Vanished? But that's impossible! I'm sure they searched for them. They must have found something."

"Nothing," he said. "At first there was suspicion that the boy who survived was involved, but no bodies were ever found, and he was cleared. They just disappeared."

The chill again shook Barbara's body.

Silence settled around them like soft snowflakes. Slowly, Barbara drew her other hand from the table and settled it on top of the other in her lap. She consciously slowed her breathing and peered into the dark eyes of the man sitting in front of her. She noticed that they were not exactly black. They were polished onyx, with barely visible swirls of dark green and blue deep inside.

"I will pay now," she whispered.

The gem maker's bushy eyebrows arched upwards. "Ah? You always intended to pay then?"

She shook her head. "I'm not sure."

He smiled slightly. "I see." His smile spread. "I am relieved. Truly I am." He looked into her eyes. He had seen those eyes before, but they were brown, not green...

"You had me wondering. Worrying. You played your hand very well, very well indeed. "He looked at her with a mixture of amusement and respect. "Perhaps there is more there" — he tapped his chest — "than meets the eye?"

"Perhaps," she replied, a small self-deprecating smile on her red lips. "But I doubt it."

The man nodded, his whole body moving back and forth gently in the chair. "Do not underestimate yourself." He pointed to the red jewel still glowing inside the clear globe. "You see, the camera does not lie, yes? I have seen many, many jewels. Few that glow red like yours. And I have seen one with the white diamond." He stared unblinkingly into her eyes. "Just one."

She felt herself flush in embarrassment and shift her eyes to the blood-red stone, pulsing on the table. She had made a decision. She did not understand what it was exactly or what it meant. But she would have her gem. And though she could not stop David's curses, his hateful invective. Though she couldn't escape his derogation or even his blows, she was not helpless. She could listen to the truth and name the liars.

"But, madam," the gem maker continued. "No matter how beautiful it is, you are seeing the gem through its shell. You are not touching it. You are not feeling it. That, I have learned, is quite another experience." He smiled. "Shall we complete our business and open up the case? Would you like to hold your very beautiful stone?"

Barbara glanced back at the man eagerly. She stood and walked across the patio to a large white leather purse she had left under a flowering cherry when the session had begun. A few pink petals had settled on the purse. She brushed them off and picked up the purse and carried it back to the table.

She pulled the top open and drew out stacks of bills carefully bundled with white paper strips. She piled them next to each other until there was a block of eight identical stacks of bills. She pushed them across the table.

"It's all there," the woman said. "$40,000. You can count it if you like. I got it out of my account before David could freeze it. "

DeAngelo smiled. "I do not think that will be necessary." His voice, never loud, was almost a whisper, gentle and hushed. He turned to the table and put his hand on the small hammer. He slid it across the table to her. "Strike with the round head. Be careful of the sharp end. It is like a razor."

She felt her eyes widen with surprise. "Me?" she stammered. "I am to open it?" DeAngelo shrugged. "Who else? It is your gem, yes?"

"Well, yes, but...but what if I did it wrong. What if I hit it too hard and broke the stone?"

He laughed aloud. "That, madam, is quite impossible. No one can..."

He hesitated and Barbara noticed a shadow cross his eyes. "Really, no one can destroy your gem now. Not me, no one you will ever meet. As matter of fact, now you are the only person who *can* free your stone." He nodded at the hammer and smiled encouragingly. "Go on."

Barbara placed her left hand hesitantly on the leather-bound handle of the hammer. Remembering its heft in the hand of gem maker when he brought it to the table, she braced herself as she lifted it. But it was not heavy. In fact, it seemed to have no weight at all. She stared at the hammer in bewilderment and wonder. She turned to the globe lying on the leather pouch and held the hammer over it uncertainly.

"Go ahead," he whispered. "Just tap it lightly."

Barbara brought the brass head down gently, slowly, and touched the clear shell. She was sure the tap was too delicate, too tentative, and raised the weightless hammer again for another blow. But as she did, the clear ball was gone. She inhaled sharply. The ball had not shattered; there were no shards on the pouch or on the table. It had simply disappeared.

And now, lying on the soft leather pouch was her stone, glowing even more gloriously, from a thousand facets, each like a tiny laser, so brilliant the gem appeared to vibrate, pulse. It seemed to hum slightly, but she couldn't be sure. She lay the hammer down on the table and stared at the jewel, transfixed.

"Pick it up," the man said. She could hear him, but it was as if he were speaking from a great distance. "It is yours. It is you."

Of its own accord, it seemed, her left hand settled slowly around the stone. As her palm covered the gem, heat from the stone spread through her hand and into her arm. Tingling warmth flowed gently upward, through her shoulder, then it crept across her chest and down through her stomach and groin, extending to her legs. She gently gripped the stone and turned her hand over.

The stone rested against her white skin like a tiny heart, throbbing, blazing crimson, then deep rose, crimson, rose. Her breath slowed as she peered at the living thing in her palm. The silver and gold threads swirled around the black pearl at the center of the glowing ruby like a nucleus, and inside that the dazzling candescent white diamond.

The diamond twinkled and light seemed to flow from it through her eyes and into her heart. She didn't know how, but it went to her heart, she was sure of it. She pulled her gaze away from the shimmering gem and looked at the gem maker, who was smiling gently at her, almost tenderly.

"Perhaps," Barbara breathed. "Perhaps you enhanced my soul a bit?"

"Perhaps." The man shrugged. "As I said, I try to make my customers happy. But I can only work with what is there. I create nothing. The machine creates nothing. It simply takes a tiny bit of your soul and makes it corporeal, material." His smile broadened. "Again, perhaps you underestimate yourself, yes?"

She sat back in her chair. Her eyes drifted upward. "Perhaps," she said quietly. "Perhaps I do."

"Ah." The man gave a brief nod delivered with a note of finality. "Well, then, keep your gem close." He pulled a small leather bag from his vest pocket, a miniature of the bag that had caught the gem, and slipped her jewel inside. He slid it gently across the table to her. "It will remind you of what you are. What you can be." He beamed. "It will remind you that you have fire in your soul as well as on your head!"

Barbara's hand flew up to her long red hair unconsciously, and she laughed. "Thank you," she said. "Thank you so much."

He stood, his suspenders dark against his starched white shirt. He brought his right arm across his waist and bowed low. Barbara smiled to herself. From anyone else it would look ridiculous. But from him...

"You are most welcome," he said, straightening. "Now, this has been a most pleasant afternoon. But I really must leave." He was aware as he spoke that he felt genuine regret. He didn't want to leave.

Dread crept up from her stomach. When the man left, what then? The excitement of the day began to wane.

"Must you?" she asked. "Wouldn't you like to stay and have a glass of wine?" She gestured to the sprawling house above them. "I have a very nice Pinot Grigio. It would be lovely on such a warm spring day."

"Indeed it would," the man smiled.

He pulled up the cuffed left sleeve of his white shirt and peered at a gold wristwatch with a worn brown leather band. "But I cannot. I must go." He looked across the table, his eyes steady. "I have to be home tomorrow morning. And to do that I have to catch the 4:00 train."

"Oh, I see," Barbara said, disappointment in her voice.

The man stretched his arm across the table and picked up the empty leather pouch from the table. As he did, Barbara reached out to touch his hand. He yanked it back, his eyes sharp.

"You cannot touch me," he said fiercely.

She drew her hand back in surprise. Shock and confusion washed over her. "I... I'm sorry. I didn't mean to be forward."

DeAngelo stood a few feet away, and his eyes became soft again. "It is nothing," he said. "But I cannot touch you. I am the one who is sorry."

"Is it your religion?" she asked. "Is it because I am a woman?"

He shook his head. "No, no. It is not that. I cannot touch a man either." His deep eyes locked with hers. "Please. Ask no more about this."

Barbara hesitated. "Can I at least know your name then?"

"No, madam, I am afraid you cannot."

Barbara studied the gem maker in silence. It had been an afternoon like no other spent with a man like no other. *Who is this man? This man with no name?*

DeAngelo took the now-empty pouch in his hand and carried it back toward the machine. He placed the pouch in the valise and began breaking down the machine. He pushed the accordion lens in and locked it. Then he carefully unscrewed the camera from the brass plate.

Barbara watched with mounting dread. "I don't want you to go," she said.

"That is kind of you. Truly." He looked back at the woman. Her white dress blended with the furniture. Her pale face was framed in the tumble of red hair and lit by her emerald eyes. "I would like nothing more than to stay."

And somehow, she knew that he meant it. "But you are so lonely," she said softly. "So very lonely."

His head snapped back like she had slapped him. His face crumpled slightly, and for the first time his intense black eyes became unfocused. He said nothing for several long moments. "Perhaps, madam," he said at last. "Perhaps. But I cannot stay. It is getting late." He hurriedly lifted the machine and fit it into the mahogany box. It slid into the red velvet lining like a glove.

Barbara stood up from the patio chair, holding the gem bag tightly in her left hand. She felt the panic in the pit of her stomach. "But how can I contact you? I don't even know where you live, where you work."

She remembered how she had met the jewel maker. Just two weeks ago. It had been 10:00 in the morning. She remembered because the 10:00 news had just begun on the radio while she sat at the breakfast room table drinking coffee. She was still in her nightgown and felt slightly irritated at being disturbed. She had pulled on her robe and walked through the hall to the door. She opened the door to a distinguished, serious man who stood on the brick porch with a leather valise. He looked so much like the Fuller Brush salesman she'd heard about that she nearly laughed. He wore gray wool pants held up by suspenders and a starched collarless shirt.

Her first impulse was to wave him away like a Mormon missionary or magazine subscription seller, but there was something in his eyes that stopped her. Even though his face was that of an average middle- aged man, perhaps 45 or 50, through his rimless glasses his dark eyes seemed old, the oldest eyes she had ever looked into.

That all seemed so long ago. She emptied the gem out of the small leather bag into her palm. "Plus, I need a chain," she said staring deep into the stone. "And a setting."

The man continued to pack up his machine. "That should be no problem. I am sure you have access to the best jewelers in New York, Madam."

She looked up sharply. "Indeed. And not one could make a chain or setting for this." She gazed off to the right. "They make chains of delicate gold links that would break at the first tug. Gold brooches with a bunch of diamonds plunked around the outside. Trinkets, beautiful trinkets for bored housewives and young mistresses." Her eyes turned back to the man in front of her. "I want an unbreakable chain." She felt her eyes burn with unaccustomed ferocity. "I want a setting that fits my stone."

DeAngelo looked up from the camera and regarded the woman in front of him for a long moment. He walked back to the table and sat down in the chair across from her.

"If you wish, I do have access to specialty jewelers. They have done work for my clients in the past. I can guarantee the strength of the chain – it will be made from an unbreakable alloy – and if you describe the setting you would like, I can have your stone set as well. Perhaps you could sketch out something for me?"

Barbara leaned forward over the table. This was her only chance. She did not want to lose him. "My stone must stay with me. And I want to meet the jeweler and speak to him directly about the setting."

He studied her, peering inside her green eyes, which were directed at him unflinchingly. "You are questioning me," she stated. "Measuring me. Why?"

The gem maker's head tilted slightly in surprise. "Yes. I suppose I am. You see, it is not as easy as taking a bus downtown. My jeweler is located in, ah, a very private studio. It is designed to be difficult to get to."

"That doesn't sound like a great business plan," Barbara said, leaning back slightly and dropping her gaze. "He won't get rich that way."

"Actually, it is a woman. And no, I do not think her goal is to get rich. She is a specialist with a very specific clientele." He looked back into Barbara's face. "She only takes clients on referral."

"Like from you?"

"Yes."

She leaned forward, her forearms flat on the white wrought iron tabletop. "Will you refer me?" She asked. "Please."

She felt the man study her intently. She saw him glance at her outstretched arms, which ended in clenched fists. Her bright red hair fell forward, framing her face. She had made a simple request, the "please" a short, blunt entreaty, but she knew her eyes danced imploringly. She wondered if he could sense her emotions, a jumble of feelings even she could not fully name. *Pain*, she thought, *and fear mixed with desperation. And perhaps* – she felt her heart jump – *hope?*

"Madam, I want you to think about this very hard," the man went on. "This jewelry shop I mention is very difficult to find."

"You already said that," Barbara pointed out.

"Yes," he nodded. "And for good reason. I would advise you to meet with a few local jewelers. Perhaps you will find someone who can accommodate your needs." He paused. "It would be far easier."

"I don't want easy," she replied. Then almost in a whisper, "I tried it. It doesn't work."

The gem maker was quiet for a long time. He looked at the woman again. His lips were drawn in a straight line as if he were trying to solve a difficult problem, weighing pros and cons. Occasionally clouds of doubt, or perhaps even fear drifted across his dark eyes. Then there were flashes of something lighter.

Finally, he reached into a small chest pocket in his vest and pulled out a black business card and set it on the table.

"You will need to consider this carefully." He pushed the card across the table. "Put it away for now. You may feel differently in a day or two. You may change your mind." He paused. "Perhaps your situation is not as bad as it seems, no?"

Barbara's eyes narrowed. "I will not feel differently. And unless something dramatic happens, my circumstances will not change in a day or two." She looked back over the hedge. "Or a year or two."

He nodded. "I see. In that case, if you wish to find me, follow the instructions on the card."

Barbara placed her gem carefully on the table, took the card and began to look at it. "Not now, madam," the man said firmly. "Put it in your purse."

Barbara nodded uncertainly and opened her purse. She slipped the card into a side pocket and snapped the purse shut. She looked back into the dark eyes of the gem maker.

She still did not want him to go. "He's having an affair, you know." The gem maker sat back in surprise. "Madam?"

"My husband, David."

He shook his head. "I am sorry. Truly."

Barbara picked up her jewel and put it in the palm of her hand again and studied it quietly. "With his secretary." Her red lips curled slightly in a wry smile. "Rite of passage I suppose." She looked up at the man, whose eyes glowed sympathetically. "Before we were married, I was his secretary." She shook her head. "What an idiot."

"No, madam," he said solemnly. "Whatever you are, it is not an idiot." His face was relaxed now, and his dark eyes radiated something she was unaccustomed to, something that felt like respect. "I have no idea how you have achieved it, but you are a most charming and… unusual woman."

Barbara tilted her head back slightly and looked at him through slightly narrowed eyes. "What's your sign?"

His eyebrows drew together. "Madam?"

"Your sign. Your zodiac sign. A Taurus I would guess."

He frowned slightly. "Yes, I guess I am a Taurus." He tilted his head quizzically. "But surely astrology is a pseudoscience, yes?"

Barbara laughed a genuine laugh from deep inside her. "Not at nine. I was looking for an identity in an empty home. So when I discovered I was an Aries, a fire sign, well, that was exciting, adventurous." She looked at him a little sadly. "Yours, I am afraid, is an earth sign."

"Indeed?" the man asked a small smile on his lips. "And is that so bad?"

"Well," she sighed in mock dismay. "I'm afraid Aries and Tauruses are just not that compatible."

"I am shattered," he said. "So it is astrology that made you different?"

"Hmm. I suspect I was already pretty different. But astrology helped me build an identity. Fire signs, you see, are exciting, mercurial, daring. We know how to have a good time. We're feisty and passionate." She laughed. "Everything I wasn't. But then," she went on, "we are also seekers. And, oh yeah – intuitive. Silly as it seems, it made me want to study people. At first it was to see if I could identify their sign, but then it was just to see the complexity of their lives play out in their voices, hand movements, eyes. The way they walked or sat."

She sat silent for a moment, her eyes straying back to the hedge. "And Aries are always on the hunt for things that light us up, you know? I remember reading this in an astrology book one time: 'The Aries hunter will not settle for something mundane but will push until the flame can burn the brightest.'" She gave him a wan smile. "I think I failed that part."

He looked at her solemnly. "Perhaps not."

They sat quietly for a few moments until the man dropped his gaze to the table. "This has been delightful, madam, but I really must go."

He stood up and walked back to his camera case and snapped a brass hasp over the staple. He reached into his valise and pulled out a tiny silver and gold padlock. He inserted the shackle into the staple on the case and snapped it shut with a loud click and removed the gold key. He reached inside his shirt and drew out a silver chain with a small clasp, opened the clasp, and inserted the tiny key.

The gem maker smiled and bowed low again. "Madam, it has been lovely meeting you." His lips spread in a gentle smile. His eyes flitted up toward the house and he cocked his head. "I believe someone has entered your house. Your husband perhaps?"

Barbara's head snapped around toward the house. Through the dining room windows she could see a figure moving toward the screened porch facing the garden where she sat.

"Barbara!" a man shouted. "Barbara, where are you?"

She stood up and smoothed her dress and looked up at the house. "I'm down here," she called. "On the patio."

"Well, get up here. I've got a game in a half hour!"

She turned back to say goodbye, but the garden was empty.

Chapter 2

"OK, I SAID YOU COULD get your little gem thing." David stood squarely in front of Barbara on the porch that opened onto the patio. "I think it's a total scam, but, as usual, if that's what you want, I give it to you. But I also told you to get him to drop his price." David's face turned red with anger. "Did you even bother to bargain?"

"It wasn't like that, David. I…I tried." Barbara looked into his eyes—jittery, hard eyes. What could she say that would make sense to this man? That the gem maker had the darkest eyes she had ever seen, like deep pools of water? That the gem he made gave her hope for something outside of the stifling tedium of her life? That she knew the real lie and the true liar, and it wasn't the gem maker?

That her magnificent gem was worth every dollar?

"Easy come, easy go, huh?" David said. "Especially when I'm the one who works for it."

"David, you've never worked a day in your life," she blurted. "You inherited every dollar you have, and you know it."

Shock washed across his face. Her words amazed even her. She'd thought them a hundred times, but now, as if she'd become someone else, some other red-haired woman she watched from a distance, she spoke to them. "The only reason you go to the office is Elaine."

"Don't start on Elaine," David said, pointing his forefinger at her.

"She's one of the best legal secretaries in the city."

Barbara raised her eyebrows slightly. "Is she legal? Just barely, I would think."

David recoiled and squinted at her as if he had just found a poisonous snake in his living room. "Barbara, what the hell has gotten into you?"

She inclined her head to one side and smiled coyly. "Me?"

"Yes you!" David shouted. "Whatever it is, I don't like it. Not one bit!"

Barbara's brow furrowed in mock concern. "David, aren't you forgetting your golf game? It's Thursday, so you have a date with Fred and Rodrigo. Every damned Thursday, remember?"

David's face pinched in confusion. He pulled up the sleeve of his blue dress shirt and looked at his watch, a giant gold Rolex he bought himself for his last birthday. A dozen diamonds were arrayed along the outer rim. It had always looked rather effeminate to her.

"It's at 5:00," she said. "Every Wednesday. And with Bernie every Saturday, Philippe and Charlie every Monday." She smiled. "Better hurry along now."

"I'm not done with this, you know," he said, leaning toward her menacingly. "Maybe it's PMS or something," he muttered, "but I want you over it by the time I get back." He turned and started up the hall then turned around and faced her. "You understand?" he snarled.

Fuck you, she thought. "Yes, dear."

David glared at her. He did that a lot. But this time his eyelids flickered slightly, and an emotion Barbara couldn't quite put her finger on flashed briefly in his eyes. Confusion? Uncertainty? Maybe a tinge of fear? That thought made her smile. "Have a good game."

He looked hard at her for a long moment then spun and stalked down the hall.

Barbara stared after him. She felt her heart beating like a bird banging to get out. What had gotten into her?

She looked down at the frills along the neckline and the hem of her dress. What was she thinking? That the session with the jewel maker was a nice little photo op? That she would dress up like Scarlet O'Hara to present the perfect feminine soul? That she would impress her jewel maker with her elegance?

She grabbed her purse and walked along the slate hallway to the stairway that wound upward from the huge, empty foyer. She rested her hand on the polished oak banister and looked at the ornate wood front doors.

Two shafts of sunlight filtered through the pink glass, giving the entry hall a kind of unreal rosy tinge. Why had she never noticed how silly it all was — the cavernous lobby, the huge carved desk against the staircase that no one ever used. The crystal chandelier hanging from the high ceiling that looked like it belonged in Versailles. The cheesy painting of an English aristocrat in his shooting tweeds, aiming a handsome shotgun at a disappearing grouse with his spaniel at his side. *Where did David pick that thing up? Probably one of those antique shops on West 24th that catered to pompous rich lawyers who wouldn't know a Degas from a tiger on velvet.*

She pulled up her hem and walked up the stairs, her high heels catching in the deep white carpeting. She stopped, yanked off one black pump and threw it down the stairs and then pulled off the other and tossed it after its mate. She felt some pleasure as the shoes bounced hollowly in the hall below. God, she hated those things.

Without her shoes she felt lighter, easier. She hooked the purse over her shoulder and danced up the stairs, holding her dress out with both hands, until she got to the landing. Another heavy chandelier hung over the carpeted hallway. Maybe she could set it to fall on David when he came back late from his golf game.

Barbara walked down the hall to their bedroom door that was surrounded with gold-painted molding carved in ivy leaves. She pushed open the door, already unzipping her dress. She folded it down from the waist and stood out from it as if she were shedding a skin, flinging it on the bed. She noticed herself in the mirror on the closet door and paused. She wore low panties and a scratchy red lace bra David had bought for her a few Valentines ago. She reached back and undid the catch and shrugged out of the bra. She raised her hands over her head and shook her hair until it spilled down her shoulders and across her small breasts. She studied herself for several moments. She had forgotten how good she looked. She twirled, admiring her slim waist and long, strong legs. Damn. *Not bad for 32.* She laughed.

She stopped and was quiet for a moment. She had laughed. It occurred to her that she hadn't done that much lately. How long had it been since she had really laughed, laughed for joy instead of out of obligation at some stupid joke David told, or some droll comment, usually about another woman in their social group, by one of his friends' trophy wives?

She stepped closer to the mirror and peered deeply into her own eyes. Was it possible that they were getting greener? Since she had turned sixteen, she had entered "grey" for eye color on her driver's license. But the eyes she stared into certainly were not grey. They were deep jade. She had read once that eyes were not really organs; that they were actually part of the brain, portals into our soul.

Maybe, maybe not. But as she studied her eyes, she realized that David was right. Somehow, for some reason, she was different. The eyes that stared back at her now glittered green and danced. There was life in there.

She turned toward the bed where she had thrown her purse. The jewel. She picked up the purse hurriedly and opened it. She drew out the soft leather case with her gem and gently shook the jewel onto the white bedspread. It tumbled out, still glowing like it was on fire, but deeper now, like an ember. As she picked it up and held it in her palm, a jolt of terror shot through her. Her heart started beating wildly and her left hand with the gem trembled uncontrollably.

What if she lost it? What if it was stolen? If someone grabbed the purse and ran off with it? She could have it set in silver and hang it on a platinum chain, but it could be easily snatched off her neck. No chain was unbreakable by a determined assailant. And she certainly couldn't leave it in the safe, not with David's papers and the two Colt pistols he had been given as the largest donor to some hunting club. He would not have access to her jewel, that was certain.

She didn't want to hide it anyway. She needed to have it near her heart all the time. She needed to know it was there, to feel it. Yes, it had to be set and made into a necklace, but it could not hang on an ordinary chain. The chain for the jewel had to be unbreakable, indestructible. A thief would have to kill her to steal the gem.

Still holding the burning stone, Barbara sat on the bed. She had to find the gem maker, have him take her to the jeweler he mentioned, that was clear now.

She turned the purse upside down and shook its contents onto the bedspread. A bottle of Tylenol tumbled out, lipstick, Kleenex, her red leather wallet, a half-used roll of Tums, a small shower of change. She kept shaking the purse, more frantically until at last, a single black card tumbled out and landed on the wallet. She picked it up eagerly, scanning the black surface for an address, phone number, anything.

But there was nothing — just a solid black shiny surface. She quickly flipped the card over and scanned the other side. Surely there had to be something. But it too was black. She held a solid, coal-black card unblemished by a single letter, number, or rune on either side.

She sat down heavily on the bed, tears of frustration filling her eyes. She had to find him, had to see him again. And this card was her only clue. She stared at it, somehow hoping it would give up some secret, but no matter how hard she gazed, it remained simply what it appeared to be — a business card that was completely black on both sides.

Waves of panic swept through her, and her body shook with sobs. Of what? Anger, certainly, even betrayal, and something else, something that felt a lot like desperation. She pulled the card to her and then grasped the jewel from the bed and drew it to her chest, clutching them both fiercely to her like a lifeline thrown from a passing ship.

She clutched the card and jewel to her naked chest until they hurt. Finally she loosened her fists and held the card and jewel away from her in her open palms. The card. The jewel. She held the jewel between her fingers of her left hand and moved it over the card in her right palm.

The jewel was still glowing vibrant ruby red, translucent, crystalline and luminous, but she could see nothing of the card through the red stone. She stood up and walked to the window. She held the gem, so sunlight flowed through in a light pink beam. Then she brought the card under the stone and held it in the rose light streaming softly from her jewel.

She peered at the card, and she saw it – three lines, all in lower case, burning as if on fire in the middle of the card:

track 61

city hall train

up

Chapter 3

BARBARA LOOKED AROUND GRAND CENTRAL Station, trying to find an information booth. How long had it been since she last took the train? High school? God, what had she been doing for the last 10 years? New York was one hour away with trains running hourly, even more frequently during busy periods.

Why the hell do we always drive? Was it just to show off his Jag? Or maybe it made it easier to spend those long evenings "working" with Elaine.

Barbara clamped her teeth and heard herself actually growl. *What an idiot she I've been.*

She had forgotten how cavernous the station was with the great arched green roof rising 125 feet above her. She craned her head upward and stared at the magnificent giant gold zodiac figures painted on the ceiling, the constellations twinkling gold, and Orion raising his gigantic sword at the muscled Taurus.

She smiled as she recalled discovering her father's astrology books when she was nine and how she fell in love with the romantic mythology.

Barbara felt someone's eyes on her and looked down from the ornate ceiling to see a thin young man with a tiny ponytail and wearing a neat pin stripe suit looking at her and smiling condescendingly.

"He raped Merope, you know," Barbara said to the man. "Orion. But he got his in the end. Died from a sting from Scorpius."

The man's grin faded; he turned and hurried into the throng that milled around them.

A hick. I look like a gawking hick. A suburban bumpkin, sheltered in her luxurious hothouse along with the other indoor plants.

She looked around anxiously. What now? Then she saw an enormous four-faced clock at the far end of the concourse. Of course, the information booth. *I remember now.*

Barbara walked to the circular structure with a dozen glass windows facing out towards the line of commuters queued in front. One line looked somewhat shorter, maybe only six or seven people, so she hurried to the back before someone else got there first.

As she waited, she pulled out the map and notes and tried again to make sense of what she had found. The three words "City Hall Station" had not been as simple as she had first thought. Unless Barbara was looking in the wrong city, a thought that nagged in the back of her head, there was no City Hall Station in New York. There was a Brooklyn Bridge/City Hall station, but that didn't seem right. The man was too precise, too particular to forget the Brooklyn Bridge.

The young woman in front of her moved away from the window and Barbara stood facing a 40-ish man in an MTA uniform.

"What can I do for you, lady," he demanded, working the keys of a computer and staring at the screen while he spoke.

"Well," Barbara began. "Well, I have a question."

"That's what we are here for, lady," the man answered distractedly, his eyes still fixed on the screen.

"Well, is there a City Hall train?"

"Green line, Number 6 train," the man answered automatically.

"No," Barbara began tentatively. "No," she said again, more decisively. "That is the Brooklyn Bridge/City Hall train."

The agent glanced up, slightly annoyed. "That's right, lady."

"But I want the City Hall train. Just City Hall."

The man looked at her curiously. "Well, lady that's going to be real hard."

Barbara's eyebrows drew up. "Why is that?"

"Because no train has stopped there since 1945."

Barbara stood in silence for a moment. "Hey, lady," a man's voice called impatiently from behind her. "Move it along, OK? You're taking all day."

Barbara looked over her shoulder nervously. "Are you sure?"

"Yes, ma'am," the agent replied. "Now, they open the station up once or twice a year for special tours, but you would have to go to the museum to find out more. Can't help you with that."

Barbara felt the annoyance building behind her. The man behind the glass motioned to the side with his head. "That's all I can tell you. But if you're lucky, you can get a glimpse by staying on the Lexington Line number 6 train. It loops around at the old station and stops at Brooklyn Bridge and then heads back uptown."

"Lady!" the voice behind her shouted.

"One more thing," she added hastily. "Where is Track 61?"

The agent eyed her with a combination of annoyance and curiosity. "Are you putting me on? Track 61 is at the bottom of the station. Hasn't been used since Roosevelt."

Barbara glanced over her shoulder at the red face of the man who had yelled at her, deciding not to pursue the issue. She thanked the agent and moved reluctantly to the side. A large woman in a print dress glared at her and bustled up to the window. Barbara stood in the middle of the bedlam that was Grand Central Station and felt her confidence wane as if it were seeping through the soles of her feet into the cold black and white granite floor.

The City Hall station had been closed for more than 70 years. And Track 61 even longer.

Barbara rubbed her eyes wearily. Now what? The agent had said she might catch a glimpse of the station, but she had no idea what good that would do since no train had stopped there for decades.

Did the gem maker laugh at her after he left, finding her hope and desperation amusing? Barbara's lips trembled and tears welled in her eyes. She sighed and looked around the terminal. At the far end she saw the departure board. The next train to New Canaan left in 20 minutes. Twenty minutes more and she'd be home. Such as it was. Sort of like this place. She glanced around the station. Cavernous, peopled but empty. *Let's face it. Like my life.*

Still, the thought nagged at her: Why would the man give her the name of a subway station that was closed? She was halfway across the echoing hall toward the New Canaan platform when she noticed a soaring, arched passageway trimmed in gleaming brass on her left. Crowds of commuters swarmed through the entrance into the station, and she looked at the illuminated black sign above the passage. It read "Subway" with two arrows pointing down the hallway. She hesitated, glancing over at the departure board. Now she only had 10 minutes. If she hurried, she could still make it and get home in time for dinner.

She wasn't aware of making a decision. She simply found herself turning left and walking down the passageway to the subway turnstiles. She edged toward a ticket machine and scanned an illuminated map of red, green, brown, blue, yellow, and tan ribbons in a bewildering tangle of subway lines along with an undecipherable legend. She did manage to find Brooklyn Bridge-City Hall stop, on the Green Line, but the fare display on the screen was almost as confusing. Finally, she punched the Metro 7-Day Pass button. She'd figure out the details later.

She took a deep breath and walked to the stile and slipped in her new Metro Card. She pushed against the bars and walked through. Dinner would have to wait.

Barbara joined the stream of passengers and was relieved to see a sign on the wall that read "Lexington Line." She joined the flow of people toward the right and down a flight of stairs until she found herself standing on a long platform crowded with passengers.

The giant tube yawned black on each side. She looked nervously down at the rails. She noted in particular the third rail that ran parallel to the tracks. She didn't know a lot about subways, but she did know that this rail carried the electricity that ran the trains. She also knew that the slightest contact with the rail would electrocute her instantly. A sign on one of the support beams read:

DON'T BECOME A STATISTIC. LAST YEAR 146 PEOPLE WERE STRUCK BY TRAINS. 47 WERE KILLED.

Barbara moved a little farther away from the platform edge.

The subway train entered the station with a loud whoosh and a blast of air and squealing brakes. The platform was packed, and she began to edge forward as the sliding doors opened and passengers spilled out as those waiting crowded on. It was a madhouse, and Barbara found herself being jostled and shoved aside as the crowd surged toward the open doors.

Fuck this, she thought, surprised at her ire. She brought her elbows to her waist, her fists clenched in front of her, and charged ahead, pivoting her body and threading through the mass of bodies, her arms swinging, just to let people know she was there.

Barbara stood near the front entrance as the train left the Canal Street Station. It was her third trip around the Train 6 circuit that swung in front of the old station, but she had been unable to catch a glimpse of it on the first two trips. A now familiar message rang from the speakers: "This is the last downtown stop on this train. The next stop on this train will be Brooklyn Bridge–City Hall on the uptown platform."

"You must be a subway buff."

Startled, Barbara turned from the window. A tall Black man with a short mustache and beard was smiling at her. He wore a blue hat with an MTA badge pinned to it and a red striped tie and white shirt under his dark blue sweater. His eyes twinkled behind dark-rimmed glasses.

"Oh, sorry," Barbara stammered. "I do have a ticket."

The man laughed. "Oh, I'm sure you do. No, I just noticed that this is the third trip you've made on the turnaround, and usually when that happens, we've got a subway buff on our hands."

Barbara looked at the man uncertainly. "I, I wouldn't say I'm a 'buff' really. I'm just, sort of looking for something."

"Like the old City Hall station?" the man suggested. "Happens all the time. You'd be surprised."

"Yes," Barbara said, relieved. "That's it exactly. I heard it is quite beautiful and that sometimes you can get a glimpse of it from this train as it passes."

"That's true. When they built the station in 1904 it was the showcase for the entire subway system. There's even a brass chandelier, if you can believe that. And most marvelous of all, there is a stained- glass skylight. Breathtaking. That's how you can see the station sometimes — if the sun is bright outside, light leaks through the panels and you can just make out the platform and some of the tiling."

"Oh," Barbara said. "So that's why I haven't spotted it, I guess.

It's night?"

"Yeah. But even on a clear day you can't see much. Sad, really. It's such a wondrous place. See, it's only a half mile from the Brooklyn Bridge stop. That's partially why they closed it. And the Brooklyn Bridge station had more riders."

The man looked at Barbara. "Tell you what. If you come up to the lead car, we have a spotlight. When we go by, I'll turn it on the station so you can get a glimpse. But keep your eyes peeled: we'll only have a few seconds."

"Really?" Barbara said. "You'd do that for me?"

The man laughed again. "I watched you go by two or three times. I thought, 'This is a woman who really wants to see the station,' so unless I do something she could be riding around in circles all night."

Barbara smiled. "That is very kind of you."

"Come on, now," the conductor said. "We have to hurry. Follow me."

The conductor led Barbara through a door at the front and into a small space with a control board sparkling with red and green lights. As the door closed the train picked up speed.

"We're almost there," the man said, grabbing a chrome handle that rotated on the right side of the cubicle. "Get ready."

The agent switched on the light and a bright circle appeared on the cement walls flashing by the window.

"Now!" he said."

Barbara has expected something special, but not this. As the train sped by, the light raked over the old station, briefly showing not one but a dozen arches, each tiled in green and white. Multi-paned skylights wrapped around the tunnel, and as they flashed by, she saw an archway over a set of steps, City Hall spelled out in tile above it. Then it was gone, and she was staring at the blank walls of the subway again.

"Well?" the man asked. "What did you think?"

Barbara was quiet for a moment. "I thought it was exquisite. Elegant. From another time." The man nodded and turned off the searchlight.

"And no trains stop there?" Barbara asked.

"Not for 70 years." He shook his head. "Too bad. Did you notice the curved platform? When the trains got longer, they didn't fit anymore. So the most beautiful station in New York stands empty and unused. Too bad."

The train slowed as it neared the Brooklyn Bridge Station, where it looped around and headed north. "So are you going to have another try at it?" the man asked. "I stay on this train north from Grand Central, so I can't help you with the light."

"No," Barbara said thoughtfully. "But thank you so much. I think I've seen enough." She smiled at the man. "You've been very kind."

The agent opened the door, and they re-entered the subway car. "Nothing, really. Just glad you got a glimpse."

"And the Brooklyn Bridge Station. You said it is only a half mile from the old station?"

"That's right."

"And only the Number six trains actually pass by it?" The conductor raised his eyebrows slightly.

"In case I want to show some friends."

"Yep. Except for the local 6, but it only runs at rush hour."

Barbara nodded her head. "Thank you again," she said. "You've been very helpful."

The man took the bill of his cap and tipped it slightly. "My pleasure."

The train groaned to a stop.

Barbara hesitated, and then reached out her hand tentatively. "Please, one more thing." The man tilted his head.

"Have you heard of Track 61?"

The conductor grinned. "Boy, you know how to pick 'em. Track 61 has been closed since the 1940s."

"Yes, so I've heard. Is there any way to get there?"

The man shook his head. "No, ma'am. No way I've heard of. They just store old trains down there." He shook his head. "Don't even think it'd be all that interesting. Nothing like City Hall."

Barbara smiled again. She felt the train slow as it completed its loop and headed north. "Brooklyn Bridge-City Hall" the voice intoned as they came to a stop. She sat down on one of the hard plastic seats as passengers heading uptown crowded onto the car. The doors wheezed shut and the train rapidly picked up speed. She stared blankly into the darkness and was only vaguely aware of the tunnel slipping by her and flashes of brightness as they entered stations.

Ten minutes later they shuddered into Grand Central Station. She stood up and was swept onto the platform in a wave of departing passengers, who streamed up stairways until she was nearly alone. Everyone, it seemed, had somewhere to go. She adjusted the leather strap of her bag and walked up the stairs.

Grand Central Station was as cavernous as it had been that afternoon, but now the giant windows looked out onto darkness. The light seemed feeble in the gigantic building. And it was cold. She shivered in her summer dress and wondered why she hadn't had the good sense to bring a sweater. Next time, she would.

Next time. What did that even mean?

She sighed and looked at the south end of the station. The giant multi-faced clock hanging from the ceiling showed it was 7:54. A train to New Canaan left on Track 8 at 8:14. She walked slowly across the expanse of floor toward the gate to Track 8. There was no hurry. It was Thursday. If David had bothered to come home at all, he would have wondered angrily where she was, why she didn't have his scotch poured for him. Then he would grab his clubs and head out to the country club with Charlie.

They would drink away until 9:00, maybe 10:00, and then he'd stagger into the house, and they would fight. Where had she been? What time had she gotten home?

And, this time, she would tell him that it was none of his goddamned business.

The return train was half empty, and Barbara found a seat at the back of the car where she wouldn't be disturbed. She pulled up the MTA subway schedule on her laptop and scanned the maze of multi- colored lines. She knew her route now, and quickly selected the green dot with the white 6, the Lexington Line. She studied the timetable. There were nine stops north from Brooklyn Bridge-City Hall to Grand Central Station. *Ten in my case*, she thought wryly.

It looked like if she was going to get to City Hall Station, she would have to walk.

Chapter 4

THE SUBWAY CAR CLATTERED MECHANICALLY as it hurtled through the dark tunnel. Friday night. Barbara glanced at her watch: 2:35 am. Well, Saturday morning actually.

The last two nights had been nightmarish. She had only been home for a half hour on Thursday before David returned, but it had given her enough time to move her things into the guest bedroom. She was done with his accusations, humiliation, his disapproval. She was done with him.

When he arrived, even more drunk that normal, shouting for her, she barricaded the door with the dresser. He stomped into their bedroom. She heard the shattering of a lamp smashing on the floor. When he realized she had moved into the guestroom, he exploded in fury. After nearly battering the door in, he finally retreated to their bedroom and passed out. She quickly stuffed the things she had brought with her into her purse and quietly let herself out the door into the damp night. She flagged down a cab and took a room at the nearby Hilton, hoping sunlight would put a new perspective on her predicament.

That night at the hotel seemed endless. She knew rationally that David couldn't find her, but his hatred and rage rang in her head. She had always known it was there, just below the surface, but to face it had shaken her. *What had she been thinking these past years? Why hadn't she left long ago? Was she that weak?*

She smiled wryly as she looked through the window into darkness. *Lots of women leave abusive relationships and shithead husbands,* she thought. *But I imagine most of them have a more considered plan than to walk through a rat-infested subway tunnel to an abandoned subway station to find a man she had met one time in the hope he could help her connect with her inner Aries.* But then she felt her jewel resting between her breasts, warm and comforting. She knew there was more of a plan than that. She just wasn't quite sure what it was yet.

Words of the old Heart song played in her head: "Try, try, try to understand, he's a magic man." *He fucking better be,* she thought. At this point, she had no Plan B.

When she woke up that morning, she knew what she had to do. She would make her run for the City Hall station that night. Move while her resolve was strong.

Fearing that David would try to cancel her credit cards, she took a cab to a nearby mall and found a sports shop, where she bought a backpack, headlamp flashlight and hunting knife. She had explained to the helpful young clerk that she wanted a pack that was light and clung close to her body. Ah, he had said, a day pack.

"Actually," she had replied, "a night pack."

He had looked at her quizzically but found her just what she wanted: a grey and black Osprey Daylite pack that rode high on her shoulders. In the same mall there was a RoadRunner store she had remembered from years ago when she had jogged nearly every day. *Why did I stop?* She bought two pairs of black tights, a couple of sports bras, and a pair of Brooks Ghost running shoes that she chose mainly because they were astonishingly light. Plus, she liked the name. Then she picked out a black Under Armor fleece hoodie that fit snugly.

Back at the hotel she had pored over the subway tables once more. She removed essential items from her purse and stuffed them into her new backpack. Everything else she would leave at the hotel. She had no idea when or if she would return. In fact, she had no idea if she'd be alive the next day. And if she did make it to the old station, what was she supposed to do then? The card read "up." Up was desperately lacking in specifics.

As those thoughts piled up in her head, she had laughed. Lightly at first, and then in a full roar. For the first time in a very long while, she felt alive.

The train was about two minutes from the Brooklyn Bridge station. Even though she knew she could abort if the timing wasn't right or the station was unexpectedly jammed with passengers, her pulse quickened. She picked up the new backpack on the seat next to her and shrugged into the straps, mentally reviewing its contents: a headlamp designed for night cross-country skiing; a backup flashlight; wire cutters in case she encountered a fence barrier; her cellphone, though she had no idea how that would help if she were run down by a train. A pair of leather and nylon work gloves. She had also bought a hunting knife in a leather sheath. She wasn't quite sure why, but it had something to do with the images of giant, red-eyed rats that nagged in the back of her mind. And her jewel, wrapped tightly in its leather pouch and zipped safely into an inside pocket.

She looked around the car and confirmed that she was the only passenger. The train slid into the station, and she stepped onto the platform, consciously minding the gap. As she did, she selected the stopwatch function on her watch and pushed the start button. It was set to alarm in 18 minutes. She had chosen the fire engine signal.

She had checked and rechecked the subway table a hundred times. She had accounted for every train using the Lexington route. After the 2:37 departed, she had 18 minutes before the next scheduled downtown train would be on the tracks. Eighteen minutes to cover the half mile between her and the old City Hall Station. She couldn't afford to run – too much risk she might stumble and fall headlong onto the dreaded third rail. But she had plenty of time. A careful walk covered two to three miles in an hour. A half mile in 20, 25 minutes tops. She figured she could easily do it in 15.

She hoped she wouldn't need the three-minute cushion.

Barbara was joined by three others who stepped out of cars farther down the track. She moved quietly toward the northern end of the platform as the other passengers disappeared up the stairs as the train pulled out, whining into the cavern on her right. Then she was alone on the long platform. She glanced across the tracks to the northbound platform and was relieved to see it was deserted as well.

She had expected to be the only person in the station, but what she hadn't expected was the silence. It was beyond quiet. As if noise had been sucked out of the station by the train like a giant vacuum. She looked nervously at the blinking red numbers on her watch.

Barbara hurried to the far edge the platform, which stopped just short of the mouth of the black subway tunnel. She turned and looked behind her. She was still alone. She glanced down and was relieved to find what she'd expected – a simple four-rung metal ladder imbedded into the concrete led down to the gravel surface below. There could be no surprises. She needed to be sure she could descend and, assuming there was another ladder at the old City Hall station, ascend.

She turned and put her foot on the first rung and then stepped down quickly to the final rung. As she did, she noticed a sign screwed to the left side of the ladder. The figure of a man arching in pain with a jagged electric bolt slicing through him was just below giant red letters: "DANGER! Do NOT Enter!"

Thanks. I needed that, she thought grimly. Barbara glanced down at the glittering subway rails as she descended. The two main rails looked just like a conventional railway, but on the near side, just a few feet away from her, there was another rail, raised maybe a foot off the ground on white insulators. The third rail, the one that carried over 600 volts, enough to kill her in a few short moments. Across from her, on the other side of the station, the northbound rails were visible over a concrete separating wall.

Her fear of the third rail was not just paranoia. She had found that the wooden cover over the rail was designed to protect it from water and debris and would more than likely collapse if she were to fall on it. She also discovered she probably wouldn't die instantly if she came in contact with the rail. Instead, she would be paralyzed until the voltage rushing through her body finally caused her heart to stop.

She did not find that reassuring.

Her right foot crunched as it reached the gravel. *OK, this part I can do.* She glanced over her shoulder into the yawning hole of the tunnel, the rails disappearing quickly into the darkness. *It's that part I'm not so sure about.* She turned toward the dark mouth of the tunnel.

Suddenly she froze. Above her, two passengers made their way noisily down the stairs onto the platform maybe 60 feet away. They were a couple in their 40s, well dressed, swaying and giggling. They seemed pretty drunk, but still able to spot her slinking down the gravel and into the tunnel. Barbara ducked down behind the cement platform wall and watched the couple anxiously. She hadn't figured on this. If spotted, the whole plan could be ruined. What if they called the police? And she had no appetite to crouch on the ladder until the next train left the station.

She studied the couple. Their clamor echoed in the cavernous station. Barbara looked at her watch: she had been there four minutes. Fourteen to go. Should she risk it and make a run for the tunnel? The couple was leaning against a pillar, laughing loudly, but they kept looking her way. Even if they were drunk, seeing a red-haired woman in black tights and a black hoodie sprinting along the subway floor was sure to catch their attention, especially when the slightest noise was amplified in the silent, tiled chamber. And climbing back over the edge to the platform didn't seem like a great idea. *Oh, Hi there. Just checking the switches, you know.* She drew away from the ladder against the subway wall.

Finally, from deep in the tunnel on the far side of the station, she heard a low rumble that built into a full roar as the train she had taken, having completed its loop and now heading uptown, neared the station. Barbara pulled the hood over her head and crouched deep in the corner against the platform wall, hoping she wouldn't be spotted from the train. The couple stopped talking and stared at the platform directly across from them as the train exploded into the station and screeched to a halt.

Using the clamor as a distraction, Barbara sprinted for the tunnel entrance. She stepped into the darkness of the shaft and heard the doors sigh shut across the barrier from her and the low shriek as the train moved from the far platform. It was 2:42, and it was all quiet again. She had 13 minutes to make it to the abandoned station.

She found it hard to believe that she would either be there in the next few minutes or be dead. Though she preferred the first, either alternative seemed acceptable.

Chapter 5

BARBARA STOOD IN THE DARKNESS at the mouth of the tunnel for a few moments, willing her heart to slow. Thirteen minutes. She shrugged off her pack, pulled out her headlight and strapped it on before trying the switch. A bright swath of white light cut into the blackness ahead of her, and she walked deeper into the tunnel.

Barbara had not really known what to expect inside the subway. She had envisioned a black cave, dripping with water, pitch dark and slimy. But what she found was even more unnerving. Instead of being black, the tunnel was lit every 20 feet by blue lights that cast an eerie glow over the wall and reflected off the shiny rails. Graffiti artists had preceded her, situating pictures of giant rats, knives dripping blood and obscenities under the lights as if they were displays in a gallery. Wires and cables looped loosely along the concrete walls. Sensors were mounted at intervals high on the walls. Barbara couldn't be sure if they were connected to cameras but ducked to avoid them. Trash, piles of newspapers, and empty water bottles were piled along sections of the track. Just where rats would hang out, she thought, grabbing the hilt of her knife.

For the first few hundred feet, the two rails, northbound and southbound, ran parallel, separated by a low concrete wall. Up ahead, lit by a dull red light, there was a junction and another line curved to the left and disappeared into the gloom. It had to be the City Hall loop, didn't it?

Suddenly a red light on the wall separating the north- and southbound tracks began to blink sending her heart racing. She could try to outrun it, hoping she made it to the City Hall loop first, or she could lie down beside the rail. She had read that there was enough space so that most trains would pass over a prone person on the ground. Most trains.

The light blinked frantically, and she heard the rushing of the train, close now, louder. How had she miscalculated so badly?

She yanked off her backpack, throwing it in front of her in a panic before diving headfirst onto the gravel and sliding as close to the tunnel wall as she could, eyes squeezed shut.

The roar was deafening and the ground shook, but there was no terrifying screech of steel wheels just inches away. No subway cars rushed over her. Slowly the noise subsided, and Barbara lifted her head. The train was passing on the other side of the concrete wall northbound, not a few inches but a few feet from her head.

She lay flat again, relief washing through her. She stood up, still shaky, as the end of the train disappeared in front of her, and she was in silence again. The red light had stopped blinking.

Barbara reached the junction and swung her headlight into the tunnel that opened to her left. She stepped carefully over the rails and walked until the tunnel mouth of the main line was lost behind her. She looked nervously at the seconds ticking away on her watch as she squinted her eyes. Ahead of her the blue gloom seemed to lighten slightly. Barbara walked faster, and then slowed. She knew the rule: take every step slowly. She had time. Each step confirmed she was moving toward light, real light.

And then she was in a dim cavern that she recognized from the pictures she had seen on the web and the few seconds from the train. Even in the gloom, she could make out the soaring arches, the white and green tile, the wide stairway.

She followed the beam of her headlight as it scanned across the white wall until it lit a sign in green tile. She could just make out the words: City Hall.

Barbara rushed forward to the platform, looking anxiously for the cast iron ladder, but she found nothing. Panic rising, she followed the curved station platform to the far end, and there it was – a metal ladder that led to the top of the deck. She grabbed the third rung with her gloved hand and climbed the rusty bars until she was able to crawl over the edge.

She gave one last push and sprawled on the tiled floor, breathing hard. She looked at her watch. *Forty-seven seconds.*

Barbara lay prone, her heart thudding. She heard a muffled growl in the tunnel behind her and jumped to her feet. The noise grew louder, shrieking, rushing toward her. She glanced at her watch again. The 3:15 Lexington Local, right on schedule. A single brilliant light glared from the onrushing train. If the conductor spotted her, the MTA cops would be all over her in minutes. She turned off her headlamp and scrambled up a broad stairway in front of her and pressed her back against a tiled wall, staying in the shadows until the train streaked by.

She leaned her head against the wall and closed her eyes, feeling her heart slow. She took a deep breath and looked around her. The leaded glass skylights sifted the city lights into the abandoned station, silvering the tile floors and curving walls. The green and white tile became shades of grey, walls of a sepulchral tomb, silent except for the vague hiss of traffic above her.

She stepped back onto the landing into a dim column of light from the skylight high overhead. There was no sound or color, no movement, just shadows and silence.

God, she was so tired. She shook her head to clear it and studied her surroundings. Behind her the stairway where she'd hidden led upwards to the old station entrance on Broadway.

Up. City Hall. Up.

As she climbed the main stairway from the platform, she lost what little illumination there had been from the skylight. She switched her headlamp back on and scanned the broad stairway anxiously for rats. She only managed about 12 steps before she encountered a sliding metal gate stretched across her path. It was rusty and padlocked where the two sections met. She rattled it in frustration and then sat on the top step and stared into the darkness. Now what? *Goddamn it. I get this far only to run into a dead end?*

She walked slowly back down the stairs to the landing and sat down cross-legged on the floor in the dim circle from the skylight, facing the stairway and the tiled walls on each side. What was she missing? She studied the walls in front of her, slowly rotating the beam of her headlamp from left to right. Just to the right of the curving staircase, she stopped and squinted into the darkness. There was something there, a rectangle that blended into the shiny white tile. She stood and walked toward the object, keeping it in the beam of her headlamp.

As she neared, it became clear that she was looking at a steel frame enclosing what appeared to be a smooth metal door some seven feet high. She scanned the surface carefully, looking for a handle, a keyhole, something. But even though she studied every inch of the surface, there was nothing — just a brown metal slab with a seam down the middle. Barbara took a breath and stood back. She ran her hand over the cold surface, thinking there might be a recessed handle, but again she detected nothing.

She shone her light on the door frame. She started at the bottom left and carefully moved her light upwards. About halfway she stopped. Set into one of the tiles was a tiny rectangular panel.

She leaned forward and saw that the panel contained two almost indiscernible white buttons in a vertical line. She slipped out of her pack, dug out the flashlight and directed its beam, blazingly bright in the darkness, on the buttons. As her eyes adjusted, she realized there were dim letters above each one. She could just make out the words: "Up" and "Down." She stared at the panel for several moments.

Then she pushed the Up button with her gloved finger.

Barbara listened desperately for some response, but the silence only seemed to deepen. She pushed the button again with the same results. She knew she was right. But it made sense that there had to be more to unlocking the door than simply pushing the button. There had to be some activation mechanism.

She remembered the hotel room at the Hilton. The door unlocked with a plastic card issued at the desk. Barbara turned the light to the backpack on the tiled floor and rummaged through it until she found the small, zipped pocket. She opened the pocket and pulled out the gem maker's black card. She grasped the card by its edges and drew it across the metal plate. Suddenly the buttons began to glow white like tiny moons. She pushed the Up button again.

Immediately a low grinding sounded from behind the door, and then a low hum and a thump that shook the floor slightly. There was a moment of silence before the twin doors began to draw open. Gradually the gap widened, allowing a shaft of dim light to escape from inside.

The doors moved so slowly that it seemed to take several minutes for them to draw fully open. Barbara watched with a mix of apprehension and excitement. She slipped the card into the pocket of her hoodie and pulled the thong with her jewel bag over her head. She shook it gently until her gem, gleaming blood red, fell into her palm. She took a deep breath and held the gem in front of her as a talisman against whatever might emerge.

Then the doors stopped, fully open, and Barbara stared into what looked like a perfectly ordinary, perfectly empty elevator car. She shone her flashlight inside. The compartment was small, maybe four feet by four feet, and the back was decorated in gilt and a beautifully etched mirror that reflected the beam of her flashlight into her eyes, blinding her. She switched it off and realized the elevator was lit with a soft light from a frosted glass circle in the center of the roof of the car. She swallowed hard, slung one strap of her pack over her shoulder and stepped inside.

Almost immediately, the doors began to slide shut. She fought an impulse to jump through the narrowing opening and remained motionless in the middle of the car. The doors closed fully, and Barbara was sealed inside like a tomb. She examined the panels on each side of the door, looking for some sort of button, when suddenly the elevator jerked upward, nearly knocking her off her feet. She reached out and caught a brass rail that ran around the inside of the car, her right hand gripping the cool rail fiercely, the left wrapped around her gem.

She had no idea how long she was in the elevator. It was if time had stopped; there was only the sense of moving upward, the dim light in the ceiling, the low grind of the machinery. So it was something of a shock when the car shuddered to a stop. Barbara stared at the closed door. For several seconds nothing happened, and then the doors slid slowly apart. She looked out the doorway, slipping her gem back into its bag and over her head, and prepared to exit. The door gave a low clank and stopped. She had clearly arrived.

She stepped forward into a foyer lit by a crystal chandelier hanging from the high ceiling. Waist-high dark wood wainscoting lined the wall. Directly in front of her was a framed photograph of a woman in a white dress sitting in a chair, smiling.

Barbara studied the photo. The dress and hairstyle made her think of pictures she had seen of her grandparents, pre-war, maybe early 1940s, she guessed. The picture was exquisitely detailed, clearly taken by an accomplished photographer, and she could make out the delicate pattern of the lace around the woman's low neckline, the ribbons that tied back her long hair, the pearl buttons of the bodice. The woman's face was strikingly beautiful, the smile wide and warm. This was no posed photo. Even in the dim light of the foyer the tenderness in the woman's eyes was unmistakable.

A long, burgundy-carpeted corridor, lit by a dozen small chandeliers similar to the one in the foyer, opened to Barbara's left. At the far end she saw an ornately carved wooden door. She adjusted the straps of her bag and walked toward it. Along the hallway other photographs hung in old frames, all of the same model that appeared in the first photograph she had seen. Sometimes the woman was walking in a wood; other times she sat at restaurants or cafes, but those shining eyes left little doubt it was the same person.

Barbara stood in front of the door. It was heavy and old, possibly walnut, mythical animals and birds carved along its edge. In the center was a single brass peephole just above an enormous ivory door knocker carved in the shape of a boar's head. She paused for a moment, aware of her heart beating wildly. She rapped sharply on the door with her gloved knuckles.

The knock seemed to be absorbed by the dense wood. She stood, biting her lower lip, listening for some response. She knocked again, this time more forcefully with the side of her fist, but still there was only silence. *Maybe he's not home.* Her shoulders slumped. The man worked. All over the country, or all over the world for all she knew. Why had she just assumed he would be home?

She grasped the ivory doorknocker and raised the boar head, slamming it hard against the wood. She jumped back as the noise boomed around her, echoing along the long hallway. In a few moments, she heard a tiny squeak and her eyes darted to the peephole above the doorknocker. Had it opened?

There was another squeak and the tiny crystal eye seemed to close.

She was sure now. There was someone inside. She stood in silence, her eyes riveted on the peephole. Seconds ticked by, maybe a minute, and then she heard a lock being unbolted. After a few seconds, the door opened, and she was looking into the glittering black eyes of the gem maker.

He looked at her dumbfounded. He stood in front of her in a blue silk housecoat, his silver hair swept back behind his ears. He held a pipe in his hand, and she could smell the sweetness of the tobacco. He tilted his head and stared at her, whether in astonishment or anger she couldn't be sure.

"Madam," he said at last. "Whatever are you doing here?"

Barbara remained frozen with fear. She couldn't speak. In fact, she wasn't even sure she knew the answer to the man's question.

"Are you alright?" the man asked, his bushy eyebrows pinching together in concern.

"Yes," she finally managed. "I think so."

The man looked at her, his mouth open in dismay. "I want to ask you in, but it is not allowed." The man's black eyes were wet and glistening. "I am so sorry. So very sorry."

She stared at him for a long moment and then groped inside her pocket and held out the card. "You did invite me," she said evenly, masking a surge of despair. "The chain?"

He looked at her silently, and she felt the swirl of emotions in him as if they were her own. Fear fought with loneliness; kindness and generosity struggled with dread; a certainty of some terrible consequence mixed with resignation and something else. Hope, perhaps.

Despite herself, tears began to leak down her cheeks. She was so tired. She leaned wearily against the wall of the corridor and closed her eyes.

"So I did," the man said gently. "So I did. Please, excuse my lack of hospitality." He smiled. "I am not used to visitors. Now, you must come in, yes?"

"But..." Barbara sniffed and wiped her nose with the back of her glove. "You said I couldn't. That it's not allowed."

The man reached down and took Barbara's hand between both of his own. "That is true," he said, holding her hand as if it were a tiny rabbit. "That is true. But sometimes...sometimes it is necessary to break the rules, no?"

As he spoke, he smiled, but Barbara sensed the gravity of his invitation. He had made his decision, and there would be repercussions. For both of them.

She looked at his hands holding hers. "And you said you could not touch others."

He withdrew his hands. "That is also true, but...Well, we shall see. But no more standing in the hall. Come now, come into my apartment. Please. I welcome you."

Barbara stood awkwardly in the doorway. "I don't want to get you into some sort of trouble. I can go back the way I came."

His eyebrows arched. "And I am looking forward to hearing about that. No outsider has visited me on a Saturday night in perhaps 40 years. Now, don't worry. Let's just go inside and have a cup of tea, yes?"

Barbara hesitated, wiping away tears. "I am the one who needs to apologize. I don't know why I fell apart like that. So much has happened." She looked into the man's face. "And all of it because of you."

He stood in his doorway, holding the door open for her. "I am not sure that is a compliment. In any event, you give me too much credit."

"No, I don't," Barbara continued, stepping through the door.

As the man closed the door quietly behind her, Barbara surveyed the living room and gasped. It was vast, with 12-foot ceilings. Carved oak molding ran along the bottom of the walls, which were painted in gold murals of mountains, lakes, and forests. Heavy maroon velvet curtains hung over the windows, blocking out the night. The room was lit by a single magnificent chandelier that hung from the ceiling by a gold chain. The chandelier glowed and glittered like a colossal jewel. It was four feet high and at least as wide. Lights were arrayed in three tiers, each dripping with swags of cut crystal that refracted the light like tiny rainbows. And hanging from the bottom was a large crystal ball, cut like a gigantic round diamond. By some device, light was directed through the bottom of the chandelier, so it glowed as if it was lit by inner fire.

"Beautiful, isn't it?" the man asked from behind her.

Barbara realized she was gaping at the shining creation like a schoolgirl. "Yes, yes it certainly is."

"It's Italian. A Marie Theresa. Dates back to about 1910."

"There must be 300 crystals," Barbara said, still staring up at the chandelier in awe.

"Over 500, actually. Both pear drops and slab drops. And 40 lights. The arms are gilded in gold."

"I've never seen anything like it."

"Nor are you likely to, unless perhaps in Venice."

Barbara dropped her eyes from the chandelier and began to notice the furnishings. The glowing maple floors were covered in elaborately woven Persian rugs. An embroidered sofa and love seat sat in one corner with a mahogany table holding a Ming horse lamp. Around the room were scattered armchairs, their deep green leather contrasting with the gold tacks along their seams. Across the entire back wall a bookcase, stuffed with books, many in leather bindings, stretched from the floor almost to the ceiling.

A ladder on a runner that slid the length of the bookcase provided access to the upper shelves. Along the top of the shelves a deep recess was lined with stained glass windows. A mahogany desk was pushed against the side wall, and a massive stone fireplace stood on her right, its broad mantel intricately carved from a dark brown wood. On it were heavy brass candleholders with large black candles. Between them was a framed picture of the woman Barbara had seen in the hall.

"It is all so beautiful," Barbara said.

"Thank you, madam. You are kind. But please, sit down. I will make us some tea, yes?"

She looked gratefully at the man. "Tea would be nice, so nice."

The man motioned Barbara to a leather sofa with a marble coffee table in front and three other matching chairs around it. "Please sit. I will be only a minute."

Barbara collapsed into the soft seat and leaned against the back. She closed her eyes and could smell the faint scent of leather and polish. She could fall asleep right here, right now.

"Here we are, Madam."

Barbara awoke with a start. "Oh, I'm sorry. I must have dozed off."

"Only for a few moments, perhaps. Some tea, and then…" He paused. "I do not know your intentions, madam, but if you wish, you may stay here the night. It is late, and perhaps we could discuss your chain later?"

My intentions, Barbara thought. *Do I even know my intentions?*

"That would be very kind," she said.

"Very well. Finish your tea. Then I can show you to a bedroom." He smiled. "I believe you call it a guest bedroom, no?"

Barbara nodded. Her eyes began to close in exhaustion.

The man placed a silver tray with a gilded Limoges tea set on the marble table. He poured her a cup and handed it to her. "Would you like sugar? Cream, perhaps?"

"Some sugar, yes, please."

The man picked up a silver tongs and lifted a white cube from a crystal bowl. "One?"

Barbara nodded and he dropped the cube into her tea and then poured a cup for himself. He sat in one of the chairs across from Barbara and took two cubes. "I take two, sometimes three. Learned that in Australia, I believe."

"I am so sorry to impose on you so," Barbara said. "I'm not even entirely sure why I am here."

"Perhaps, but here you are. Your husband. He will be angry?"

Despite her exhaustion, Barbara felt anger rise inside of her. "I certainly hope so," she said sharply.

The man nodded. "But I find it hard to believe he will do nothing. He will come looking for you?"

"Probably," she smiled slightly. "But I doubt he will find me here."

The man nodded. "Indeed. That is very unlikely. But perhaps that will make things more difficult when you return home?"

"I have no home." She sat upright in the sofa and looked at the man intently. "I have no life. Surely you can see that."

The man took a sip of his tea and sat back deep into his chair, looking at her, saying nothing.

She sat back in the sofa. "This is not like me," she said. "At least not like who I was." She was almost in tears again. "It's all been a lie, of course. I knew that but didn't want to look too closely. And when I did it all just went, 'poof!' Up in smoke." She was staring at the rich carpet on the floor, her hands clasped around the warmth of her cup. "But no, you are right. It is not all because of you."

The man continued his silence, studying her with his black eyes.

"But it did have something to do with the gem, didn't it? The beautiful stone you made for me. It did something, didn't it?"

"No, Madam. As I told you, the stone does nothing. It is simply a part of you. Perhaps a part you do not know well. Perhaps a part that we recognize with a start, no?"

"Maybe," she said doubtfully. "Anyway, what I said earlier isn't entirely true. You see, I do know why I came here."

The man looked at her, cocking his head in interest.

"I want you to take me to the jeweler you mentioned who will make me a chain that will never break," she said rapidly. "I want to have my jewel placed in a setting that will never tarnish. I want to have my stone on a chain that has no clasp. I want my stone between my breasts," she said fiercely, "so that it can only be removed if my head is chopped off."

The man was quiet for a long moment and then nodded. "Yes, of course. As we discussed. But you are tired. Perhaps we can talk later after you have slept, yes?"

Barbara leaned forward, her eyes searching the man's face. "But is there such a chain? Please, tell me. Do you know such a silversmith?"

"Oh, yes, Madam. Truly, that is the least of our problems."

Relief washed through Barbara, and she felt her eyes closing.

"But after the chain, perhaps there is more you want, no?"

Barbara looked wearily at the man, now standing. "I don't know," she said. "I don't know." Her eyes closed. "But yes, there is more. I just don't know what it is exactly."

He smiled. "When you wake up. There is plenty of time for talk. Now, may I show you to your room?" He motioned to a door to the left of the bookcase. "Please, Madam, follow me. I believe you will find nightclothes in the chest of drawers. They may be a bit musty, however."

Barbara stood and followed the man. She had never felt so safe.

Chapter 6

THE MESTER. VICTOR CARALDO LOOKED at the clock on his bedside table. Who the fuck else would call at 4 fucking 27 in the morning?

He considered not answering; then he rolled over and grabbed his cell phone. It was healthier to answer the *Mester's* calls, no matter when he phoned. At least if he didn't want to wind up dead in a ditch.

"Yeah?"

"Don't 'yeah' me, Vic," the old man snarled.

He hated being called Vic, and the old man knew it. Son of a bitch. One day he might have to kill him. He sat up in bed. "Sorry, Boss."

"That's better. I need you over here. Now."

"Boss, it's not even five in the morning!"

"I know what fucking time it is, you moron!" the voice exploded. Even over the phone the anger was edged with menace. "Just get your ass over here. Now." The cell went dead.

Jesus, didn't the son of a bitch know the trains didn't run until 5:00? No, of course he didn't know. In the 16 years Victor had worked for the *Mester*, Victor had never seen him outside of his office. Rajiv told him about monthly disappearances, when, the staff whispered, the *Mester* would simply vanish. Some said they could hear a helicopter on the roof, but no one had seen it. The next morning he would be back at his desk. Victor didn't know if the rumor was bullshit or not. And didn't much care. If the old man did leave the compound, wherever he went, he sure as hell didn't take the tube. How would he know when it ran? Not that he would give a damn anyway.

Victor pulled himself naked out of bed and dropped onto the Persian rug and ripped off 50 push-ups, his dick slapping the wool with each descent. He burst up and completed 30 leg thrusts. He was beginning to wake up, feel strong again. He grabbed the bottle of Laphroaig 18 on the table and poured the crystal tumbler full, then twisted off the top of the bottle of Dianabol and threw two into his mouth. He washed them down with the scotch. *Breakfast of champions*. He pulled on his Manchester United shirt and silk pants and black Lobb battle boots and made his way through the dark hallway of his Sloane Gardens townhouse.

Outside, he strode in darkness along Holbein Road headed for the Sloane Square underground station. As he walked down the street, the few pedestrians he met stared, but not for long. They quickly stepped aside to let him pass. Even in London, where residents viewed boarding the Tube or pushing along crowded streets as a contact sport, people sensed that Victor was a man to avoid, and that was the way he liked it.

At the station entrance he glanced at his watch — 5:00. He loped down the steps and automatically brushed his transit card against the reader and walked through the metal fingers as they swung inward. Victor rarely felt happy, but this morning he was particularly displeased. It was bad enough the *Csúnya Mester* – "Ugly Master," a Hungarian nickname the old man had acquired somehow over the years and used only far out of earshot – expected him to take a 45-minute tube trip to that goddamned fortress he lived in, but at 5:00 in the morning?

As his was the first train of the day, Victor saw few other passengers until they reached Kings Cross, when early commuters began to push through the doors. Victor remained in his single seat, glaring balefully at his companions, who seemed only too happy to study the dark that flashed by the windows. At Barbican he climbed the long flight of stairs two at a time then headed through the Smithville Market. *Crazy old son of a bitch. Lives in the middle of nowhere. The meat district, he says. Likes to live in the meat district.*

He walked three blocks south to the locked gate of the mews where the bunker was located. Victor took out a blank white card and inserted it into a slot in the rusty gate. The lock clicked audibly, and the gate swung open, closing behind him with a snap.

The compound was a line of three early Victorian red brick homes, ornate, glaring crimson in the rising sun. The old man had bought them years ago, long before Victor had gotten involved. The old man had connected them into a warren of dark hallways, great rooms with heavy green curtains on the windows, sitting rooms and a library filled with ancient books and smelling of dust and leather. Victor knew that one of the houses was the old man's personal quarters, but he had never seen it. He was limited to the compound itself, the original middle house of the three. Downstairs a large meeting room opened off a cavernous foyer. A spiral staircase curved to the second floor and the old man's office, but business access was limited to the ancient elevator with a brass folding gate.

When he got to the compound gate, Victor used the same card to open the ornate gate and then strode to the front door. Shaped in the form of a goat's foot, the brass door knocker was a reminder of the original owner's profession. He lifted the heavy hoof and slammed it onto the plate screwed into the door.

Almost immediately the door swung open and Rajiv, The *Mester*'s servant, said by some of the staff to be a eunuch, bowed in the doorway.

"Mister Caraldo," he said, "you are expected."

Victor brushed by him toward the elevator. He stepped in and the open cage moved reluctantly upwards, the cable looping inside the shaft. Staff members stared at him impassively as he rose into and out of their sight.

The cage came to a trembling stop, and Victor slid the gate aside. He stepped onto the soft carpeting and stepped straight ahead to a white door trimmed in gold. He knocked.

"Come in, for God's sake," the old man roared from inside. "It's about fucking time you got here."

Victor turned the gold handle and walked into the old man's office.

Over the years he had seen The *Mester* maybe 35, 40 times. Usually, he got his orders from Madame Matin, as well as his money, but there were times, special tasks, that had taken him into the old man's office. But no matter how many times he saw the *Mester*, each encounter still stopped

Victor dead in his tracks.

The *Mester* was small, very small, barely able to lean his scrawny elbows on his huge mahogany desk even though the matching desk chair was at its maximum height. Enormous ears stood out of the sides of his head like fleshy satellite dishes. Sunken cheeks, always covered in a scruffy beard that looked like mold, set off thick, deeply frowning lips that pulled downward nearly to his whiskered chin. A large, bulbous nose fell from a high forehead with just a fringe of grey hair at the edges.

All that aside, it was his eyes Victor never got used to. The old man's eyelids were pouched and red, framing huge sockets sunk deep under great bushy eyebrows. But the eyes. They were the color of amber jewelry, deep yellow-orange, and most peculiar of all were the pupils. They were not round. They were oval, like that of a cat, but where a cat's pupils tapered from top to bottom, the old man's ran from side to side, like elliptical black seeds. Yellow, orange, and red streaks ran from the pupils to the very edge of the eye. Only a thin wedge of white framed the flaming pupils on each side.

Victor approached the desk and stopped two feet from the edge at a spot in the deep maroon carpet where he'd been instructed to stand when talking to the old man. As usual, O'Brien, the *Mester's* bodyguard, sat in a red leather chair to the *Mester*'s right, looking bored. Victor folded his large hands behind his back and leaned forward expectantly. The *Mester's* yellow eyes raked his face, a grim fury drawing his lips down in a sharp V underneath the overhang of his nose.

"There's trouble in New York," the old man said.

Victor quickly inventoried the agents in the New York area. "Madison?"

The *Mester* shook his head. "DeAngelo."

Victor's head snapped up in surprise. "Are you sure?" he asked in disbelief. DeAngelo was one of the *Mester's* oldest field agents. It was Victor's job to know each agent, all 27 of them, and DeAngelo was one of the few he had only met at the agents' meetings held every four years or so at the bunker.

Unlike most, there had never been any need to see him more often.

The old man rose halfway over his desk in fury. "Am I sure?" he roared. "You are asking me whether I am sure or not. You of all people? You've always had a nose that could snort bricks. But you're gettin' a big head now, too?"

"Sorry, boss," Victor hurriedly apologized. "It's just there's never been a whiff of a problem with DeAngelo. I've been here 16 years. I've only met him a couple of times, at the conferences. Checked in with him at The Building once or twice. Barely heard his name mentioned."

The *Mester* settled back into his chair, still glaring at the tall man in front of him. "Listen, vulture head, sometimes those are the most dangerous," he growled. "When they turn it can be a fuckin' disaster. They figure they've got nothin' left to lose." His mouth twisted into a snarling smile. "'I can't take living like this,'" he said in a high, mocking tone. "'The million pounds I make every year isn't enough. I need people.' Isn't that their usual line?"

"More or less," Victor agreed. There had been 24 agents when Victor had begun working for the *Mester*. He had been brought in by the old man during a crisis 16 years ago, a revolt the old man had called it. Whatever it was, after Victor reduced the number of field agents to 22, the trouble seemed to go away. That and the emergency meeting the old man called at the bunker where Victor was officially introduced as the killer of the two troublemakers. Of course, replacements had to be trained and monitored, and when agents, old or new, violated terms of their contracts they needed to be disciplined. But he had never needed to remove one permanently since the purge.

The *Mester* steepled his fingers and stared at the red blotter on his desk. "DeAngelo. The old fool. He's been with me so damned long. Stationed all over the world. He won't be easy to replace."

"You want him out?"

The old man rocked back and forth in his chair. "Not sure yet. I need you to check out the situation and report back. I'll let you know once you size things up."

Victor nodded. "What am I looking for?"

"Not certain. There's a person involved, a young woman. A client." He shook his head, his fleshy lips pressed together. "Sooner or later it always gets them. A client. Can be love, or boredom. Seduction. Get caught up with the client's troubles. Christ!" the old man exploded. "Of course they have troubles! Why else would I send my agents there? I tell them over and over, 'These are fucked up people. That is why they buy our product. Take their money and stay out of their goddamned lives!'"

Victor stood silent.

"Knowing DeAngelo, my guess is he's been sucked in by some needy, spoiled little princess. Trying to help her. But he knows the rules." The old man's cold eyes turned upward and stared into Victor's face with a fury that caused Victor to unconsciously straighten. "I will brook no disloyalty." His voice had become flat, metallic, chilling. "He is no different."

Victor nodded. "Observe and report."

"Yes, and be quick. I want this resolved, one way or the other. With his knowledge things could get messy." The old man paused, his lips drawn into an upside-down U. "And there's something else."

Victor looked at him expectantly.

"This girl he's taken up with. He made her a gem."

That makes sense since that's what he does for a living. "So?"

"So there's something about it. Felt it when it was made. Figured she'd just take it and disappear like the others. But she hasn't. That makes me uneasy." He eyed Victor. "And I don't like feeling uneasy."

Victor nodded assent.

"But he is one of the best. I don't want to liquidate my holdings unless necessary, understood?"

"So I should talk to him."

The old man nodded. "Watch him. And her. Document his contract violations. I can overlook a slip now and then, but my gut says this time he's gone too far. Confront him. I want to know what he has done and how he responds, understood?"

"Yes, sir. He is still in The Building?"

"How the fuck should I know?" the old man boomed. "That is your business. *Is* he still in The Building?"

"Of course," Victor added hastily. "I have full coordinates on all agents. I just wondered if your information indicated he had moved."

"My 'information,' as you put it, indicates this guy is fucking up. My 'information' tells me you need to find him, examine him, and recommend rehab or liquidation, understood?"

"Yes, sir," Victor nodded. "I'll be on the next plane out of Heathrow."

"I doubt it," the old man growled, "since there's one leaving every 20 minutes. But I want your first report tomorrow by 22:30."

"Sir, that would be 3:30 in the morning here."

"Aw, isn't that sweet," the old man mocked. "Vic is worried about waking up the old man."

"No, sir. Just wanted to make sure we were on the same page."

"I doubt that will ever happen, Vic," the old man snorted. "But don't be concerned about waking me up. Since I don't sleep, there is no reason to worry." His enormous eyes glittered. "Or maybe there is."

Chapter 7

BARBARA LAY IN BED, AWARE that she had no idea where she was. She fought through the haze of sleep, trying to remember. She turned her face from the down pillow and looked groggily into the room. It was a grand bedroom in white and gold, the gilt crown molding, carved in a rope design, glowed along the high ceilings in the soft light filtering through heavy curtains drawn across the windows. The canopy above the bed draped around the sides and enclosed her like a silk cocoon. The mattress was soft, so soft she felt like she was melting into it, safe and warm. She squeezed her eyes shut. Where was she?

Slowly bits and pieces of the previous day began to stick. The subway. Then an elevator and a long hall with the pictures of a woman on the wall. The door. And then the gem maker.

She turned onto her back and stared at the silk above her. The gem maker. She was in his apartment.

The fog began to lift. Judging from the light, it must be day. She guessed she had slept through to the afternoon.

Barbara lifted the down comforter and looked at herself. The red pajamas were wonderfully soft and fit her as if they had been made for her. The heavy silk and brocaded sleeves and cuffs gave them a faintly old-fashioned feel. And she remembered what the man had said — they did smell a little musty, but in a rich, earthy way, as if they had been stored for many years in cedar and fragrant leaves.

She sat up against the carved headboard and took a better look around the room. A single door in the far corner led to the hallway outside. The two windows, one on the wall to her right and the other to her left, were high and curtained. She slid her legs over the edge of the bed onto deep wool carpeting and stood. She smiled. Something was different. She thought about it. She was in a room in an apartment in a building and she hardly understood how she had gotten there. It was as if she had no past, that this was day one. *Perhaps this is how Alice felt after falling down the rabbit hole.*

She pulled back the gold velvet curtains. The soaring windows behind were shuttered from the outside, leaking slivers of light through their slats. She left the curtains open, allowing her to better study the room she was in. A red silk robe hung from a heavy wood coat stand near a matching bureau. She padded across the deep gold carpet and pulled the robe on, marveling again at how well it fit. A pair of embroidered Chinese slippers in matching red silk, richly decorated with gold thread, rested against the base of the stand. The smooth, quilted silk felt luxurious on her feet. She pulled the robe's belt tightly around her waist and opened the door.

She instinctively followed the hall past several closed doors until she emerged into the great room. Daylight was stifled by the curtained windows. She squinted as she scanned the dim room hoping to spot the gem maker.

"Madam," the gem maker said, emerging from a door on her right. Barbara started, bringing her hand to her chest.

The man stopped in his tracks. "I frightened you," he said apologetically.

"I'm sorry," Barbara said, dropping her hand. "You surprised me."

"Of course. It has been an odd time for you, I am sure." He bowed slightly toward her. "In any event, I am delighted to see you."

Barbara twirled, the edges of her robe spinning. "What do you think?"

The man stood back and looked at Barbara for so long that she began to blush. "You look beautiful," the man said softly. "Beautiful."

She laughed. "And you were right. Everything fits perfectly." She gave him a mock glare. "Have you been entertaining other women, sir?"

The smile slipped slightly. "Not for a very long time," he replied. "I assure you." He brightened. "Perhaps too long, yes?"

She looked at him closely. He wore an impeccably cut dark suit with an open-collared white linen shirt underneath. He was taller than she had remembered, his silver-grey hair swept back gracefully. Had she ever really looked at him? Or had she just seen him as another tradesman? His ancient eyes belied the soft, lineless face and full lips. His nose was small, almost delicate, but it fit his long, thin face. She grinned sheepishly. He was obviously way too old for her, but he *was* kind of handsome.

The man cocked his head. "Madam, you smile. You are particularly lovely when you smile. It was something I said, perhaps?"

"No, no," Barbara muttered self-consciously. "I was just thinking..." The man looked at her expectantly.

"I was just thinking that you are not as old as I thought." She dropped her eyes to the polished wood floor. "You are actually very handsome."

The man laughed aloud. "Madam, you are, truly, too kind." His smile slipped again. "And I assure you, sadly, that I am quite as old as you thought." His eyes darkened. "Considerably older, I suspect."

Barbara looked puzzled. The man waved his hand dismissively. "It is of no matter. Now, shall I make you some coffee? Or perhaps you prefer tea?"

"I'm not sure I should have coffee this late in the afternoon."

"Afternoon? No, madam, it is 9:00 in the morning."

"In the morning?"

"Yes, madam. You slept all day and all night. You must have been very tired. Very tired indeed."

Barbara brought her hand to her mouth. "You mean I've been sleeping for, like..." she made some quick calculations "like, 24 hours."

"Twenty-eight," the man corrected.

"Oh, my."

He gestured to the leather chair she had sat in the morning before. "So, will it be coffee? And perhaps some eggs?"

Barbara sat on the edge of the chair. "That would be lovely. Can I help?"

"Absolutely not. I will not have you in my kitchen. It has hardly been used for..." the man paused. "For a very long time. I will not have you judging my ship by the disrepute of my galley."

Barbara smiled. "I doubt it's all that bad. Let me see."

The man hesitated then relented. He bowed slightly and pushed open the swinging door through which he'd just entered.

Barbara stood up and walked through the doorway, sensing that she was passing more than just a physical threshold.

The room opened up in front of her like the kitchen of a Parisian restaurant. Copper pots hung suspended from cast iron hangers set in the high ceiling over a massive walnut island. A gigantic gas stove occupied half of the far wall flanked by black granite counters. An old-style ceramic sink with a few plates in the bottom was beside a black two-door refrigerator that looked like it could hold an entire side of beef. Brown wood cabinets with glass panes lined the walls, but except for some dishes in the cabinet near the sink, all were empty. Barbara had a feeling the cupboards along the wall at the end of the kitchen would be equally bare.

"It's lovely," she said. She looked at a shuttered window over the sink. "But can we open the shutters and let some light in?"

The man hesitated. "There are shutters on the outside as well, madam. I doubt you will find much light gets through."

"I see," she said. She looked back toward the living area. "I guess you like it sort of dark?"

The man shrugged. "It is better that way."

Barbara looked hard at the man and saw deep sadness in his eyes once more. *What is causing such pain,* she wondered. *Such desolation?* She swept her hand around the kitchen. "Well, anyway, I want to make us an omelet. You have such wonderful copper pots and pans. Are they French?"

The man raised his eyebrows pretending to be insulted. "*Mais, oui. Où d'autre?*"

Barbara laughed and pulled down a seven-inch copper frying pan off the overhead rack. She ran her finger along the outside, leaving a long streak in the dust that covered the skillet. She frowned disapprovingly. "A pan, sir, is only as good as the cook that uses it, regardless of its origin. And the dish washer that washes it. It would appear that you have done neither for some time." She carried the heavy pan to the sink and began running hot water. She looked at him sternly. "I do believe we have a bit of work to do in here. Do you have dish soap?"

"Oh, yes," the man replied. He rushed over to the sink and opened up the cupboard underneath. He pulled out a large yellow bottle of soap that looked like it had lasted him for several years.

"Good. Now, since you offered me eggs, I assume you have some in the fridge? And butter?"

"Ah, yes," the man said, moving to the great refrigerator and peeking in. "Both."

"And a little parmesan cheese?"

The man looked back into the refrigerator. "I'm afraid not."

Barbara gave an exaggerated sigh. "Tarragon, then? Or perhaps some chives or chervil?"

The man looked at her. "Chervil?"

Barbara walked over to the refrigerator and opened the door wide. Inside the vast interior were empty shelves. Along the side she spotted a quart of milk, some coffee cream, and a Dr Pepper. The dozen eggs and quarter of butter looked lonely on one of the wire shelves.

"Well, I see parsley is out of the question. Can I hope for salt and pepper?"

The man opened a cabinet and took out a crystal salt and pepper shaker and handed them to Barbara sheepishly. "I'm sorry madam. I had not expected company."

Remembering the night before — or was it the morning before? — she laughed. "No, I suppose not. Well, this will be very basic, sir, but as you recently pointed out to me, we make the most of what we have to work with."

The man smiled broadly. "And in your case, it seems, that was perhaps more than met the eye, yes?"

Barbara washed the pan in the warm water. "Maybe," she said, concentrating on scrubbing the dusty pan. "We'll see, I guess." She turned on the gas and set the pan on the burner.

The man stared. "May I watch?"

"Of course." Barbara pointed to a kitchen chair next to a small wood table in the corner. "But sit down and keep out of the way." The man walked obediently to the chair and sat, studying her every move.

"Spatula and bowl?"

"Middle drawer."

Barbara opened the drawer and pulled out a bowl and an old wooden spatula and cracked three eggs into the bowl. She beat them lightly with a fork then dropped a pat of butter into the pan until it sizzled.

She dusted the eggs with a little salt and pepper and poured them into the pan. After the eggs began to bubble, she gently drew the mixture in from the sides of the pan with the spatula a few times, so it gathered in light folds in the center. She waited for a few seconds and repeated the procedure until there was barely any uncooked egg left. With the pan flat on the heat, she shook it back and forth a few times to settle the mixture. She turned up the heat for a moment and then tilted the pan down away from her and rolled it gently toward the edge. She then coaxed the rolled omelet onto a plate, seam side down. She picked up another pat of butter and rubbed it over the omelet, giving it a bright glaze.

The man stared at her as she carried the plate to the table. She looked at him, smiling. "What?"

"That, madam," the man almost whispered, "was magnificent."

She waved him away. "It's an omelet. Nothing to it."

"Not the way you made it," the man said, still looking at her intently. "You made it into a concert, a ballet."

Barbara hadn't blushed in years. Now she seemed to be doing it every day. "It's an omelet. Just eat the damned thing!"

The man laughed. "Gladly."

"Good. But then, sir, as you would say, we must talk, yes?"

Chapter 8

THE MAN LOOKED AT HER incredulously. "Madam, you *walked* to the subway station?"

"There was no other way." Barbara glared at him reproachfully. "After I deciphered your card, and then found out the station you directed me to had been closed for nearly 70 years, I didn't have a lot of choice."

The man sat across from Barbara, an urn of coffee along with two cups on the table between them. "I am so sorry. You see, there *is* a train."

"I hate to disagree with you, but I assure you, you are utterly mistaken. Believe me, I looked at every schedule and every connection."

The man took a sip of coffee. "You are quite right; there are no scheduled stops here. But there is a train. It arrives and departs here four times a week. It leaves Grand Central from the Track 61 station at 4:00 am every Wednesday, Thursday, Sunday, and Monday mornings. It is a very old train, with just three cars."

Barbara looked at him with a mixture of exasperation and disbelief. "First of all, *nothing* leaves from Track 61. And hasn't since FDR was president. Secondly, *nothing* stops here either, for just about as long." She shook her head. "Plus, how could a train operate four times a week and not be noticed?"

The man sighed and shrugged. "It is complicated. You will understand more after we visit the Market. But suffice it to say that there *is* a train, it *does* leave from Track 61, and it *does* stop here." He waggled his head uncertainly. "Well, not here exactly."

"Not here, *exactly*?" Barbara asked, leaning forward. "What does that mean?"

"You see, it stops at the Market Terminal. Which is under the City Hall Station."

"Under it," Barbara said, leaning back in her chair, nodding as if that made perfect sense. "This train you insist operates four times weekly that nobody knows about, doesn't appear on any schedule, and departs on an unused track doesn't stop here. It stops at an unmarked terminal located beneath the deserted City Hall Station." She tilted her head slightly. "Do I have that right?"

The man smiled slightly. "I understand this is hard to comprehend. But then, there is the gem, yes?"

Barbara's hand strayed to the leather bag around her neck underneath the silk robe and felt the contours of her jewel.

"And this train. It carries passengers?"

"Indeed. As well as food and materials needed by the workers here. The people are generally Market representatives seeking outlets for their products and, very occasionally special buyers, carefully screened by Market security. A special pass is issued when one leases a workshop or apartment here. It is the only way to enter the train." He shook his head and shuddered. "You walked! You could have been killed!"

"Yeah, or attacked by rats." She looked at him reproachfully. "I appreciate your concern, but it would have been helpful if you'd mentioned this train of yours."

"But Madam, I did. Do you not recall?"

"Sir," Barbara began. "Oh, for Christ's sake. I feel like an idiot calling you 'sir.' I don't even know your name."

"Sadly, that must remain the case."

Barbara frowned. "I think the fact that you can't tell anyone your name is ridiculous." Her voiced rose in anger. "Who made up that rule, anyway? Names are important. They are part of who you are!"

"Madam, madam..."

"And would you please stop calling me 'madam'? It makes me sound like I run a bordello. My name is Barbara."

The man seemed shocked. "I am so sorry. I meant no insult."

"That's OK. I was kind of kidding. But look. With all due respect, you said nothing about a special train. Not a word. Not a hint. Much less what time it departed."

"That's not entirely accurate," the man said, a small smile playing across his lips. "If you will recall, as we were finishing our delightful afternoon session, I said I had to refuse your kind offer of a glass of wine as I had to catch my train. It left at 4:00."

"Exactly!" Barbara said in exasperation. "And I scoured every timetable. *No* train leaves at 4:00 on the Green Line. Number 6 or 7 or any other number." She rolled her eyes in frustration. "And even if there *was* a 4:00 departure, how was I supposed to know it was some mystery train that left from a subway stop that has been closed for 75 years?

The man smiled slightly. "Because I told you."

Barbara sat back heavily in the kitchen chair. "You told me."

"I looked at my watch. Do you recall?"

Barbara nodded curtly.

"I told you that I had to catch my train that left Grand Central Station at 4:00, yes? And that I had to be home the following morning?"

"I recall," Barbara said.

"What time was it when I made that remark, Madam?"

Barbara was too puzzled to rebuke him for calling her Madam. "Well, I guess it would have been 4:15 or 4:30. David had come home to get ready for his 5:00 golf game." She looked up toward the ceiling. "It was after 4:00. You couldn't have made the 4:00 train."

"Exactly."

"So it had to be 4:00 in the morning." She paused. "Thursday morning since we met on Wednesday."

The man beamed at her.

"I see," Barbara said, tapping her fingers on the table. "And 61?"

"Track 61. On the card, of course. I thought that would be the easy part. It is known."

"Barely. Plus there's no access to it!" Barbara said in frustration. "I asked."

The man held up a placating hand. "Ah, but there is. Through the adjacent Waldorf Astoria hotel's basement. A very singular elevator."

Barbara looked at him in irritation. "What is it with you and elevators?" She settled back in her chair. "And I presume my card – your card – would have opened this 'singular' elevator for me?"

The man smiled in agreement.

"And 'City Hall'?"

"The train – it stops only at Track 61 and here, but we wish not to call attention to The Market. So, the destination placards read 'City Hall.' Believe it or not, other trains — special purpose trains shall we say? — stop at the Track 61 station." The man smiled wryly. "It is not as quiet as some would have you believe."

Barbara was silent for a moment, staring over the man's shoulder at the heavily curtained windows. "So, this was a test of some sort. One that could have killed me."

The man raised his hand apologetically. "It was, perhaps, indeed a test, but not one that could be failed," he widened his dark eyes. "Short of being run down by a train, of course, which I promise you, was a possibility that had not occurred to me."

"Hmm. That's reassuring."

He paused. "You see that you have entered a different world, yes? Someplace where the rules don't seem to apply in the way to which you are accustomed."

Barbara felt the air around her shimmer and considered the cypher of the man sitting in front of her. She nodded.

"Most people would not persevere in seeking out such a place given so many obstacles." He shrugged. "Nor should they. They belong somewhere else, not here. It is not for most. So it is made difficult to find." He looked deeply into Barbara's green eyes. "And very few have. Very few. A handful of seekers, outsiders." He paused. "Watchers. To find this place, you must want to do so very badly."

Barbara dropped her gaze to the glossy marble tabletop, noticing the dark swirls that broke up the white surface. "Well, I guess I passed. And managed to do it without getting killed."

"For which I am most grateful. And yes, I would quite agree. You passed. With an A- perhaps?"

"I'd say an A+," Barbara shot back. "For doing it the hard way."

The man laughed. "Excellent point; an A+ it is." The man studied her. "Madam, why did you want to find me, this place? For more than a chain, yes?"

"As I have already pointed out," she replied sharply, "my name *is* not Madam. It's Barbara."

"Very well, Bar-ba-ra." He pronounced the name slowly, sounding out each syllable, as if he were trying out a new language.

"And in absence of a real name, I think of you as the Gem Maker. So, that's now your name: Gem Maker."

The man's bushy eyebrows arched. "Jim Maker? That is what you are going to call me? Madam, I hardly think 'Jim' fits me, do you?"

Barbara shrugged. "Since you won't tell me your real name, Jim will have to do."

The man was silent for a long moment. "Jim. I cannot abide it. Perhaps we can come up with a compromise?"

Barbara arched one eyebrow. "I'm listening."

"I cannot give you my name, no. But the name I have gone by for many years? My *nom de plume*, if you will?"

"Depends."

The man looked puzzled. "On what?"

"Whether I like it or not."

"Ah, I see." He smiled slightly. "And do you like DeAngelo?"

Barbara tilted her head slightly and stared at the shuttered windows. "DeAngelo." She looked back at the man. "From the Angels," she said solemnly. "Yes," she said, nodding her approval. "I do."

The man smiled. "I am so pleased."

"DeAngelo," Barbara said, trying the new name. "So you are Italian?"

"No, I am Hungarian."

She looked at him quizzically.

"My father was from Budapest. I was born there."

Barbara sat quietly. "Yes. But how did you acquire 'DeAngelo' then?"

The man stared at the shuttered windows. "It is complicated."

Barbara snorted. "Surprise, surprise. But I still like it." She looked into the man's eyes. "But I have a feeling it describes just one part of you."

"Do you, madam?"

"Yes, I do. And *stop calling me 'Madam'!*"

"Yes, madam. Uh, Barbara." He paused. It is a name that can be pronounced in many ways, yes?"

"Barbara? Yes, I suppose so. I hadn't really thought about it."

"You should. A name, as you say, is very important. The pronunciation is as significant as the name itself. Each creates different waves, resonates in our ears differently. Which do you prefer?

"I don't know. I guess most people just usually say 'BAHR-bruh.'"

The man nodded. "That is only because they are lazy. There are three syllables in your lovely name, not two." He narrowed his eyes. "Since you have approved my name, I will approve the correct pronunciation of yours. I will use the German version: BAHR-bah-rah. It seems to fit you. It is a bit edgy, as they say, yes? Barbed, perhaps?"

Barbara laughed. "Perhaps. You wouldn't be the first person to say so."

"I am not surprised," the man smiled. "And it is a name that fits in other ways, no?"

"Such as?"

"In Greek, it means 'foreign woman.'" He paused thoughtfully. "A woman who travels from a distant land."

"Really?"

"Quite so. You know the story, yes? Of Saint Barbara?"

"Sort of. Wasn't she killed by her father?"

"Indeed she was. With his sword because she would not do as he ordered. But afterwards he was struck by lightning and died a terrible death. So, she became the patron saint of artillerymen, gunsmiths. Anyone who worked with fire and explosives."

She leaned back in the high, leather chair, looking at the man curiously. "Go on."

"Ah. This is not enough? So. You have heard of the Cuban religion of *Santería*?"

Barbara shook her head.

"It is an ancient religion from Africa that came over with the slaves. Like all religions, they mixed their old beliefs with new ones. In *Santería* Barbara became *Chango*, the deity of fire, lightning, and thunder."

Barbara leaned forward, unconsciously tugging at a strand of red hair that had fallen across her face. She settled into the chair. "How do you know all of this?"

The man waved his hand toward the library. "I do not have much of a social life." He smiled wryly. "So I spend a good deal of time with my books. They are knowledgeable friends who put few demands on me."

"It must be a lonely life for you."

The man shrugged. "It is the life I chose."

"I see. And the woman in the pictures in the hallway." She nodded at the portrait over the fireplace. "Was she your mother? Grandmother perhaps?"

The man had been sitting upright in his chair, but now he sank back into the leather. He lowered his eyes and fidgeted with a brass tack on the arm. "That is my wife."

Barbara looked at him in confusion. "Did you say she was your wife?"

The man was silent for several seconds. "Yes, madam."

Barbara did not correct him. "But…Did you marry her when she was a very old woman? I've heard of relationships like that," she offered.

"No. Actually I was two years older than she."

Barbara shook her head. "I must be missing something. Those pictures look like they were taken before the War. Maybe in the 30s?"

"Quite astute. The photographs in the hallway were taken in 1938 and 1939." The man looked at the portrait. "That was made shortly before she died in 1940."

"Look…" Barbara began, wondering if she had read the man wrong. Perhaps he was simply mad, delusional. That would explain a good deal. "I think you must be mistaken," she said softly. She'd heard that you never wanted to confront psychopaths about their inventions, or they could turn violent. "The woman in those pictures could not be more than 25."

The man nodded. "She was 24 and 25 in the photographs. Twenty-six when the portrait was painted."

Barbara felt like she was getting sucked deeper into the rabbit hole.

"Mr. DeAngelo, that doesn't make sense. If you are right, she would have been born in 1914. And you, well, you would be over a hundred."

The man gave Barbara a sad little grin. "I look good for my age, don't you think?"

Barbara stared at the man silently. He was not lying; she could tell that from his eyes, which were clear and kind. But that did not rule out insanity.

"I understand that this is quite a shock."

Barbara said nothing.

The man sighed. "I warned you, no? I told you that mine is a complicated story. I did everything I could to keep you away. I did not expect you to appear at my doorstep."

"The test."

"Yes, and very few clients have ever figured out the code. And only two…" He smiled, "Well, until now, that is. Only two others have actually found me. But for them it was a challenge, a puzzle. They were quite delighted to arrive at my door. But that was all. They had solved the mystery. But you. For you it is something else, no?" He paused. "I asked why you came. I believe you changed the subject."

"I came…" Barbara began. "I told you yesterday. I came because I wanted a chain for my jewel that would never break. You said there were such chains, and you knew who made them." She paused for a moment, and then added defiantly, "That is why I came."

The man brought his hands together, steepled under his delicate nose. "I see. Well, then, we should waste no more time, yes? We will visit the shop I mentioned and have your chain made. Then you can return home."

Barbara felt an edge of anger creep into her voice. "I told you. I have no home. You know that."

"Yes, sadly, I do know that. And so you have come here out of desperation. Hoping that I can be something I cannot. That I can do something I cannot."

Barbara leaned forward, her red hair fanning across her face, her voice tight. "Please, sir, do not pretend. You are not some itinerant jewelry salesman.

You are far more than that." She paused. "It is true. I have a peculiar ability to see who people are, what they are, and you are a sad, lonely man, but a man of enormous compassion and power. I felt that the day you made the jewel."

She pushed her hair behind her ears. "And yes, it is also true I *was* desperate, desperate for a way out. You were mysterious, otherworldly. Maybe you were a door or a black hole I could pass through to another life. A place to hide while figuring it out. Maybe not. But I had nothing to lose. And a great deal to gain. That much I understood."

Barbara glared at DeAngelo. "You, it seems, feel that you have much to lose and little to gain." She paused. "But I do not believe you."

DeAngelo glanced up at the woman, still leaning toward him, demanding a response. "Madam, Barbara, you do not understand what you have begun. This is not a game. Or if it is, it's a very dangerous one, no?"

Barbara placed both hands on the arms of her chair, as if bracing herself. "Nor is this a game to me, I assure you. You are right; I have no idea what I've wandered into. I only know that I was living a life as empty as an unfurnished house. That somehow meeting you freed me from the desperation of knowing another life was possible without having the courage to seek it. I understand there are great forces at play here, though I have no idea what they are. But I don't care. For the first time in a very long time, maybe forever, I feel alive."

She stared at him across the marble table. "Unless you say to me you do not want me here. That your days are full and satisfying and that I am only complicating things. That I am ruining your wonderful life."

The man idly turned a simple gold ring on his right index finger, looking back down at the table. "I believe we should see about that chain." He looked up at her grimly. "Then, perhaps, you will know more about what it is you have become involved, yes?" He stared intently. "You may not be quite so sure this is the life you want to trade for."

Barbara sat upright and gripped the leather arms. "Whatever I've gotten into, as you put it, I chose it. And I am in. Totally in. I will not go back." She stood, her hands braced on the arms as if preparing to lunge forward. "Ever."

Chapter 9

WHEN THEY STEPPED INSIDE THE elevator, DeAngelo said, "Down, Market." The brass doors closed, and the old car jerked downwards.

"It responds to voice commands," Barbara observed. "That's why I couldn't find any buttons." The man nodded.

"Is this the only way up and down?"

"Unless you have an apartment, yes."

"And if you do?"

"There is an emergency stairway. The entrance is hidden in the kitchen, actually. You can reach the Market Level, but it is a very long way down. The elevator is so much more convenient, yes?"

Barbara nodded thoughtfully. "But last night, I took the elevator from the City Hall Station level."

DeAngelo nodded. "Like the stairway, it is an emergency exit and entrance. Rarely used by residents in order to avoid detection but critical if we had to evacuate."

"But how did the elevator know I wanted to go to your floor?"

"Because you used my card. It was the only way you could have entered by yourself."

Barbara nodded. The elevator clattered softly. "You said you have made scores of jewels, right?"

"Yes, that is correct."

"So do you have a jewel of your own?"

The man stared intently above the door, as if reading floor numbers.

"Mr. DeAngelo, I asked if you had a jewel of your own."

"Yes, Barbara. I heard you."

"Well," she asked in exasperation, "do you?"

"It is not as easy a question as it might seem. Yes, I had a jewel made. Many years ago. But I do not possess it."

Barbara looked puzzled. "So, you do have a jewel but it's not here. Did you lose it?"

"No, no," the man replied softly. "Someone else has it."

"What?" Barbara thought about her own jewel. The idea of anyone else having it was horrifying. And frightening. "You gave it away?"

The man lowered his eyes and looked steadily into hers. "It is being held."

"Like for ransom?"

"More as blackmail, yes? For discipline. To ensure loyalty."

"I don't understand."

The elevator clamored to a halt. "I will explain. But not right now. We are here."

The door opened silently onto a broad platform. They stepped out onto ancient wood decking that smelled faintly of creosote. Barbara glanced behind her to a single subway track that stretched into dark shafts to her left and right. Above her the subway tunnel roof was rough-hewn rock.

"Market Station," she whispered.

DeAngelo nodded and motioned to a high arch in front of them decorated in black and white mosaic. Bright light and a tumult of voices leaked out into the deserted station area.

"Not to be found on an official subway map," DeAngelo said. "But as you can see, it is quite real." He nodded toward the arch. "Please."

They passed through the arched entrance and Barbara looked out on a tiled cavern. An immense vaulted roof rose above them, but no light filtered through this ceiling. Instead, a soft yellow glow shone from a central ball that shined like a tiny sun, its light sifting through the dust and noise in front of her to the black and white tiled floor of the Market. Around the base of the vast dome, dozens of small storefronts lined the circular walls as far as she could see on each side until they were lost in the eddying crowd.

Brightly painted sandwich boards advertised the products within – leather goods, clothing, tools, paintings, hats, and things she could not decipher. Each shop was dominated by glass display windows, many with their brightly painted wooden doors wide open. Hundreds of men and women, most in bright red and black uniforms, strolled across the tiled floor, some chatting, others clearly on business.

"My God," she whispered. "It's huge. It must be as big as Grand Central Station."

"Larger, actually," DeAngelo said. "By some 20,000 square feet I understand."

Somewhere a bagpipe was whining, and a dog barked, cutting through the low babble of voices. Smells of sweat, leather and what she would have sworn was bread infused the air.

Barbara felt as if she had wandered into a dreamscape. "But…how can this be? DeAngelo?" she whispered, her eyes roaming around the gigantic open space. "Where are we?"

He glanced behind him. "That is the Market Station." He turned back and waved his arm expansively. "And this is the Market." He nodded at the stalls strung in a circle around the base of the dome. "Each of these stores sells very special items, no two alike. Many have workshops in the back. Others work in their lofts in The Building."

"Yes, but *where* are we? Are we underground?"

"Oh, yes. Deep underground. Let's go in, shall we?" DeAngelo suggested.

She realized she had been standing still in the middle of the entranceway as if turned to stone, her jaw slack and her eyes sweeping the gigantic, seething space in front of her.

She moved forwards slowly. "But how can this be?"

"Yes. Quite astonishing when you see it for the first time, no?" He ambled slowly into the brightly lit Market. At his side, Barbara stared around her as if she had just emerged onto another planet.

"It is an interesting story. Most people think the New York subway opened in 1904, and in a way they are correct. But 30 years before that, there was a subway that failed, the Beach Pneumatic Transit. Alfred Beach – modest man; he named the subway for himself – had grand plans. Miles of underground tunnels, dozens of stations, Beach subway cars. And what could be grander," he waved his hands in a wide arc, "and attract more investors, than an enormous main terminal, glorious and stunning? So, he started here. Only a few miles of tunnel were ever built before his grandiose plans were shattered in the stock market crash of 1873. All that remained of his dream were those tunnels."

"The line behind us," Barbara said, looking over her shoulder at the old station.

"Yes. Those and a vast, half-finished terminal. When the subway was finally built, they simply sealed off the original tunnels and abandoned the old station. And built City Hall Station above it."

"OK, the Market train switches off the main line," she nodded back toward the platform where the elevator had stopped, "and disappears down this hole onto a 150-year-old track no one remembers and winds up at this station no one knows about."

"Something like that," DeAngelo agreed. "After the Market's founding, residents realized they needed a route for supplies, to export products. They opened the old rails, connected them with the Lexington Line and purchased an old train, the very one that services the community today."

"So that's why no one notices comings and goings at City Hall Station. The maintenance men, the conductors, the visitors. The train doesn't stop there."

DeAngelo continued nodding.

"But the train *does* stop at Grand Central Station. Four times a week. Even at 4:00 in morning on Track 61, *someone* must see it. Not to mention the odd subway spelunker who notices this little chuffing engine disappear into a secret tunnel to get here."

"Yes, you are right, Madam. It no doubt does happen, but once the train has left the platform, they forget. Oh, for a few moments they might have a vague recollection of an odd train they thought passed by, but within seconds they forget."

"Forget."

DeAngelo smiled. "Twilight amnesia. Anterograde. An inability to form new memories. You can speak, are perfectly aware at the time, but no memories of an event are stored. It is a hypnotic state, apparently." He shrugged. "Have no idea how it works. A frequency issued by the train."

"And on the train?"

DeAngelo nodded. "It is a way we can bring agents and suppliers here without their remembering the exact location." He paused. "Once they leave the train anything that occurred on the trip out is forgotten. It is better that way, no?"

"And me?" Barbara looked hard at the side of DeAngelo's face. "When I leave here, I'll forget this place? Last night?" She waved her hand across the Market floor. "All of this?"

DeAngelo cleared his throat. "Not necessarily, Madam."

"What? Unless I walk out the way I came in?"

DeAngelo smiled. "That should not be necessary. Resident cards render us immune, as do the very limited number of visitor cards issued to us. I don't know the physiology, but they do."

Barbara reached into her backpack, unzipped a small pocket, and pulled out the man's black card.

"Exactly," DeAngelo said. "Please, do not lose it. We do not give them out easily."

She tucked the card back into her pack then looked around her. They had begun to stroll across the floor, mingling with the crowd that circulated among the shops. In front of them was a small grocery, its canvas awning covering an enclosure with rows of displays filled with oranges, apples, and melons.

Baskets of blueberries and raspberries crowded tables near the wood picket fence. Behind the fruit there were shallow bins of carrots, tomatoes, and potatoes. On the other side of the aisle into the grocery, stacks of bread – long baguettes, round loaves, flat circles of focaccia, oval loaves of dark rye – covered a long table dusted with flour.

"I knew I smelled bread," Barbara said happily.

"Indeed you did." DeAngelo nodded toward a man helping a customer in the bakery section. He wore the regular red and black garb covered by a white apron. "That is Mr. Clement. He joined the Market only about 10 years ago. Before that he had won medals for his breads across Europe."

Barbara stared at the man as they walked by. He looked up and smiled briefly. Barbara gave a small wave.

"He gave it all up to come here," Barbara mused. "And what about you, Mr. DeAngelo? What brought you here?"

A few people mumbled a greeting to the man as they walked, some touching the brim of their hats, but most paid them no attention.

"As you have seen, my apartment is in a rather special building. The residents here are a curious but talented collection of men and women, most of whom work here in the Market. Some are crafts people, other artists, and writers. For a variety of reasons, each of us lives somewhat — how do you put it? Off the grid?"

DeAngelo hesitated. "The organization I work for is also non-traditional. My colleagues are generally introverts. Reclusive I suppose. It fits our work. Some years ago, a gem maker was transferred from New York shortly after I arrived from Australia. He thought I would be happy here."

Barbara looked at him. "Are you?"

DeAngelo's face darkened and he said nothing.

"OK. So back to your story." Barbara swept her arm around the bustling, noisy market. "This is hardly a hole in the ground," she pointed out. "It's mammoth. And the tiled walls, the floor. How could it have been forgotten?"

DeAngelo nodded. "Surprising, no? Have you heard of the Terra Cotta Army?"

"I think I saw something about it in National Geographic. It's in China."

"Yes. Just outside the city of Xian. It was built by China's first emperor, Qin She Huang, more than 2,000 years ago. It is really an underground palace, built as a tomb for the emperor. There are four pits, all larger than a football field, filled with life-size horses, warriors, officials. Over 8,000 figures, each face different. There are chariots, weapons." He shook his head slightly. "Astonishing."

The two of them were circulating around the perimeter of the Market. Barbara smelled coffee and looked at a small café. A low picket fence enclosed a courtyard with small tables covered in red-checked tablecloths. People sat talking excitedly or scrolling across the screens of small computers.

"Can we have a coffee later, after we see the jeweler?" Barbara asked as they passed the café.

"Most certainly."

They walked silently for a few moments. "DeAngelo."

"Yes, Madam?"

"What does the Terra Cotta Army in China have to do with this place?"

DeAngelo laughed. "Of course. You see, as vast and magnificent as the tomb was, despite 700,000 people working on it, despite many contemporary accounts of its brilliance, within a few generations, it was forgotten. Buried and lost. And it was not rediscovered until 1974, nearly 2,100 years later."

As they neared the center of the floor the vast dome dampened the chatter and noise of the lively marketplace, but somewhere in front of her, Barbara heard the clanging of a hammer on an anvil. The bagpipe had been replaced by a horn section off to her right. Two men, one in what seemed to be the red and black uniform of the Market and the other in khakis and a white polo shirt, walked by them toward the elevator. The man in street clothes carried a large leather valise.

"Let me know how they go," the Market man said.

"Oh, they'll go, my friend," the one in the white polo shirt said. "They're gorgeous, as always." The Market man beamed and put his hand on the other's shoulder. "Have a good trip back."

Barbara shifted her attention back to DeAngelo. "Well, somebody seems to have remembered this place."

DeAngelo nodded again. "Indeed. Like the Terra Cotta Army, rumors persisted and, with a little digging…"

"So to speak," Barbara offered.

DeAngelo looked at her and laughed. "There were old newspaper accounts of the work. Letters. And yes, about 50 years ago it was rediscovered."

Barbara's eyes scanned the crowd in front of her. People of all shades were talking, walking arm and arm. Looking seriously at the floor as they walked, deep in thought.

"But who *are* they? All of these people?"

DeAngelo was silent for a moment. "Misfits. Outsiders. Inventors. Shapeshifters. Geniuses. Seers. Gifted artisans. People who look different, are different." He paused again, studying the crowd that filled the tiled floor. "This world is, perhaps, larger than you know, yes? More varied. Not so predictable as that to which you are accustomed?"

"I'm beginning to get that impression, yes."

"There are more types of people," he went on, "than fit neatly into the *Minnesota Multiphasic Personality Inventory*."

"That's the test that measures personality types, mental illness."

"Yes, yes. Quite right. But here, well, there are people who have special skills, knowledge, instincts. Some would say powers perhaps. And those who have found forgotten skills — or perhaps discovered new ways of enhancing them."

"Like your gems."

"Yes." Beside her, DeAngelo's face settled into a grim frown. "And no. All such people do not live here, of course." His eyes clouded. "That is the case with my employers.

"Every time you mention your employer, something dark sweeps through you. You fear them."

"Perhaps that is the case, Madam. I have come to respect your intuition."

"Will you…can you tell me more?"

The man sighed. "I will, yes. I must. But later, please? There is no time now. We are here on business. And to understand my employment situation, you must also understand the Market."

"You are deferring quite a bit of information until 'later."

"Yes, yes," the man agreed. "My regrets. But can we return to my elucidation?"

Barbara nodded reluctantly.

"As I was saying in reference to my employer's compound, there are other pockets where the world as you know it is frayed, torn slightly. Where those who have unusual ways of being in the world collect. Where the rules are bent slightly." He glanced briefly at her. "Do you see?"

"No," Barbara's eyes swept across the crowd. "Actually, I don't see."

DeAngelo sighed and glanced over at Barbara. "Madam…" he began, catching Barbara's glare. "Excuse me. Barbara, have you ever been to a circus?"

Barbara looked at him quizzically.

"Ah, perhaps that dates me. Have you ever seen a contortionist?"

Barbara shrugged. "Sure. On TV I guess." She paused, thinking. "Oh, wait. There was this one woman – she was on a documentary. I think she'd just been named to the *Guinness Book of Records* or something as the greatest living contortionist. She was Russian. Zlita, Zlata; something like that. My God, she moved like a snake. Her head seemed separate from her body. She bent over backward until she was looking out between her legs!"

"Yes, yes. And what did you think when you saw her?"

"I don't know. Mainly that her body sure didn't move like mine. What she did seemed humanly impossible."

DeAngelo nodded once more, this time toward the people in the shops and walking across the tiled floor.

"Precisely. And not everyone's mind works like yours either. Or mine. There are people who can do things cerebrally, mentally that seem…humanly impossible. They are up there," he said, motioning upward, "walking on the streets talking with a being from another dimension that no one else can hear. Predicting the future in run-down tarot parlors. They are living in monasteries, hogans, learning ancient rites and forgotten arts. They have grown up in isolated corners where old knowledge is still passed down. They are the children in school who devise a chemical theory so advanced the teacher scorns it as rubbish."

DeAngelo stopped and looked directly into Barbara's eyes. "They are sitting in the back of classrooms, watching, knowing how those around her feel and think." He held her eyes for a long moment. "Come. I am anxious for you to meet Mrs. Harlow."

They began to walk more purposefully, veering slightly to the right.

Barbara looked above her. The ceiling was a colossal mosaic configured in concentric circles of multicolored tile that became lighter until they met in a central glowing ball. "It's like a miniature sun."

"Indeed. It is precisely that. Created by three of the original colonists here. Brilliant physicists. "

Her eyes swept down to the rows of shops. "It's right out of a Dickens' novel," she marveled. "But with an artificial sun." She paused, watching the people swirl around her. "You mentioned the first colonists. How did it start, the Market?"

"Ah. There are always those looking for a refuge, yes? A place where they can be who they are, where they are safe. Where they can escape the mayhem of the world. A few came together to look for such a place. They followed the rumors, explored the old subway lines. Used diagrams they found in forgotten libraries. Dug through the walls to the abandoned tunnels until they found what they were looking for." He raised his eyes to circular walls embracing them like vast arms. "When it was rediscovered, only a few artisans located here. At first, they lived in tents but as their numbers grew, they built more permanent structures. Over the years artisans and architects, masons and carpenters settled here. Together they built this." He looked at the rainbow dome overhead. "It is very beautiful, yes?"

Barbara was still trying to make sense of the place. "It is so vast. Is the subway the only way to get here?"

"Yes. As I said, that is partly why the elevator stops as the City Hall platform. In an emergency, we can reach the platform and exit through the tunnels if necessary."

"Wouldn't recommend it," Barbara murmured.

The pair made their way through the crowd, most of whom moved courteously out of the way though they seemed largely oblivious to DeAngelo and Barbara.

"The people," Barbara said quietly, her voice almost lost in the murmur of conversation and the immense space of the vaulted building. "They look like they are from every country in the world."

"Yes, around 60 I believe. The Management seeks diversity."

"Management?"

"There is a Market Council. It is not easy to operate such a place. To feed those living here. And to sell the wares. Each trade — the jewelers, potters, tailors, cobblers — operates as a syndicate, and the syndicates select their representatives to the Council. And of course, remaining obscure, hidden, it is very important."

"Twilight amnesia."

He nodded to a man hurrying by with a mug of coffee. "The goods made here are, what would you call them? Specialty items, yes? They are sold to special buyers."

"Like your jewels."

"Exactly. So the Council has salespeople on the outside."

"And you? How do you find your clients?"

DeAngelo's dropped his eyes. "My situation, it is different, yes? You see the people in uniform?"

Barbara paid closer attention to the red and black clothing worn by most of the crowd, a simple long- sleeved, collarless red cotton shirt with wood buttons and a pair of what looked like black jeans. Men and women wore identical items, though some had adorned their outfit with jaunty scarves, black berets and other hats, and jeweled pins.

"They are members of the Market Syndicate. I am not."

"You are on your own?"

The man shook his head. "It is not that simple. My clients are identified for me. Just as you were."

"I've wondered about that," Barbara said. "It must have been a mistake, your coming to the house looking for me. I'm no CEO or budding politician. I'm a housewife. Maybe you were supposed to see David?"

DeAngelo raised a hand in dissent. "First, madam, you are far from a housewife." He glanced at her. "Do not underestimate yourself. No mistake was made. It was you who was identified."

"Identified? By whom?"

They had been making their way across the floor and now neared a shop with "Necklaces/Settings" painted across the glass front in perfect red letters rimmed in gold.

"It is a difficult question." He paused in front of the shop. "I will attempt to answer later. But now, you came for a special chain, yes?" The man waved his arm toward the door. "After you, madam."

The shop was larger than Barbara had expected from the outside. Wood floors extended deep behind a glass display case positioned a few feet inside the door, and though there were curtains separating the rear of the building, Barbara could make out work benches in the back. The shop smelled of floor wax and dust.

She had expected it to be dark inside, but instead it was bright and cheery. The ceiling of the shop was glass, lighting the interior with the glow of the artificial sun in the tiled roof.

A tiny bell dinged on the display case. Almost immediately a small woman of indeterminate age appeared from behind the partially drawn curtains. She wore the syndicate uniform brightened by a necklace of glistening gold beads. She wiped her hands on a soft blue cloth.

"Madam," the woman said, nodding to Barbara. "Mr. DeAngelo. It is good to see you again. It has been a long time."

"Indeed, Mrs. Harlow. It has indeed. Too long, no?"

As the two spoke, Barbara's eyes had strayed to the items in the case, and she gasped. "Those are your jewels." She turned to DeAngelo. "I can tell!"

"Ah, Mrs. Harlow. This is Barbara, a client of mine."

The woman's eyes arched in surprise. "I have been privileged to make necklaces for your clients before, sir, but I have never met one."

"Yes, well, this client is a bit unusual, no?"

"DeAngelo," Barbara continued, still staring at the glowing jewels in the case, each encased in filigrees of gold or silver and attached to exquisitely delicate chains. "I recognize them. They *are* yours, aren't they?"

The shopkeeper looked at the man, puzzled. "In all the years I have known you, I have never seen you with another person." She looked at Barbara. "And certainly not an outsider on a first-name basis."

The man waved his hand, looking slightly embarrassed. "It is a long story." He turned to Barbara. "Barbara, this is Mrs. Harlow. She is the chain maker I mentioned to you."

Barbara tore her eyes away from the case and extended her hand. "I am sorry. I was just startled to see the gems in your case."

The shopkeeper shook Barbara's hand gently. Barbara was surprised at the softness of the woman's hand, like kid leather.

"I understand. They are indeed striking."

"You see," DeAngelo explained, "these are reproductions of some of the jewels I have made. Some, alas, that were later destroyed." The man nodded to a particularly spectacular jewel. It was an amber tear drop, glowing yellow and red exploding in a shower of orange flakes. At its center were tiny black, red, and white specks. "You recall the sad story of the musician, no? Who did not pay for his jewel?"

Barbara thought back to the conversation on her patio. Could it have only been a few days ago? "Yes, of course. But you said his jewel disappeared from your vault."

The man nodded. "That is true. But as you can see, there are great artisans in the Market. Before it vanished, I had a jeweler make a replica. It was not, of course, like the original. It contained none of the man's soul. But otherwise it is an exact likeness. I use them as samples occasionally, for clients." He gestured to Mrs. Harlow. "And to show how they might be set."

"May I see it?" Barbara asked.

The woman drew the sliding door in the back of the display case open and drew out the jewel, carefully draped over a black velvet neck by a gold necklace. Barbara lifted the jewel and then ran her fingers along the gleaming chain. "It is so fine." She held the chain in her palm. "It weighs nothing. Is it really unbreakable?" she asked dubiously.

The shopkeeper looked into Barbara's green eyes. "You could tow a semi-truck with it."

Barbara picked up the necklace and grabbed the chain in each hand. She yanked viciously. "Ouch," she winced, looking at the red welt on her palms.

"You did not believe me?"

"I don't know. It is so fine, so beautiful. I just wanted to make sure, I guess."

"So, are you satisfied now?"

Barbara nodded meekly.

The man had watched silently. "Barbara," he said gently. "This is not an ordinary chain, nor is Mrs. Harlow a normal jeweler."

"No," Barbara sighed. "It seems like nothing much is normal anymore."

"I understand it is hard for you to grasp," the woman said. "Few outsiders venture here." She glanced somewhat askance at the man. "And fewer understand this place." She waved her arm to include the entire Market. "We work with materials unavailable to others anywhere in the world. We have learned techniques that are centuries old and that are practiced nowhere else."

She took the necklace out of Barbara's hand and laid it on a black velvet square on the glass top of the case. "The chain is a modified *forcat* style, but it has 52 links per inch." She paused for emphasis. "The most links anywhere else on earth is 38. Each link is hand forged from an alloy of several precious metals, including osmium, rhodium and meinterium, the hardest metals on earth. It is a formula known only to us."

"I think I've heard of rhodium and maybe osmium," Barbara said, "but never meitnerium,"

"I am not surprised. To most, it is still a theoretical metal. It is solid under normal conditions and assumes a face-centered cubic crystal structure, similarly to iridium. But in fact it is the second heaviest metal in the universe with a density of around 37.4 g/cm3."

"But if it's so heavy, then how can the necklace be so light?"

The woman laughed. "Here we are speaking of the number of electrons, the atomic weight as well as the lanthanide and actinide contractions. Density, really. Together they form an alloy that cannot be melted and remains lustrous at even the highest temperatures. It is impervious to any acid known. Oh, and the meitnerium isotope has another unique characteristic. It is radioactive."

"You mean, like, hot?"

"Yes and no. We craft the chains so that the owner is not affected by the radioactivity. It is normally low anyway. For the owner, it has only beneficial effects."

Barbara looked skeptical.

"It is true," the woman continued. "Low amounts of radioactivity can be healthy and strengthening.

"But not so with a person who attempts to steal your necklace. We adjust the atomic emission with your own nuclear rhythms. For a person not synchronized, touching either the chain or the jewel setting results in an instant radioactive burn." She smiled. "It is very unpleasant. Only you will be able to remove the chain from your neck."

"The settings for the jewels. They are made from the same material?"

"Yes. All settings are made from the same alloy." She pointed at the jewel lying on top of the velvet. "We use a prong method for setting your jewel. Do you see the tiny arms holding the stone?"

Barbara nodded.

"This method shows off each jewel to its best advantage. We use 52 arms attached to the base loop. Then we cut a 'bearing' into the arms."

Barbara frowned slightly.

"Excuse me. A 'bearing' is a notch that corresponds to the angles of your stone. Then the stone is inserted so that it rests snugly in all of the bearings. A specialized tool then bends the prongs gently over the crown of the stone and sets it permanently. It cannot be removed, nor can it be harmed in any way. It is a tiny impermeable cage that protects your stone, forever."

Barbara stared at the stone on the countertop. "It is lovely."

"Each tip of the arm is rounded then hand etched with a symbol of your choice."

"A symbol?"

"This setting," DeAngelo explained, "enhances your stone. Not just its beauty, but it's inner content, its potency. The arms hold the gem, yes, but they also project its energy."

Barbara looked at the man, her head cocked. "But you said the gem has no power. That it only crystalizes what is inside of me. How then can the setting project a force that is not there?"

The man nodded. "That is partly true, but as what is 'inside of you,' as you put it, grows, that change is reflected in your stone. It amplifies your strength. The setting acts as its antennae."

Barbara put her hand on the counter. "I see. I think."

"So," the woman said. "We should get started with your chain. I am sure you would like your gem back as soon as we can complete the job. I think we can get at it later this week."

Panic surged through Barbara. She grasped the pouch hanging from the leather cord and held her gem to her chest. "I don't understand. I can't leave my stone." She looked frantically at the man. "I thought I made that clear!"

DeAngelo reached out toward Barbara then checked himself. "I don't think there is any other way," he said, concern in his voice. He turned to the woman behind the counter. "Mrs. Harlow, is there any possibility we could wait here while you make the chain and setting?"

"Sir," the woman began, "this is not a drive-in jeweler. You know the work that is entailed." Her face darkened. "And you and your client are not our only customers. You are aware of that, I am sure?"

The man nodded contritely. "Yes, Mrs. Harlow, I am most aware that your skills are in great demand. And I know what a great favor I am asking of you. But as you can see," he repeated, "this is not an ordinary customer." He held his hands together as if he were pleading. "I would be most indebted."

The woman glowered at the man then turned to Barbara.

"It is not possible to have it done today. The alloy needs to be carefully cast and the links worked."

Barbara felt an ache of dismay that must have shown in her eyes.

Mrs. Harlow sighed. "But I will work through the night. It will be ready tomorrow morning."

"Oh, thank you!" Barbara burst out. "Thank you so much!"

The woman nodded to Barbara and then turned to DeAngelo. "You have been a very good customer over many years, but" she added disapprovingly, "in the future, sir, would you please leave your customers outside of The Market?"

The man smiled.

"Now, miss," the woman said. "Let us have a look at your gem."

Barbara loosened the strings of the pouch around her neck and gently shook the stone onto a velvet mat on the countertop. Somehow, her jewel seemed even more ravishing than she'd remembered. The hundreds of facets glittered in the light from the overhead sun.

The woman gave a small gasp. "It is magnificent." She looked at the gem maker. "Surely one of the most spectacular you have created." She glanced at Barbara. "I wouldn't have thought it."

She picked up the stone and studied its deep red core with the appreciation of a master jeweler and the awe of a novice. "Yes, I believe we can make a setting that does such a stone justice. Now, just a few details." The shopkeeper looked at Barbara. "Miss, I do not believe you want this jewel on permanent display. Despite its protections, you would attract much attention." She glanced at DeAngelo. "Attention I suspect you do not want."

"Yes," Barbara said uncertainly. "I guess you are right."

"I would recommend a 70cm chain." She looked at Barbara appreciatively. "That would place the gem directly between your breasts, but, unless you wore very low necklines, out of sight of the casual observer."

"Yes," Barbara managed again. Things seemed to be moving very fast now. "That sounds fine."

"Good. Now, I wish to take your molecular synchronization." The woman pulled out what looked like a thin blood pressure cuff from underneath the counter. "Please, may I put this around your neck?"

Barbara nodded, and the woman stepped out from behind the display. She gently fit the Velcro tape around Barbara's neck, which was attached by a wire to a small digital display on the counter. She stepped back behind the display case. "Now, please be still. You will feel nothing, but it is imperative that you not move."

She nodded again, and Mrs. Harlow pushed a button on the console. She had been right; despite her fears, Barbara felt nothing. After perhaps a half minute, the woman pushed the button again. She reached over and undid the Velcro strap.

"Very good," she said. "Now, there is just one more thing. What symbol is it you want on the arms of your setting?"

Barbara looked uncertain, and then turned to DeAngelo. "What should it be? You know better than I do."

He bowed slightly. "Madam, I assure you, that is not the case. You know yourself the best, no?"

Barbara's mind turned to the conversation they had had, just hours earlier. "You said Barbara became Chango, the deity of fire, lightning, and thunder in Santeria?"

The man nodded.

Barbara smiled. "And I *am* an Aries."

DeAngelo nodded once more. "Indeed you are."

She turned back to the jeweler. "Mrs. Harlow, I would like my symbol to be fire."

Mrs. Harlow smiled. "A good choice. Now, since the two of you are so impatient, I really must get to work." She lifted Barbara's gem gently from the velvet and rested it in her palm. She looked directly into Barbara's eyes.

"I assure you, I will protect your jewel. It will not be harmed."

Barbara realized it was more than a promise; it was a vow. She nodded.

Barbara leaned across the counter and gave the woman a hug. "Thank you, Mrs. Harlow."

The woman returned the jewel to the leather case and waved the two of them away. "Shoo, now. Come back tomorrow morning."

Barbara glanced back as the two of them left the shop.

"Please, do not worry," DeAngelo said. "It could not be in safer hands."

Yes, Barbara thought. *Safe hands. And what about me?*

"Mr. DeAngelo," Barbara said as they entered the main Market area. "Could we have that coffee now?"

Chapter 10

THEY EMERGED FROM THE SHOP into the swarming courtyard. Barbara looked at the glowing ball embedded in the center of the ceiling high overhead. "Does it ever get dark?" Barbara asked softly.

"No, the sun stays on day and night. Here, night and day mean little. People work when they like."

"How do they sleep?"

"Most have rooms in the Building, as I do. This is their workshop, their social center, their town square." They drifted toward the rambling café against the far wall Barbara had noticed when they entered. As they walked, Barbara became aware of the low thrum of an electric motor, the shrill of drills and routers, and the dull thud of drums. Singing arose from somewhere in the maze of shops and people.

She smelled coffee, sawdust, and steel.

Suddenly DeAngelo stiffened beside her, and she was dragged out of her reverie. She followed his gaze to a far corner of the Market. She could see nothing. She looked into his stricken face. For the first time, fear glinted in his black eyes.

"What is it?" she whispered.

"Nothing."

"Don't lie to me. You're not good at it."

He looked at her, his mouth set in a grim line. "Let us get our coffee."

He walked ahead, making Barbara almost trot to keep up. DeAngelo stopped at the small gate in the wooden fence that surrounded the café and spoke to a waiter in a black coat over his red shirt. The man nodded and led him to a table near the door to the interior of the café. Barbara hurried behind. DeAngelo sat in the chair facing the Market square as Barbara slipped into the chair facing him.

"What is it?" she asked quietly, looking intently into his drawn face. "What did you see?"

"Not what, madam. Whom." He motioned to the waiter, who approached the pair with a small notepad.

"Can I help you, sir?" the man asked, genuine concern in his eyes.

"I wish you could, Albert." He breathed deeply. "For now, two espressos?" He looked at Barbara, who nodded. "Yes, two espressos, please."

After the waiter had left, Barbara leaned forward. "Please. You must tell me. Who did you see?"

The man sighed. "He did not waste any time."

Barbara felt her frustration rising. "Who? *Who* didn't waste any time?"

DeAngelo sat back in his chair, fighting to slow his breathing. He nodded briefly toward the far wall of the Market. "There is a man there. You wouldn't have noticed, but I did."

"Yes. Go on."

"He is a very dangerous man. Someone I had hoped I would never see again."

"Dangerous in what way?"

"Dangerous in the way he could kill us both with his bare hands in a matter of seconds. That kind of dangerous."

Barbara looked anxiously over her shoulder. A sea of people was flowing across the vast black and white tiled floor. "Where?"

"Look slightly to your right. He is standing in the doorway of the leather shop. He is looking at us."

Barbara let her gaze travel down the line of shops against the far wall. Near the end was an awning over the entrance to a store specializing in exquisite leather goods. Standing in the shadow of the awning was a tall man, his shaved head shiny and pale. Even from their distance, she could see a great hawk nose and small mouth frozen in a thin red line.

She turned back to DeAngelo. "Who is he?"

The waiter approached their table and set down two expressos. They stared up at Barbara like two dark eyes in their fine white China cups.

"DeAngelo," Barbara repeated, "Who is he?"

"His name is Victor Caraldo." DeAngelo continued to stare at the figure. "He works for the *Mester*."

"DeAngelo!" Barbara said sharply. "Look at me."

The man tore his gaze away, startled.

"I can see you are frightened, but I don't know why. I don't know Victor Caraldo, and I don't know the *Mester*." She leaned forward across the table. "Don't you think it's time you let me in on what's going on? Let me into your life just a little?"

The gem maker stared into Barbara's eyes. "Madam," he said quietly," it is precisely because I have been imprudent and let you into my life that Caraldo is here." His voice remained even, but the intensity of his glowing black eyes caused Barbara to sit back in her chair.

"Did I not say you had no idea what you were getting into? Did I not say you would be in danger, as would I?" He narrowed his eyes slightly. "I *have* let you into my life, no? Too much, perhaps?"

Barbara averted her eyes from his angry stare. She sat up straight in her chair and picked up the espresso and sipped it thoughtfully.

"I am sorry that I have put you in danger," she said, glancing back at him. "I realize I acted impetuously without understanding the risk involved. And if I have caused you any harm, I sincerely apologize." She set her cup down. "But I do not apologize for seeking out a man who I understood was extraordinary. A man who could not only see me but see through me." She glared at him. "And a man who I thought had gained the wisdom and courage to see to the core not only of others, but of himself." She took another sip of her espresso. "Perhaps I was wrong."

The china cup rattled in its saucer as she placed it roughly on the table. She nodded vaguely toward the man on the far side of the Market. "Clearly my being here has triggered some response. I don't understand why, but I can see that you are in peril, and that somehow, I am the cause." She stood.

"I think I can find my way back now." She smiled slightly. "I think I will take the train next time, though. I will come back on Thursday for my gem."

She looked at the man, who was staring into his expresso. "I really am sorry," she said quietly. "I hope everything works out for you."

Barbara turned and walked out of the café into the swirl of men and women toward the elevator at the far end of the station. *What now?* Tears blurred her vision and crept out of her eyes. She bumped into a woman, who scowled at her.

Suddenly a hand fell on her shoulder. She whirled, terrified it was the tall man DeAngelo so feared. Instead, she stared into the glistening black eyes of the gem maker. He held her at arm's length for a moment then dropped his hand to his side.

"I am the one who should be sorry, madam. Not you."

She looked at him silently for a long moment. "Isn't it dangerous for you to touch me? Especially with this man here watching you? Back at the house you said it was forbidden."

The man looked down at the tile and then back up into her eyes. "It is beyond that." His voice shook slightly. "And, madam, I am glad it is." He nodded back toward the café. "Please, will you finish your expresso? I believe we have a good deal to talk about, yes?"

Barbara gave a brief nod. "Yes, I believe we do."

Chapter 11

THEY RE-ENTERED THE CAFÉ AND sat at their table. The waiter hurried over. "Is everything alright, sir?"

"It is fine." He glanced at the worried expression on the man's face and smiled. "Really, Albert. But thank you for your concern."

The waiter nodded and left the table.

DeAngelo dropped his eyes and pulled a hand through his silver-grey hair, brushing it behind his ear. He put an elbow on the table and rested his chin in his palm, then lifted the cup to his lips. He rolled the espresso around in his mouth for several seconds before swallowing it.

"It is bitter, yes?"

"Espresso usually is."

"Yes, yes. And truth? That can be bitter as well, no?"

Barbra tilted her head slightly, looking at him. "It seems so, doesn't it? I had a life laid out for me. Comfortable, luxurious even. It was so seductive, so safe, you know? There was nothing I wanted. Yet somewhere I knew that I had nothing that I truly needed." She sat back, looking thoughtfully over the man's shoulder. "How does that work? How do we live on two planes? The material and the spiritual?"

"Perhaps. Or, as Nietzsche saw it, the conscious and the unconscious."

"Like Freud?"

"Yes. Later. Nietzsche understood we did not always know where our thoughts came from. He knew that we often push unacceptable feelings and thoughts into the unconscious and that these can come out in ways we do not even recognize." The man paused thoughtfully. "At first, this repression, it makes us feel better, yes? We don't have to confront our urges, our fears, our sadness. We can get on with our business. But then, someone, perhaps a kind woman, makes us think about our own emptiness and hurt. And do we thank her? No, no. For she is the villain now. We regard her with hostility, anger, for she is threatening to expose us.

"Those repressed feelings, they do not go away, yes? They simmer deep in our unconscious." He paused and looked into Barbara's eyes. He moved his hand from his cup and reached across the table and gently covered her hand with this. "They make us forget who our enemy is and who is our friend."

Barbara stared back. The heat of his hand was like a warm compress, damp and soft.

The man withdrew his hand and sat back, staring over the crowded market. "My name…" he hesitated then laughed self-consciously. "It has been a long time since I have spoken this to another, no? My name is Zoltan József."

"Zoltan," Barbara said slowly, concentrating on each syllable. "I like it. It fits you."

"My father would be so pleased."

Barbara smiled and extended her hand across the table. The man grasped it lightly. "Nice to meet you, Zoltan," she said. "Now that I know your name, who are you?"

The man's eyes twinkled. "As I said, my father and mother were Hungarian. I was born in Budapest." He looked directly into Barbara's eyes. "October 10, 1913. Almost a year before the Great War began."

Barbara was vaguely aware that she wasn't even shocked anymore. "Yes, go on."

"My parents were Jewish. My mother died just six days after I was born. An infection called puerperal. It is caused by a streptococcus bacterium."

"I am so sorry," Barbara began.

The man smiled sadly. "That was a very long time ago." He stopped and stared into the cup.

"What about your father?"

"My father could not bring me up. He was a professor at the University of Budapest. Philosophy. His family was wealthy, and we lived in a great home off Andrassy Ut adjacent to the Jewish Quarter. My father was a communist, you see. After the War, he joined other revolutionaries who wished to see a socialist Hungary." The man sighed. "The Red government was a failure, and in 1919 it was crushed by reactionary forces. They attacked and murdered sympathizers of the old government. We knew it as the White Terror— Tens of thousands, many Jews, were imprisoned, tortured, and killed. My father was shot by a firing squad with six other men."

"That's horrible," Barbara said. "So you were an orphan," she added softly.

"Yes. That is so. I was nine. It was a terrible time, and even as a child I could feel the hatred and the fear. I lived in the big house, almost never going outside, only surviving because of my nanny, Raza. Three months after my father was killed, my uncle Ödön came to the house. He was a successful merchant and left alone by the fascists. He brought a train and boat ticket that would get me to England, where we had relatives. He said I had to leave. That I would be killed if I stayed. The next day I left for Italy with just a tiny leather suitcase."

"That's how you happened to grow up in London, then."

He nodded. "But first I went to live with my aunt, yes? I wasn't yet 10. My aunt, she was not cruel, but she had children of her own, older than me. Their father had died in the War. They were not interested in this strange Hungarian boy who had fallen from the sky. We could not communicate. You see, then I spoke only Hungarian." The man chuckled. "Hungarian, and Latin, of course. That was very handy."

Barbara smiled. "I like it when you do that." When he cocked his head quizzically, she went on, "When you laugh. You don't do it very much."

He was quiet for a moment. "No. No, I suppose I do not. Perhaps there has not been much to laugh about, no?" He looked at her. "I feel more like laughing now than in many, many years."

She looked at her coffee, cooling in the small cup in her hands, embarrassed.

"Shall I go on? Perhaps you are bored. Tired of this long story."

Barbara looked up sharply. "No! I mean, no, please. I want to know more about you." She was startled at her vehemence. *He's a magic man.* "It's important."

The man described the isolation and depression he felt at his aunt's, followed by six years at a remote boarding school in northern England. Books his only refuge, he excelled and was accepted into Cambridge and later worked as a professor at a university near London.

"A professor, yes, but I was not very good. The sadness, you know. My students saw it. I was not, I am afraid, very much fun." The man paused again, deep in thought. "And then the defeat of the Republican forces in Spain. The rise of fascism. The anti-Semitism. Such a dark time, inside and out."

He looked up, his black eyes suddenly alive. "And then I met Rebecca. She taught at the college. I did not notice her. I did not notice anyone, yes? Then one day I was sitting in the library, reading, Nietzsche most likely. Suddenly a hand touched my shoulder. I jumped like it had been an electric shock. When I turned, I looked into the most beautiful face I had ever seen, the softest, kindest eyes. She was smiling. I remember that smile, broad, warm, and real. 'I wondered how I'd ever get your attention,' she said. 'I've been flirting with you for months. You didn't seem to notice, so I took the direct approach.'"

The man's eyes glistened, a tenderness smoothing the lines in his face. "Can you imagine? She wanted me! My heart pounded. I was joyous. I was terrified. I was in love. That was in 1937. I was 27 and she was 24. We married three months later. Only my aunt came, but I did not care. Now I had Rebecca. That was all that mattered. They were such happy years, yes? We loved each other. She found kindness and love in me I did not know were there. We danced. We made love. We talked. We took walks. Every minute away from her felt stolen."

His eyes darkened as if a light switch had been turned off. "Then, it was early September 1939. It was only weeks after Hitler had invaded Poland. The Second War had begun. She found a small lump in her breast. I kissed it, joking that my kiss would make it better." His eyes dropped. "How stupid of me. I didn't understand. It was cancer. In those days, they only knew how to remove. There were no treatments. The cancer spread. My sweet Rebecca died December 1, 1940."

Tears welled in Barbara's eyes, and her throat closed in sorrow. She reached across the table and took his hand in hers.

"I cannot describe the darkness that swallowed me," the man continued. "I could not get out of bed. I was paralyzed. I took a leave from the college. I almost hoped to be called into the army so I would be killed. But I was already too old for the draft. Our home only reminded me of her death. The red carpeting she so loved faded to grey. The poppies in the garden were black. The sky ash. I remained lost in that bleakness for more than a year. The only contact I had with the outside world was the newspapers I read each day. I became morbidly fixated on the obituaries.

"One day there was an unusual notice. Small. It read, 'Lost parents? Other loved ones? We understand. Lift the darkness. Create gems.' Then there was a phone number. I did nothing, and then I lost the paper somehow. But it haunted me. I read the obituaries for the next week to see if the notice would appear again. Two weeks later, there was another notice in exactly the same place in the paper. This time the text read, 'Lost parents? Rebecca? We understand. Lift the darkness. Make gems.'"

Barbara gave a small gasp. "It actually named Rebecca?"

The man nodded. "Of course I first assumed it was a coincidence, some nasty trick of fate. But then I began to wonder. Remember, I was not really in my right mind, yes? Who had written this note? Was it meant for me? Who else? How did they know? Was there some magic at work? Ah, and here is the catcher: Could this person somehow bring her back to me?"

The man saw the perplexed look in Barbara's eyes. "I know. It was totally irrational. But I was desperate, yes? Any hope, no matter how foolish, was a tiny star in a black sky."

Her coffee long forgotten, Barbara cupped her chin, her eyes wide. "So what did you do?" she whispered.

"I called the number," the man said dully.

"And?"

"When I called, the voice on the other ended, high and reedy, began: 'I've been waiting. It's about time you called.'"

"He actually said he'd been waiting for you to call?"

"He gave me directions to his office near Smithfield. I was in a trance. It was Christmas Eve." The man shook his head sadly. "Somehow, I still had this idea he had brought Rebecca to life, or that maybe he could. I found his home, a sprawling red brick Victorian mansion. On the massive door was a heavy brass knocker. It was goat's foot. A man in a white turban answered. He was flanked by two bodyguards, who led me upstairs and into an office."

Barbara leaned forward.

"I had no fear of the thugs who met me, the rambling house, nothing. I was beyond fear. Until, that is, I met the Ugly Master, as I heard him called behind his back later. The door was opened by the robed servant, Rajiv, and I walked in. This hideous little man sat on an elevated chair behind a vast desk. It wasn't just his sunken cheeks or his giant ears flaring from the side of his head like fleshy shells. Or the small mouth pulled downward deeply at each corner. That was merely repulsive. My fear, that came from his eyes. Huge, yellow green eyes under drooping eyelids and bushy eyebrows. They glowed."

Barbara frowned.

"No, really, they glowed as if there was some terrible sulfurous chemical burning just behind them. When I looked into them, I felt my heart sink. They never blinked. He stared at me for a long moment. Then he said something quite extraordinary. 'Rebecca is dead. She will not return. You will never find another love.' His voice was high, reedy, raspy, cold. His sneer turned his words into a curse. I said nothing. 'You work for me, or you will die. You have no will to live. I will give you a purpose. And an income.'"

"Oh, my God," Barbara exclaimed. "Who was this man, this Ugly Master?"

Zoltan waved his hand gently. "Let me finish and you will see. After he spoke, I stood there, dumb, staring into the man's eyes, transfixed. 'Come,' he said. He slid from his chair and walked toward a door on the right side of the office. I became aware of the guards watching my every move. 'I am a gem merchant,' he explained. It was 1940. The war was not going well. The Master assured me the Nazis would win, but in the meantime, the European market for his jewels had plummeted. He needed an agent in the Australian market. And later in the US. I was it."

"But why you?" Barbara asked. "How did he even know about you?"

"Why me? Yes, I have asked myself the same question many times. You see, I think he can sense heartbreak. Depression and sadness. He told me he only hired orphans—no families, fewer complications. And if possible, widowers. He didn't trust women, he said. Too independent. How did he know I was an orphan? I do not know, but he did. I only had to sign an agreement."

"Did you do it? Surely you knew it was all wrong, Zoltan."

He shrugged. "I had nothing, so I felt I had nothing to lose. I would not live forever, he told me, but he would assure me an unnaturally long life. As long as I complied. He demanded total loyalty to him.

"There could be no compromise. I could not marry. I could not touch another person. I could not give anyone my real name. He assigned me the name DeAngelo. A joke I think."

The waiter approached their table. "Can I get you something more, sir?"

"No, thank you, Albert," he smiled. "We will be leaving soon. Just the check please."

The waiter pulled a bill off his pad and placed it on the table. "There is no hurry." He glanced out over the crowd, still milling about in the Market. "The man you were looking at, the man with the bald head and large nose."

"Yes?"

The waiter nodded to his right. "He is approaching."

The gem maker's eyes darted upwards. Some distance away, perhaps 50 yards, he saw the shiny head bobbing above the crowd, slowly advancing toward the café.

"It is safe here," the waiter continued. "We have refuge status."

Zoltan continued to stare into the crowd then turned toward the waiter and nodded. "Thank you, Albert," he said gratefully. "Thank you for the warning."

The waiter gave a slight nod and moved onto the next table.

Barbara stared nervously over her shoulder then turned back to Zoltan. "Refuge status?" she asked. "Does that mean we are safe?"

The man's face was tense. "There are many powerful forces in the world. Many of their representatives, their agents, reside here, do business here, or socialize here. The Market also draws assassins or enforcers if there is a conflict within one of the consortiums. There were killings many years ago, right here in the Market. Brutal and frightening. Craftspeople began leaving, and many others threatened to go if the Council did not act. They did. I don't know how they did it. It is a mystery to me, yes? But somehow, they made most of the market shops and restaurants refuges. That meant that no one could be harmed while inside the perimeter. If anyone attempted to harm another person in a refuge, even to become aggressive, that person became immobilized."

"Like frozen in their tracks?"

"Exactly," the man nodded.

"Then why didn't they make the entire Market a refuge?"

"I believe they tried, "the man replied. "Whatever protection they used could not extend over the entire area. So they designated most of the cafes and many of the shops as refuges."

Barbara looked back over her shoulder. "Have there been more killings outside of the refuges?"

The man shook his head. "There is greater monitoring of who enters. Stricter screening at the street level entrances. Fewer train passes issued." He stared at the shaven head bobbing toward them in the crowd outside the cafe. "But they cannot screen everyone, no? And the *Mester* has his ways."

"But no one can hurt you here, in the café, right?"

"That is the theory," the man smiled. "Perhaps we shall see, yes?"

Barbara turned back to look at the approaching bald-headed man. "So we just wait?"

The man shrugged. "If not here, he will find me wherever I go. But that does not mean you have to stay. You are not his concern, yes? It is me he wants." He nodded at the gate of the café. "Perhaps it would be best if you left now. This café may have refuge status, but the *Mester* is very powerful."

"Zoltan, do you really think I'm just going to get up, walk out the gate and wave goodbye? Especially now that we are on a first name basis?"

The man managed a tight smile.

"You were telling me about the Ugly Master, but I don't understand what that has to do with this man," she nodded vaguely backward with her head "that's after you."

"Yes, you are right. Let me finish quickly. After I signed the agreement, the *Mester* took me into a large room — like a laboratory, yes? — attached to his office. In the center of the room, on a slightly raised round disk, maybe five feet in diameter, there was what looked like an old camera. It was very much like mine, but slightly larger. The old wood had been painted black. This was the chief gem maker, he told me. I remember asking him what he meant, that I thought he dealt in precious gems. Oh, yes, he assured me. Very precious indeed. But first he and his agents had to create them. He introduced me to the camera and its settings. He showed me how to focus. How to adjust the settings. How to enhance the customer's natural character.

"'Now,' he said. 'I will demonstrate on you.' I remember his cruel smile. 'But keep in mind it will take part of your soul.' My soul? I asked. He laughed a high, harsh laugh. 'You have already lost most of it, haven't you?' he said. 'With the death of Rebecca? What do you have to lose?'"

"Did he do it?" Barbara asked eagerly. "Did he make your gem?"

"Yes. He created my gem."

"What did it look like? Was it beautiful?"

The man paused for a long moment, as if remembering an old sadness. "It was a teardrop, a stunning iridescent blue green," he said. "And in the middle was a glowing green sphere, perfectly round, yes?" He paused. "And at its center was a tiny white diamond, shimmering."

She gasped. "The diamond. Like mine." Her eyes widened. "You said you had only seen one other like it. It was yours."

For a moment, the man's eyes cleared. There was a warmth there she hadn't seen before. "Indeed."

"What happened to it? Do you still have it?"

The man shook his head sadly. "He took it and put it into a red leather bag. Then he opened the safe behind his desk and hung the bag on a peg. There were maybe 20, 21 other bags hanging in the vault. Just a little insurance, he said. He explained how the jewels could be destroyed by a tiny hammer, and then he pulled one out of a drawer in the vault. It was exactly like mine — a round brass head at one and the other sharp, like a tiny axe blade. He stared at me with those dreadful eyes. 'Should you ever violate the terms of our contract,' he told me, 'I will destroy your gem, and with it, a part of whatever soul you still have left.'"

"How could you agree to work for such a horrid man?" Barbara asked.

He shrugged. "Why not? If I complied with the terms of the contract, he said, and produce ten gems a year, that's all, and you will be wealthy — forever." He gave a small ironic smile. "You see, he could also extend my life. Not immortal, but I would age far more slowly."

"But Zoltan," Barbara protested. "He was evil. Surely you could see that?"

The man nodded sadly. "You are right. But he too was right, you see. I had no reason to live. I never wanted to touch or be touched again. I wanted only to be alone. To live with my books and my loneliness. The lengthened life? It was no incentive, of course. In fact, the thought of living an extended life of misery almost made me walk away. He saw me hesitate, and, as always, he got it. If the depression increased, became unbearable, he assured me, I could simply kill myself. Or, he could have me killed. And that's what he would do in any event if I violated my contract."

Barbara sat back. "That is where this man out there comes in. You have violated your contract. He is here to kill you."

Zoltan nodded. "Somehow, some way, the old man knows. About…" The man's eyes drifted over Barbara's shoulder. He stopped speaking abruptly and sat upright in his chair. His face shifted, became darker, grimmer. Barbara turned. The hawk-nosed man was walking through the entrance to the cafe. His eyes were fixed on their table. She felt a surge of fear and turned back quickly to Zoltan. "Now what?" she whispered.

The jewel maker said nothing. His gaze was fixed on the man approaching them. Barbara sensed he was beside their table, and she looked up slowly into ice blue eyes set deeply in a face dominated by a long, beak of a nose. He was a big man, and she was aware of other patrons staring at them.

There was a long silence. Zoltan sat rigid in his chair, staring expressionless into the bald man's face. The man looked back at him, a slight smile pulling up the edges of his thin lips.

Suddenly the waiter was standing just behind the man. "Sir," he began quietly.

The bald man ignored him, still facing the jewel maker. "Sir!" the waiter said more loudly.

Barbara saw the man's jaws clench and his eyes narrow. His head swiveled slowly, like that of a giant vulture, until he glared at the waiter, inches away.

The waiter's eyes lit up with fear, but he returned the man's stare. "This is a refuge, sir," the waiter said. He nodded toward a corner of the awning at what looked like a security camera, a small green light blinking at regular intervals from the lens. "Any violence will be neutralized."

Barbara sensed the big man tense and heard his breathing become shallower. His hands formed fists at his side. After several seconds, his fingers unclenched, and his breathing returned to normal. The slight smile returned to his face. "I am well aware that this is a refuge," he said.

Barbara had expected the man's voice to be deep, threatening, but it wasn't. It was light, lilting, almost affable. But the eyes gave him away. They glared like blue lasers into the waiter's face.

"There will be no violence here," he said. "I am simply meeting with an old friend." The waiter broke away from the man's stare and looked at the gem maker.

"It is all right, Albert. Thank you."

Albert nodded, looked warningly at the bald man, and withdrew.

"DeAngelo. It's been a long time."

The jewel maker gave a cursory nod. "Victor."

The man glanced at Barbara, who was watching the drama play out with wide eyes. "I don't believe I have met your companion."

"No," Zoltan said. "I don't believe you have."

The bald man waited expectantly several seconds and then gave a low laugh. "Where are your manners, DeAngelo? You have a reputation for being a gentleman."

"I am Barbara," she blurted.

The man's gaze shifted to Barbara for the first time. The eyes were meant to freeze her, she knew. Their iciness to frighten, to intimidate. But she saw something else in the gaze. Uncertainty.

"My name is Barbara," she said more evenly. "And I am not Mr. József's companion. I am his friend."

Barbara was amused to see the facial muscles above his eyes shift upwards. If he hadn't shaved off his eyebrows, he would have raised them.

"So that's who *I* am," Barbara continued. "Who are you?"

Barbara took some satisfaction in the brief look of confusion that drifted across the man's eyes.

"This, my dear, is Victor Caraldo," Zoltan said quietly. "Victor works for the Ugly Master."

The man's thin lips curled into a genuine grin. "*Csúnya Mester.* Ugly Master. I haven't heard that for a while."

Zoltan started. "Did you say *Csúnya Mester*?"

"Yeah. I got that from Dezső. It's Hungarian or something."

"It is indeed Hungarian, yes."

"Dezső told me that's what they used to call him in the old days. Said it translated as Ugly Master. The rumor is the little bastard grew up on the streets of Budapest." Caraldo shrugged. "Don't know if it's true. That's just what I heard."

"Excuse me," Barbara broke in. "Can one of you tell me who Dezső is exactly?"

Zoltan turned toward Barbara. "He was another agent, one of the first I believe."

"Retired now," Victor added.

"Yes," Zoltan said. "Under circumstances I never fully understood." He looked at Caraldo.

Victor shrugged. "I had to retire him. If it had been anyone else, he would have been killed." He shook his head slightly. "I guess if that ugly sonofabitch had a friend, it was Dezső. Supposedly knew him before they got into the jewel racket."

"Ah, as I suspected." As the *Mester's* enforcer, Victor had killed two agents and terrorized many others. Zoltan held Caraldo's eyes for several moments before turning back to Barbara. "Dezső too is Hungarian. Lives in Budapest still, I understand."

Victor nodded. "Stumbles from one bar to another, I hear." Victor shrugged his massive shoulders. "Poor old bugger."

"I see." He tried to assess the situation. If the *Mester* had wanted him dead, he would have already been killed. So what was Victor there for?

"What else have you heard, Victor? The Ugly Master, the *Csúnya Mester*, does he still call you Vic? Still taunt you for being stupid? Humiliate you in front of agents like he did in London?"

The man's face clouded.

Zoltan knew the danger, but his anger flared. "Does he still use you to kill agents who dare to disagree with him? Whom he fears?"

Caraldo' hawk-like face had become flushed, his bald scalp glowed pink. "It's a job."

"A job that means being used like an expendable tool. Just like the rest of us," Zoltan added quietly.

Caraldo shrugged. "I live in the real world, DeAngelo. I realized a long time ago, the smart kids used their brains to get what they wanted; I used what I had. Fair enough. They had a future being smart. Mine was in being big and mean. Strong. Started taking kids lunches in 3rd grade. If they reported me, I beat the shit out of them. Because I could, see, and then the next one was easier to persuade. Worked pretty good. Still does."

"Guess that's why killing people comes so easily to you. Like when you strangled Fitz in Tokyo, or when you beat Welser to death in Buenos Aires."

"Didn't mean to kill Welser."

"Ah, I see. Just cripple him for life, yes? And when the *Mester* introduced you in London, what? Fifteen years ago? When he told us that you had killed two agents. Do you remember, Caraldo? He dressed you up in black. He even had you wear a cape, yes? He said you were a wild animal. A sociopathic killer. Do you remember him screaming 'I will not tolerate any insubordination' with you at his side?

"Spit, I remember, sprayed from his mouth. After that, you visited us, unannounced. Watched us. We never knew."

Caraldo shifted his feet uneasily. "I never killed anyone since."

Zoltan sat back in his chair. "No. No you haven't. Just used fear to keep us in line, yes?"

Caraldo shrugged again. "Like I said, it's a job."

Barbara noticed a change in the man. His tone became flat, almost defensive.

"So you say. And what is your job today, Victor? What brings you to New York? Maybe to catch a play?"

Caraldo glared at the gem maker, who returned his stare with unblinking black eyes.

"For goodness sake," Barbara said loudly. Both men turned to her, startled. "Can we be a little civilized around here? If the two of you need to talk, please, Mr. Caraldo, sit down!" She nudged the chair between her and Zoltan with her foot.

Caraldo stood uncertainly.

"Please."

He slowly pulled the chair from the table and folded slowly into the seat.

Barbara nodded. "Now, isn't that better?"

Chapter 12

ZOLTAN BECKONED TO ALBERT, WHO hurried to the table, eyeing Caraldo. "Everything is fine, sir?"

"It is, Albert. Could you bring us another espresso?"

The waiter looked at Caraldo and then back to Zoltan. "Will that be two or three?"

"Three, Albert. Thank you."

Zoltan sat back in his chair. "So somehow he knew almost immediately about Barbara."

Caraldo nodded. "It seems so."

"How does he know?" Barbara wondered. "How *could* he know?"

The two men looked at each other. "I hope you will never meet him, my dear," Zoltan said. "But if you do, you might understand."

He nodded at Caraldo. "You've been here for 24 hours. Watching us, no? What have you seen?"

"Enough."

"And what have you reported to the *Mester*?"

"That you seem to have met a woman with whom you are very friendly. That the two of you left your apartment together. That you visited a shop in the Market. But my guess is he already knows that. Just needed me to confirm what he sensed."

The black-coated waiter arrived with the espressos and carefully placed them on the table.

"Thank you, Albert." He waited until the man was out of earshot. "And what has the *Mester* told you to do about it?"

"Nothing. Yet. He is expecting one more report. Then he will give me instructions."

"To kill me?"

Caraldo shrugged. "Possibly. But you are one of his oldest agents. He might just have me bring you in for 'reeducation.'"

"Torture," Zoltan said.

"I don't know what they do. That's not my department."

Zoltan was quiet for a long moment. "Why are you telling me this, Victor?"

Caraldo's eyes flitted to Barbara and then back to Zoltan. "I have nothing against you, DeAngelo."

"Zoltan," Barbara corrected. "Zoltan József."

Caraldo glared at Barbara and then turned back to Zoltan. "The truth is I am ready to move on. I'm tired of his humiliation. Tired of living by scaring the shit out of people." He downed his espresso in a single gulp and slammed the cup down on the saucer, still holding it in his hand. The people at the next table looked up from their conversation in alarm.

"Plus, I might need you sometime. And you sure as hell need me."

Zoltan studied the big man in front of him closely. "I can't tell whether you are lying or not." Caraldo shrugged. "What if I am? You're screwed anyway."

There was a long silence. "Mr. Caraldo," Barbara began, leaning forward. "I don't believe you're lying." She looked into the big man's face. "What should we do?"

Zoltan glanced at Barbara. He had already seen her empathic powers, but what was she doing? She had no idea who or what she was dealing with.

"I cannot speak for you, Ms…?"

"Just call me Barbara."

Victor nodded. "Yes. He mentioned you, the *Mester*. He said your jewel was 'unsettling.'"

Barbara stared at him in shock. "He knows about me? About my jewel?"

"I think that's why he got me over here so quickly. I don't know what he has in mind for you, but DeAngelo…Mr. József's life is in grave danger. In a few hours I may be ordered to go to his apartment and kidnap him." He turned the cup in his enormous hand. "Or kill him."

"I thought that's what you did," Barbara said. "Kill people."

Caraldo glanced down at Barbara. "I've done lots of things. I ran drugs as a mule when I was 15 until I was busted at Heathrow and did six months at Her Majesty's."

Barbara looked puzzled. "Her Majesty's?"

Caraldo laughed bitterly. "Her Majesty's Young Offender Institution. They had a good gym there. Nobody fucked with me. Met a few mates who were street fighters. Taught me a lot. So I get out and started beating plonkers up for a living."

The gem maker swirled the coffee in his cup. "Did you enjoy it?"

"Sometimes. Mainly if it was a bad dude. But mostly it was just business. But then one day I'm working out and the guy who owns the gym comes over and says there's someone who wants to meet me. The gym owner's a little shady, you know? Dope here, break a leg there. So I'm wondering what this is about. I walk into the owner's private office and there is this tiny little fucker with huge ears sitting behind his desk. Weirdest looking dude I'd ever seen. Little, almost like a dwarf or something, but he's not. And damned if I could tell how old he was. Just fuckin' weird, with these huge yellow eyes. Stared at me for a long time. I stared back. I don't give a fuck.

"So he asks me if I want a job." He looked up at Zoltan. "He has this squeaky little voice. You've heard it. Just weird, eh? Anyway I ask him doing what. He says just what you've been doing, but for more money and less shit. He gives me this figure – fuckin' more money than I've ever had. 'Who do I have to kill,' I joke. 'Hopefully nobody,' he says. No smile. 'But you never know. I run a jewelry business. Just want you to make sure my salesmen don't cheat me.' OK, I said. That doesn't sound too hard."

He paused. "Then he makes my gem. He had this big camera thing; sort of like De…Zoltan's but larger. The most beautiful thing I'd ever seen, that jewel."

Barbara had been looking into the man's blue eyes as he spoke. "Grey, wasn't it?"

Victor looked at her in surprise. "Yes, grey." He tilted his great head slightly. "How did you know?" Zoltan smiled. "Astrology."

Caraldo looked at Barbara warily and went on. "Yeah. Grey with black threads and a magnificent green diamond in the center. After I had a chance to hold it, he put it in a bag and hung it in his vault. Guess it's still there."

Zoltan looked darkly at the bald-headed man. "That's all very interesting. But then you kill Fitz and Welser. They heard Welser screaming for an hour."

Caraldo ran his hand over his bald head. "Those guys were raising hell. Demanding changes to their contract. Fuck, I didn't even know what their goddamned contract said. I flew to Tokyo to talk with Fitz. Son of a bitch charges me with a knife. I broke his neck. What was I supposed to do?"

"And Welser?"

Caraldo leaned back in his chair, shaking his head. "Man, that was a fuck up from the word go. After Fitz, Welser starts trying to contact other agents. Wants them all to revolt, bring the old man down somehow. Never got the details. So the old man sends me to Buenos Aires to knock some sense into him. Tells me not to kill the guy. Takes too long to train new agents. Just knock some sense into him. No one was sure where he was, but the *Mester* got a tip. So I track him down at this apartment. The fucker opens the door with a gun on me. I knock it aside and break his arm. He's screaming bloody murder, so I slug him. Again and again. He won't stop." He stared at the empty cup in his hand. "Finally he was quiet."

"The *Mester* happy about that?"

Caraldo's face darkened. "Called me an undisciplined ape. Said he should kill me. And then…" He paused.

"Then what?" Barbara asked.

"Then he took my jewel out of his vault. I hadn't seen it in years. He put it on his desk. Do you know about his little brass-headed hammer? With the sharp end?"

Barbara nodded.

"He pulled my jewel out of the leather bag. When I saw it, something gave inside of me. It was so beautiful. Grey with that green diamond in the center. I could feel it, you know? Feel it pulling at me. He raised the hammer. I thought he was going to smash it. I screamed."

"Did he? Did he smash it?" Barbara asked, her eyes wide.

Victor shook his head. "At the last second, he turned the hammer. He struck my jewel with the sharp end. It was like…It was like I had been stabbed in the heart. The pain was terrible. I fell back. I thought I was dying. He leaned over me, those glowing yellow eyes fixed on me like a vulture's. 'Never disobey me again,' he hissed. 'Or I will use the other end.' The pain slowly went away. I was able to stand. Then he said, 'Maybe it's for the best. Scare the shit out of the rest of them.' He gave me that sneer, you know?"

Zoltan nodded. "The one that passes for a smile."

Victor chuckled humorlessly. "That's the one. Then he said, 'Think we'll have a little gathering of the agents, Vic. Sort of a coming out party for you.'"

"That was when he dressed you up like Zorro."

He nodded again. "What could I do, man? I tell you what I could do – whatever that little son of a bitch told me to do."

Zoltan pulled a gold watch on a delicate chain from a pocket in his vest. "It's 11:30. What time do you have to report back?"

"Told him I'd have a final report by one o'clock."

"Not much time."

Caraldo nodded. "And if he tells me to go to your apartment and kill you," he looked grimly at the gem maker, "I will go to your apartment, and if you are still there, I will kill you."

"You wouldn't!" Barbara exclaimed. "You couldn't after what you've said."

His blue eyes, now dim and bitter, turned to Barbara. "I would and I could."

Zoltan nodded. "Thank you, Victor. I will leave immediately."

"I do not want to know where you are."

"Of course."

"Wait," Barbara broke in. "What about me?"

"We will talk about it after Mr. Caraldo leaves, yes? But Victor, you are caught, no? What way out is there for you?"

"Either he kills me, or I kill him. There is no other way. But I will not be his fuckin' slave anymore. I'm done."

"Caraldo, is it not true we are all really slaves to the *Mester*? Not just you, but the agents as well?"

Victor nodded. "Sure. But the agents, they don't have any contact with him. To them the Master is just a name, a bank account, a salary. They don't have to ask how high every time the little bastard says jump."

"Perhaps, but, like me, all of us were recruited at times when life was of little or no meaning, no? For some, I fear, things have not changed. But for others…" the gem maker looked across the table at Barbara. "For others the harsh conditions of our contract have become intolerable. You are not alone. And it is true. It appears that the only way to extinguish our contracts is to nullify the *Csúnya Mester.*"

"Yeah. But killing him, I can't see how. He's surrounded by security. The compound is impenetrable. The only chance is if I catch him unaware."

"But he's never unaware, no?"

Caraldo was silent.

"Don't be too sure there is not a way. We just have to find it." He leaned toward Caraldo and spoke softly. "Ironic, isn't it? I cannot stay and you cannot leave, and yet that gives us something in common." He paused. "We have nothing to lose. People with nothing to lose can be the most dangerous, yes?"

Chapter 13

"I AM *NOT* STAYING HERE." Barbara waved her arm around the giant hall. "I don't even know where *here* is!"

"Barbara, please. Calm down." The gem maker raised his index finger to his lips to quiet her. "You do not understand. I will almost certainly be killed. If you are with me, very likely you will be killed as well. And if you are not, you will be in a strange city, no? No friends, no hope."

Barbara felt the anger rising in her like a wave. "When will *you* understand? You *know* that I threw my lot in with you when I walked through your goddamned apartment door. Just as much as you did with me. There is no going back for me, and you know it." As she spoke, her voice rose. "You do know that don't you?"

Zoltan glanced around the café nervously. "Please, do not attract attention."

"Attract attention?" Barbara hissed. "I've already attracted attention. Attention that you say might get us both killed." She glared at him. "Your Ugly Master seems to have me firmly on his radar. I'm into this up to my neck. Whatever happens, you are not going to get rid of me."

"I am only thinking of you. You are young. You have so much life ahead of you. My life is old."

"And I am sick of you pronouncing yourself dead," Barbara whispered sharply. "You did it after Rebecca died. You are not going to do it with me. *Yes*?"

Zoltan sat back in his chair and studied Barbara. She was leaning forward, her emerald eyes alight. Her face was framed in a mass of flaming red hair. He shook his head, smiling ruefully.

"What?" Her eyes narrowed. "Are you laughing at me?"

Zoltan's smile broadened. "No, my dear. I am just thinking two things."

"And what might those be?"

"First that you are one of the most stubborn people I have ever met."

"I am not being stubborn, I'm…"

"And second, that you are very beautiful. Especially, as they say, when you are mad, yes?"

Barbara glared at him. "You infuriate me."

The man's dark eyes opened in surprise. "I infuriate you? But, madam, why?"

"For starters, you keep calling me 'madam'."

"You are right. I apologize."

"And you can be so fucking patronizing." She glared across the table at him. "Last night, I told you I didn't know why I'd come, what I expected from you, do you remember?"

The man's smile faded. "I do."

"Well, that wasn't entirely true. Sure, I was wringing my hands over my precious, stupid little life. But I *did* know why I came. And it was because of *me*." She leaned forward slightly, her face set. "But I also knew what I expected from you."

Zoltan sat back in his chair. "More, I suspect, than an unbreakable chain."

"Do you remember when I told you I was an Aries, the day you made my stone?"

The man steepled his hand on the table. "And that I was, most regrettably, a Taurus."

Barbara nodded. "We laughed it off, but I told you things about Aries, about me. About being seekers, being daring, exciting."

"And that you were none of those things."

Barbara's head shook sharply. "Not that I *was* none of those things, but that I had failed to *become* any of those things. There is a difference."

The man continued looking at her intently.

"And I also told you that we won't settle for the mundane, remember? That we will push until our flame blazes as brightly as possible."

The man nodded. "As I remember, you indicated you had indeed failed in this quest."

"And you, sir, said what?"

The man was silent.

"You said, 'Perhaps not.'"

"I recall."

"But you were wrong, you see. I *had* failed. Up to that point. And I hated it. Hated myself most of all."

"And I…"

"Was the trigger, the catalyst. The fire."

"You knew this when you sought me out?"

Barbara waggled her head from side to side. "More or less." She waved her hands around the Market. "Although I hadn't expected all of this."

The man smiled slightly. "No, madam. I suppose not." He paused. "What did you expect?"

Barbara settled back. "An adventure."

The man raised his bushy eyebrows.

"When I was younger, I used to plan out great adventures, research them. When I was nine or ten, I looked up the word in the dictionary, and I still remember the definition: 'an exciting, unexpected event or course of events involving risk and resulting in unknown outcomes.'" Her eyes became less hard and twinkled slightly. "Or something like that.

"All that time in school. The years with David. All the crap. I knew it for what it was. But you see, I was waiting for you." She smiled broadly. "And when I met you, when you made my magnificent jewel, I knew what I wanted from you, sir." She paused and peered deeply into his black eyes. "I wanted adventure."

The man continued to study her silently.

"But enough of that," Barbara continued. "That's not what you asked. You asked me why I found you infuriating."

The man nodded slowly, his eyes not leaving her face.

Barbara leaned forward again. "So let me tell you why. You've just been told you have an hour and a..." Barbara looked at her watch. "Well, now, an hour and 15 minutes to disappear or you will most likely be murdered, and what do you do? Make plans to get the hell out of here? Sprint for the emergency exit, wherever that is? Phone for a plane ticket to Buenos Aires? Oh, no. Instead you sit here arguing with me when you know full well that I will follow you if it kills me." She sat upright, breathing hard.

The man said nothing, his black eyes gleaming and moist. "Well?" Barbara demanded in exasperation.

"Well then," the gem maker said at last. "I guess we should begin to make plans."

"It's about time," Barbara grumbled, folding her arms.

"Barbara." The man leaned forward and tugged Barbara's hands away from her chest and pulled them gently onto the table. He took her left hand in both of his raised it to his lips. "You do me a great honor, perhaps one I do not deserve. It has been so long since someone has..." He held her hand softly. "But I have little to offer. No life, really. You can have no future with me, no?"

"Would you shut up and listen to me," Barbara said fiercely. "Is that what I said I wanted from you? A future? Did I ask you for a future?" Her eyes flickered with green flame." I *do* have a future with you. It is this minute, then this day, and then this week. That is all the future I want."

"Perhaps that is enough for now," Zoltan said doubtfully." But you will want more. You deserve more, so much more."

Barbara pulled her hands away and laid them in her lap, shaking her head. "God, you really are exasperating," she muttered. "Not to mention arrogant and presumptuous."

She breathed deeply. "Can we worry about that later? Right now, sir, I believe *your* future is in more immediate jeopardy."

The man looked amused. "Have it your way, my dear." He chuckled. "Though I doubt it could be any other way." He gestured with his head out the gate of the café. "And you are right. I have little time to lose."

"We," Barbara corrected. "*We* have little time to lose."

"Yes." He paused. "We. We have little time to lose." He smiled slightly.

"I haven't thought in those terms in a very long time." He drew a brown leather wallet from the inside pocket of his blue corduroy coat and pulled out several bills unlike any Barbara had seen before. He placed them on the table. "*We*," he said, smiling, "have a few errands. We will talk as we prepare, yes? We will be less likely to be overheard."

Barbara stood up and took Zoltan by his hand. For a moment she looked into his shimmering, black eyes, which were almost even with hers. And the words came to her again: *He's a magic man.* "Come on," she said. "We must hurry."

They strode through the gate and made their way to the far side of the Market. In the extreme corner – Barbara had totally lost her bearings but sensed it was the northwest – four stone columns held a carved marble frieze over high wood doors. A black plaque read "Market Syndicate Bank."

"Stay right here," Zoltan said. "Please, keep your eyes open, yes? If you see Caraldo, you must get me at once." The man's eyes scanned the crowd milling around the Market. "And he is not the only one we need to fear, yes? The *Mester* has darker, more ruthless men."

Barbara nodded. "How will I know them?"

"You won't. I shall be back in a few minutes."

Zoltan turned and hurried through the doors. Barbara walked up the first marble step and stood with her back against one of the columns. She looked over the crowd, focusing on the odd person who wasn't clad in the Market's red and black. There was a tall man, his long grey hair bound by a blue bandana, that she studied as he neared the bank, but he veered off and entered a nearby market selling koras and stringed instruments she did not recognize.

The gem maker reappeared at her elbow. "That is a relief. I had feared the *Mester* had frozen my account. He tried it seems. But the Market bankers, they are loyal to their depositors. They do not like to be threatened, no?"

The man pulled a brown envelope with a metal clasp from inside his coat and handed it to Barbara. She looked at it uncertainly.

"Open it. Please."

Barbara unclasped the flap and looked inside. The envelope was stuffed with $100 bills, perhaps 50 or 60.

"There is something else."

Barbara pushed her hand deeper and touched a plastic card. She drew it out and looked at it. It was completely black on both sides. She looked up at the man quizzically.

"It is a credit card. It has a million-dollar limit."

Barbara examined the card. There were no discernible numbers or letters. "But there is nothing on it."

"I assure you, it will not be refused. No one will ask you for identification. It will also serve as your train pass and elevator entry card. It will work only for you, but you must guard it carefully, yes?"

Barbara nodded. She pulled off her backpack unzipped a side pocket and slid the card into a Velcro closured pouch inside. She took the envelope and pushed it into the main section of her pack.

"What's next?"

"Travel agency."

"The Market has a travel agency?"

The man has started walking. "Several, actually, but I deal with Madame Jeanine's Travel." By this time they were near the center of the station.

"Does she give you better prices?"

The man guided her gently with his hand through a knot of arguing men.

"That is not her specialty, no. But she can get you anywhere without anyone else knowing, yes? No trail. And places, too, where one cannot be found. Places on no map. Places dark even to satellites."

"That sounds like a great idea," Barbara said, breathing heavily as they hurried toward a line of shops.

"It does, yes. But that is not what I am looking for."

The man stopped under an awning and grasped the brass handle of a bright red door. The glass window to the right of the door read "Madam Jeanine's Travel. We Specialize In Where No One Else Goes."

Zoltan opened the door and held it open for Barbara. At first the office looked much like any other travel agency. A counter ran halfway across the room, and several small tables were strewn with travel magazines. Posters were tacked onto the walls. But as she studied the posters, Barbara began to feel uneasy. They were pictures of an abandoned prison, what looked like the surface of Mars, a vast cemetery, a selection of shrunken human heads, a shuttered and dusty ghost town. And the lights. She looked up at the ceiling and saw a ruby glass skylight that gave the interior a dark red tinge.

"Mr. DeAngelo," a soft voice purred. "It is so good to see you again."

Barbara shifted her eyes from the ceiling into the face of a tall woman in a red sheath dress that clung to her body like paint. Tattoos of fantastic flowers and foliage grew out of the high neck and climbed up her cheeks and across her forehead into a thicket of crimson hair. Her lipstick seemed too red to be real until Barbara realized that her lips had been tattooed scarlet.

"I understand you may need to travel. Quickly."

Zoltan gave a small bow. "Madame Jeanine, my companion, Barbara."

The tattooed leaves over the woman's lavender eyes grew upward as Barbara watched, and yellow roses at the corner of Madame Jeanine's eyes crinkled as her cherry lips opened in a broad smile, showing white teeth filed to a point. She stepped forward and extended a long hand, also tattooed with vines, her two-inch fingernails painted in violet and purple blossoms. Barbara took the hand and, for a reason she didn't understand, curtsied, pulling slightly on her Lycra tights.

The woman's smile broadened. She held Barbara's gaze. "Mr. DeAngelo, I am so pleased for you." She studied Barbara, still smiling. "I just love the hair."

"Ahem," Zoltan interrupted.

"Of course. What is wrong with me," Jeanine said, dropping Barbara's hand and turning to Zoltan. "You are in a hurry. And you want to go to Budapest."

Barbara turned to the gem maker. "Budapest? Zoltan, you're…we're going to Budapest?" Then she looked at Jeanine. "And how did you know?"

Jeanine glanced at Barbara and cocked her head as if puzzled. "I am a travel agent, dear. What good am I if I do not know where my client wishes to go?" She returned to the counter and opened a drawer, drawing out two thin leather cases the size of a checkbook. She walked from behind the counter and handed them to Zoltan.

Now her face was serious, her eyes fixed on the gem maker's face. "You are starting a dangerous journey, DeAngelo." She paused. "Be careful.

I would miss you if you did not return."

"Thank you, Jeanine." He took the cases from her hands and slid them into the breast pocket of his coat. He smiled. "But life is something of a dangerous journey, no? And the outcome is never in doubt?"

The woman nodded slowly. "Just the same…"

"You are very kind. I look forward to seeing you again soon. Perhaps when I am not so rushed? Perhaps over a nice glass of Primitivo?"

"I look forward to it," the woman said. "Now, you must leave."

Zoltan bowed low from the waist. "Madam." He turned to the door and opened it. Barbara glanced over her shoulder and walked back into the bustle of the Market. Zoltan started across the tiled floor and Barbara rushed to catch up.

"Zoltan, can you slow down a bit?" The man eased his pace slightly.

"Budapest? That's where you were born." She was walking beside him now, speaking quietly. "Is that why you are going there?"

The man shook his head. "No. You may remember Caraldo's name for the Master?"

"Yes. *Csúnya Mester.* Ugly Master."

"That is right. It is Hungarian, yes? And Caraldo's story that the *Mester* grew up on the streets of Budapest. You recall?"

Barbara nodded, hurrying alongside.

"And that the rumor started with Dezső. He was one of the original gem makers."

"Yes, I remember."

"I met him at several of the gatherings, but he said little. He never left Budapest. I always wondered why."

"Is he still there?"

"Yes, I believe so. But old. Very, very old, no?"

"You mean…"

"Yes, we do age. But slowly. He must be… Ah, here we are."

Barbara looked up, confused. "This is the chain maker's shop."

"Indeed. And a place of refuge." He opened the door to the tinkling of the bell. "Please, step inside. I will explain."

Chapter 14

AFTER A WHISPERED CONVERSATION BETWEEN Zoltan and Mrs. Harlow, the woman led Barbara and the gem maker behind the curtains and through the workshop, full of benches draped in red velvet. A woman wearing what looked like a welding mask with a tube extending from the top to a small tank on her back looked up from a glittering chain in a thin mold. The smell of enormous heat emanated from a glowing furnace in the far corner.

At the back of the shop was a simple wooden door. Mrs. Harlow opened it into a dark room. "You will be quite safe here," she said. "It is deafened."

Zoltan nodded. "I cannot thank you enough, Mrs. Harlow."

"No need, Mr. DeAngelo. There are rumors afoot."

As she pulled the door closed, a light began to glow from the ceiling until the area was fully lit. They were in a hallway that ran between a wall on their right and a series of doors. The hallway opened onto a large, round sitting area, the light above like a miniature of the sun in the Market. The floors were covered in deep blue Berber carpet, and low chairs and ornately tooled leather hassocks were arranged in a large circle.

Zoltan motioned to one of the hassocks. "Please, sit down. I have much to say and little time." Barbara settled into the soft leather as Zoltan pulled up a stool and leaned forward.

"Now, you must listen very carefully, yes?"

"Yes," Barbara said automatically.

"I must leave today. Almost immediately. The key to the *Csúnya Mester* and his undoing lies in Budapest. I sense it." He drew his hand through his hair. "God, all these years I have been such fool."

"Zoltan," Barbara began.

He held up his hand. "No, truly, a fool. I saw the *Mester*, what he was, the first time we met." He nodded at Barbara. "As did you."

Barbara looked at him quizzically. "I've never had the pleasure."

"And I hope you never will. But when I told you how I was recruited, how I agreed to the *Mester's* terms, do you recall how you responded? You asked how I could work for such a horrid man. 'He is evil,' you said. 'Surely you could see that.' Even then I made excuses, to you and to myself. I had nothing to lose. This gave me something to live for. What harm could there be in making gems for people?"

He leaned further forward until his face was only a few feet from Barbara's. "But, you see, I *did* know it was all wrong and that, somehow, I was part of that evil. Over the years it became clearer and clearer. The brutality of the Mester and his staff. The killing of Fitz and Welser for speaking out. But it wasn't just that. The gems I made…"

Barbara saw his dark eyes cloud as if a thunderstorm was passing behind them. "Yes, go on."

"I didn't make a point of following my clients. Perhaps I knew better. But occasionally a name in a newspaper article would catch my eye, or I'd hear a name I recognized on a radio report." His voice tensed. "A Chilean army colonel responsible for torturing thousands. The CEO of an oil company that funded climate change denial. A media owner who promoted lies and hatred. An evangelist who flew from megachurch to megachurch in a $50 million jet purchased for him by his congregants."

He leaned back and stared at the glowing ceiling.

"Zoltan," Barbara said softly. "I am so sorry."

He looked back at Barbara. "Madam, I am the one who must be sorry. I saw all of this, knew all of this, and what did I do?" He grimaced. "Nothing. I did nothing. I did not want to rock the boat, as you say. I never balked at an assignment, no matter how loathsome the client. I took my money and lived my sad little life."

"And now?"

"And now it is time to do something. I must."

Barbara leaned forward and took his hands in hers. She held them softly for a moment. "Yes," she said. "You must, I see that. But why Budapest? You said the Mester's compound is in London."

"True. But as Caraldo said, he is unassailable in his compound."

"What then?"

"The key to his undoing is in Budapest. If I have any chance, I must find out who the *Mester* is, what he is. How he can be reached." He gave a wry smile. "If there is a way."

"Dezső."

Zoltan nodded. "If anyone knows him, his weakness, it is Dezső." He nodded toward the door of the room. When I leave here, I will exit through one of the secured elevators and disappear. Only you and Madame Jeanine know where I have gone. And she will happily die before giving up this information."

Barbara nodded, grasping the gravity of his words.

"If you are determined to do so, you will follow me after your chain is complete, yes?"

"Where will I stay until then?" She smiled. "Think I'd like to skip the apartment for tonight."

"The rooms along the hallway are living quarters for some of Mrs. Harlow's workers. She has a room you may use for the night. She will fit your chain tomorrow morning."

"And then I can leave?"

Zoltan shook his head. "Tomorrow is Wednesday. You will need to be here to have your necklace fitted, no? You will have to wait for the Thursday train. Even if they are looking for me on the train, they will not recognize you. You will be safe."

"And here? What if Caraldo comes here looking for you?"

"He will not. However, as I have told you, the *Csúnya Mester* has other, even more ruthless thugs. When Caraldo reports that I have disappeared, he will almost certainly send them after me. But not, I think, for a few days. Perhaps not until Victor returns. But no matter. This is a refuge. You will be safe here."

Barbara raised her eyebrows. "That's the theory. But, Zoltan, won't the *Mester* just destroy your gem?"

"I do not believe so. As Caraldo put it, we are expensive to train. Also, if he did, I would know. I would be wounded but not dead, at least for a while. He would have no more control. Without that, he understands I could do a great deal of harm. I have files that could prove very damaging, including the name and contacts of all the gem makers. He knows I could create a great deal of trouble for him." He paused. "And then there is you."

"Me?"

"As you said earlier, you are clearly on his radar. Caraldo said your jewel unsettled him. I don't know why, but he is afraid of you. I do not believe he wants to provoke you. Not yet."

"I hope you're right."

"Not so much as I."

"Will he know you are in Budapest? Can the *Mester* detect where you are?"

Zoltan was quiet for a long moment. "He always knows."

"Like he did about me. He knew I had come to your apartment."

"Yes, but he has limits. He senses things, but not always clearly. That is why he sends Caraldo, to give him the details. To make sure what he intuits is accurate. I believe it is a feeling, unease, followed, perhaps, by some hazy image." Zoltan shook his head. "I cannot be sure, of course, but he hunted Welser for months before Gunter made the mistake of returning to his apartment in Buenos Aires."

"When Caraldo killed him."

Zoltan nodded. "But I will not make that mistake, no? The *Mester* could not seem to pinpoint Welser when he disappeared as long as he was on the run. Only the area he was in. He had Ahmad and Salazar after him as well as Caraldo. They interrogated each of us, hoping we would know something of Welser's whereabouts."

"I see. But sooner or later he will know."

"I believe you are right."

"And he will send his men after you."

"Yes. That is why I will stay on the move and remain in Budapest no longer than necessary to find out more about our *Csúnya Mester.*" He smiled slightly. "And while I am there, I will, what is it you Americans say? Keep my eyes peeled, yes?"

"It's not funny, Zoltan."

"No, madam, it is not."

She ignored the address. "I don't want to go all the way to Budapest just to see you killed. Does he know you are Hungarian?"

"No. My records show me as British. He will guess from my accent, perhaps, that I emigrated from somewhere in Eastern Europe, but not which country. I never spoke Hungarian to him. I did not know until today that he himself might be Hungarian."

"OK, so back to our travel plans. I take the train tomorrow night to Grand Central Station. By the way, there really is a train?"

"Yes. It is quite real, I assure you." The man pulled one of the leather cases he had received from Madam Jeanine. "This is the ticket you will need to board the Grand Central Station train. Once you disembark, you will take a taxi to the Teteboro Airport. "

"Teteboro?"

"It is a private airport. The driver will know it. When there you go to the Moonachie Air desk."

"Moonachie Air."

"You will hand the attendant this ticket." He passed the wallet to Barbara. "It is a dark ticket. It is not traceable. You will board an aircraft with others who will neither know nor be interested in you. When you land in Budapest, you will take a taxi to the Danubius Hotel."

"May I write this down?"

"No. You must remember. It is too easy to lose a backpack. Or have it taken, no?"

Barbara nodded. "OK. I check into the Danubius Hotel. What then?"

"You will be at the hotel for two or three nights. It is very beautiful. In the heart of Budapest."

"So I act like a tourist."

"Yes. But each morning, perhaps while enjoying coffee in the Café Astoria next door, you will read the *Daily News Hungary*, the English language paper."

"That sounds pleasant."

"Yes, but you concentrate on the obituaries. Not so pleasant. And you look for an entry under the name of Ernő Kiss. An easy name to remember, no?"

"And, again," Barbara smiled. "A pleasant one."

"Not so much, I am afraid. He was one of the martyred generals who led Hungary to independence in 1849. After their defeat by the Russians and Austrians, he was hanged."

"Lovely."

"The obituary will announce a phone number where you can leave condolences. Call the number and leave the number of your room. Just your number, yes?" he asked. "Nothing more."

Barbara nodded.

"I will have found a safe place to meet and will send you directions."

"How?"

"I don't know. It will depend on the situation. If possible, I will send you a note. But I will reach you. I promise."

Barbara looked into the gem maker's face. "Where will you be while I am waiting?"

"Looking for Dezső. I have some leads to follow, but no matter. I will be there."

"Are you frightened?"

The man glanced at the ceiling in thought. "I am hopeful. For the first time in many years. I am hopeful I will be free, or I will die." He smiled. "Perhaps I am more afraid of the hope than of death, yes?"

"I remember an old saying: The world is too full of possibilities to give up hope."

The man lowered his head, and when he raised it again tears filled his eyes. "I am sorry you have been drawn into this. I fear for you. But you give me courage." His face softened. "For that I thank you."

He stood and began walking toward the doorway.

"Zoltan," she called quietly. He turned back toward her. "See you in Budapest."

Chapter 15

BARBARA OPENED THE DOOR OF her room and peeked down the hall. It was barely 6:00 am, but she could not sleep. For nearly an hour she had lain in the soft feather bed staring at the dimly glowing pink ceiling, wondering what she had gotten herself into. And when she thought about her gem — now, she hoped in its setting and suspended from a fine, unbreakable chain – her heart beat faster as if she were a little girl again on Christmas morning.

The hall was empty. Barbara pulled her fleece hoodie over the tights and crept toward the door at the far end. When she reached it, she hesitated. Through the door she heard a quiet hum, perhaps a buffing wheel, and the higher pitch of another tool she could not identify. The workshop was awake.

Barbara pushed the door open slowly and peered inside. Whereas the hall was lit dimly with a soft light emanating from the ceiling, the workshop was as bright as midday. A dozen workers hunched over velvet-covered benches or polishing rings and chains. She watched the activity silently.

"Barbara, you are awake early."

Barbara jumped and brought her hand to the neck of her hoodie.

"Excuse me," Mrs. Harlow said. "I didn't mean to startle you."

"No, no. I'm just a little bit, I don't know, jumpy I guess." She nodded at the activity of the workshop. "And all of this. I had no idea."

Mrs. Harlow arched her eyebrows. "Perhaps you thought elves made our jewelry?"

Barbara closed her eyes and exhaled deeply. "I'm sorry, Mrs. Harlow. It's…it's just a lot to take in."

"Of course. I was going to say I understand. But I suspect I don't. I have worked in the Market for more than 30 years. I was astonished when I first arrived, I remember, but it has been so long. And this business with Mr. DeAngelo. It must all be rather unsettling."

Unsettling, Barbara thought. *You could say that.*

"Now, would you like some breakfast?"

"I would, but…" She hesitated.

"Yes?"

"Mrs. Harlow, is there any chance my chain is done?"

"Ah, I see. First things first." She nodded toward the curtains that separated the workshop from the front of the store. "Come with me."

As they walked between the rows of benches, workers glanced up curiously. At the front of the shop, Mrs. Harlow drew the curtains back and motioned Barbara into the store. Bright light from the Market sun poured through the front windows and glassed roof. Mrs. Harlow closed the drapes behind her and stepped behind the display case. She motioned Barbara to stand on the other side and turned to the wooden cabinet behind her. She raised a gold ring on her right index finger and swiped it across a metal plate in the cabinet. A green light blinked, and Mrs. Harlow pulled the door open. She took down a tall red cylinder from a shelf and set it on a velvet mat on top of the case.

She looked at Barbara and lifted the cylinder revealing a piece of dark wood fashioned in the shape of a neck.

"Oh, my God!" Barbara gasped.

Mrs. Harlow smiled. "Yes, it is very, very beautiful, isn't it?"

Barbara stared at her round jewel, now clasped in a setting that hugged her stone in blazing red gold, that ignited a glow in the stone so intense it looked as if it were aflame. A thin chain, made of the same deep red material as the setting, fashioned into hundreds of impossibly fine links, suspended the blazing red stone.

Barbara reached out and began to touch the chain, then pulled her hand back. "It is radioactive?"

Mrs. Harlow nodded. "But it is safe for you to touch. Only you."

Barbara took the chain in her hand and felt its exquisite lightness. "It must have a thousand links in it," she whispered.

"1,534."

Barbara ran her hands down the chain until she fingered her jewel. She lifted it slightly and studied the setting. Fifty-two tiny red-gold arms clasped her glowing jewel, front and back. At the end of each was a minute burning flame. She looked more closely.

"Mrs. Harlow," she said. "These look like real flames!"

"I believe you said you wanted your symbol to be fire, is that not correct?"

"Yes," Barbara breathed. "But I didn't know they would be, you know, real."

"Lift your jewel to the light."

Barbara carefully raised the gem and looked at it in the bright light from the Market's sun. As she did, the miniature flames at the end of the arms contracted and she could see that the end of each tiny arm was an exquisitely carved red and yellow flame, like those of a diminutive candle.

"It is…magnificent." Tears welled in Barbara's eyes, and she hugged the jewel to her chest.

"Yes," Mrs. Harlow agreed. "One of our finest settings. It was crafted by Mrs. Sunkara." Mrs. Harlow paused. "She reported something rather odd."

"Odd?"

"Yes, when she placed the gem into your setting, the arms folded over the jewel. On their own. Quite extraordinary."

"Please," Barbara murmured, "please thank her for me."

"Yes, yes I will. And there is something more."

Barbara looked up from the gem.

"As the arms closed over your gem, they cast a protective webbing around the entire necklace. Mrs. Sunkara described it as a small pinkish net."

Barbara looked at her, puzzled.

"Yes," she said, arching her dark eyebrows. "After several seconds, the web drew back into the arms, and she was able to complete the polishing."

"What does all of that mean, Mrs. Harlow?" Barbara asked, gazing at the necklace lying cool and subdued in her palm.

"We have no idea," Mrs. Harlow conceded. "It would seem that your gem has capacities we have not seen before." She looked at Barbara closely. "It seems that you have a very special jewel, my dear."

Barbara looked back solemnly. "May I put it on now?"

Mrs. Harlow reached under the counter and pulled out a pair of what looked like white silk gloves. She took the chain from Barbara. "Please, remove your sweatshirt."

Barbara grasped her black fleece at the waist and pulled it quickly over her head. She stood in the shop, her shoulders bare and glowing in the Market sunlight, her black sports bra dark against her skin. Mrs. Harlow carefully held the chain in both hands, the tiny clasp open. Instinctively, Barbara bent her head forward, and Mrs. Harlow slid the chain through Barbara's tangle of red hair and around her neck. A sharp crack sounded as the clasp fused shut. Mrs. Harlow withdrew her hands slowly until the red-gold chain was taut and the stone blazed against Barbara's black bra.

"A stunning outfit," Mrs. Harlow commented.

Barbara took the gem in her hand and studied it. It shone ruby red but as she peered deeply into the glowing stone, the filigree of yellow and white threads swirled in their blood red arms. The miniature black pearl in the center seemed bolder, more vivid. And the tiny ivory diamond imbedded in the pearl, even though encased in the deep ruby of the jewel, blazed white hot at the heart of the stone.

Tears streamed down her cheeks.

"I could hardly bear not having it," she murmured. "It was like a part of me was missing. Zolt… Mr. DeAngelo says it contains a fragment of my soul."

"Yes, I have heard that."

"Can you see it in the gem? My soul?"

"No, dear. We work at the molecular level, matter. Perhaps souls are energy that we cannot see." She shrugged. "Each gem has its own vibrational signature. We employ lattice dynamics that calculate atomic force constants. This provides us with the jewel's vibrational spectrum, which can then be matched to other elements, such as the red gold alloy we have used in your setting."

"I see."

"Do you?"

"Well, not really. But I understand that each gem is unique with specific vibrations?"

"Yes. Take a simple mineral such as quartz. Quartz crystals, when cut along certain planes, can be made to vibrate, if you apply the right type of electrical energy. Your cell phone has at least two such crystals in it. These crystals come in various sizes, and like bells, each size resonates at a different frequency — six, 10, 60 up to 100 million cycles per second. But gems such as yours are far more complex, multi- molecular crystals. No two are the same, so no two have the identical vibratory pattern. "

Barbara continued to stare at the gem in her hand. "Zoltan said they do not give us power. They only amplify the powers, the character, we have."

"That is very possible. The quartz crystal, for example, is completely inert until electrical energy is introduced. It only gives off reflective energy — the energy the crystal picks up, it gives out."

"So, theoretically, the energy of a person could activate a gem? The gem, as you say, could reflect the energy it picks up?"

"Theoretically that is so. But with natural gems, they would simply vibrate at the frequency commensurate with the energy captured. We have set many of Mr. DeAngelo's gems, dozens, and in each there is something more."

"More?"

"Yes. In each we find a molecular cluster that seems to act as a sort of accelerator. It enhances the vibrations of the billions of molecules around it." She smiled. "Perhaps that is the home of soul."

"So each is different but has the same general configuration."

Mrs. Harlow nodded thoughtfully. "But it is odd. In some gems there is something else, something we can see but not analyze. It is very strange."

"Like a flaw?"

"Rather, but not in the sense we usually use the term. It is an anomaly. A tiny portion of the gem that is out of the expected molecular order. It's as if it a speck of unidentifiable material has been placed there independent of the surrounding mineral elements." She shook her head. "Almost as if it were inserted after the gem was made." She adjusted her round eyeglasses. "Strange."

"Could it be just an impurity of some sort?"

Mrs. Harlow shook her head. "As I said, all gems, all crystalline formations, vibrate at a predictable frequency. No matter how many elements there are in a gem, once analyzed we should be able to identify the vibration frequency of each. But in these…flaws, as you put it, the frequency is erratic, as if activated by energy outside of the gem itself."

Barbara caught her breath. "Mrs. Harlow, does my gem have such a flaw?"

"No, dear," Mrs. Harlow smiled. "Yours is beautiful, clear. Molecular perfection."

Without knowing exactly why, relief flooded through her. Her gem was perfect. Unflawed. She looked at it in wonder. Did she deserve such a stone?

"We find the anomaly mainly in the dark gems, regardless of color – blue, green, black, red. And often in the gems we set into men's rings."

"Rings?"

"Yes, dear. Many men are still reluctant to wear necklaces, it seems."

"Of course," Barbara said. She clutched her jewel to her chest. "I'd just never thought of putting my jewel on my finger."

Mrs. Harlow looked at the young woman in front of her admiringly. Barbara's red hair tumbled over her bare shoulders in untamed waves. The stone glowed between her breasts. "Before you leave, I wish to say something."

Barbara looked at her in surprise. "Of course."

"You are different from the girl who entered our store just yesterday. Your green eyes shine like trapiche emeralds, brighter and deeper. And there is strength there I did not see when you first visited. I must confess I wondered if Mr. DeAngelo had misread you, had projected qualities onto you that weren't there." She gave a slight nod. "I was wrong. Your gem tells me that you are as extraordinary as the jewel itself."

Heat flushed her cheeks and spread down into her neck. *Damn it. Stop blushing. Right now.*

Mrs. Harlow slid Barbara's black fleece across the countertop. "Here. I think you should put this on. Even here you would stop traffic like that. And where to next?"

Barbara thought a moment. "An adventure."

The chain maker nodded in approval. "Breakfast first?"

Chapter 16

"I DID JUST WHAT YOU said, but he wasn't there." Victor was aware he sounded whiny, but the *Mester's* sulfurous stare had evaporated his usual bravado. He could see the fury build in the *Mester* like a deepening hurricane. The yellow-green eyes seemed to swirl faster and faster.

Out of the corner Caraldo saw O'Brien sitting in his usual chair, pretending not to listen but smirking.

"I was at his apartment at, I dunno, no later than 1:00," Caraldo stammered. "I had scouted them out at the Market, just like I told you. I talked to him then reported right to you. When you told me to grab him, I went directly to his apartment." He paused and glanced away from the malignant glare. "Honest."

The *Mester* had both hands on the desk and leaned toward Caraldo menacingly. "You are either an incompetent moron," he hissed, "or a traitor." Suddenly the *Mester's* eyes seemed to explode. Victor fell backward as if pushed violently by a gigantic hand. He crashed into the wall, smashing his head against the plaster, and began to slip to his left. He caught himself and straightened up. Fear and hatred welled up in him like a volcano.

"A fool or a traitor," the *Mester* hissed again. "And I have no use for either."

Victor tensed against the wall, wondering if he could reach the small .38 in the shoulder holster under his coat in time.

"That would confirm you are a fool," the *Mester* snarled. "You would be dead before your hand moved."

Victor tried to breathe deeply, his eyes scanning the room. "There is nowhere to go, Vic. Nowhere."

"I told you, I..."

"Shut up!" the *Mester* roared. His voice seemed magnified, huge, as if it were booming from a far larger man. "Shut up! I want no excuses. You failed me."

Caraldo's heart raced as he watched the old man's eyes simmer with rage.

Slowly the *Mester* leaned back until he was sitting again in his elevated chair. His hideous stare never wavered, his gigantic eyes never blinked.

"You will bring DeAngelo in." The *Mester's* voice had returned to its usual barking hiss. "You will bring him to me alive if possible. If not, you will break his neck and bring his head to me."

Caraldo's breathing returned to something approaching normal. "I don't know where he is, boss. I told you. It was just yesterday when I went to his apartment. I turned it upside down. Nothing had been taken or moved. There was no clue, nothing."

"Yes, you told me. And that is one thing you have said I believe." The *Mester's* oval pupils dilated slightly. "And I don't know where he is either." He was silent for several seconds, as if concentrating. "But I will. I will. And when I do, you will fetch him to me, is that clear?"

"Of course, boss. I've always done what you've asked."

The sunken eyes narrowed slightly. "And that's the only reason you're not dead, Vic. The only reason. And because you're too stupid to defy me." A sneer curled one side of the fleshy lips. "You know you're nothing but an ignorant loser, don't you, Vic?"

Caraldo stood silently against the wall.

"An imbecile. That's why I hired you. A musclebound halfwit that would obey. Right, Vic?" Suddenly the bizarre, eldritch voice bellowed, "Right Vic?"

Caraldo was pushed hard against the wall again. He glared at the small, gnome-like man in front of him. He gave a curt nod.

"Say it," the *Mester* said, returning to a piercing hiss. "Say it. 'I am a moron. I do what I am told.'"

Caraldo looked down at the red carpeting. "I am a moron," he said quietly. "I do what I am told."

The *Mester* leaned back in his chair. "That's better, Vic. And if you try a runner?" The old man's hideous head gestured slightly to the safe in the wall on his right. He picked up the hammer on his desk. "I will use this hammer." He fingered the razor-sharp end. "But not this end." He grasped the round gold head. "This one. I will smash your gem into nonexistence."

Chapter 17

ZOLTAN STARED AT THE OLD agent across a faded blue tablecloth crowded with empty wine bottles.

"So, you would like to know about the *Mester*." Dezső's thick eyebrows arched. "Wouldn't we all? But yes, perhaps I can recall a story or two."

It had taken Zoltan three days to track down the old agent. Dezső had stopped attending London meetings years ago and Zoltan had no address, but he did have a picture from one of the early gatherings. Dezső had always been a drunk, and after two days of visiting every bar, Zoltan was about to give up. He knew Caraldo had reported that Zoltan had fled the Market days ago. It wouldn't be long until the old man would place him in Budapest, if he hadn't already. He couldn't waste any more time. He'd give it one more night.

And this night he hit it lucky. The *Klub Vittula* was buried deep in the old Jewish Quarter in an ancient brick cellar, a maze of tiny windowless rooms lit by a few red lights in sconces on the dark walls. It seemed a perfect fit for the fat drunk he remembered. He approached the young bartender who recognized the picture immediately — Dezső came there every night. Usually late.

He would wait.

He took a small table hidden in the shadows of an alcove and watched the shifting clientele — young hipsters, wrecked druggies, old drinkers — walk in and stumble out. And an hour passed, and Zoltan began to wonder if this night Dezső had gone elsewhere. Tried a new bar. Passed out in his apartment.

Dezső appeared near midnight. Although it had been years, Zoltan recognized the man immediately. Like the rest of them, he had barely aged. He wore an old brown herringbone sport coat split open by a giant stomach, too large to be fully covered by a greying white shirt that hung over his belt. An unruly mop of brown hair was topped by a tattered black beret. Zoltan saw the bartender nod toward his booth. The old man turned and squinted. Recognition suddenly lit his face. He grabbed a bottle of wine from the bar and made his way through the crowd to Zoltan's table. He paused, his head cocked inquisitively. Then he held out his hand.

"Zoltan József," he said.

Zoltan stood and grasped the old man's hand. "It has been a long time, a very long time."

They chatted, catching up, Dezső drinking at an alarming rate, but they both knew this was hardly a coincidental meeting. After a half hour of small talk, Dezső leaned across the beat-up wooden table. His eyes were set deeply in his puffy face.

"I never knew you that well, Zoltan, but you always seemed like an honest man." His eyes narrowed. "What is it you want from me? Are you in trouble?"

Zoltan hesitated. How closely involved was Dezső with the *Mester*?

"Are you still making gems, Dezső?"

The old man's face clouded. "Not for many, many years. You could say my license was revoked."

"By…?"

The man shrugged his shoulders. "Who else?"

"Ah. Caraldo said you were retired."

Dezső flinched. "Caraldo?" he asked huskily, fear lighting up his dull eyes.

"Do not worry," Zoltan said, raising his hand slightly. "My visit has nothing to do with him. He is not after you. But I always wondered why you stopped attending the agent meetings."

Dezső licked his lips nervously. "I made a mistake. One of my clients, he couldn't pay. I lied for him. I was supposed to destroy his gem. But I couldn't." He stared into the throng of people crowding the bar. "He was a friend. I told the *Mester* I had hammered it."

"But he knew better."

The old man nodded. "Called me to London. Screamed at me. Told me he would have killed me, but we went back too far." Dezső poured more wine into his glass and drank it as if it were water. "His goons, led by Caraldo, came to my apartment. Took everything. My camera, my money. He emptied my bank account. I had nothing."

"Did he..." Zoltan paused. "Your jewel. Did he return it?"

Dezső gave a harsh laugh. "In London, he brought it out. Had it on that huge desk of his. He picked up the hammer. The one with the gold head on one end and the sharp blade on the other?" Zoltan nodded.

"He started to smash it, and I screamed. At the last second, he changed ends. He struck the stone with the sharp end." The man's eyes winced at the memory. "It was the most excruciating pain I have ever felt. As if a dull blade was jabbed through my chest, into my heart." He rubbed his chest and winced slightly. "It's still there, you know. The pain. Every day." He tapped above his heart. "A dull ache."

"I am sorry."

The man looked into the smoky noise that filled the cellar bar. "Then he put the stone, my beautiful blue jewel, back into his safe. I assume it is still there."

Both men were quiet for a few moments, idly listening to the din of the bar. *Yes, it's still there*, Zoltan thought. *Like mine. And they will stay there until he doesn't need us anymore. Until we become a liability. Or until we take them back.*

"You asked me what I wanted," Zoltan said. "I want to know about the *Csúnya Mester*. I think you may be one of the few people who can help me."

Dezső stared intently into his wine glass. "*Csúnya Mester*," he mused. He looked up at Zoltan. "Why now?"

"Yes," Zoltan said nodding. "Why now indeed. Perhaps because I have already waited too long." He stared into the deep red of the wine his glass. "Perhaps I have finally awakened."

There was silence as both men sipped their wine. "You want to kill him," Dezső said. A flicker of recognition flashed in his dull eyes. "Talking could be dangerous. For you and me."

"Perhaps," Zoltan replied. "I don't know. I'm not even sure what it is I am looking for. Or what I could do if I found it."

Dezső drained his glass again. "Let me think. Tonight. If I decide to speak with you, I will meet you tomorrow."

Zoltan nodded. "Of course. I understand."

The old man suddenly leaned across the table until Zoltan could smell the wine on his breath. "No you don't," he said fiercely. "He destroyed me. I too would like to kill him." He sat back heavily, breathing hard. "You know the Liszt *Ferenc tér?*"

"The square? Of course. It is very near where I lived as a boy."

The old man raised his eyebrows in surprise. "There is a cafe there, the *Cafe Vian.*"

"I know it. It is just two blocks off of *Andrassy.*"

The old man nodded. "I will be at the last table outside on the square at 2:00." He paused and looked into Zoltan's face. "If I have anything to say."

Zoltan spent an uncomfortable night on the floor of a deserted house near *Andrassy.* It had been empty for years, at least since the 1956 revolution. Zoltan recognized the house from his childhood and knew that along with a quarter million others, the owners had fled, leaving the rambling mansion to the rats and homeless. He spent the day in the dusty rooms, wondering if the *Mester* had located him yet.

And he wondered about Barbara. What had he gotten her into? It had been three days since he had seen her. If she was at the Danubius, was she thinking the same thing?

In the afternoon he left the house and walked the short distance to the café. It wasn't quite 2:00 yet, but Dezső was already sitting at the table alone with a nearly empty glass of red wine, probably a cheap *Gamza*. He wore the same brown herringbone coat and white shirt with a stained red tie. The beret slouched to one side of his head. Zoltan approached the table and sat across from him.

"I've given it some thought," Dezső said as Zoltan settled into his seat. "I will share with you what I know." He was speaking rapid Hungarian, and Zoltan was relieved that he could follow most of it. After only three days in Budapest, he was pleasantly surprised how quickly the language had returned.

"Thank you."

"No need. But I must have your word that this is between you and me. It can go no further. Do you understand?"

Zoltan nodded. "Of course. But…" He hesitated. "There is a woman."

"Isn't there always?"

"It's not like that. This is a young woman, a client. She has been drawn into this, somehow." He shook his head slightly. "It is very complicated. But she is here."

Dezső's bushy eyebrows rose in surprise. "Here? In Budapest?"

"Yes. At least I believe so. She has changed my life. She thinks more of me than I do. She is my…" Zoltan struggled to find the right words in Hungarian. "*Ő az én bátorság,* yes?"

"She is your courage?"

Zoltan nodded. "I am being hunted. She insists on aiding me. I would like her to meet you."

Dezső leaned back in his weathered wood chair and stared at the umbrella overhead, his broad hands clasped across his fat belly. "You are being hunted by…"

Zoltan smiled wryly, remembering their conversation the evening before. "Who else?"

Dezső gave a curt nod. "Alright. But no one else, understood?

"Understood." Zoltan motioned to the waiter for another bottle of *Egri Bikavér.*

Dezső was quiet for a long moment. "You called him the *Csúnya Mester?*"

"Yes, the Ugly Master. I had heard agents call him that behind his back, but always in English. It wasn't until Victor Caraldo said it in Hungarian that I realized the *Mester* had a Hungarian connection."

The bottle of dark red wine arrived, and Zoltan poured Dezső's glass half full. The old man stared at the glass and frowned. Zoltan quickly filled the heavy tumbler.

"Caraldo," Dezső said, shaking his head slightly. "That boy is going to get himself into trouble." He took a deep drink from his glass.

"He said you were the one that told him it was Hungarian."

The old man glanced up sharply from his wine, a spark of fear lighting his brown eyes. "He told only me."

The old man relaxed and leaned back in his chair again, balancing the wine on his protruding stomach. "I hope that is the case." He finished the wine and put the glass on the table with a thump. Zoltan picked up the bottle and filled the glass again. "For his sake as well as mine."

"He meant nothing." Zoltan said. "He knows nothing. But when I realized the *Csúnya Mester* might be Hungarian, I thought you might. You were one of his first agents."

The old man adjusted the tie around the collar of his worn white shirt. "One of the first, yes. And the only one of that group left alive. And me just barely."

Zoltan poured wine into his own glass and sat back. "I am glad you decided to come."

Dezső opened his hands on the table and shrugged. "Perhaps I also have waited too long."

"If I am to survive, I must understand the *Mester*. You may be the only person who can help, no?"

"As I said, I may have a few stories that could be helpful."

"I would very much like to hear them."

"Yes? Well, they are not short stories. I think we will need another bottle of wine to properly appreciate them."

Zoltan nodded and called the waiter over and ordered wine along with *langos*, fried bread covered in cheese.

"Of course," Zoltan said. "Wine is a fine lubricant of the memory, is it not?" He smiled. "But I must ask you to not tarry on details. As much as I would like to hear your stories in their fullness, I am in something of a hurry."

Dezső drained his glass. "I will do my best."

Chapter 18

"HIS REAL NAME IS GAVRILO. He was an orphan, you know."

Zoltan shook his head. "I did not know that, though he always said he only hired orphans. Claimed they had no other loyalties."

"No doubt true. But he hates families, people with partners. Friends." Dezső laughed bitterly. "Of *course* he was an orphan. If he had parents, can you imagine how they must have reacted when they saw his hideousness?" His eyes squinted as he stared out into the narrow square just outside the café's black metal fence. "I wonder if they screamed when they first saw him. What do you think?"

Zoltan gave a small shrug.

"I like to imagine the look on his mother's face when he popped out. Jesus, the horror, the horror. Damn, that would have been good. Now that's assuming he had a mother."

Zoltan's eyebrows furrowed. He wondered how badly the years of hard drinking had compromised Dezső's ratiocination.

The old man's face clouded in anger. "Go on and laugh. But I'm not so sure. Odd things, unnatural things happen." He glowered at Zoltan through bloodshot eyes. "You of all people should know that."

"Of course. Please, continue."

"There were two rumors in the orphanage. One was that he had no mother. The other one was that he had killed her when he was a baby."

Zoltan tilted his head. "You said these rumors were heard in the orphanage, yes?"

Dezső nodded his head drunkenly.

"And how would you know that?"

Dezső sat immobile for several seconds, his eyes fixed on the table. "Because I was in the orphanage too."

Zoltan poured himself a half glass of wine and leaned back slightly. "I see. I meant no disrespect. You were there when the *Mester* was brought to the orphanage?"

"No, no," the old man growled. "He had been there for years before…"

"Yes?"

"Years before I was brought there. In 1903. I know nothing of my past. I was told as an infant I was left in a pew in a church, *Szt Anna Templom*."

"Saint Anne's Church. Across the Danube, yes. And he had been at the orphanage for many years before you arrived? "

The man hunched his shoulders noncommittally. "I do not know how long." He looked up from the table. "But for as long I can remember, the *Mester*, Gavrilo, he was there."

"You are sure about the date?"

The man gave a curt nod. "It's the only document I have. Not a birth certificate. A file card. I went back when the place was still standing. 1919. The country was in chaos. Can you imagine? A million and a half Austro-Hungarian soldiers dead. First the Red Terror, then the Romanian War. They took everything – cars, food, cattle. And when they left, the White Terror. Horthy's revenge, eh?"

"Yes. It was a terrible time. My father was killed. Firing squad."

"Jewish?"

Zoltan nodded.

The old man jerked his glass upward, spilling wine down his chin. "They killed hundreds. I remember bodies hanging from trees. Militias shooting whole families. All through the night, gunfire, flames. Screams."

The two men were quiet. Traffic on *Andrássy út* hummed softly. The airbrakes of a bus hissed. "You were a young man, a boy. How did you survive?"

Dezső stared blankly toward the green of the square. "I met the *Mester.* He was in Budapest. I was 15 and the war had just ended. Kun and his Bolsheviks had seized power. His thugs were everywhere. Then the Romanians came…"

The man lifted the bottle to pour more wine into his glass. Only a few drops leaked into his empty tumbler. He slammed the bottle down on the table hard. He looked up at Zoltan under his heavy eyebrows. Zoltan waved to the waiter and held up the bottle, wondering how much more he would get out of Dezső before he passed out.

The waiter brought the bottle and pulled the cork. Dezső grabbed the bottle and sloshed the wine into his glass.

"Gavrilo had already formed a troop of orphans. He was glad to see me. I was older than most. I became a sort of officer. His lieutenant. Really, there were so many of us, living like starving dogs on the street. Like he says, orphans have no past, no hope for the future. We lived for the minute. We didn't fear death because we had no life. We were ruthless. We stripped corpses. And if they weren't quite dead, we helped them long. Jewelry, rings, guns. We slipped into houses, occupied or empty, and stole – food first and then what we could sell. We were jackals. And we ruled much of the city. No one came near us. The *Mester* became rich. We set up headquarters in an abandoned mansion on *Bajza Utca.*"

"I know the area. I walked there sometimes with my nanny. When we weren't cowering from the Terror. Such a beautiful street lined with tall plane trees and lovely homes. So many had been damaged during the Romanian War, abandoned by Jewish families fleeing the Terror."

Dezső's eyes began to close.

"Dezső!" Zoltan said sharply.

The old man's head jerked up, his black beret tumbling onto the brick floor. He squinted at Zoltan. "You said the *Mester* had set up headquarters in an empty mansion on *Bajza Utca.*"

Dezső nodded boozily. "He lived in the master bedroom. A vast bed, I remember. I slept downstairs, but I had my own room. For the first time, I had a room of my own. We stole a car. I had one of the boys drive me to the orphanage. It was in *Tatabánya.* You know where that is?"

Zoltan nodded. "An hour northwest."

"Yes. It was a dark place, red brick blackened by soot and time. My men walked with me to the front door. It was locked. We shot off the locks and I went in. It had been abandoned for years, but the office was still like the day the staff had left. I went through the files for hours. What to look for? I had no last name. I finally found a file box. There were a hundred cards in it, each with a single name arranged alphabetically. Gavrilo. I pulled the card and studied it on the desk. It was blank. No mother's name, no father's. Age at time of arrival – blank. Birth date, blank. Family members, blank. There was only one note, penciled at the bottom: 'Grotesque. Unplaceable.'"

"And you? You found your card?"

Dezső's head nodded toward the table. "I too had no last name," he mumbled as his head settled onto his arms crossed on the table. "But I had a date. Born 1903. And there was a note on my card. 'Name tag in a woman's writing pinned to blanket. 'Name of baby is Dezső.'"

The man became quiet, and then began to snore.

Chapter 19

SHE HAD BEEN IN BUDAPEST for four days, eagerly scanning the obituaries each morning. And each morning she had found nothing. Today had been the first day she had begun to really wonder. What if Zoltan never appeared? What if he had been caught, killed? Certainly not out of the question. What if she was going mad? She fingered the black card in her pocket, finding some reassurance in its cool, plastic tangibility.

The opening chords of the toccata shook the pew Barbara sat in. The air around her trembled as the great organ thundered Bach's masterpiece into the magnificent sanctuary of St Stephen's Basilica, which glowed a dull gold and red in the low light of the evening. The arpeggios gave way to the driving fugue. She glanced over her shoulder at the lone figure on the balcony attacking the keyboard, his hands bouncing high into the air. How could one man create this stunning, towering sound? She turned back to the front of the basilica, closed her eyes, and let the music wash over her.

Four days, and a million miles, a thousand years away from anyplace she knew, any time she could remember. The music filled her chest, pushed her head gently from side to side. This seemed right, to be in this glorious church, glittering with gilt, draped in heavy red velvet, a place she had never heard of in a city she knew only through rumors and fairy tales, old history lessons, exotic travelogues, listening to music that filled her up as if she were drowning gloriously in the shattering chords from the giant pipe organ.

There was a brief lull, and then a flute floated its song into the now still air. She looked up at the balcony again. A golden-haired woman in a white blouse and black dress, her eyes closed, swayed slightly as her notes drifted into the sanctuary below. The organ joined her, and the music, thunderous pipe organ now muted, danced delicately in the shimmering air. They intertwined, separated, rejoined, one playing to the other, holding notes, sharing soaring harmonies.

Barbara looked up at the dome above her, imagining the notes rising, collecting at the top like heavy steam, condensing, raining back down on the hundred or so listeners, their faces upturned as if to catch the drops on their cheeks, breathe them into their lungs.

Barbara closed her eyes again and let the music take her. Four days, and not a word from Zoltan. Sometimes, late at night in the darkness of her room, she wondered if he were even real, if all of this was some sort of elaborate illusion.

How had she gotten here? The dark plane, each seat enclosed by a black curtain, no one speaking except the lone stewardess, and then in hushed tones, asking if she would like champagne. Cognac perhaps? Each passenger being invited to deplane separately, many met by chauffeured sedans on the tarmac. The quick cab ride through the night streets of the strange city, wipers clicking rhythmically against the steady rain, the driver speaking almost no English but nodding when she told him the name of the hotel. Paying him silently with the black card. Checking into the hotel, its lobby all polished brass, deep blue carpets, pink marble columns.

"Yes, madam," the man at the desk in a black suit and red tie had said in broken English when she gave her name. "Your room is waiting."

The music shifted to more gliding arpeggios, the brilliant organist showing his dexterity as his fingers danced up and down the keyboard.

It had rained steadily since she arrived. The old stone buildings reflected the slick grey of the skies, the streets gleaming black. At first, she had been afraid to leave her room, never knowing when Zoltan might contact her. But then the hours passed into days.

She bought an umbrella and walked the narrow streets of the Jewish Quarter, eating duck breast at a small café and listening to klezmer music, tasting Hungarian wines in a booth at the *Doblo* and enviously watching the couples sitting together, laughing, their faces close together. She studied a Hungarian phrase book. She tried saying *"köszönöm"* to waiters hoping they would recognize thank you, but she was always disappointed by blank stares that reminded her that Hungarian was not even an Indo- European language, less similar to English than Hindi. There was nothing to connect, no words that resembled English, written or verbal.

The menus might as well be written in Swahili. How did *szeretnék egy üveg bort* connect with "I would like a bottle of wine?" She was grateful for the English of the staff, no matter how halting.

Suddenly the organ shuddered into silence, the air still shivering. She stood up with the rest of the audience, applauding, and turned to the musicians, small and insignificant behind the gilt railing of the balcony high above her. They bowed as the crowd continued to clap until they waved briskly and disappeared into the darkness behind them.

She made her way slowly out of the church, listening vaguely to conversations in a language that was so alien she could not pick out a word. The steps outside the basilica spilled onto a plaza, an intricate pattern of red and blue circles inlaid in the brick. Barbara pulled her scarf around her neck, glad that she had bought some warmer clothes and happy to ditch her black tights and hoodie. The wind whipped off the Danube to her right, carrying a cold rain under her opened umbrella.

Head down, she walked along *Károly* to the steps of the pedestrian underpass at the intersection with *Rákóczi út,* the busy avenue that ran beside her hotel. The streetlights barely lit the cement steps that led down into the tiled circle below. She moved out of the entranceway into the bright light, lowering her umbrella.

The underpass was large, maybe 100 feet in diameter, with a confusing set of entrances that gave the place a maze-like feel. Barbara studied the interior, trying to figure out which stairway to take to her hotel. As she did, she noted the buskers and beggars clustered around the walls, some already asleep in raggedy sleeping bags.

She flinched and quickly stepped back into the dim stairwell. From the gloom she studied a man across the circle, sitting against the tiles, a grey wool blanket pulled over his head. The head swiveled back and forth, its beak-like nose pausing at the end of each scan like a metronome. The blanket threw a shadow over the man's face. Surely, she was imagining things. She could feel the tension knotting her stomach. She couldn't do this much longer.

Then the man she was watching pulled back the blanket and ran his hand over his bald head. She had not been wrong. Caraldo sat against the curve of the far edge of the underpass, scanning the broad circle like a hawk.

Barbara slipped back into the darkness and flattened herself against the cold cement wall of the stairwell, her breath quick and shallow. She watched the man to see if he had noticed her, but he drew the blanket back over his head and continued his sweep.

Barbara withdrew up the stairs, her eyes on Caraldo until she was out of his sightline. She turned and dashed up the last steps to the glistening street. She ran to the intersection, glad that the evening traffic was light, and sprinted across the four lanes, dodging a honking taxi and reaching the other side safely. She hurried into the lobby of the hotel and into the open mouth of the elevator and punched the button by her floor number and waited impatiently as the old elevator clanked upward until lurching to a stop. The door slid open, and Barbara walked quickly to her room.

As she opened the door, a dark object, perhaps a piece of paper, fluttered onto the floor. She scanned the empty hallway, closed the door, and turned on the lights. A black business card lay at her feet, a dark rectangle on the burgundy carpeting.

Chapter 20

BARBARA HELD HER UMBRELLA AGAINST the cold drizzle and studied the address she had scribbled on a sheet of Danubius Hotel stationery. Finally. Finally the night before she'd heard from Zoltan. Well, not heard from—he had left a card under her hotel door.

She held her scribbling up to the garish red light leaking out of the building's front doors: 12412 *Kazinczy u, Szimpla Kert. Up. Left rear.* It was the right address, but why would Zoltan want to meet here?

She stood at the bottom of a short flight of steps that led up to the warped, unfinished wood double doors of the building. Once it must have been magnificent, but now stucco crumbled off the walls, exposing worn red brick. Unpainted windowsills, most with framing broken or missing glass panes, rotted with ferns growing from the wood.

Two burly men stood on each side of the entrance, arms folded, as crowds of young people shuffled in and out of the entrance. Barbara walked hesitantly up the stairs. She turned to one of the bouncers. "Excuse me," she said. "Is this the *Szimpla Kert*?"

"*Nem beszélek angolul,*" the man grunted nodding toward the other man. Barbara turned to him. "Yes," he said in a heavy accent. "This is the *Szimpla Kert.*"

"It is a club?"

"Yes," the man answered curtly. "Do you wish to go in?"

Barbara peered into the gloom inside. The air throbbed with heavy rock music. "I am supposed to meet a man here."

"That is often the case."

Barbara felt herself blush. "No, I mean a friend." The bouncer shrugged indifferently.

"It doesn't…I mean, no offense, but it doesn't seem like his kind of place."

The large man rolled his muscled shoulders under his black t-shirt. "People like different places for different things. This is a good place if you want to be together. It is also a good place if you do not. No one will bother you here."

Barbara nodded and unconsciously fingered the jewel hidden under her new sweater. She was glad she had stayed noir— all black seemed to be the dress code. She shifted her pack onto one shoulder, climbed the final steps, and entered the club.

Inside, a curving mahogany stairway, once grand but now chipped and worn, led to the second floor.

In front of her, a gigantic room stretched into darkness, lit by multi-colored Christmas lights and dim red bulbs illuminating various bars along the walls. Smells of cooking food and sweat mingled with a faint odor of decay.

The cement floor was crowded with a jumble of mismatched tables and chairs, worn sofas and several bathtubs filled with cushions and pillows. The old plaster walls, broken in patches with grey laths behind, were decorated with spray-painted graffiti and occasional posters. An old car with no doors or windows was parked against the remains of a soaring wall. Young couples sat on cracked seats drinking from glasses perched on the dashboard. The room was a gigantic crypt trembling to the bass of a metal band playing loudly somewhere in the desolation.

She shook her head slightly and moved toward the relative calm of the stairway. Up.

Staying to the left, she made her way toward the rear of the building, weaving through crushes of dancers, small tables of men and women deep in discussion, and people lined up at small bars, sipping beer. She passed by empty windows and doors reduced to shells and decorated with spray paint and markers. Each held a few tables and some chairs, perhaps some cushions in a corner.

The hallway narrowed into mazes of small passages and dark closets. She kept walking, scanning each room, each face, hoping to see Zoltan. The crowds began to thin, and she sensed the hall was coming to an end. Was this a wild goose chase? Had she misunderstood the note? Worse yet, had she been set up?

Would she find not Zoltan but Caraldo waiting for her?

Barbara walked slowly toward the last door in front of her, her breathing shallow and fast, and edged into the windowless room beyond. Even by the gloomy standards of the club, the room was dark, the few tables lit only by several candles and a single green light bulb hanging from a twisted cord. She stood cautiously just inside the door and searched the murky interior.

"Barbara," a voice called softly from a dim corner.

She turned and spotted a man rising from a wooden chair. As he stood, he nudged the table and a glass of beer rattled slightly. He opened his arms.

"Zoltan!" she cried, running toward him. She crashed into his arms, hugging him tight. "Thank god it's you."

Zoltan pushed her away gently, kissing her gently on the forehead. "You were expecting someone else?"

She took a deep breath, slung her pack off her back and slid into a worn rocking chair with a dark leather seat. "Caraldo, for one," she muttered.

"Caraldo?" Zoltan asked in alarm. "He is here?"

"He is, but can we talk about that later?" She rocked sharply toward Zoltan and grabbed the edges of the table. "Jesus, Zoltan!" she hissed. "I thought you were dead, or captured, or, I don't know, maybe not even real. Where have you been?"

Her eyes were starting to adjust to the dim light, and she realized Zoltan was smiling broadly at her. "I don't see what's so funny," she said angrily. "I've been worried to death. What was I supposed to do if you never showed up?"

"I am sorry. Really, but it is so good to see you. Until right now I feared I might not see you again."

"You really thought that was a possibility? That at the last minute I would decide not to come? Or that I would get to Budapest and take your black credit card on a shopping spree to Paris?" She gripped the arms of the rocker fiercely. "Damn you, Zoltan. What is wrong with you?"

His wide grin faded, but his face remained soft, his black eyes warm like coals in a fireplace. "You are right. There are many things wrong with me." A small smile played around his lips again. "But we are working on that, yes?"

"Ooh," Barbara muttered, sitting back so hard in her chair it smacked loudly against the brick wall. "You can be *so* frustrating. And after four days of hearing nothing, reading the damned classified ads every day, I find this black card stuck in my door. That's it. Just a black card."

"And how long did it take you to figure out how to read it?" the man asked, his head tilted, enjoying her tantrum.

"That is not the point. OK, sure, I remembered your business card and used the flashlight through my gem to read it, but that wasn't easy either."

Zoltan looked at her quizzically.

"Did you know it takes a strong shaft of light to illuminate the letters?" Barbara didn't wait for a reply. "No, of course you didn't. So there I am holding the damned thing between my jewel and the ceiling light. Nothing. Then I use the table lamp. Still nothing. So I'm thinking, *Now what? My gem doesn't work. I am truly up the creek.* Do you get it, Zoltan? There I am stuck with a card I can't read and no way to contact you."

She quieted, her shoulders shaking. "I was scared." She looked at Zoltan, tears glistening on her cheek in the dim candlelight. "Really, really scared." She sniffed. "I've never felt so lonely."

Zoltan's face sagged. He leaned over the table and placed his hand over hers. "I am sorry. So sorry. But you found me, yes?"

Barbara sniffed again. "Well, yes. But you didn't make it easy."

Zoltan's eyes lit again. "It was for your safety, madam. And mine. It was not supposed to be easy, yes?"

Barbara leaned back in the rocking chair and ran her hands through her mass of damp red curls and shook them. "Well, then you were successful."

"You look absolutely lovely, madam."

Barbara glared but made no attempt to correct him. "What is this place, anyway?"

Zoltan tried to stifle a chuckle by holding his fist to his mouth and coughing slightly. "It is a *romkocsma*, a ruin pub."

Barbara was still looking around the room. "They got that right," she muttered.

"It was once a magnificent mansion, maybe two. But during the war, right at the end – ah, so tragic." He closed his eyes for a moment. "Those who survived the Nazi's and returned were attacked by the White Terror, and anyone who could find a way fled the county. Then during the communist reign, these houses were left to crumble And were abandoned after the revolution. "

Barbara's eyes returned to Zoltan's face. "That is so sad."

Zoltan nodded. "Most were beyond saving, the mansions. But even after the collapse of communism, the country was so poor they could not be repaired or torn down." He stared briefly into the gloom. "But then, something began to happen. Young people, desperate for a place to meet, to join with others, to talk, began to simply take the houses over. They had no money, so they bought chairs from secondhand stores, salvaged them from dumps. Fixed the wiring a bit…"

"Hopefully," Barbara added, eyeing the cord hanging from the ceiling warily.

"…and opened them up as bars. Ruin bars."

Now Barbara was rocking gently back and forth in her chair. "I see. But what I don't see is why in the world you would have us meet here."

"Ah. That would be because of Dezső."

Barbara stopped rocking. "The agent here in Budapest. The old one. You found him?"

"Indeed. I am sorry, my dear, that I was not able to greet you properly and earlier. But I have not been idle. You see, I not only found him, I have spoken to him several times."

"About the *Mester*."

"Who else?" Zoltan lifted the glass and drank deeply. "Please excuse me. I have been impolite. Would you like a beer, or a glass of wine perhaps?"

Barbara settled back. "Some wine would be nice. Maybe a glass of *Egri Bikavér?*"

Zoltan raised his eyebrows. "Ah, I see you too have been busy. Yes, but I will get us a bottle. Maybe three."

Barbara looked at him, puzzled.

"No, not for us, madam. Or at least not *just* for us. I am confident that the guest that will be joining us will consume the lion's share."

"Guest?"

"Yes, you see Dezső will be here shortly. Let me get the wine. Then I will share with you what I have learned." He stood up. "Oh, and Barbara. He is frightened. That is why he wanted to meet here. He felt vulnerable outside. "

"Does he know about me?"

Zoltan nodded. "Yes, but he is still nervous. I assured him you were safe."

"If he is so concerned, why is he taking the chance of talking with you?"

"I will explain," he said. "But the answer is quite simple. He hates the *Mester* more strongly than he fears for his life."

Chapter 21

"YOU DON'T BELIEVE THAT, DO you? That the *Mester* didn't have a mother?"

Barbara and Zoltan sat speaking softly in the corner of the dark room. Zoltan shrugged and took a sip of wine. He needed something to drink after recounting what he had learned from Dezső the previous day.

"No, I do not. I imagine he was simply born deformed and abandoned. But as Dezső says, strange things do happen. And the *Mester* is one of them."

Barbara shivered slightly. "His story…" She paused. "I don't know whether I feel more sad or frightened."

"Indeed." Zoltan looked up. "Ah, he is here." Zoltan began to stand then leaned toward Barbara. "One thing. Once he begins drinking, which is as soon as he sits down, he is only good for an hour or so. It is important that we listen, yes?"

Barbara nodded. "My lips are sealed."

She turned and looked over her shoulder at the heavy-set man moving toward them. Even in the dim light she could see the red bulbous nose and jowly face.

"This is the lady you mentioned?" the man said in heavily accented English as he neared their table.

"It is. Barbara, I would like you to meet an old friend." He smiled slightly at the man. "A *very* old friend. Dezső, this is my very *young* friend, Barbara."

The man tilted his gigantic head slightly and removed his beret. He took Barbara's hand and raised it to his lips. "Madam, it is lovely to meet you." He looked at Zoltan. "Young, yes. And very beautiful. You failed to mention that."

Barbara felt herself flush. This was becoming a pattern. She had never thought of herself as beautiful. She wondered if she just appealed to Hungarians.

Zoltan motioned to a straight-backed chair at the end of the table. "Please, sit down. Join us for a glass of wine."

The man's puffy face lit up. "Thank you. But that chair…"

Zoltan looked at him quizzically. "Ah, I see. It does not look comfortable."

"I can hardly imagine myself falling asleep in it."

Zoltan quickly scanned the room and strode to a table near the door. He pulled an old green easy chair, the high back worn and soiled, from underneath the table and dragged it back to where Barbara was sitting. He replaced the wood chair and Dezső settled into the upholstery heavily.

"That is better," he said, pouring himself a glass of wine as Zoltan returned to his seat. He took a long drink. "Much better. And the wine – it is lovely."

Zoltan nodded toward Barbara. "You can thank Barbara for that. She has been doing some serious research since arriving in Budapest."

Dezső raised his glass to Barbara. "Thank you, madam. I drink to your good taste and good health."

Zoltan extended his hand across the table and the two men shook hands briefly. "I have shared your stories with Barbara." Zoltan said. "We are both most interested in learning more, if you would be so generous."

Dezső had already drained his first glass and poured himself another. Barbara looked up at Zoltan in alarm, wondering if they would get their full hour.

Dezső smiled at Barbara. "In such charming company, I would be pleased hold forth, even if, for the lady's sake, it is in my abysmal English. At least as long as the wine holds out," he added, "and if the lady is interested."

Barbara returned the man's smile. "Zoltan has told you how we met? And our current situation?" The man nodded solemnly.

"Sir, I am interested, most interested."

The man grinned. "Very well then. Let me see. Where did I leave off?"

Zoltan leaned forward slightly. "You had returned to the orphanage and found your card as well as that of the *Mester*."

"Ah, yes. Yes. So, I had met the *Mester* in Budapest and was working for him. I told you that?" Zoltan nodded.

"I had not seen him for many years. He had walked out of the orphanage – just walked out – several years before I left. We knew each other. We were not friends, but I learned from him. We were always hungry, so he showed me how to steal food. At night we hid to watch the staff grope each other in the hallways. Listening, always listening. Watching other children leave with families. Sometimes when I was with him, we would overhear their remarks – 'He is so monstrous!' And as I came to know him, I found he was indeed hideous, hideous in ways neither you nor I understand."

Dezső licked his lips nervously and tilted the wine into his mouth. "You see, he embraced it, the monstrousness. A year or so before Gavril left, the director of the orphanage died. She fell down a flight of marble stairs. They never proved anything, but Gavril told me what had happened. He hated her. She was always kind to me and most of the others. But not to Gavril. When she looked at him, it was with disgust, loathing. That night he heard her in the hallway." Dezső turned toward Barbara. "Such ears he has," he whispered. "Huge. They can hear…anything."

"Please go on," Zoltan said, noticing the quickly disappearing wine.

"Gavril told me he slipped into the hall. He saw her at the top of the stairs. He snuck up on her in the shadows." He looked at Barbara again. "So quiet, he can be so quiet. He comes up on you unheard."

Barbara nodded.

"He kicked her in the back and watched as she fell screaming down the stairs. We all heard the screams. And then the screaming stopped."

Dezső wiped his lips with the cuff of his filthy shirt and began on the second bottle, nervously pouring his glass full. "And then, just a month later, he killed a kitchen maid when she caught him stealing bread. I asked him why he killed her. He said she screamed at him, and he didn't like it, so he used a bread knife and cut her throat. Then he finished eating the bread."

Dezső threw back his head and drained the glass. "Again, they couldn't prove anything. But they left him alone I can tell you that. The whole staff was terrified of him. That's the way he likes it, you see. Everyone frightened of him."

Barbara had been watching the man's fleshy face as he spoke, noticing the fear rise in his eyes and how his mouth tensed as the pitch of his voice rose. As shocking as his revelations were, she knew he was telling the truth without embellishment. She shivered slightly in the dark room.

Dezső spun the red wine around in his glass then drank it.

"Then he left the orphanage?" Zoltan asked.

Dezső nodded. "I was about eight or nine then, I guess. I didn't see him again until after the war."

"When you met him once more, in Budapest."

Dezső's eyes began to close. Barbara uncrossed her legs and kicked Dezső gently under the table. He looked up startled.

"Oh, goodness," Barbara said. "I am so sorry."

He looked at her blearily. "Quite alright, my dear. Now, where was I?"

"You are in Budapest, now, Dezső," Zoltan interjected. "What happened in Budapest?"

Dezső leaned back in the old chair, staring at the cracked ceiling above him. "Many things," he whispered. "Many things I do not wish to share. But there is one occasion I must tell you about."

Barbara sensed the man was trying to rally from his drunkenness, but it was a losing battle. His eyes fluttered and his chin sank forward.

Later she wasn't sure what it was. A shadowy movement by the doorway, or possibly a noise. Maybe it was nothing. But as Dezső's head fell forward, her pulse raced as if she'd been injected with adrenalin. She sat bold upright, and her head snapped around. She stared at the entrance to the room they were in.

Zoltan's eyes darted toward the doorway. "What is it?" he asked, his hands gripping the sides of his chair.

"I don't know. Maybe nothing."

Zoltan shook his head. "You do not react to nothing." He stood up and slid into the shadows of the peeling wall, easing himself toward the empty doorway.

Barbara's heart rate had slowed, but there was a metallic taste of fear in her mouth. Her gaze locked on the dark rectangle of the entranceway as Zoltan edged to the battered doorframe. With a single fluid motion, he swung around the edge and disappeared into the darkened hallway.

Barbara turned to face the door, half rising from the rocking chair. Next to her, Dezső snored gently, apparently unaware of their movement. In a few moments, Zoltan returned, his face dark and solemn. He knelt next to Barbara's chair.

"What did you see?" he whispered so as to not wake up the sleeping Dezső.

"Nothing really," Barbara said quietly. "It was more what I felt." She paused. "Terror."

"When you turned to the doorway, was there anything, anything at all?"

"Maybe," she replied. "I can't be sure."

"Go on."

"A shadow, large and menacing, like a bear." Zoltan nodded his head slowly.

"Yes, a bear. A Russian bear, I fear."

"What?"

"I caught a glimpse of a man descending the stairs down to the main floor. I can't be sure…"

"But what do you think?" Barbara persisted.

"It might be Zhukov."

"Zhukov?"

Zoltan ran his hands through his hair. "He works for the *Mester*. A thug. Former KGB agent I understand."

Barbara stared back at the door. "That would mean what's his name, the Ugly Master, knows where you are."

Zoltan nodded. "To be more precise, knows *we* are *here*."

Barbara took a deep breath. "So what do we do?"

Zoltan stood up and nodded toward Dezső. "Wake him up. If it was Zhukov, we need to know as much as possible and as quickly as possible."

Zoltan walked around the small table toward his seat, and Barbara leaned toward Dezső on her left. She reached over gently and ran a finger around the old gem maker's ear. He twitched slightly then began to lift his head as she pulled lightly on his earlobe.

His eyes fluttered and then opened. He looked directly into Barbara's face and smiled.

"Madam, I do not believe in heaven, nor that I would reside there should it exist. But surely you are an angel."

Barbara sat back in the rocking chair. "Shit," she muttered, looking at Zoltan. "Am I blushing again?"

Dezső gave a low, boozy chuckle. "And it only makes you more lovely. Now, where was I?"

Zoltan leaned forward. "You were about to share something important. You said there was an incident, an occasion we should know about."

Dezső nodded his great shaggy head. "Yes, of course." He looked first at Zoltan and then into Barbara's eyes. His were the frightened eyes of a man reliving a long-buried horror.

"I will tell it as I remember it. You must make of it what you will. When you hear the event I describe, you might think, 'Dezső, that old drunk. He is cracked.' But I assure you. It happened."

Zoltan nodded. "What happened? Please, tell us."

"It was in 1920. Despite all the horrors, the city was becoming normal, picking itself up. There was pressure on our operations. Several of our gang members were arrested demanding protection money from businesses along *Andrassy.* One was killed in a shootout. They really wanted him, of course. They knew he was the..." He paused and looked at Zoltan. "*Agyvelő?*"

"Brains."

"Yes, yes. The brains of our operation. The police had begun to call him the *Csúnya Mester,* the hideous master. He heard this from police informers we hired. He laughed. 'Ugly,' he said. 'Monstrous. Yes, to all!'"

Dezső put his glass down and held onto the upholstered arms as if to steady himself, bowing his head slightly in concentration. "I heard through our prison network that they were torturing one of the men that had been captured. I smuggled knives into them – we owned the jail. They escaped, killing five guards, the torturers, and the guard who had informed. I could not afford for him to talk."

He looked up and shrugged. "It was a war. People die. But that was too much for the police. They had found out where we were headquartered. We woke up and saw that they had ringed our house with gunmen. Snipers were on the roofs on other buildings all around us." Dezső's face darkened and his eyes returned to the stained tabletop. "That's when he came to the front door. Just like that. Knocked on the door! Can you imagine? We're under siege. Our men are pointing guns out of every window. Armed guards around the entrance. But he paid no mind and walked right up to the guards as if he were coming over for tea."

Zoltan held up a hand. "Dezső, *who* knocked on the door?"

Dezső continued as if he had not heard. "They yell at him to stop. He doesn't. Laszlo raises his gun to shoot. He looks at the man. His eyes are not eyes. They are flames. That is what he told me later. Blue flames! Flickering in the night. Franjo answers the door, pointing a shotgun at his chest."

Barbara looked at Zoltan and raised her eyebrows. How much of this was true? How much were the rantings of delusional old drunk?

"The man, the tall man brushes the gun aside." Dezső is speaking in a low voice, as if in a trance. "I'm in the *Mester's* room, figuring out how we can survive the police assault. I hear the commotion and step out onto the landing where I can see what is going on. The man is standing just inside the door. He is tall, maybe 6'3 or 6'4. It is raining outside, and he wears a dark brown wool cape with the hood up. I can smell the wet wool all the way up the stairs. 'I want to speak to the *Mester*,' he says to Franjo. Not *Csúnya Mester*, just the *Mester*, the Master."

Dezső's shaggy eyebrows knit, and his eyes closed. "But he doesn't actually speak. Later you cannot remember the sound. Only the words. Franjo nods up the stairway. The tall man climbs toward me, silently. Not a sound. My heart is beating fast and hard. I retreat down the hall from him, but he pays no attention to me. He stands outside the *Mester's* room and opens the door. He stands still in the doorway for a few moments, his head swiveling, swaying a little, as if he is trying to catch an odor. Then he laughs. Or so it would seem. It was a series of loud hisses, like escaping steam. He walks inside and the door closes."

Dezső was bent over at the waist, his head not far from his ballooning belly, his eyes closed. For a moment Barbara was afraid he had passed out again, but he shook his head and continued.

"I creep up to the room, to listen. And inside I hear him, or at least I understand what he is saying. I don't know. 'Gavrilo,' the man says. It is a statement, not a question. I wonder how he knows the *Mester's* name. He hated the name. Never used it. He had me swear I would never use it. How did the brown-robed man know?"

Dezső pulled himself almost upright, his eyes still closed. "'I think it is time for you to work for me,' the tall man says to Gavrilo. I hear the squeak of his desk chair. I wonder if he is scared. 'I am doing fine,' Gavrilo tells the man in that high-pitched voice of his. I thought it would tremble, but it didn't. He seemed like he knew the man."

He paused, thinking. "Not well, but maybe like an uncle you met when you were a small child? Familiar. Then the tall man gives that hissing laugh again. '*Are* you doing fine? You are surrounded by heavily armed men. Every way out is barricaded. They are preparing to burn you out then shoot every one of you.' That laugh and then a pause. 'What is it you want, Gavrilo?' he asks. The *Mester* is quiet for a long time. I begin to wonder if they have moved to another room out of earshot.

"Then I hear Gavrilo say, 'Power. I want power.' The tall man says, 'And so you should. We are masters, Gavrilo, you and I. We are *here* to wield power. We are noble, courageous, warriors, are we not? They are pathetic weaklings who live in a hell of their own making. And then they call *us* evil.' He hisses again, but this time it is the hissing of a snake, filled with hate and loathing."

Dezső opened eyes were glowing with fear. "I can remember it like it was today. What he said, word for word, but I do not recall his voice." He looked at Zoltan curiously. "How can that be?"

"Please, Dezső, go on," Zoltan said. "Finish your story."

Dezső's head began to slump toward one side. Barbara reached out and took the old man's hand and brought it to her face. Dezső straightened, staring at Barbara and tracing the lines of her high cheekbones with his blunt fingers.

"So soft," he whispered.

Barbara leaned toward him, still holding his hand against her face.

"Please," she said gently. "Go on."

The man's stricken face relaxed, his eyes became clear again. He withdrew his hand and replaced it on the arm of his chair. He looked into Barbara's face. "Madam, you make me feel young again. You remind me of red tulips and cherry blossoms." He smiled. "Yes, before I go to sleep. I must finish the story."

Dezső took a deep breath. "This is what he said: 'We are the strong ones, Gavrilo, you and I. *We* are what is noble, what is courageous. They call you the Ugly Master, the Monstrous Master, do they not? But that is because they fear you. We need power, yes, to avoid victory of the weak and pitiful over the strong and good. And for that you need wealth, Gavrilo, as well as power. I can give you both.' I hear them moving, over toward the window.

"Then I hear him again, just as clearly as before. 'I too need power,' the tall man says. 'And I have it. But not as much as I would like. I need you for that. I will give you a machine,' he says, 'that will steal people's souls. You will have the souls of those who serve you. They will be yours. And they will steal the souls of others and place them in gems with power that the owners do not know what to do with. But we do, do we not Gavrilo? We know how to use them, the nobles like us, the warriors. We will strengthen their goodness. We will show them the joy of watching suffering, of realizing *all* the human joys the weaklings have made evil. And the power, Gavrilo, think of it. It expands, compounds. It feeds and strengthens us, the Masters!'"

The last words seemed to empty the old man. He crumpled sideways over the arm of his chair. His eyes closed again, and his mouth became slack. Barbara reached out to cover the old man's hand. Suddenly he turned his head slightly to smile at Barbara, his eyes still shut. "I am not quite done," he muttered. "Tomorrow, I will tell you what happened then. How we…"

His head slumped again, and he breathed the shallow, regular breath of the unconscious.

Chapter 22

BARBARA AND ZOLTAN WERE QUIET for a long minute, both staring beyond the slumbering man and into the murky darkness of the room. It was as if a spell had been broken. Suddenly outside the single empty doorway, they heard crashing music and the low babble of voices. The acrid smell of a hundred cigarettes filled Barbara's nostrils. For the first time she tasted the rich flavor of the wine on her tongue. She looked at Zoltan across the table, lost in thought.

"Zoltan" she said.

He looked over at her as if he were awaking.

"I'm not sure we should stay here too long."

He cocked his head but said nothing.

"Earlier tonight, in the pedestrian underpass. The one underneath the Astoria?" Zoltan nodded.

"I saw Caraldo."

"Yes, you mentioned he was here. Are you sure?"

"95%. He was posing as a beggar, sitting against a wall with the hood of his black sweatshirt over his head. At first, I wasn't certain, but then he pulled back the hood. It was him."

"Damn," Zoltan muttered under his breath. "First Zhukov and now Caraldo." He looked up. "Did he see you?"

Barbara shook her head. "I caught sight of him before walking into the light. I stayed in the shadows to make sure, but he didn't look my way or change his position. Then I walked back up the stairs to the street. I waited for a minute, but he didn't come behind me."

Zoltan nodded. "Still, there is Zhukov." He looked broodingly out the murky doorway. "He will report he found us. They will both be in pursuit. I am afraid you cannot return to the hotel room."

"I figured that might happen." She nudged the pack at her feet. "I took everything from the room I need."

Zoltan looked at her admiringly. "Madam, you never cease to amaze."

"Zoltan, do we have to go through the whole 'madam' thing again?"

Zoltan dropped his eyes. "I do apologize. But somehow, it suits you."

Barbara sighed. "Let's talk about that another time, OK? Right now I think we should get the hell out of here.

"Yes, of course. It is not safe here."

"Is anywhere safe?"

"There are several deserted houses near here. I stayed in two that were easy to get into. Last night, I moved to another." He paused. "My family's old home."

"Your old house?" Barbara said. "Where you grew up? Is that smart?"

"As you say, is anywhere safe? But yes, I believe so. Caraldo knows I am in Budapest, but not where. The house is simply another abandoned mansion."

"Do you think the *Mester* knows we've been found?"

Zoltan nodded. "I imagine so. But neither he nor Zhukov nor Caraldo know anything about my past. They would have no reason to single out the house. And as I said, the *Mester* seems unable to pinpoint agents' locations unless they stay in one place for several days. Last night was my first there. I believe we will be safe for one more."

"Perhaps we should leave now. Leave Budapest." Barbara shivered. "It feels like it is closing in."

"I wish we could," Zoltan said. "But I need to hear the rest of Dezső's story. I have learned much, but no chink. No opening that would provide an advantage." He paused. "The incident he related, the conversation he overheard between the *Mester* and tall man…"

Barbara leaned forward. "Do you know this man?"

Zoltan shook his head. "No. But it gives credence to the rumors."

"Rumors?"

Zoltan sighed. "That the *Mester* was not acting alone. That he was part of something larger. I wish I had listened more carefully. Asked more questions."

Barbara glanced nervously at the doorway into the room. "About what?"

"Who the *Mester* worked for." He looked up at the dimly lit ceiling. "The Company," he said quietly, almost to himself. He looked back at Barbara. "But we must leave now."

Barbara nodded toward Dezső, snoring softly in the chair. "What about Dezső?" Uncertainty clouded Zoltan's face.

"I mean the first place they'll come looking is here," she continued.

"But we cannot carry him. Not to the house." He went to Dezső's side and hooked his forearm under the sleeping man's arm. He gestured to the other side of the chair. "Please take him by the other arm. We will move him to another room."

Barbara bent slightly and hooked her arm under Dezső's. Even with both of them lifting, she wasn't sure they could get the man to his feet. It was like lifting a 250-pound sack of corn. They finally got him upright, his legs rubbery and useless. Zoltan lay Dezső's left arm over his shoulder. Barbara did the same, and together they slowly dragged the old gem maker up from his chair and into the hallway.

Although patrons passed in the passageway, few paid them any attention. Dragging an unconscious comrade through the smoky halls did not seem particularly remarkable. But the man was heavy. Within a few minutes, she was gasping. "Gotta stop, Zoltan," she puffed.

Zoltan nodded through another doorway, on his left, this one fit with an ancient wood door that was once painted green. "This is good enough. We cannot afford any more time in any case."

Barbara leaned forward and pulled the door fully open. Inside a couple on a sofa in a far corner was entirely preoccupied with each other. On their right there was a small, shadowed alcove, possible a closet at one time in the mansion's history, containing two old, upholstered chairs, their covers worn to an oily slick.

They dragged Dezső's dead weight to one of the chairs and lowered him into the deep cushions. He promptly slumped over one arm and resumed snoring.

Will he be all right?" Barbara asked.

"I think he spends most of his nights in chairs like this."

"And Caraldo and Zhukov?"

"They are looking for us. If Zhukov did see us, he will take Caraldo to the room we were in. It will be empty, and they will take their search elsewhere." He nodded at Dezső. "He is of no interest to them."

"It's sad," Barbara said, looking at the old man. "I like him. I believe, despite all he has done, he is a kind man. To end your life like this…"

"Yes, it is sad. Sadness I do not want to experience. I see more and more clearly that I cannot continue while the *Mester* is alive, while he controls my gem, my life."

"Does it have to come to that?" Barbara breathed. "You or him? One or both of you dead?"

"I don't know. Perhaps not. But after tonight, I fear that it does."

He stood and moved around the slumbering man and extended his hand to Barbara, who was kneeling next to the chair they had deposited Dezső. Barbara got to her feet and gave Zoltan a small curtsy. "Thank you, sir. It is so refreshing to see that chivalry is still alive."

A small smile played across Zoltan's lips. "For the moment, madam."

It was late when they left the bar, but the same two security men were still at the door. The man Barbara had spoken with saw them as they walked down the stairs.

"Te vagy a legjobb, amit tehetett? " he called out to her. Barbara stopped and turned back toward the man. "What did you say?" Barbara demanded.

The man sneered and ignored her. She looked at Zoltan, who took her gently by the elbow. "What did he say?"

"It is nothing. Come, please let it go."

Barbara yanked her elbow out of Zoltan's grip and squared off with the bouncer. "I am not leaving until I know what he said."

Zoltan sighed. "He just asked if I was the best you could do. He was kidding. He meant nothing."

Barbara walked back up the two steps until she was standing on the landing next to the security man, her hands on her hips, glaring at him through narrowed eyes. His look of smug certainty faded, and he edged away from her.

"You are a stupid thug," she said slowly to make sure he caught each word. She pointed down the steps toward Zoltan. "He is more of a man than you could ever hope to be. *Megért?*"

The bouncer looked at her apprehensively. He gave a curt nod.

Barbara turned sharply and walked to Zoltan. When she got to him, she put an arm around his neck and drew his head toward her and nibbled on his ear. She turned back toward the bouncer. "You should be so lucky," she yelled.

"Barbara, Barbara," he said. "What are you doing?"

"Sorry, but he gave me a hard time when I got here. Bastard."

"But you don't want to call attention to us, please."

They walked silently for a while. "Alright," she said. "I'll try to be more careful. But what I said was true. You have more character in you little finger than that muscle-bound jerk will ever have."

"I think he was commenting more on my age, yes?"

"Ha. If he only knew."

Zoltan chuckled, and soon they were both laughing, drawing looks from passersby, huddled under their black umbrellas in the wet night.

"Madam, you are a wonder. And where did you learn to say 'understand' in Hungarian?"

"Well, I remember the word from a phrase book. But I wasn't sure if it meant 'understand?' or 'where is the train station?'"

Zoltan laughed even harder, wiping tears away with the back of his hand. "Oh, madam. Barbara. It has been so long since I laughed."

Together they walked the narrow streets under Barbara's umbrella, the dark buildings on each side muffling their laughter.

Chapter 23

FROM THE RUIN BAR THEY made their way down *Andrassy* past the opera house. The commercial area was replaced with grand homes, mansions with turrets, stained glass windows, great arched windows, and cupolas. Some had been maintained in their original magnificence. But with each block Barbara noticed more and more of the chateaus were without windows, their walls sprayed with graffiti. Long-dry fountains stood in once beautiful gardens, now unkempt and neglected.

They neared an intersection and stopped in front of a sprawling mansion separated from the street by a high fence, cast iron spears thrust into a low cement wall. The main house was flanked by two three- story square towers. Stucco walls were crumbling, revealing the red brick underneath. Tall rectangular windows were boarded up with faded wood.

"My god," Barbara whispered. "It's magnificent."

"Fifty years ago perhaps. Now? No. It is just…empty. Come."

They walked to the iron gate in the fence and Zoltan pulled it sharply toward them. It opened reluctantly, creaking loudly. They slipped through the gate and hurried across the weedy courtyard along the side of the mansion until they reached the rear of the building. High French doors once filled with panes of glass were covered with heavy wood planks, black with age.

Zoltan motioned to a window to the right of the door and grabbed the bottom of a wide piece of wood covering. The board swung outward and held it open for Barbara. She closed her umbrella and squeezed through the opening. Zoltan followed, and the piece of wood slammed shut behind him pitching them into complete darkness.

Zoltan took her hand. "This way," Zoltan said. "The hallway leads to the great room."

She was aware of the high walls ending suddenly, opening into a vast dark gallery. Small shafts of light leaked around boarded windows in front of them, revealing grey lumps of ancient furniture, some covered with rotting sheets, strewn around a room larger than most houses. She looked up but could not see the ceiling.

"This is where you grew up," she whispered, reluctant to speak in the hush of the vast, darkened great room.

"Not really." Zoltan said. "For the years I was here, I spent most of my time in my room on the top floor. I remember looking out over the city from the windows. Afraid. Knowing that I was only safe in this old castle. Like a fairy tale, yes? A sad fairy tale."

The melancholy of his voice echoed in the still room.

Barbara felt the weariness wash over her. She put her hand on Zoltan's arm and leaned against him. "Your sorrow," she murmured. "It is exhausting."

He looked down at her kindly. "Yes. And you, madam, help it be less so. But here." He led her to a long settee with a curved back. He pulled off the sheet, revealing the rotting brocaded fabric underneath, deep red and still beautiful, even in its decay and the gloom. He shook the sheet, sending dust in clouds lit by the dim light from the streetlamps outside that seeped through the shutters. He turned the sheet over and tucked it into the sofa.

He motioned grandly at the settee. "Madam, your bed awaits."

She looked at her watch. It was 7:45. She was surprised to realize she had slept for six hours. It was light outside, but the rain spattered against the glass and the sky remained grey. The room was cold and dank. She shivered and put her hands inside the pockets of her sweatshirt. Zoltan slept on a chair pulled in front of the double front door, his head against the upholstered wing.

She studied him silently. She couldn't put her finger on it, but he had changed. Physically he seemed younger, the lines on his forehead less deep, the tightness around his mouth more relaxed. His hair was longer, swept back in grey waves over his collar. He held his round glasses in one hand, and she noticed his long eyelashes.

She turned back to the window, thinking about Dezső's words the night before. What did it all mean? What were they up against? She snuggled into the corner of the sofa, drawing her legs underneath her and pulling Zoltan's jacket around her.

She wondered if they would get out alive. Her mind turned to her life before meeting Zoltan, and for a brief moment wondered what David was doing. She shook her head. How long ago had it been? A month? A year? A century? And as for David, he'd be doing what he always did. Drinking, playing golf. Hitting on women at the club. Bonking his secretary. How had she ever thought that was a life?

She sighed and watched the rain drops run down the window in front of her.

"That was a deep sigh."

She turned, startled, to see Zoltan standing at the end of the sofa, smiling gently at her.

She smiled in return. "I suppose it was." She pointed to the window with her chin. "I think it's the weather."

Zoltan stared outside for a long moment. "And perhaps many other things as well?"

"Maybe. But I know one thing that would raise my spirits. Some of that thick, heavy coffee they serve around here."

"And perhaps the best cherry strudel in Budapest?"

Barbara's eyes lit up. "Now you are talking, sir. Lead on."

They went back through the kitchen to the window they had climbed through the night before. Zoltan pushed the heavy board outward and scanned the yard.

"Well?"

"The good news is that there does not appear anyone in the immediate vicinity anxious to murder us."

"And the bad?"

"It continues to rain, I am afraid."

"Seems like a fair trade."

After clambering out the window, Barbara put up her umbrella so Zoltan could crowd under. He led her through the garden, overgrown with high bushes and weeds, to the front gate.

"What was it like," Barbara asked, "to return. To go back to your old home?"

Zoltan pulled his coat around him more tightly. "It was…odd."

He said nothing for so long, Barbara wondered if the conversation was over.

"I remembered it all. I went to a window in the back and saw the board had been pried loose. When I climbed inside, I knew at once I was in the old kitchen. I could hear the maid clanking pots, smell the goulash. I went upstairs to my old bedroom. It is hard to believe, but my bed was still there. I recognized it. I lay on it and cried."

They walked in silence, walking in cadence under the umbrella. "Ah," he exclaimed. "We are here."

Zoltan opened the door of a small bakery with a cluster of tables covered in red-checked tablecloths in one corner. As soon as she walked inside, she almost swooned from the overpowering smells of coffee and the indefinable sweetness of sugar and rich cherries baking. How long had it been since she had eaten? She put out her hand and grasped the back of a wooden chair to steady herself.

"It smells like heaven."

Zoltan smiled. "I cannot verify that personally, but I should not be surprised."

He led Barbara to a table against the far wall and pulled out a chair for her. He walked to the marble counter and said something in Hungarian to the young woman working there. She nodded and began pulling strudels from the glass display case. As the woman completed their order, Zoltan stepped aside and picked up a paper lying on a table nearby. He scanned the first page and then idly flipped through the other pages. Suddenly he stopped. He pulled the paper closer, his face tense.

"*Uram!*" the waitress called.

Zoltan continued to stare at the paper.

"Uram," she called out again, a tinge of annoyance in her voice. *"Megrendelese keszen!"*

Zoltan looked up at the woman, his face ashen. He took the tray and put the folded paper under his arm. He carried the strudels and coffee to the table and sat down heavily, staring out the cafe window.

"Zoltan," Barbara whispered, leaning forward. "What's wrong? You look like you saw a ghost." She quickly surveyed the small bakery, half expecting to see Caraldo at a corner table. "What is it?"

Zoltan unfolded the paper and slid it across the table to Barbara. Her eyes swept over the page. In the right-hand corner a brief title stood out in boldface: "Grisly Murder Occurs in Jewish Quarter."

She scanned the article rapidly. A man, who had not been identified, had been found dead in an abandoned building off *Kurt U.* It appeared the crime had occurred sometime around 2:00 am, only hours before a homeless man found the body. There was no identification. What made the crime especially shocking was that the head and hands had been cut off and removed. At this time, the police had been unable to establish the man's identity. The man was obese and appeared to be in his 80s. A black beret was found near the body.

"Oh, no!" Barbra cried.

Zoltan picked up his cup between his hands. He stared at the black coffee. "Yes. I am afraid we have heard *Dezső's* last story."

Chapter 24

"POOR *DEZSŐ*," BARBARA SAID. "HE was so broken, but I liked him."

"Yes," Zoltan said. "And it appears that I got him killed."

"Zoltan, you cannot blame yourself," Barbara protested. "You did nothing wrong."

He shook his head sadly. "We need to leave. Now. We will stop by the house. I must pick up my bag." He stared out the window. "I'm sorry. I should have brought it."

"Must you stop?" Barbara asked, looking around the bakery uneasily.

"Unfortunately, yes. There is too much risk of it falling into the *Mester's* hands. Notes of my conversations with *Dezső,* the plans to breach the security based on his knowledge of the Compound. It is quite detailed. If the *Mester* finds it, we will have no chance."

"Then we will take a cab to the airport?"

Zoltan rose from his chair. "Yes," he said. "And I think we will use the main airport this time."

"There are others?"

"Yes, not dissimilar from Teteboro."

"Where I flew out of."

"Yes. These are the airports we used as agents. But I believe Caraldo and Zhukov will be guarding them. I think we may be better off using *Ferenc Liszt.*"

"Tickets?"

"We will purchase them when we arrive. There are many flights to London."

Barbara took a last sip of her coffee and ate the final bite of the delicate strudel. They exited the bakery and took a side street. In a few blocks they reached a broad boulevard.

"This is *Karoly*, isn't it?"

"It is, madam. You are gaining a keen sense of the city."

They hurried across the wide thoroughfare, crowded with cars, articulated buses, and even a few bikes. "I like it here."

Zoltan glanced at her. Her red hair flew across her face in wet tresses. She had always reminded him of someone. And now he realized it was Rebecca. Not so much the looks. That is what had puzzled him. No, it was her joy, her aliveness.

She looked at him and he turned away in embarrassment. "What?" she asked, smiling at him.

"Nothing. I am just happy you like it here. I am sorry it is under such circumstances."

She took his arm. "Perhaps we can visit sometime under *different* circumstances."

"Perhaps," he said.

They walked several more blocks and then went right on *Andrassy*.

"Zoltan."

"Yes, Madam."

"Last night you mentioned the Company. That you thought the *Mester* was part of it."

"Yes."

"What do you know about it?"

"Not much, I'm afraid." He shrugged. "Only rumors, as I said. Staff at the compound whispering about visits from the Company. That the *Mester* would disappear occasionally, supposedly to meet with the Company boss. An old agent saying something about Company rules." He shook his head ruefully. "Never really knew what they were talking about. Or cared."

"And the man *Dezső* described. The man in the wool cape. Who is he?"

"Yes. Who is he indeed?" Zoltan stopped in front of his old home. "Madam, please stay here. I will enter through the rear and meet you. I shall only be a few minutes."

"Zoltan, if you think I'm going to stand here and wait for you while you break back into the house, you're crazy," Barbara hissed. "I'm coming with you."

Zoltan glanced upward. "Very well," he said, opening the gate. "Shall we?"

They walked swiftly across the grounds and around the right tower and through the back window.

Zoltan walked ahead of her toward the great room where they had slept. "It will take only a moment. I left it by the chair," he said over his shoulder.

They hurried through the kitchen doorway into the living room. The great room opened in front of them, but even in the grey daylight, it was so dark Barbara could hardly see the furniture strewn across the floor.

"Now that really was stupid."

Zoltan and Barbara froze. She turned toward the voice.

Even in the gloom, she could see Caraldo sitting in a red velvet chair near the windows, watching them. He held a luger in his lap.

Fear jolted through her like an electric shock. "Zoltan," she whispered. "You said no one knew about you, about the house."

Zoltan looked steadily at Caraldo. "Apparently I was mistaken."

Chapter 25

CARALDO STAYED IN HIS CHAIR but raised the gun and pointed at them. "Stay right there." He shook his head. "Mistaken is an understatement. We had this place staked out for weeks."

"But how…"

"He tracked you to Budapest the day you left the Market. Once he knew you were here…" Caraldo shrugged. "The old man has his ways." He tapped a sphere on the side table next to him. The ball began to glow until it cast a wide circle of light.

"Now, walk toward me. Slowly." Barbara remained rooted to the floor.

Zoltan moved in front of her and faced Caraldo. "We can talk from here. Though I doubt there is a lot to say."

Caraldo waved the pistol. "Move out from in front of her."

Zoltan stood straighter, glaring at the man in the chair. "You will have to shoot me first."

"That can be arranged, DeAngelo. I assure you; no one would be happier than the *Mester*."

"And what would you do then? Cut off my head like you did with Dezső? Take it back to London to prove to your master that you had completed your assignment?"

Caraldo tensed. "I didn't kill Dezső," he said quietly. "I wouldn't have done that."

"Then who did?" Zoltan demanded.

"Zhukov, " Victor muttered.

"So, he is here."

"Yeah, along with O'Brien. But Zhukov killed old Dezső."

"And cut off his head and hands…"

"No identification. But knowing Zhukov, he especially enjoyed that part."

"The *Mester* knows how to recruit them, doesn't he?"

"Them. That would include me, too, I suppose."

Barbara edged beside Zoltan. "This is all quite chatty." She glanced at Zoltan reproachfully. "In case you haven't noticed, he's aiming a gun at us."

"Thank you for pointing that out, Ms…"

"Barbara. Remember?"

Caraldo grunted. "How could I forget? After our conversation my interview with the *Mester* was not, shall we say, pleasant. In fact, this is my final chance. I don't think he trusts me."

"I am sorry," Zoltan said. "You took a great risk for us. For which I am grateful."

Caraldo gave a small nod, still holding the gun on the pair. "You understand I cannot afford to return empty-handed this time?"

Zoltan said nothing.

"I bring you in alive, or I bring in your head."

"I see."

"I'd rather alive." Victor shrugged. "But that's up to you."

Rage rushed through Barbara. "You really *are* nothing but a cheap hood," she snapped. "After listening to your sob story, your hatred for the *Mester*. The humiliation. Your desperation to get out. Boo hoo. And now you'd kill Zoltan without a second thought."

Caraldo swung the pistol so it was pointing directly at Barbara's head. "No, lady. You don't quite get it. I would kill you *both* without a second thought. You, I am afraid, have become part of the deal."

Barbara's anger turned to fear. Her hand strayed to her chest, and she clutched her jewel though her shirt.

"Oh, yes. The *Mester* has taken great interest in you. It's not every woman who can lead an established agent astray, you see. I bring you both in alive, directly to him," Caraldo shrugged again. "Or I return with both of your heads in a suitcase."

Zoltan put his hand on Barbara's arm, still staring at Caraldo. "There is another option."

"I don't think so."

"Back in the Market, you said you had to kill the *Mester*. Remember? 'Either he kills me, or I kill him. There is no other way.'"

Caraldo's mouth tightened slightly.

He looked steadily into Caraldo's eyes. "Has that changed?"

"Maybe not, but I also said there was no way to kill him," Caraldo said. "That hasn't changed either."

"That's not exactly what you said, is it?" Zoltan persisted.

Caraldo continued to point the gun at Zoltan's chest, but he settled back slightly into the red upholstery. "Refresh my memory."

"You said the only way to kill him was to catch him unaware, no?" Caraldo gave a slight nod. "And that he is never unaware."

"From an external threat, yes, but from an old enforcer in his own office? While he is distracted by two hated prisoners?"

"Go on."

"We go back together, the three of us, Barbara and me in your custody."

Barbara regained control of her voice. "Perfect," she blurted. "And then he can watch while the *Mester* and his thugs kill us in front of him." She scowled at Caraldo. "Just your kind of entertainment." Caraldo's jaw clenched, and he swung the gun barrel toward her.

"As I was saying," Zoltan continued, "we go back together with us as your prisoners."

"Just shoot us now!" Barbara shouted at Caraldo. She thrust out her chin. "I'm not going anywhere with him."

Caraldo sighed. "DeAngelo, can you get her to quit yapping for a few minutes?"

Zoltan's fingers tightened lightly around her arm. She gave a curt nod, still glowering at Victor.

"As I was saying, we go back as your prisoners. You said you are under orders to bring us directly to the *Mester*'s office in the Compound?"

"Or your heads."

Zoltan ignored the comment. "And so you do exactly as you are ordered."

"And then?" Caraldo asked.

"And then we kill him."

There was a long silence in the huge room. The three of them faced each other in a ten-foot circle of light. Outside Barbara heard the low rumble of thunder.

"That's not much of a plan," Barbara began.

Zoltan turned to her, a spark of irritation in his dark eyes. "Madam, please."

Caraldo eyed them coolly. He nodded at Barbara. "Is she reliable?"

"She is brave."

"Yes. Yes, I can see that. But can she keep her head?"

"I can hear what you are saying," Barbara fumed.

"Yeah, you can. So I will ask you. Can you keep your head? When you are confronted by a monster with yellow cat's eyes? Who can destroy you with the wave of his hand? Who could break DeAngelo's gem and doom him in front of you? Can you keep your wits if the *Mester* hacks DeAngelo's jewel and you have to watch him scream and writhe on the floor?"

"His name is Zoltan," Barbara said. Caraldo looked at her curiously. "And yes, I can do all of those things." She leaned toward Caraldo. "I came to this nightmare late, I admit, but that does not mean I am stupid. Zoltan says I am brave. But he is risking everything, everything, for a chance, one last chance to stop this evil that has been set in motion. And I am here with him. To the end."

"Please, Barbara," Zoltan began.

"No! I mean it," she exclaimed, her blazing eyes never leaving Caraldo's face. "I am willing to fight at his side, die at his side, to end this madness. You don't know the stories we heard from poor Dezső. Do *you* understand what you are up against? Do you have any idea?"

Caraldo remained quiet, considering her.

"So don't question my motives, sir. Nor my resolve. As for my abilities, perhaps I will surprise you."

Caraldo smiled slightly and lowered his gun. "You already have. So, maybe we should sit down and discuss plans." He gestured at the scattered furniture. "Pull up a chair."

Chapter 26

CARALDO LOWERED THE REVOLVER AND placed it on the dusty oak table beside his chair as Zoltan pulled a dining room chair into the ring of light and held it for Barbara. Then he dragged up an upholstered footstool and sat facing Caraldo.

"I don't much like our chances," Caraldo began. "Too much can go wrong and not much is likely to go right."

"*Prefiero morir de pie que vivir de rodillas,*" Barbara said.

Both men looked at her.

"I'd rather die on my feet than live on my knees. Emiliano Zapata."

Zoltan's head tilted slightly in surprise. Barbara shrugged. "He was an Aries."

Caraldo grunted. "I'd rather not die at all."

"Let us make that an objective, yes?" Zoltan said, still looking at Barbara.

Caraldo ran his hands over his shaved head. "First things first. When we leave this house, from the moment we step out the door until we are in the *Mester's* office, you are my prisoners. Understood? That must be clear to anyone watching us."

Barbara leaned forward in her chair. "Who would that be?"

"Hopefully no one. I don't even know if Zhukov or O'Brien are still in Budapest. But we can't take a chance. That is especially true at the airport and on the plane. It will be bugged, audio and video. The *Mester* will be watching our every move. If he suspects anything," Caraldo pointed his finger at Barbara for emphasis *"anything,* we are all dead."

"I'm not a fool," Barbara snapped.

Caraldo nodded. "Glad to hear it. That should improve our odds of surviving to about 500 to one." He turned to Zoltan. "And I am hoping we will be alone on the plane as well."

Zoltan removed his glasses and wiped dust of his lenses with a handkerchief. "Won't they wait and fly back with us?"

"I don't think so. Dezső was their assignment. You, Mr. DeAngelo, are my personal challenge, you see." Caraldo laughed bitterly. "But we do have one thing on our side. He says I am a moron, a loser. Too simple to resist him. Maybe my stupidity will finally pay off."

"You're not stupid," Barbara cut in. "I saw that the first time we met you in the Market. There's something in you that he fears. That is why he has to humiliate you. You scare him. He can't control you." She paused. "You said your gem is grey, right?"

"What does it matter?"

"Humor me."

"Yes."

"Dark grey, charcoal?"

Caraldo shook his head. "No, it is lighter, almost pale." His voice softened. "It is round, and the light plays off its facets like sunlight on the water." He thought for a moment. "It is more the color of a grey pearl. Reminds me of fog early in the morning along the Thames." He laughed. "I sound like some sort of poet."

"It must be beautiful."

Caraldo nodded, his head reflecting the light from the burning sphere on the table. "Yes. And in the center is a green diamond. It throbs like an emerald heart."

"Yes. That's what I thought."

Caraldo raised his chin slightly in curiosity.

"The dark stones – though not all of them, I don't think – are the stones that are used."

"Barbara," Zoltan asked quietly. "Is this the time to go into all of this?"

Caraldo looked baffled. "What are you talking about? Used how?"

Barbara raised a reassuring hand at Zoltan. "It seems that the *Mester*, and possibly another, uh, someone we don't know much about, are able to use the stones to drive their owners further into evil, hatred, violence. To find joy in other's suffering."

Caraldo brushed the comment aside with his hand. "We all know that the stones make the person more of who she or he is, right? Just juices up what's there. That's nothing new."

"There's maybe more to it than that. According to Mrs. Harlow…"

"The Jeweler in the Market?" Caraldo asked.

"Yes. In some of the stones they have set, especially darker stones in rings, they have found an element they cannot identify. They believe it acts as some sort of receiver/sender."

"Of what? And what for?"

"We are not sure," Zoltan answered. "But Dezső believed the *Mester* worked for another man. Dezső believed he was a witch, perhaps. A sorcerer or warlock. He did not know. Believe that or not. But if what he told us is even half true, it seems that the *Mester* is part of some circle of power that needs evil. That breeds it to feed on. To profit from."

Caraldo stared from one face to the other. "It is hard to believe, yes?" Zoltan asked.

Caraldo nodded. "But not altogether. The *Mester* seems hardly to be human. The only trait left is cruelty. And there is something else."

"Yes?"

"Once a month…" Caraldo hesitated. "I don't know this for sure, but I heard it from Rajiv."

Zoltan glanced at Barbara. "Rajiv is the *Mester*'s personal servant."

"He was drunk one night when I went to the bunker to get my check from Matin. Anyway, Rajiv let me in and gave me a Laphroaig. So, I asked him where the *Mester* was, you know, just talking rubbish. He said the oddest thing."

"Please," Zoltan said.

"Well, it was hard to understand. You know, Rajiv doesn't talk much."

Zoltan nodded. "I thought he might have had his tongue cut out."

"Don't think so. Not all of it anyway. But like I say, he was really loaded that night. So when I asked, his eyes got all strange, spooky. 'It is the full moon. The *Mester* is at the castle.' That's what he said. He was at the castle. So I asked him the obvious question: What castle?"

Barbara leaned forward impatiently. "What did he say?"

"He said, 'The black machine came. He is at the castle.' But by then he was legless. Fell arse over tit, he did, right onto the white carpeting. Never did find out what the barmy bastard was talking about. I figured it was a bunch of tosh, you know? But then – a few days later, I guess – I was back at the Compound, and I ran into O'Brien. So I asked him about the castle and all."

"You're friends with O'Brien?" Zoltan asked.

"Well not friends, really. No one is friends with anybody at the bunker. But we get along. Same line of work I guess."

"Go on."

"So he says, yeah. The old man disappeared once a month. I asked him how he got out of the bunker without anyone seeing him, and he told me there is a hidden elevator entrance in the wall just behind where he sits when he's on duty. You know, where the door to the lab is."

"Yes. There are the two windows behind the *Mester* and then the one on the wall to the right of his desk. At least I always assumed it was a window."

"Yeah. That big curtain hanging there. You think it's a window, but it's not. There's an elevator behind it. He's the only one who can use it, see. His ring."

Barbara looked at him quizzically. "His ring?"

"Yes, De…Zoltan, you must have noticed it? He wears it on his right index finger. Large black stone, gold setting?"

Zoltan nodded. "But I didn't know it had any power."

"Yeah. Don't know how much. But you know the safe behind his desk? Where he keeps the agents' jewels?"

"Of course."

"He waves the ring across the front to open it. I've seen him do it."

"Like Madam Harlow," Barbara said. "That is how she opened the safe in her shop."

"Victor, where does the elevator take the *Mester*?"

"I don't know for sure, but O'Brien said he had to help him carry a briefcase a couple of times. It goes down to a parking garage under the bunker. Up, it goes to the roof."

"The roof?"

Caraldo nodded. "Said there's a helipad up there."

Barbara's eyes squinted in surprise. "The *Mester* needs a helicopter? Where would he go?"

Caraldo shrugged. "The castle, I guess, wherever that is."

Zoltan looked thoughtfully at the shafts of light leaking through the boarded windows. "The Company," he mused. "Of course. He takes a helicopter." Dust particles danced in the beams. "It is getting late. Perhaps we should put this aside for now and review our plan, yes?"

Caraldo nodded. "I haven't checked in with the *Mester* today. He expects a report each evening. He will be delighted at the news."

"He will send a plane?"

Caraldo nodded. "The dark plane, a jet. It will be here within hours of my call."

"You were saying that we have to play the role of your prisoners," Barbara began. "Surely we can't travel through Budapest in handcuffs."

"Yes and no." Caraldo reached into a pocket in his leather jacket and pulled out two narrow bracelets. "You will put these on. He will be able to monitor you, and so will I." He opened the jacket, unzipped the inner pocket, and slid out a sleek silver case about the size of a cell phone. "Not only monitor." He held the shiny rectangle in the light. A series of small buttons ran across the bottom of the device. "The green button? That will paralyze you in your tracks if you tried to run. The others just give me a range of deterrents, from excruciating pain to fatal heart attack."

He rose from his chair and slipped the circlets around Barbara and Zoltan's wrist. He pushed a button on the console and the bracelets contracted tightly. "By the way, I *will* use it," Caraldo said, looking at them from under his bony eyebrows. "We will take a taxi to the airstrip. Hopefully there will be just the three of us and the pilot."

Barbara fingered the bracelet around her wrist. "And if we are not?"

Caraldo shrugged. "If O'Brien and Zhukov are both there, it probably means they simply waited for the plane. We should be OK. Or if O'Brien is by himself."

"And if it is only Zhukov," Zoltan asked. "What does that mean?"

Caraldo settled back into his chair. He rubbed his right shoulder thoughtfully. "Maybe nothing. Or maybe he is there not to watch you, but to watch me." Zoltan nodded. "It will mean he does not trust you."

Caraldo shrugged.

"No matter," Zoltan said. "There will be three of us in his office. Even if he doesn't fully trust you, you will have his quarry, yes?"

"Yeah. We play it the same way."

"At the risk of being nosy, what way *is* that?" Barbara interjected.

"Once in London there will be a car waiting for us," Caraldo said.

"At Northold?" asked Zoltan.

"Yeah. It's already arranged, as you know. No questions. We land, the old man's Mercedes limousine is on the tarmac. The one with no handles inside. We leave. You will sit in the rear seats. I will be facing you. Everything will be monitored, recorded, so stay quiet."

Caraldo looked at Barbara. "I told you about the bloody bugger's ears, eh? But it's not just that he can hear everything. He can pick up the slightest hint of emotion in your voice. Fear, anger. Or betrayal. You can talk with each other before we get on the plane. Show that you are scared, you know?"

Barbara's throat tightened and she swallowed hard. "That shouldn't be difficult."

"Yeah. And I'll tell you to shut up. Push you around a bit. But once in the plane and his office, say nothing."

Barbara and Zoltan nodded.

"How will we get to the office?" Zoltan asked.

"The car will take us through Smithfield and up the lane you will stay in front of me as we walk to the house. Rajiv will take us to the main elevator. It's an old clunker but it works. We go up to his floor and I will knock. He will order us in. When we enter," he glanced at Barbara again, "do not show shock or horror. Stay calm. He will pick up on any feeling, any thought."

Zoltan nodded again. "So. We are in the office. Describe it for me."

"We won't get closer than two feet away. "If he's not suspicious, O'Brien will be the only other person in the room, sitting to the right of the *Mester*, maybe six feet away in his chair against the wall."

"And If Zhukov is in the room," Zoltan asked. "What does that mean?"

"Nothing good. O'Brien is a bit of a chav, but he's all right. Not like that nutter Zhukov. I don't know how much the *Mester* would want O'Brien to see if he means to get really nasty. He knows O'Brien and me get along. If O'Brien is there by himself, we can breathe a little easier."

Zoltan nodded. "What then?"

"You'll be cuffed, so I'll shove you ahead of me as we enter the room."

Zoltan stared out the window, streaked with rivulets of rain. "Good. Place me in the center and position Barbara to my left, yes?" He glanced at Barbara. "He will likely focus on me. If you can, edge away from me."

Barbara's left hand now rested between her breasts over her jewel. She felt its warmth spread through her chest, calming her breathing.

"Victor, you move from behind me to the right. He will almost certainly have my jewel on his desk. And the hammer. He will threaten to smash it. That is a given. But I think there is something else he's after."

"Yeah?"

"As you know, Barbara has a jewel, yes?"

"No shit," Caraldo muttered. "That's what started all of this."

"He wants it."

Barbara's hand clutched the jewel. "He can't have it!"

Zoltan raised his hand. "Please. The point is that he will try to get it. But the chain is made by Mrs. Harlow, yes?"

Barbara nodded uncertainly.

"Atomically tuned to your frequency?"

"You already know that."

"Ah, yes. But he doesn't. He will grab it. He wants to humiliate you. He wants to tear it off your neck."

"And when he grabs the chain, he will burn his hand." Barbara nodded. "I see."

"From what I've heard, 'burn' is an understatement. Yes. I regret putting you in such a dangerous situation, but I see no alternative."

Caraldo's beaked head jerked forward. "Dangerous position? No shit. It will be a wonder if *any* of us get out alive."

Barbara glared at Zoltan. "It is time, sir, that you quit treating me like your teenage daughter." She brushed back her tangle of red curls angrily. "I'm sick of it."

Zoltan gave a contrite nod. "Very well. When that happens, when he grabs your chain, we move. He will have my jewel on his desk. When he recoils, I will lunge for the jewel. Grab it." He looked at Caraldo. "You will have your revolver unstrapped in your shoulder holster, yes? As soon as I move, you will draw and shoot O'Brien. To wound if possible."

"Won't O'Brien just pull his gun and shoot you?" Barbara asked.

Caraldo looked upward at the ornate plaster ceiling thoughtfully. "No. O'Brien is a professional. He will see Zoltan lunging, assuming he is after the *Mester*. As his bodyguard, he will protect the *Mester*. By the time he reacts, it would take him five to six seconds to unholster his gun and get a shot away, and even then, he would have no time to aim. He'd risk hitting the old man. No, he will leap from his chair to stop DeAngelo. That is when I fire."

"Why not just shoot the *Mester* and be done with it?" Barbara asked.

Caraldo remained silent a moment, rocking slightly back and forth in the chair. "Because I do not think he can be killed by a bullet. Or not by one or two, anyway, which is all I could get off before he recovered."

"Yes," Zoltan agreed. "I believe you are right."

"That doesn't make sense. How do you know this?"

"Because," Caraldo said, "he told me. Sixteen years ago."

"He told you?" Barbara asked incredulously. "And you believed him?"

"The *Mester* is not one to take lightly. He also showed me."

"What do you mean?"

"It was the day he hired me. He said he had other thugs work for him that from time to time had taken a dislike to him. They had tried to kill him. Then he pulled up his shirt. There were seven scars, front and back, where bullets entered and exited. He fixed those yellow green eyes on me and said, 'They are dead now.'"

"But it's easy to fake a scar."

"But not so easy to shoot oneself in front of 25 people, no?"

Barbara turned toward Zoltan. "He did that?"

Zoltan nodded. "It was the day he introduced Caraldo."

"We were onstage," Caraldo began. "I had already threatened the agents, waving my gun around. I had put it back in my shoulder holster. He was screaming at the agents, telling them that they could not harm him. Suddenly he reached over and pulled my gun out. He held it in front of his left hand and pulled the trigger. The explosion was deafening. By the time we recovered, we could see the wound already healing."

"Maybe, I mean…Could it have been a trick? Maybe there were blanks in the gun."

Caraldo shook his head. "I had loaded it that morning."

"Like an Indian *fakir,*" Barbara mused.

"He wasn't faking," Caraldo said. "He really shot himself through his hand."

"No, like an Indian holy man, a *sadhu.* I've seen videos of them pushing a knitting needle through their arms. There's no blood, and when they remove the needle, the wound heals almost instantly."

The three were silent.

"Then I don't understand, "Barbara said. "If he can't be killed…" Both of them looked at Zoltan.

"She's got a point," Caraldo said.

"I do not think he can be killed by a gun," Zoltan corrected. "But he has chinks. I have known him for many years. He cannot tolerate sunlight. It weakens him." He looked at Caraldo. "There are two large windows behind his desk, are there not?"

Caraldo nodded his head.

"And they are always covered with heavy curtains made to keep out all light, yes?" Caraldo nodded again. "Every sliver."

"How do you know this? About sunlight weakening him?" Barbara asked.

"Once I was in his office. Rajiv accidently pulled a curtain open while cleaning. The *Mester* screamed and clutched at his eyes, as if he were blinded.

His office is always dark, lit only by a few indirect lights."

"Yeah," Caraldo added. "O'Brien told me one time he heard a noise outside and rushed to the window and pulled back the curtain. Old man screamed like a stuck pig. Sunlight seems to cripple the old bugger, blind him. And maybe more."

"Yes," Zoltan said nodding. "Dezső said the same thing. He always abhorred sunlight."

"Fine, but I still don't see how this helps us," Barbara said. "The room will be dark."

"Yes, but not if we can get to the curtains and drag them down." Zoltan looked at Caraldo. "This is where you come in. After I have grabbed my gem, the place will be chaotic. As soon as you immobilize O'Brien, run to the windows and rip down the curtains."

Caraldo nodded his great head slowly. "Could work."

Zoltan glanced at his watch. "How long will it take us to get to London?"

"If I call in the next hour, we will be in his office around 5:00, 6::00 at the latest. Sunset would be at...."

"About 9:20," Barbara said. "I've been watching it set over the Danube the last few nights."

"The windows face west, yes?"

"Yeah," Caraldo agreed. "When I get the curtains down..." He paused. "*If* I get the curtains down, the light will flood into the room. But is that enough to paralyze him?"

"Possibly not. But as you are tearing down the curtains, I have grabbed my jewel from his desk. Those sulfurous eyes cannot tolerate light. He flinches even when the door opens to the hallway. So. I seize the jewel and race to the window. I hold my jewel in the sunlight. Focus it like the beam of a torch into his eyes so it will blind him."

"And if it doesn't?" Caraldo asked.

"Then we are doomed. But the agents' jewels are powerful. I believe it will work."

"I appreciate your confidence," Barbara said. "Then what?"

"Then," Caraldo said deliberately, "I will take that damned hammer off his desk. I will turn it to the blade. And I will split his head open like a melon."

"I see," Barbara said.

"Then I will lead us out the back exit through the laboratory. I know the way."

"Wait, wait," Barbara broke in. "What am I doing all this time?"

Caraldo leaned forward. "Trying to stay alive."

Chapter 27

A BLACK SEDAN WITH DARKENED windows waited for them outside Zoltan's house. The driver was separated from the rest of the car by glass panels. Caraldo gave him instructions through a grated metal disk in the glass.

During the trip to the small airport outside of Budapest, Barbara's anxiety built steadily until her heart was stuttering uncontrollably. The rhythm of the wiper blades and deathly quiet in the back of the cab gave her time to think. They were not good thoughts.

Caraldo sat in the passenger seat, turned toward them, his deep eyes menacing and bright. She looked out the window at the grey buildings slipping by them, rain dripping in rivulets down the glass. The more she thought about what was to come, the more desperate it seemed. What were they up against? And as for a plan, Barbara could personally come up with a very long list of things that could go wrong. She fingered the silver wrist band.

What if this was all a set up? What if this was the simplest way to capture them, if Caraldo and the *Mester* had come up with the whole scheme to get them to the *Mester's* bunker with as little trouble as possible?

In the front of the cab, Caraldo's cell phone toned. Seven chords that seemed familiar, as if she had heard them recently. Then she remembered. It was the opening to Bach's Toccata and Fugue in D Minor at the cathedral. When? She desperately tried to recall. Could it have only been two nights ago? Surely that was not possible. It must have been weeks, months ago.

Caraldo read a text and grunted. He turned around and looked through the windshield at the glistening pavement, slick with rain.

Zoltan laid his hand over hers and squeezed it softly. She glanced away from the window and gave him a small smile. His coal black eyes were like obsidian behind his glasses. She saw concern in them, but something else. It might have been determination, conviction. She wasn't sure. But it had not been there when they first met. That she knew.

The car finally pulled up to a gate in a red-brick fence that enclosed a number of low hangars.

Caraldo got out and spoke to the guard, who said something Barbara could not hear and pointed to a small, sleek jet on the runway ahead of them. The guard opened the gate, and the driver pulled onto the tarmac and drove to the waiting plane. He stopped by a ramp of steps that extended from the open door. Caraldo jumped out and quickly opened the rear door. He motioned to Barbara.

"Out," he ordered curtly. His hand was in the pocket of his leather coat. They all knew it was clutching the bracelet monitor.

Barbara swung her legs out of the cab and stared apprehensively at the plane. Zoltan crawled across the seat and stood beside her. He took her hand.

Caraldo pushed Zoltan forward. "Move it. Up the stairway."

Zoltan knocked Caraldo's hand away and turned on him angrily. "Don't touch me," he said.

"Sure," Caraldo said, his thin lips in a sneer. "No problem." He squeezed a button in his pocket, and Zoltan screamed, falling to his knees on the runway. He grabbed at his chest.

Barbara knelt beside Zoltan, holding his arm. Her head snapped up toward Caraldo. "You bastard," she spat.

"Get up, both of you," Caraldo commanded.

Barbara helped Zoltan to his feet, her green eyes flashing angrily at Caraldo. "Into the plane. Now!" he roared.

Zoltan was trying to get his breath, still holding his chest. Barbara held his elbow and guided him toward the ramp. Suddenly the door filled with the stooped body of a large man.

"So you do have them," the man said in a heavy accent. "I was beginning to wonder."

Behind them Caraldo snarled again. "Move. Up the stairs." He shoved Zoltan lightly. "Wonder what?"

"Oh, if you could really pull it off. You being such a *glupaya svin'ya.*"

"Stupid pig. Yes, you've called me that before." He trailed Barbara and Zoltan as they stumbled up the stairway. "It's nice to see you again too, Zhukov."

Barbara stared at the man leering at them from doorway. Her stomach turned in fear and despair. She figured the odds of any of them getting out alive were back to about 1000 to one.

Chapter 28

THE PLANE TRIP WAS SILENT and dark. All the windows had been blackened. Of the eight seats in the plane, four were occupied. Barbara and Zoltan sat in the second row from the rear, Caraldo behind them.

Zhukov hulked in the seat nearest the doorway, glancing back at them occasionally, his square face gashed by a wide mouth set in a constant frown. A large, squat nose spread out from expressionless brown eyes set under heavy black eyebrows.

What had just happened? Barbara wondered. Had she seen what she feared most – evidence that Caraldo had betrayed them? That the whole scheme was a charade? Or that Zhukov's presence proved otherwise, that Caraldo was really on their side? If that were the case, what did it mean that Zhukov was on the plane by himself?

She put her head back against the black leather of the seat and tried to sleep, but it was no use. There was nothing soothing in the whine of the plane's engines.

The steady drone deepened, and the plane slowed. She looked nervously at her watch. They had been in the air for nearly two hours.

"Keep your eyes forward," Caraldo barked. "We are landing. When we depart, stay in front of me."

Minutes later the plane eased onto the runway and taxied to a stop. Barbara desperately wanted to scrape the paint off the window next to her, to see where they were. She knew that made no sense, but the blackness was closing in on her like a coffin.

The engine whine slowly abated, and Zhukov stood, flipped a handle, and opened the hatch. Barbara watched him carefully. He was a large man, possibly even fat, but the ease with which he raised the door, as if it were cardboard, suggested enormous strength. He pushed a button and the stairs folded out from the plane. Zhukov turned his blank face toward them and gave a sharp nod.

"Up," Caraldo directed. "The girl first."

Barbara fumbled with her seat belt and crouched in the aisle, looking straight ahead. Behind her she heard Zoltan edge into the aisle behind her.

"Slowly down the stairs. Into the car."

They emerged into a soft summer afternoon. It occurred to Barbara that she hadn't really seen the sun for a very long time. And that she might never see it again.

Zhukov stood at the bottom of the stairs. He motioned to the limousine parked 20 feet away. A man in a turban stood by an open door. Barbara looked back to see Zoltan behind her.

"Straight ahead," Zhukov roared.

No. Appearing frightened would not be hard.

Barbara sat on the leather seat at the far back of the limousine and slid up against the far door. A moment later, Zoltan stooped to enter the car. Caraldo gave him a savage shove that sent him sprawling across the seat. Zoltan straightened, glaring at Caraldo. Barbara studied Zoltan's eyes. There was an emotion there she had not seen before. Hatred.

Caraldo crouched on the bench seat opposite them, and Zhukov sat in the passenger seat. As soon as the doors closed the limousine quietly accelerated.

The drive into London was a blur. Barbara was aware of leaving the expressway then winding through narrow streets, but she had no sense of direction, no idea where they were. Caraldo kept his hawk-like eyes on them the whole time.

Caraldo turned his head sideways toward Zhukov. "Where's O'Brien?"

"What's the matter, Vic? You don't like me?"

Caraldo said nothing and turned back to Zoltan and Barbara. She could read nothing in his eyes.

The limousine approached an iron gate that swung inward as they approached. They drove through and the gate swung shut with a clang. Barbara felt fear churning in her belly. Her breath was shallow and fast. She felt sick.

Zoltan turned toward her, took her hand, and brought it to his cheek.

Caraldo leapt across the space between them and brought his fist crashing into Zoltan's jaw, snapping his head hard against the seat back.

Zoltan shook his head dazedly and glared into Caraldo's eyes. "You cannot hurt me anymore." Barbara had never heard the tone in his voice before either. Deep, hateful. Defiant.

"You think not?" Zhukov rasped from the front. "Don't be so sure." He gave a short, cruel laugh that sounded like the bark of a dog. "And anyway, it will certainly be fun to try."

The car came to a stop in front of a sprawling brick complex. Ornate white frames enclosed darkened windows set in the red brick building. There were several wings, the main one three stories high. Zhukov opened the rear door and motioned Barbara out. He waited while Zoltan exited and slammed the door.

Caraldo joined them. "I was told to bring them directly to the *Mester*."

Zhukov gave another barking laugh. "Of course you were, Vic," he scoffed. "And I was told to make sure you did just that."

Caraldo studied the man's face for a moment. "You always were an arsehole, Zhukov."

Zhukov's mouth curled into a sneer. "*Glupaya svin'ya.*" He spit on the stone walkway at Caraldo's feet. Barbara saw red rise in Caraldo's face like a hot tide. She tensed.

Caraldo gave out a long hissing breath. "Then do your job, *mudak*."

Zhukov flinched and moved toward Caraldo. He breathed heavily for a few moments as Caraldo squared off, his great shiny head lowered, his eyes burning underneath his bony brows.

The wood door in front of them opened. A man in a long white robe stood looking at them intently.

Both Caraldo and Zhukov turned toward him. The man opened the door wider and stepped to one side of the porch, holding the door. The man's thin, dark face was covered by a neatly trimmed white beard.

"Arsehole." Caraldo edged behind Zoltan and Barbara. "Move it," he snarled. "Into the house."

Zhukov entered first with Barbara and Zoltan and then Caraldo following. Once inside, the robed man shut the door and pushed a button beside it. A metallic *click* echoed throughout the vast house.

The man turned and began walking toward an ancient elevator against a far wall.

"I know the way, Rajiv," Zhukov barked. He pushed by the man and walked to the elevator door. He pulled the brass gate open and glowered at the rest of them.

"Quit wasting time," he said. "You are keeping the *Mester* waiting."

Caraldo grabbed Zoltan hard by the shoulder and pushed him toward the open elevator cage.

The cage was not meant for four people. As they crowded in, Caraldo and Zhukov stared into each other's eyes, just inches away, neither flinching. The cage clattered to a shuddering halt and Zhukov motioned them out and walked to a white door just to the left of elevator. He stood for a moment and then raised his hand to knock.

A voice roared from inside. "Goddamn it, open the fucking door and get in here!"

Zhukov turned the brass handle and swung the door inward. Caraldo shoved Barbara and Zoltan sharply, and they stumbled into the room.

Barbara had heard the *Mester* described many times: hideous, ugly, monstrous. Huge fleshy ears hung at the side of his head. His thin mouth curved to his chin in a scowl of pure cruelty. Enormous green- yellow eyes with slits of black irises like those of a cat.

She had expected all of this. But when she faced the *Mester*, she looked into a face of pure malevolence, a grotesque mask made more hideous by the malice that shone through its sulfurous eyes and spread like malignant spores from his leathery skin.

She swallowed hard and drew her hand instinctively to the jewel at her chest.

Caraldo pushed her roughly aside and pulled Zoltan in front of the desk where the *Mester* sat eyeing them from his elevated chair. Zhukov stood close to Caraldo on his right.

Bile rose in Barbara's throat. She glanced at Zoltan. He faced the freak in front of him, glaring at the *Mester* fearlessly. His head was high, his back straight. Those black eyes she knew well by now were blazing with hatred, and contempt. He glanced over his shoulder at her with a sad smile and nodded.

She began to breathe again. She heard noises, sharp voices, shuffling of chairs. Her vision broadened. She could not afford to panic.

Barbara's gaze quickly swept the room. It was larger than she had expected, but much as Caraldo had described it. The ceiling was high, the two sets of windows rising 14 or 15 feet from the floor. The *Mester*'s desk made an ell, an extension on his left leading to the two windows behind him, both covered in thick gold brocade drapes. The heavy drapes stretched along a bar bolted into the plastered walls. Another bar near the floor held them in place along the bottom. Between the curtained windows the safe door, heavy and black, was set into the wall.

Underneath the safe was a small table with a large jar. Dezső's head floated inside.

Barbara stifled a scream. She closed her eyes, then forced herself to reopen them, avoiding the sickening sight on the table.

To her left a man with a sandy crew cut sat alertly in a green leather chair against a wall, watching the activity closely. O'Brien? Another set of curtains to the *Mester*'s right hung to the carpeted floor. Behind those, she knew, was the elevator entrance. To the left of that was a closed door.

She returned her attention to the desk and started. Two gems now lay on the table. One was blue green, almost turquoise, the other pearl grey. Between them was a two-headed hammer, maybe twelve inches long. One end was a gold sphere, the other a wide blade that glinted sharp and brutal, even in the dim light of the office. She glanced at Caraldo. He stared at the desk, his face pale.

"Well, well," the *Mester* cackled. "DeAngelo. Of all people. Who would have thought you could be such a pain in the ass, you miserable crybaby. Woe is me. My poor Rebecca. My life is over," he mocked. "I just want to die."

Zoltan flinched, but his eyes never left the *Mester's* face.

The *Mester* cackled again, placed his hands on the desk, and drew himself violently toward Zoltan. "This time, you will not be disappointed," he roared in a voice that did not seem his own, a shuddering bellow too big for the scrawny body in front of them.

He sat back and quieted. "O'Brien, leave."

"Boss?"

"Out, out, out!" he roared.

The man stood uncertainly, staring first at Caraldo and then at Zhukov. "You want me to guard outside the door?"

"I want you downstairs. And I don't want you up here again until I call for you. Is that clear?"

O'Brien started toward the door, his eyes darting around the room. He left, shutting the door behind him. The *Mester* pushed a lever with his foot and the door lock clicked. He leaned back in his high- backed chair. The deep lines of his mouth drew into a smile of such cruelty that Barbara looked away.

"Ah, I'm going to enjoy this," he said. "Now, where was I? Oh, yes. Discussing Mr. DeAngelo's brief future. But..." he purred. "First things first." He turned quickly from Zoltan and faced Caraldo. As he did, Zhukov pivoted and drove a knife deep into Caraldo's stomach. Caraldo bent over and Zhukov slammed his fists into the back of Caraldo's head, pounding him onto the floor. Zhukov began kicking him savagely in the kidneys.

"Zhukov!" the *Mester* barked. "That's enough for now."

Zhukov moved back reluctantly, breathing hard. He stared, emotionless, as Caraldo groaned in pain on the white carpeting, staining it with a widening pool of blood flowing from his wound.

"Nicely done, Comrade Zhukov!" the *Mester* enthused, looking down at the writhing figure. "You know, Vic, I'm still not sure if you betrayed me or not. I don't think so because you are too stupid, too much of a moron to hide it from me." He shrugged his bony shoulders. "But you are no longer of use to me. You've gotten soft, Vic. You don't have that old killer instinct anymore. You worry me, and I don't like to be worried." He rocked back and forth with satisfaction. "But don't die on me yet, eh, Vic? I want you to see something."

Caraldo managed to roll onto his back, his eyes closed in pain. "No, no, Vic. You can't see with your eyes shut."

Caraldo forced an eye open and looked up at the *Mester*.

"That's better. Now watch closely." He picked up the hammer on the desk and hefted it. "You see, Vic, I knew you were coming so I took the liberty of taking your gem out of the safe." He looked at Caraldo with feigned concern. "You don't mind, do you, Vic?"

"You bastard," Caraldo gritted out, his teeth clenched in agony.

"Now, now." The *Mester* turned the hammer around several times, alternating the blade end and the round end, each time pretending to bring it down on the grey jewel lying on the table. "Let's see. Now, the last time, I believe I used this end." The *Mester* brought the blade end down sharply, stopping just inches from the gem. "But that didn't seem to work. You weren't humble enough. Why, you even thought about shooting me, even though you know that would do you no good." He sighed. "But it's the attitude, Vic. The attitude."

He flipped the hammer over and brought the round end crashing onto the jewel.

Barbara inhaled sharply. She didn't know what to expect. An explosion, perhaps. Or at least puff of smoke. But instead the jewel simply disappeared as the hammer head slammed into the table. It was there and then it was gone. Instantly a wail erupted from Caraldo that caused Barbara's heart to stutter, her eyes fill with tears. It was a cry of such anguish, such loss that it seemed impossible to bear. Black images of abandonment, beatings, loneliness swept through her. The terrible cry hung in the air like dark dust. And then there was silence.

The *Mester* swiveled back toward Zoltan, his face set in a macabre grin. "I haven't had that much fun in a long time." He nodded to Zhukov, who had moved behind Zoltan to Barbara's side in the melee. He grabbed her upper arm with a hand that felt like a vise. She cried out and brought her knee into Zhukov's crotch. He let out a groan and brought his right fist crashing against the side of her face.

Barbara staggered, held up only by Zhukov's hand, still clamped on her arm. She tasted blood. Zoltan whirled and lunged toward Zhukov but doubled over after a few steps.

"DeAngelo," the *Mester* cackled. "So predictable. Such a gentleman." He held up a metal case like the one Caraldo had. "Maybe you forgot?" He held up his bony wrist.

Zoltan grimaced in pain and turned back toward the *Mester*. "You are a hideous monster," he croaked.

The *Mester* pounded his hands on the desk in delight. "Yes, yes! Yes, to all! But the question is, what do we do with you?" He picked up the hammer again and held the round end over Zoltan's blazing blue- green jewel. "Do I just smash you now? That would be fun. But," he spun the hammer and brought the blade end down on the gem, "why not extend the pleasure?"

When the blade struck, a scream erupted from Zoltan that cut through Barbara like a knife.

"Zoltan!" she cried, struggling to free herself from Zhukov. He slammed a vicious backhand against her cheek, snapping her head to the side. She stilled, feeling his hand burning on her skin. In front of her, Zoltan had fallen to the floor and lay, twisting in pain, in front of the *Mester*'s desk. He looked up at her, his eyes filled with sorrow, helplessness.

"So, who do we have left? Ah, yes. The red-haired girl that started this whole fiasco. Come. I would like to get a good look at you."

Zhukov shoved her forward, slamming her against the edge of the desk so that she pitched forward at the waist, her breath knocked from her. She put her hand on the desk and pushed herself upright. She stared into eyes filled with such barbarity that she nearly retched.

She drew her head back and spit into his face.

She would die. That was clear. But seeing that brief moment of uncertainty, of shock, in the brutal face in front of her made it almost seem worthwhile.

Zhukov grabbed her by her hair and yanked her head back savagely and drew back his fist.

"Stop," the *Mester* ordered, wiping the spittle from his face with the back of his skeletal hand. "Pleasure after duty."

Zhukov shoved Barbara's head forward, sending her sprawling across the desk. She braced herself with her hands and raised her head, trying to regain her breath.

Suddenly a movement caught her eye. She kept her head down. There, by the far wall. In the dimness, she saw it again. A hand reached upward and grasped the heavy drapes. Then she saw Caraldo pull himself up onto his hands and knees facing the curtains. Concealed by the desk extension, he had managed to inch his way along the floor to the far wall. He now knelt at the curtain bar at the bottom of the drapes, breathing hard.

Zhukov faced the windows, but he had been distracted by her attack on the *Mester* and had not yet seen Caraldo. She continued twisting and struggling to keep him preoccupied. But now the *Mester's* hideous face pressed near hers.

"I can see now," he hissed. "Yes. Your jewel. It is a powerful one. Bet you didn't know you had it in you, did you?" he cackled.

Barbara glanced at the windows. Caraldo nodded at her.

Suddenly the *Mester*'s huge eyes narrowed. "What is it? You suddenly seem very excited." He began to turn his head. Barbara slammed her elbow into Zhukov's gut. He grunted and yanked her arm upward until she screamed.

The *Mester* turned back to her and gave a hissing laugh. "I see. Maybe you enjoy Zhukov's methods? You like it rough, huh? Well, when we are done here, Zhukov can show you more. Yes, and for as long as he likes, eh Zhukov?"

Zhukov gave her arm another jerk. She cried out in pain.

"Yes, until he tires of you. And then he will kill you. Slowly, I imagine. But before I leave you two love birds alone," the *Mester* paused, and then the roar, the deep, shattering roar erupted again, "I will have your gem."

He leaned forward across the desk, breathing hard. "We can do this two ways. You will remove your shirt so I can take your necklace, or," his great eyes narrowed slightly, "Zhukov can tear it off of you and strip the necklace from your neck!"

Barbara twisted once more in Zhukov's grip then stood still, panting. She glared into the terrible face in front of her. She nodded.

"Let her go."

Zhukov reluctantly took his hand off Barbara's arm. She took a deep breath and carefully avoided looking at the far wall. She crossed her arms, gripping the edge of her sweatshirt, and pulled it over her head. She let it drop to the floor and stood straight. She felt her jewel throbbing slightly between the cups of her black sports bra. She thought of Mrs. Harlow's comment so long ago: stunning outfit.

The *Mester* leaned forward, entranced by the flaming red jewel against the white of her skin.

"It is beautiful," he hissed. "More than I realized." He reached his hands out, his fingers flexing, just out of reach. "Push her forward, you idiot!" the *Mester* snarled.

Zhukov grabbed Barbara by the back of the neck and shoved her forward until she was leaning across the desk. Her gem glided forward on its intricate chain, swinging slowly, back and forth. Zhukov held her head down.

The *Mester* leered greedily and shot both hands forward and grasped the chain. And then he screamed.

As he drew his hands back, watching steam rise from the wounds on his palms, Barbara drove another elbow into Zhukov's stomach and pivoted away to her right. As she did, Caraldo gave an agonized cry and leapt high into the curtains, embracing them with his arms. Zhukov stared, stunned, and grabbed for the pistol in his coat.

Before he could draw the gun, he pitched forward on the desk, his pistol clattering across the desk onto the floor. Zoltan had regained his feet and had tackled Zhukov from the back. She whirled toward the curtains and watched Caraldo give a last push with his feet against the windows. The brackets holding the curtains creaked and then give way with a crash. Caraldo fell backward, the curtains covering him like a shroud.

Light flooded the room. Barbara squinted into the sun, temporarily blinded. "I will kill you," Zhukov roared behind her.

Her eyes adjusted to the light just in time to see him grab the gun from the desk and point it at her head.

She heard a sharp crack and a red dot appeared on Zhukov's forehead. He stood still, a look of puzzlement on his face, and then crumpled to the carpet. Barbara's head snapped toward the sound. Caraldo lay on his back, motionless, his lower body still under the drapes, his right arm outstretched. In his hand he held his .38.

A sudden howl jolted the room. The *Mester* swung his arm toward

Barbara, hands over his eyes. Barbara leapt out of his reach and ran to the windows. Zoltan grabbed the edge of the desk and pulled himself up. He lunged for his jewel, still glittering on the desktop.

The *Mester* pounced like a cat, snatching the jewel and the hammer and held them in his leathery hands.

"You think I am blind," he screamed. "That I am defeated." He held Zoltan's jewel in his left palm and raised the hammer. "You can never defeat me!"

"*Csúnya Mester*!" Barbara shouted. He turned around with a snarl.

Barbara stood on the broad windowsill, her jewel in the fingers of her left hand, her right palm in front. As the *Mester* turned toward her in fury, she dropped her hand.

The light from the window seemed to be drawn like a funnel into the stone, which throbbed in her fingers. The tiny arms of the setting burst into flame, and a beam of red light shone outward like a laser. As the *Mester* turned, the beam slashed into his eyes.

He howled in pain, throwing his head back and clawing at his eyes, dropping the jewel and hammer on the desk. He turned from the blinding beam of fire, still howling, his hands spread on the desktop as he shook his head in torment.

Barbara dropped the gem and dashed to Zoltan. "Can you stand?"

"My jewel, please. Give me my jewel."

Barbara grabbed the gem, avoiding the *Mester*'s flailing hands that were blindly groping for the hammer, and placed the stone into Zoltan's hand.

On the desk the hammer had been pushed to the far side of the desktop where the *Mester's* desperate clawing had not found it. She seized the hammer and hurried to Caraldo, who lay motionless on the floor. She kneeled and raised his great shaven head and hugged it to her chest.

"Don't die, you magnificent man," she cried. "Don't die on us."

Zoltan struggled to her side, dragging his left leg. "Can you hear us, Victor?"

Barbara heard a weak whisper. "He's alive!" she cried. She turned her ear toward Caraldo's mouth.

"His ring," he said faintly. "The compound is locked down." He stopped. His eyes fluttered. "You can only escape by the elevator."

Barbara stood. The *Mester* was still wailing, but he had stopped slashing the air with his arms. Now his hands were splayed out on top of the desk, his head swaying back and forth in blind wrath and pain.

"I can hear you!" he roared as Barbara approached. "You will never escape. They are coming."

She paused for a second, feeling the soft leather handle of the hammer in her hand. She stepped back to the desk. Then she brought the sharp end down on the *Mester*'s index finger right at the knuckle. The *Mester* roared again and drew his hand back, screeching in pain. Barbara picked up the finger and stripped off the ring, shoving it into the watch pocket of her jeans, vaguely surprised that there had not been more blood.

She heard pounding at the hallway door and gunshots as bullets were fired into the lock. She rushed back to Zoltan and Caraldo.

"You must go," Caraldo ordered faintly. "I am done." Barbara watched as a slight smile spread across his face. "I want to thank you," he whispered.

"No," Zoltan said firmly. "It is we that need to thank you, Victor,"

Caraldo's breathing was increasingly labored. "You don't understand. You see, for the first time in my life, no one has a part of my soul except me. Honor me and go. This is not the end."

Zoltan nodded and rose. "Goodbye, my friend."

Barbara continued to kneel next to Caraldo, weeping. Zoltan reached down and helped her to her feet. The *Mester* was still shrieking, though more feebly, his head lolling from side to side. The clamor outside the door was growing louder.

"We only have seconds," Zoltan gasped. Come. We must make it to the elevator." He began edging toward the curtains but stumbled, wincing in pain.

"Here," Barbara said. "Put your left arm over my shoulder. Then move your right foot forward."

Zoltan nodded, grimacing, and they started toward the elevator. Suddenly Barbara stopped. She put Zoltan's hand on the window frame so he could brace himself.

"Barbara, what is it? We have no time. We must leave now."

Barbara jumped over the curtains on the floor and faced the safe. Underneath, Dezső's head swam in the jar sitting on the table. She took a deep breath and shoved the vessel aside, hearing it crash as it hit the floor. She tried not to look, but she couldn't help herself. She glanced toward the carpet to see the head looking up at her. It seemed to be winking.

She took the *Mester's* ring from the small pocket in her jeans, placed it on her finger, and waved it across the front of the safe. There was a sharp snap. She grasped the chromium handle and pulled downward and out. The heavy door swung open.

Behind her an explosion blew a hole in the wall to the hallway, the concussion throwing the *Mester* backward onto the floor. Dust clouded the air like fog. Barbara leaned into the safe and swept out leather bags filled with gems. She stuffed as many as she could into her pockets. Zoltan had pulled himself along the windowsill and shoved more bags into his shirt. He put his arm around her shoulder again, and they stumbled toward the curtains on the far wall.

Barbara braced Zoltan's hands on the second windowsill and dashed to the curtains. She wrapped them in her arms and yanked, but they hardly moved. She tried again.

"They're too heavy!" she cried. "I can't move them."

Behind her frantic voices yelled. She heard booted feet kicking the blasted hole wider. "Slide!" Zoltan yelled. "Slide the curtains, yes?"

Barbara grasped the edge of the drapes and pulled them to one side. They slid easily along the rods. In front of her was a small door. She raised her finger again and dragged the *Mester's* ring around the perimeter. Suddenly the door drew straight up into the wall, revealing a small cage.

Zoltan dragged himself to Barbara's side, and the two of them stepped into the elevator. "Stop!" a man yelled, clambering through the wall and trying to see through the dust.

Barbara waved the ring the ring frantically. "It won't work! It isn't working!" Zoltan reached out and held her hand. "Up," he said, and the door slid shut.

Chapter 29

THE SMALL CAR ROSE SWIFTLY and quietly as Barbara steadied herself against the paneled walls. She closed her eyes and rubbed her hands across her face.

"Zoltan," she asked, "why are we going up?"

"I believe they will expect us to go to the garage. They may already have the exit covered. I do not think they will look for us on the roof."

"Maybe that's because they know there's no way down. Just a thought." Zoltan gave her a small smile. "Madam, do you know me no better than that?"

The cage slid to a stop and the door rumbled downward. They stood in a four-sided cupola high on the roof of the sprawling complex. Arched windows on three sides had been blacked out. In front of them a door opened onto the flat roof.

Zoltan exited the elevator and grabbed the handle of the door. It swung outward reluctantly, groaning on rusted hinges. He stepped through the door and quickly surveyed the situation. The flat tar and gravel roof spread over several buildings, broken here and there with wide chimneys and brick walls. As Caraldo had reported, a large yellow circle had been painted on the section directly in front of them.

They were three stories above the street below, and he could see for a mile or more over the green tops of oak trees and the roofs of hundreds of houses. To the west he could just make out the long green warehouses of

Smithfield Market.

Barbara stood in the doorway, shocked to realize it was a bright afternoon. She raised her hand to her eyes.

"Madam," Zoltan said. "I do hope we have thrown them off our trail. But I would nonetheless urge you to hurry."

Barbara lowered her hand and rushed through the open door. She scanned the low wall around the perimeter looking desperately for a stairway, another door leading into the house. She saw nothing. She slammed the cupola door shut.

"Please, follow," Zoltan ordered.

Zoltan limped across the roof and over a low wall separating the section they were on from the adjacent roof. Barbara glanced behind her and ran after him. As she slipped over the wall, the elevator behind them hummed.

"They're in the elevator," she said, reaching Zoltan.

"But going down hopefully, yes?"

"How did they get it to work? I thought they needed the ring."

"No matter." He turned nodded toward the far corner of the roof at the back of the mansion. "Come. Stay low in case they are looking for us."

Hidden by the low brick dividing wall, they crouched low and crept forward toward the edge. "Zoltan," Barbara whispered, breathing heavily. "Where are we going?"

"Just a few more feet."

They reached the corner and Zoltan motioned Barbara to stay low. He raised his head above the outer wall of the roof and scanned the rear garden far below them.

"It looks clear."

"Clear for what?" she hissed. "What are we going to do? Jump?" He planted his hands on the wall and swung his legs over the side. "Zoltan!" Barbara screamed.

He stood on the other side of the wall, smiling at her. "Jumping would be faster, but a ladder would be safer, no?" He disappeared, and Barbara peeked over the edge.

An ancient cast iron ladder was bolted into the bricks. It arched out slightly from the side of the building and extended all the way to the graveled walkway far below. Zoltan was already descending rapidly. She looked nervously at the treed garden below but saw no one. She took a deep breath extended her leg tentatively over the edge toward the first rung.

Fifty yards away, shouts burst from the cupola. She glanced toward the voices. Rajiv and a man she didn't recognize were standing in the dome. Rajiv pushed the door open just as Barbara slid over the edge. She clung to the top of the wall with her fingers as her foot desperately groped for the ladder. Finally she felt the iron rung and clambered down several steps until she was hidden. She huddled against the rusting iron, her arms locked around the back of the ladder, and tried to quiet her breathing, listening for any sound on the roof above her.

Voices yelled back and forth as the men searched the tarred surface.

"No one!" a voice bellowed. The man couldn't have been more than 20 feet away. She held her breath and glanced downward. Just below her Zoltan was flattened against the ladder.

"They're not up here!"

"Back to the elevator," Rajiv called. "I didn't they would be here. They are in the garage." The other man's boots crunched on the gravel as he turned back toward the cupola.

She closed her eyes and started breathing again.

"Barbara," Zoltan called quietly from below her. "Down the ladder. We must hurry."

She took a deep breath and slowly descended, trying not to look down. Finally her foot struck the ground, and she joined Zoltan against the brick wall.

He reached out and took her hand reassuringly. "I believe the worst is over."

"You believe?" She rested the back of her head against the rough brick. "That's reassuring."

They were at the back of the mansion. A broad gravel walkway separated them from a line of ancient oaks some 50 feet away. Beyond the oaks, a ten-foot brick fence enclosed the compound.

Zoltan nodded at the gravel walkway that separated the mansion from the trees in front of them. "We just have to get across that undetected."

Barbara glanced up at a series of security cameras mounted along the roof. "What about those?"

Zoltan nodded. "It is a risk. But I do not believe they will be checking the monitors. That is Rajiv's job, and he seems somewhat distracted, no?"

"OK. So we get into the trees." She pointed to the high brick wall that enclosed the garden. "How do we get over that?"

"There is a gate in the southwest corner. I do not believe it has been used in years. But I do hope it is open. It was the last time I was here."

"You do hope," Barbara said, rolling her eyes. "Well, I do hope so, too."

He squeezed her hand. "I will count to three. Then we both sprint across the walkway, yes?"

Barbara nodded. "Yes."

"One, two…"

It took only a few seconds to cross the graveled pathway, but it seemed like an hour. She felt exposed, vulnerable and half expected a siren to scream from the house, or to hear shots fired as they ran. But she reached the cover of the trees without feeling a bullet rip through her back or hearing the shattering screams of detection.

Still limping slightly, Zoltan led them through the oaks and plane trees between the pathway and the brick fence. After several minutes, they neared the corner. Covered by a giant oak, Zoltan scanned the fence, which extended to their right around the mansion. Directly in front of them was an old wooden gate, its timbers grey with age, laced with rusting metal straps riveted to the thick boards. A large hasp joined the two sections, and a shiny new padlock hung from the staple in the hasp.

"*Átkozott*," Zoltan swore. He glanced at the walls to each side, shaking his head. They were too high to scale, and the lower branches of the trees along the fence line were pruned so they could not climb up and over the wall.

"Zoltan," Barbara asked, looking furtively over her shoulder. "What now?"

"The padlock. This is new."

"Fine. But like I said, what now?"

Zoltan ran to the gate and inspected the lock. It was a large keyed brass padlock with a thick steel hasp. He yanked on it in frustration. Behind them, shouts were coming from the roof of the compound. Their escape route had been discovered.

Zoltan turned from the gate and returned to Barbara, who was looking anxiously toward the mansion. "I think they know we went down the ladder," she whispered.

Zoltan said nothing. He gazed at the great oak they stood under, his eyes moving up the trunk to the green mosaic of leaves above them.

"Zoltan," Barbara hissed. "Not a great time to be admiring trees."

Zoltan reached into his pocket and pulled out the red leather jewel bag. He drew the drawstring open and emptied his gem into his right hand. The blue-green stone pulsed gently in his palm. He walked forward and embraced the broad trunk of the tree.

Almost immediately, Barbara sensed the tree stir. She stared as the lowest limb, as thick as a man's leg, dipped toward them. The old oak seemed to lean forward slightly.

The branch reached the ground at their feet. Loud shouting came from the courtyard and moved rapidly in their direction.

"The gate!" O'Neil yelled. "They've headed for the gate."

Zoltan pocketed his gem and clambered onto the broad limb. He looked back at Barbara, his hand extended. "Come," he said softly.

She jumped forward, grabbed his hand, and swung herself onto the limb. Together they crawled upward into the leafy branches until they were concealed in the leaves. The tree straightened and drew its branch upward so swiftly Barbara's stomach dropped. She clutched the branch fiercely, her face buried in the rough bark.

When she dared peek out from the leaves, she saw that they were about 12 feet above the ground, just above the top of the brick wall to her right. The branch steadied as two men charged up to the gate.

"Fuck," O'Neil cursed. "The gate's still locked. There's no way they could get out this way."

"I told you, *bevakooph*," Rajiv shot back. "I put the lock on myself. You've wasted time. They still have to be in the garden. We must check the mews."

The two men turned and ran through the woods onto the gravel walkway and out of sight.

The limb they were on began to sway as if driven by a fierce wind. It twisted over the brick wall and bent down sharply until they were only a few feet from the ground on the other side. Zoltan slid from the branch and dropped to the earth, covered in a deep layer of soft leaves. Barbara disentangled herself from the branches and swung her legs over the limb, landing on all fours, breathing hard.

The branch rose above them, cleared the wall, and glided back into its original position. The tree stood motionless above them.

Zoltan stood by the wall and looked upward. "Thank you, my friend," he said softly. Barbara thought the top of the great oak bent slightly in a bow, but she couldn't be sure. Zoltan turned to Barbara, smiling.

She smiled back.

"We should get out of here."

"Indeed," Zoltan agreed. Follow me."

"Might I ask where we are going?"

"The tube. To Paddington Station. Then Heathrow."

"Heathrow?" Barbara took a step back. "In case you haven't noticed, I have twigs in my hair, and I am wearing a pair of filthy blue jeans and a black sports bra."

Zoltan looked up at her from beneath his eyebrows. "No, madam. There you are wrong. I have indeed noticed."

Barbara felt her face redden.

"As, I assure you, will every man we pass. But the tube, well, anything goes, yes? At Paddington, we shall go shopping."

"Yes, and then the Paddington express to Heathrow. We must return to the Market." He paused thoughtfully. "There is much to do."

Behind them shouts came from several points in the garden.

Barbara looked back over the wall to the red mansion beyond. She could just make out the glass cupola at the top of the elevator. She quickly replayed the last hour in her head, swallowing hard at the memory of Victor dying on the carpet. *And then I cut off the Mester's finger?* She thought. *And took his ring?* She saw *Deszo's* head swimming in the bottle of formaldehyde and gagged as she smelled the acrid liquid when she pushed it to the floor.

She looked at her crimson jewel, warm against her skin. *Who am I?* she wondered. She took a deep breath and nodded to Zoltan.

He bowed slightly and swept his left arm toward the end of the lane that ran outside the compound. "After you, madam."

Chapter 30

TRAVELLING WITH DAVID, BARBARA HAD visited many airport lounges – David loved to make a display of entering lounges and presenting his platinum card at the desks with a world-weary look – but she had never seen anything like this one. To get to the lounge, Zoltan had led her to a small, unmarked escalator located in an alcove in one of Heathrow's miles of non-descript brown hallways. The escalator ended at a small landing with a single grey metal door in the far wall. Beside the door there was a plain black box with a single red light. He slid his black card through a slot and the light blinked for several seconds followed by a click and a steady green light. Zoltan pushed the door open, and they entered a small windowless room. In front of them was a blank wall with a card reader and a keyboard. He inserted his card and a yellow light blinked above their heads.

"Now yours."

"My what?"

"Your card."

"I have to insert my card too?" She looked at him, puzzled. "Isn't yours enough?"

"The mechanism knows there are two people in the foyer. Each must have the proper card to enter."

Barbara shrugged. She put her shopping bags down and opened the magnetic clasp on her new dark brown waxed leather handbag. She had chosen it because it slung over her shoulder and snugged securely against her hip. She pulled the black card from a satin pocket and pushed the card across the reader. The yellow light stopped blinking. Barbara stood staring at the blank wall, waiting for something to happen.

"Now," Zoltan said, "push in 042814 on the keypad."

"Your birthday?"

"No." Zoltan hesitated. "It is Rebecca's."

Barbara turned to the pad. Nine numbers were set in a perfect square. "There's no zero," she said, frowning.

"No? Place your palm over the keys."

She reached out her hand and rested her palm on the pad. When she removed it, a new zero key had appeared below the numbered keys above. She glanced briefly at Zoltan, and then punched in the full code.

As she struck the seventh key, the yellow light turned green, and the wall sighed silently and disappeared. One second it was there; the next it was gone. In front of them a narrow escalator rose quietly into darkness. She looked uncertainly at the moving steps, but Zoltan walked to the bottom and waited. She glanced around, picked up her bags and walked through the passageway onto the escalator.

Almost immediately, the partition began to reappear behind them until the foyer they had been standing in disappeared behind a solid grey wall. She looked quizzically at Zoltan, a step behind her.

"That was rather odd."

Zoltan chuckled. "Yes. I suppose it was."

As the escalator ascended, small lights on each side twinkled for a few seconds, then darkened. At the top, they stepped off the moving steps into a perfectly round anteroom, perhaps 20 feet in diameter, lit with an amber glow. Identical doors, all, made of the same burgundy wood and rounded at the top, studded the circular walls. Barbara glanced around the perimeter. There were 12 doors. An exit passage opened directly in front of them.

Zoltan slipped by her and moved to the third door on their right. He typed in a code on the adjacent keypad and opened the door inward.

Barbara had not known what to expect, but it wasn't this. The room they walked into soared three stories overhead. Deeply tinted curved windows looked out onto a runway, and a circular stairway wound up to the second and third floors. A great round bed dominated the second level, and above that the stairs climbed high into a tower sheathed in glass. The room where they stood was semi-circular, a kitchen curving along the wall to their right. Soft dark brown leather chairs and a sofa curled around the stairway. On the far left a frosted glass door opened into a white tile bathroom hung with heavy white towels.

Zoltan walked to the huge stainless-steel refrigerator and opened one of the doors. He glanced inside. "Champagne, madam?"

Barbara's gaze roved over the glistening space, entranced.

"Madam?"

Barbara pulled her eyes away and focused on Zoltan. "What?"

"Champagne. Would you like a glass of champagne?"

"Why, I guess…" She took a deep breath and felt her eyes close. She could never remember feeling so weary. She forced her eyelids open. "Sure, that would be nice."

She shrugged off her bag and set it on a glass table beside the sofa and then slid into the sofa's buttery leather. She slipped off her black wedge sandals and rubbed her feet.

"I don't care how much they cost, they're still not very comfortable."

Zoltan approached carrying two flutes of bubbling wine. "But they complement your dress, yes?"

Barbara stood up and spun around, digging her toes into the deep maroon carpeting. "You like it?"

Zoltan set the glasses on the black granite top of the coffee table and stood back while Barbara spun around once again, smiling at him, her arms loosely at her side. Her dress began with a rounded collar at her neck, then tapered to a wide belt at her waist, baring her shoulders. The skirt flared outward ending mid-thigh.

"Madam, it…no, *you* are absolutely exquisite."

Barbara brushed her hair back over her shoulder. She dipped her head. "Please, sir. You are too kind, surely." She looked back at him, her green eyes sparkling mischievously. "But don't let that stop you."

Zoltan laughed and sat in a chair beside the sofa. "There is just one thing."

Barbara sat back down on the sofa. "Yes?"

"The colors, the black, greens, greys – they go marvelously with your hair."

Barbara's eyes narrowed dangerously. "Is there a 'but' coming?"

"No, no," Zoltan said quickly, waving his hand. "But you chose a print that is, well, it is all different sizes and shapes of cacti, yes?"

Barbara sat up straight and smoothed her skirt primly. "They are indeed, sir. Do you have a problem with that?"

"No, no. Not at all. I just…find that interesting."

"Look, I can wear Versace, but that's not really me, you know?" She nodded at the sandals on the floor. "I can wear stupidly uncomfortable shoes if that's what the situation calls for, but that's not who I am."

"So the cacti are a statement perhaps?"

Barbara shrugged and rummaged through the bags she had dropped on the floor. She drew out her old runners and slipped them on her feet. She leaned back. "That's better."

"Madam, you are indeed a…"

"What?"

"A marvel. A prickly marvel, to be sure, but a wonder nonetheless."

Barbara picked up her champagne glass and sipped it. "I will take that as a compliment."

Zoltan inclined his head. "As it was intended."

Barbara looked around the shining half-cylinder and out onto the runway in front of them, jets silently taxiing across the tarmac.

"Where are we?"

"Heathrow, of course. Terminal 2."

Barbara waved her hand around the glittering tower. "But this? What is this?"

"Ah, this. It is, shall we say, a very exclusive airport lounge."

"But it's huge." She pointed at the turret rising three stories above them. "It should stand out like a sore thumb. But I've never seen it. Never heard of it."

"Yes. You see, it is not visible from the ground." He shrugged. "Or from the air."

Barbara settled back into the soft cushions of the sofa and closed her eyes. "Whatever."

"Madam," Zoltan said anxiously. "You are exhausted."

"That's true," she said, her head resting on the back of the sofa. "That is very true. But I can't go to bed yet." She felt sleep creeping under her eyes. "We can talk about what happened today tomorrow. But I need to know what we do next. I need to have a plan."

"Can we not wait to discuss that until tomorrow as well?"

Barbara jerked her head forward, sending red curls dancing in front of her face. "No. We cannot. What do we do now?"

Zoltan nodded and sat back in his chair, cradling his champagne glass in both hands.

"There are still many things that are not clear to me. Many things." He lifted his glass to Barbara and nodded gravely. "Though wounded and possibly blinded, I doubt the *Mester* is dead. Even if he is, we do not know what other forces are involved. We do not know if they have the capacity to trace us, though I suspect there is enough disarray to give us some time. We do not know their end game, if there is one." He paused. "There may be no hooded man. It may be only an old drunk's story."

Barbara thought of Dezső's head on the carpet of the *Mester*'s office and shuddered. "I don't think he made it up."

"Nor do I. But we know nothing beyond his account, yes? So we have to proceed with what we do know. The compound will be in chaos. If the *Mester* is alive, without his ring, does he still have the capacity to detect us? If he does, will it take time for him to regain his sensory reach? Will they even bother with us at this point? After all, in your handbag you have a trove of agents' jewels. We don't know what that means, but they are powerful."

"Yes, and you have yours, Zoltan."

Zoltan's face lit in a smile. From the other vest pocket he pulled out the red leather bag. He drew the cords apart and emptied the jewel onto his palm. It glowed lucent blue green, like a shimmering drop of living ice from deep inside a glacier, throbbing rhythmically in his hand.

"Yes, yes, I do. When you gave it to me, when you took it from the *Mester*'s desk..."

"Yes?"

"It was as if…I don't know exactly how to explain it. It was like I was whole again. Even though we could have been killed at any time, I felt alive. More alive than in so many years."

Barbara smiled.

"Before you gave me the jewel, I could not walk. My leg was paralyzed, a dead weight. The pain was agonizing. But when my hand folded over the gem, I could feel strength flowing back from my palm, warmth coursing through my body. I could feel that there was a reason to live." He hesitated and leaned toward Barbara, his black eyes glistening with tears. "And that, madam, is entirely because of you."

Barbara reddened. Damn, she was so tired of blushing. "That is not true, Zoltan, you…"

"Madam," Zoltan said kindly. "Do not try to correct me. This is a truth of the heart."

"OK, look," Barbara said, flustered. "Let's get back to the plan. Or whatever."

Zoltan sat back, smiling. "So, we have the agents' jewels, though not all. And the *Mester's* ring, yes?" He inclined his head and looked intently at Barbara. "What do we do with them?"

Barbara shrugged. "Give them back to the agents?"

Zoltan nodded. "Very likely a good idea. And then?"

Barbara thought for a long moment. "I don't know. I don't know what we should do," she said, frustration in her voice.

"None of us does, of course. But as Caraldo put it, I do not believe this is over. We have confronted the *Mester*, but if Dezső is correct, we may have to do the same with the *Mester's* overlord. I do not know. But if that is the case, will the agents see it that way and wish to join us? Or would they side with him?"

"They would fight against us?"

"Most, no. I believe they would only argue that we should, how do you say? Let sleeping dogs lie?" Barbara nodded.

"But others, I am not so sure."

"How do you mean?"

"When we transferred the jewels to your locked case, what did you notice?"

Barbara thought about the lead-lined wallet, closed with a cylindrical combination lock, buried deep in the brown leather handbag. That afternoon she had locked herself in the private stall of a restroom in one of the boutiques and transferred the jewels they fled with into the case. It was more like a personal bathroom, and she had been able to examine each of the jewels as she placed them carefully in the case.

"About the gems?"

"Yes."

Barbara looked upwards toward the far wall. "They were all different shapes – square, oval, round, teardrop, like yours. And each was glorious in its own way." Her eyes closed as she remembered. "They shimmered and glowed like a fierce, concentrated rainbow."

"Yes," Zoltan agreed. "Beautiful. And the colors?"

"Each almost defied a distinct color. Glowing yellow, burning orange with blue streaks, green like new leaves. Blue, deep as a hole in the ocean…" Barbara stopped.

"Yes. Dark, inky. And the red. Like yours?"

"No. It was heavy, the color of dried blood." She hesitated. "The grey stone, too. It was dark, shadowy, so different from the way Caraldo described his jewel."

Zoltan nodded. "It is as I thought."

"What do you think?"

"I do not know, but from what you have learned from Mrs. Harlow, I believe some of the agents' stones may be part of the *Mester's* circle. Those agents and their gems may be arrayed against us."

"I see." Barbara struggled to keep her eyes open. "So what do we do?" Barbara could feel herself slipping into sleep again and shook her head. "Tell me something we *do* know."

"We know we managed to get 11 jewels out of the safe, thanks to your quick thinking, madam. With mine, we have 12 agent stones. We also know…" Zoltan hooked his finger into the watch pocket of his new wool vest. He pulled out a large gold ring set with a perfectly round black jewel and placed it in his palm.

He peered deeply into the jet stone. Unlike any jewel he had made or seen, nothing shimmered in the depths, no glow or streaks of other colors. The black stone stared back at him like a dead eye.

"Zoltan?"

He looked up.

"You were saying?"

"Yes. We know we have the *Mester's* ring."

Barbara gazed at the ring. "Is that good or bad?"

Zoltan closed his palm and put the ring back into his pocket. "Yes, madam. A good question. A good question indeed. And that is why we need to return to New York."

Barbara's eyes snapped open. "You said that earlier, Zoltan, but surely that's a bad idea," she said. "That is exactly where they will expect us to go."

Zoltan shrugged. "Perhaps, perhaps not. At the very least we have some time. We travel to the Market. There are sanctuary rooms there. We will have the stones analyzed…"

"And the *Mester's*," she added.

"Yes. Then we should know more about what we are fighting. And what we have to fight with."

"And then we will return the gems to their owners?"

"Perhaps, yes. And it will be better to do in in the relative safety of the Market, no?"

Barbara looked at him, weariness and tension lining her face. "We cannot stay long there, please. I am afraid, Zoltan. I don't want to be caught. I don't want *you* to be caught."

Zoltan smiled wanly. "Nor do I, madam." He looked deeply into her eyes. "And I beg you to leave here now. You can walk out that door and make a life for yourself. You can buy a ticket to anyplace in the world. You have given…"

"Would you shut up, Zoltan!" Barbara snapped. Zoltan flinched and sat back.

"If we are flying to New York tomorrow, I need to get some sleep. I'll take the bed upstairs." She stood up and picked up her bags and leather purse. She started toward the stairway and stopped. She strode over to Zoltan and kissed him on the cheek.

"Go to bed, you kind, wonderful man." She turned toward the stairway and climbed up the spiraling steps.

Chapter 31

THE EXIT HALLWAY FROM THE round foyer of the lounge Barbara had seen when they entered led to a small waiting room with a counter against the far wall. Behind it a woman in a red beret and blue suit tapped rapidly at a keyboard. Zoltan handed her their tickets, still in the leather wallet provided by Madam Jeanine.

"The plane will be fully loaded in five minutes," she smiled. "You will be able board then."

"Are there others here? Boarding the plane for New York?"

"No, sir. You are alone. No one else is expected." Zoltan nodded. "Do you have a New York paper?"

The woman reached under the counter and drew out several newspapers. "Of course."

Zoltan took a paper and put his arm through Barbara's. He nodded toward a pair of leather recliners behind a screen near the entryway. "Madam."

As they sank into the chairs, the woman behind the desk walked to a refrigerator set in a dark wood cabinet and took out a bottle of Dom Perignon. She poured two glasses and carried them to Zoltan and Barbara, returning to her desk without a word.

Barbara took a sip, leaned back against the soft leather, and shut her eyes. It had not been a good night. The bed was wonderfully soft and welcoming, but her sleep was restless, interrupted by nightmares. She awoke twice, her heart beating rapidly, and it had taken several long, disoriented moments for her to remember where she was.

"Oh, my," Zoltan exclaimed.

Barbara raised her head. Zoltan was staring at the paper. "What is it?"

He shook the paper and folded it in half. He held it to her and pointed to an article in the lower right- hand corner. She took the paper and focused on the article.

She caught her breath. She was staring at a picture of herself. She quickly scanned the headline: "Husband Held in Steubenville Disappearance."

"What?" she mouthed, turning to the text.

"The mysterious disappearance of Larchmont socialite Barbara Steubenville took another turn yesterday when police brought the missing woman's husband to the station for questioning. Through his lawyer, Sabrina Chetty, David Steubenville insisted he knew nothing of his wife's whereabouts or why she might have left without notifying family or friends.

"Mr. Steubenville contended that the police had no evidence and were harassing him for publicity purposes. Westchester County police said that no charges had been filed against Mr. Steubenville. A spokeswoman for the police, Sandra Hendricks, said only that 'Mr. Steubenville has been brought in for routine questioning. We continue to explore all leads in the case.' Ms. Steubenville disappeared nearly ten days ago after a violent domestic dispute overheard by neighbors."

"Shit," Barbara breathed.

"Exactly," Zoltan said.

"It never occurred to me…"

"Madam, madam," Zoltan said patiently, shaking his head. "So much did not occur to you." He smiled slightly. "For which I am glad. Your impulsivity has been a most welcome, how do you put it? Kick in the pants?"

Barbara lowered the paper and looked at him nervously. "They're looking for me all over the city." She motioned to the paper. "My picture is everywhere. How are we going to get to the Market without being identified?"

Zoltan raised his eyebrows. "How indeed?"

He took the paper and stared at it for a few moments and then held it toward Barbara. "The picture. What do you notice?"

Barbara studied the photo in the article. It had been taken two years earlier at a fundraiser for the Larchmont Yacht Club David had dragged her to. Her hair was pulled into a tight bun on top of her head. She wore a string of fake pearls – David insisted no one could tell the difference — and a high-necked sequined black dress with butterfly sleeves. It was hideous. What had she been thinking?

"Well?"

"I hate that dress."

"Madam. Perhaps you should have a good look at yourself. Do you have a mirror?"

Barbara nodded and dug into her green handbag. She pulled out a small silver Sephora folding compact she had bought with the purse. She opened the slim case and peered into the mirror.

The woman who stared back was barely recognizable, as if she were looking at the image of a younger sister, a cousin perhaps. She leaned closer. Her hair burst in a glorious red tangle of curls and waves that swept in front of her face. When she pushed the curls aside, she met bright green eyes, alight and steady. Her face, always pale, now seemed to glow, and her full red lips were set firmly in an expression of determination. She realized she hadn't used lipstick for days, and she liked it. For years she had tried to cover her freckles with makeup, but now they scattered defiantly along her nose and across her cheeks.

But there was something else she couldn't quite identify. She squinted at the mirror.

"You won't see it there."

Barbara looked up, surprised. "What do you mean?"

Zoltan cocked his head and looked at her thoughtfully. "It's not one thing. It's not visible."

Barbara returned to the mirror. Her eyebrows, beginning to regain their strawberry glory after being plucked and penciled for years, furrowed.

"What isn't?"

"What is so different about you? Why you don't recognize yourself."

She glanced up at him again. "Thank you, Edgar Cayce. And what might that be?"

"You have found your soul."

Barbara saw her lips curl skeptically in the mirror.

"Ah, you think I am exaggerating, yes? That perhaps I am just an old charlatan."

Barbara rolled her eyes. "No, it's not that, it's just…"

"That a 'soul' is so hard to grasp, yes? And so it is. It is your heart, your spirit. The French have a better term, perhaps: *élan vital,* yes?"

"My French was never that good," Barbara murmured.

"It does not translate well. Vital impulse. Life force, perhaps? Madam, you are unrecognizable. You are not your old self."

"Maybe, but will that play in New York?"

Zoltan laughed. "That and a large pair of sunglasses, a baseball cap and, just to be sure, your hoodie. Yes, I believe it will."

"Sir," the attendant said from her counter. "The plane is ready for you now."

Zoltan rose from the chair and held out his hand. Barbara took it and stood. She shouldered her bag and pulled her carry-on case toward a door the attendant held open.

The boarding ramp led directly to the first-class section of the plane. A flight attendant met them at the cabin door and led them forward to a pod separated from the rest of the cabin by curtains she drew behind her. They settled into seats that Zoltan showed Barbara how to convert into a bed. She gratefully sank into the soft cushions, almost asleep before the plane taxied for takeoff. As her eyes closed, she was aware of Zoltan spreading a blanket over her and tucking it under her chin.

Chapter 32

THE BA FLIGHT GOT THEM into JFK just after 11:00 at night. They had left at 8:00, and though she knew the flight took about seven and a half hours, it never quite made sense to her that she had been in London only three hours earlier. They exited the plane in the same way they boarded – a flight attendant escorted them to an exit ramp before the screen was drawn back from the regular first-class cabin. They disappeared quickly up the ramp and into the yawning airport terminal.

"Well, madam, at least this time you will arrive at the Market in a train rather than being chased by one."

Barbara thought back to her dash through the subway tunnel and felt her heart race as she remembered the terror that swept through her when the red warning lights had begun to flash, when she was sure a train was bearing down on her.

"Goodness," Zoltan exclaimed. He stopped, his hand held against his chest.

Barbara turned back toward him. "What is it? Are you OK?"

"I think so. But I felt this surge of panic." He took a deep breath. "Just came out of nowhere."

"Are you having a heart attack?"

He smiled. "No, I am fine now." He looked curiously at Barbara, his thick eyebrows drawn together behind his glasses.

"What is it?"

"Nothing. Just a coincidence, I am sure." He glanced at his watch. "We have five hours before the train leaves Grand Central Station. Given your new notoriety, I think we should go looking for those sunglasses, yes?"

Barbara glanced around nervously, suddenly conscious of the crowd around her.

"Yes, I think that's a good idea." She looked at the rows of shops lining the broad concourse. "Should we try some of these places?"

Zoltan steered her through a hallway to their right. "I think not. It seems we should avoid large crowds, no?"

"Of course; you're right. But that's kind of hard to do in New York."

"Perhaps not so difficult. I know some stores in the city. They have contacts with the Market. You will be their only customer."

Barbara looked at a digital read-out of the time on a departure screen. "At 11:45 at night, I'm not surprised."

Zoltan laughed. "Yes. I will call and make an appointment."

"I like it when you do that."

"What is that, madam?"

"Laugh."

They made their way through the sprawling terminal to an inconspicuous exit. They pushed through the doors, and Barbara took a deep breath. The late summer air was heavy and scented with diesel fuel, but she felt relief after being in airports and planes for so many hours.

Zoltan had walked to the rear door of a black Mercedes that waited at the curb. He opened the door for Barbara and then slid in next to her.

"That was convenient," Barbara commented as Zoltan shut his door.

Zoltan smiled. "Yes, we are fortunate that my good friend Mr. Godwin was available tonight."

A huge Black man in the driver's seat turned toward Barbara. He wore his hair in medium-length dreads, and a pair of dark aviator glasses wrapped around his face.

"Madam," he said, nodding at Barbara.

"Good evening," Barbara replied. She leaned toward Zoltan, "What is it with you guys?" she whispered. "The 'Madam' thing?"

"Mr. Godwin," Zoltan said, ignoring Barbara. "Would you be so good as to call Laurine at Wolf in Sheep's Clothing? How long will it take us to get there, Mr. Godwin?"

"Traffic is light," the driver rumbled. "We should be there in an hour."

"Very good."

"Wolf in Sheep's Clothing?"

Zoltan just smiled.

Four hours later, they stood on the deserted platform 61, deep inside Grand Central Station. Barbara adjusted her new sunglasses, pushing them further up her nose. She tucked a few stray hairs under her Mets baseball cap and pulled the hood of her black sweatshirt back over the cap and looked nervously at her watch.

"It will be here," Zoltan assured her.

She swept her gaze around the empty platform and looked back at the inconspicuous door behind them. It did indeed open onto an elevator that could be accessed from the Waldorf Astoria. But getting there had been rather a blur, and she wasn't sure she could navigate it again. They had taken two sets of stairs down from the glittering lobby to a long hall studded with unmarked wooden doors and turned left. The hallway ended in a heavy steel panel with no handle or visible hinges. Zoltan held his card to the surface and pushed. The panel swung upward. From there they climbed down several flights of metal stairs until they reached a landing with a single oak door, dark red from age. An incongruous card slot was the only feature, and it glowed green when Zoltan slid in his card. The door clicked and swung open onto an arched brick passageway that extended for perhaps 50 yards before ending in yet another steel door, a horizontal seam splitting the panel in two.

This time Zoltan ran the card along the door frame, and the doors slid in two halves, upward and downward, to reveal a surprisingly large and ornate elevator car.

They stepped inside. "Down," Zoltan had said, and they sank rapidly until coming to a stuttering stop. "Open," Zoltan ordered, and the doors opened onto a rough cement landing. To their right, several subway tracks ended in massive buffer stops. They stepped out onto the simple platform and moved to the far end away from the elevator.

"I do not believe we have any concern here on the platform, madam. *If* they are after us," Zoltan looked away from the old station, littered with abandoned subway cars and dusty tools, and smiled at Barbara. "And hopefully they are not, yes? But if they are, accosting us on the platform would be too conspicuous. If they are looking for us, they will be on the train."

"On the train? You mean it makes other stops?"

"Yes, one other at 125th. Mainly for supplies, but people can board there as well."

Barbara fingered the black card in her jeans pocket. "I thought you said everyone had to have a card to board the train. And that they were carefully vetted."

Zoltan nodded. "So I did," he said, staring back down the rails. "But there are ways." They stood silent in the hushed cavern of the deserted subway station.

Barbara turned to Zoltan. "What is it?" she asked. "There is something else bothering you."

Zoltan continued looking straight ahead at the platform across the tracks. "Isn't that enough?" he said lightly.

"Zoltan," Barbara said. "You are not telling me everything. Like I said, you are not a good liar."

He glanced down at the tracks. "At least with you, it seems."

"Look at me."

Zoltan sighed and turned his head toward her.

"What is it?"

"Some of the *Mester's* men may be fanning out to look for me. I suspect we have crippled his operation, if not destroyed it, but that might only invite intervention from other entities, yes?

"The Company?"

Zoltan shrugged. "Perhaps they have traced me through my gem and know exactly where I am."

Barbara tilted her head slightly, perplexed. "I know that. That's why we will be on lookout when we get on the train. In case they have traced you. But as you said, once we get to the Market, we will have sanctuary and can plan our next moves."

Zoltan nodded. "That is what I said. But they know that too. In which case there would be little need to hurry, yes?" He stopped and stared at the dusty surface of the landing. "If they are on the train, they may be here to retrieve something from my apartment that would be more important to the *Mester's* employer than the *Mester* himself."

"Like what?"

Zoltan's eyes looked upward. "The one thing I wanted before we had to flee. The same thing I was hoping to reclaim while here. A very special flash drive."

Barbara looked back toward the elevator, relieved to see that they were still alone. "What is on it that's so important?"

"Financial records. Numbered bank accounts. Names of all my clients, some in very influential positions, who would not be happy if their names were to be made public. And, most important, contact information for all of the agents."

"But why would they care? They have all that information anyway, don't they?"

Zoltan stared out the window as a darkened station slid by. "Yes, most of it. But given my rather strained relationship with one of the Company's star employees, I suspect they are concerned about how I might use it."

"Such as?"

"They would think of blackmail, of course, that I would threaten to divulge the inner workings of their enterprise, complete with secret bank accounts and names of clients, but for me it is protection. As long as I have the drive with the data and they do not know where it is, I believe they will be reluctant to kill me." He nodded formally at Barbara. "And my associates."

He paused. "But that's not all. There are 26 agents that I know of. We are not supposed to have direct communication with each other, of course – by keeping us alone and divided the *Mester* avoided the sort of resistance Fitz and Welser posed. But I was never comfortable with that. Somehow even then I knew I might need to connect. Over the years I have accumulated contact information on all of them."

Barbara turned back to the tracks. "I see. And without that information you have no way of reaching the agents whose gems we collected."

"Exactly. But they can. Imagine what lies they will spread."

Barbara turned back toward Zoltan. "Where is it?"

"Bottom drawer of my desk." He exhaled deeply. "Not all that clever, I am afraid."

"You had no idea it would come to this."

"No, madam, you are quite right about that. Quite right." He sat in silence. "However, if they are after the drive, they will have a very difficult time breaching security. They may not be able to enter without blowing out the door to the apartment."

"Would they do that?"

"It would be very risky. The Building is not directly part of the Market, but it is carefully protected. Too many Market artisans live there." He shrugged. "But who knows? If they are desperate enough, perhaps. By the time Building security could respond, they might be able to grab the drive and escape. So, when we arrive at the Market, I will take you directly to a safe room at Mrs. Harlow's."

Barbara turned her head slightly. "And what will you do?"

"I will return to my apartment and retrieve the drive."

"Zoltan," Barbara hissed. "That's crazy. If they are tracking you, to kidnap or kill you, they will know your every move. They will know you've left sanctuary and be waiting for you."

Zoltan stared straight ahead. "That is a possibility."

"And even if they aren't out to grab you but just want into your apartment, the easiest thing to do would be jump you and force you to open the door."

"I would not do that, madam."

"That's not the point, you principled idiot. They don't know that." Zoltan said nothing.

"Now, listen to me. If they know you are on the train, they will think you are too sensible to go the apartment, right? They will instead follow you to the Market. Figure out how to get into the apartment without creating a ruckus. Maybe try to trick you into leaving Sanctuary and force you to open the door."

"That might be," Zoltan said mildly. "But we're not at all sure there will be anyone on the train. We may be somewhat paranoid, yes?"

"You know what they say," Barbara muttered. "You're not paranoid if they're really after you." Zoltan chuckled. "Quite. But even if they are trailing us, I must get the drive first."

Barbara took his hand. "It's simple — I go."

Zoltan's head snapped toward her. "That is out of the question!"

Barbara waved her hand. "Shh, shut up," she breathed. "Listen to me. If one of the agents is on the train, would he act alone?"

"Probably not, but he could be meeting someone at the Market."

"Exactly. And they will be looking for you. Could it be O'Neil?"

Zoltan shook his head. "Even if he could pull himself away from the chaos at the compound, I would recognize him. He would send one of his fellow thugs, possibly Eric Paulson. He seemed to do the dirty when Zhukov was busy."

"That's the point – they are all the *Mester's* agents; I doubt they will know much about me, if anything. At the most they will have been told you might be travelling with a red-haired woman." Barbara pulled the bill of her Met's cap down and adjusted her round sunglasses. "I saw myself in a mirror in the station. I don't think they'd even know my gender. They have no idea what happened when we escaped. If we split up, if I'm still in London. They may be able to locate you through your gem, but not mine. Anyway, they want to grab you and, first, get into your apartment. Then take you back as a prisoner." She paused. "Or kill you. This is all about you."

"I cannot let you do this," Zoltan whispered sharply. "It is too dangerous."

Barbara found herself laughing. "You silly man. The last few days have not exactly been a vacation at the beach."

"But that is not the point," Zoltan said. "They will see you are with me and know you are the companion O'Neil will have no doubt mentioned." He looked at her, from her black and white sneakers to the black hoodie and baseball cap. "Even if you do look like a 16-year-old boy. And if there are two, one will follow me and the other you. No, it is simply too dangerous."

Barbara shook her head in exasperation. "Look, the solution is simple. We separate here. I get on one car – there is more than one, right?"

"Four. Three passenger cars and a freight car."

"Right. I'll stay here." She nodded back the way they had come. "And you go back to the other end of the platform. When the train pulls in, you get into the first car, and I'll get into the third. They won't connect us." She pulled her card out of her pocket. "Just swipe this across the door?"

Zoltan started to speak, but Barbara held up her hand. "When we get to the Market station, you go directly inside. That is what they will expect. I will exit with from the last car and go to the elevator and up to your apartment."

Zoltan looked at her dubiously.

"You are the decoy. If someone is tailing us, he will follow you. I will go up to the apartment and hide in the closet at the end of your hallway and wait for five minutes. If there is an agent and he decides to go directly to the apartment or to follow me, I will know it. I will call your cell phone and let it buzz three times. That means he is in the hallway or breaking into your apartment. You can alert security. I will stay hidden in the closet. OK? If no one is after us, no problem. I will be in and out of your apartment with the flash drive in five minutes and back at the Market in 15."

"And if there is?"

"He'll most likely be busy tailing you." She smiled. "I'm in and out and we meet at Mrs. Harlow's."

Zoltan was shaking his head furiously, "No…"

"In the meantime," Barbara shoved the leather handbag into Zoltan's hands. "Here. Doesn't go well with the teenage boy look. All of the agent jewels are in there. Plead with her to analyze the stones as quickly as possible. Now, I need to know how to get into your apartment."

"Barbara, I cannot let you do this."

"Sir, you cannot stop me. And please, no one, not you or anyone else will ever again tell me what I can and cannot do." She turned her head and faced him. "And that's because of you. Now, the instructions."

"I don't like this," Zoltan said.

"Instructions," Barbara repeated.

Zoltan sighed heavily. "About shoulder high there's a carved shield in the middle of the door. In the shield there is a griffin looking to the left. Slide the griffin upward; there's a nine-button keypad behind it. Place your palm over the pad. A zero will appear at the bottom of the pad."

Barbara nodded. "Like at the lounge."

"Yes. Use the buttons to enter the code."

"Let me guess – Rebecca's birthday: 042814."

Zoltan gave her a small smile. "You know me well. Am I that predictable?"

"Afraid so. Go on."

"Once the code is entered, the panel underneath the shield will open. Reach inside and take out the key. Insert the key in the keyhole. Turn it left twice, right once, and left again."

Barbara nodded. "The train should be here any minute." She turned and began walking toward the other side of the empty platform. After several steps she stopped and blew Zoltan a kiss.

Barbara heard a low rumbling on her left. 4:00. The small train swept up to the platform and creaked to a stop. Zoltan stepped forward to the lead car and pulled his black card through a groove beside one of the doors, which slid open silently. She held her card in her hand and walked to the third car. Behind it was an old boxcar. She slid the card in the slot and stepped onto the train.

It was like entering a subway museum. The car was ancient. Cracked red leather seats were framed in brass, and the floors were wooden slats. Above the doors, fading posters advertised circus performances that had occurred 80 years ago, classes in stenography and typing, soap brands that had been discontinued for decades. Two people shared the car with her. They sat together in the rear of the care and paid no attention to her.

She slid into a seat near the front and hunched down, her arms across her chest.

Chapter 33

BARBARA WAS SURPRISED HOW EASILY the train joined the main subway line. She had expected a magic door to open or at least a spark or two as the old train emerged from Track 61, but instead they switched smoothly onto the Lexington line as if they were connecting from Queens. She began to recognize the stops she had studied so closely – 28th Street, Spring, Canal. What would happen as they neared City Hall?

Suddenly the train swerved slightly onto a single rail that sloped downward, the tunnel darkening. They took a dip and the low interior lights extinguished and the car went utterly black. There was not a flicker of light inside or outside. They rode in darkness for several minutes and then the train slowed and creaked to a halt at a dimly lit platform. The doors slid open onto a wood platform and the two other passengers exited and walked toward a broad arch that opened onto a brightly lit space. She was at the Market.

Barbara rose from her seat and walked onto the station planks. She sensed passengers disembarking from the forward two cars but paid no attention. Most hurried toward the Market entrance, but a few stood by the elevator, waiting for a car to take them up to their apartments. She moved slowly toward the group, keeping her head down and staying in the shadows as much as possible.

"DeAngelo!" a woman's voice called out.

Barbara looked up for a second, noting the woman that had hailed

Zoltan and quickly studied the rest of the passengers. The woman had short dark hair, bangs framing her round face. She was older, but even from a distance Barbara could tell she was striking with arched black eyebrows and a wide smile. She had been walking toward the elevator but stopped and strode instead toward Zoltan.

Several people hung back from the elevator entrance, apparently waiting for the privacy of an empty car. A woman in a red and black Market uniform swiped a card across the face of the small button panel, and Barbara remembered her terror and confusion when she had helplessly tried to figure out how to access the elevator from the City Hall Station, when only her jewel had opened the doors to the ornate car inside. Her hand went unconsciously to her chest, feeling the gem, warm underneath her shirt. That had been…less than two weeks ago? A lifetime? She reflected briefly on the girl standing in front of the elevator that night, afraid and desperate. She was a memory, like an old friend that one remembers warmly but hasn't seen for a very long time.

The woman in the Market clothes clutched a satchel and waited impatiently for the door to slide open. A young man, dressed in the loose black pants and red tunic of the Market, stood to her side. A second man stood not far from where he had exited the train. He stared at the elevator door but glanced continually toward Zoltan, who walked toward the approaching woman. The elevator doors opened and the woman with the satchel boarded. The young man waited his turn.

The woman who had called out to Zoltan rushed up to him and held out her hand.

"Milly," he beamed. "How great to see you." He gave a small bow. "May I accompany you to the Market?"

The woman's smile broadened. "I'd be honored," she said. "We really must catch up. How long has it been?"

As she spoke the next elevator car arrived. Zoltan offered his arm to the woman, and they walked together toward the Market entrance. He never glanced up.

From the corner of her eye, Barbara saw the elevator door slide open and the young man step into the car. She hurried over before the door could close and moved by the man, who looked at her in surprise. She slipped to the rear of the car and stared at the floor.

The door closed but the car remained motionless, quiet. The silence lengthened, becoming uncomfortable. She adjusted her sunglasses and looked at the man. He stood by the door, glaring at her.

She met his stare but said nothing. "Do you mind?" he asked irritably. "Sorry?"

"I'd like to get to my apartment before daylight if it's OK with you." Suddenly she remembered.

"Oh, 'Up, three,'" she called out.

The car gave a low growl and heaved upward.

"Sorry," Barbara said. The man turned toward the door, shaking his head.

They ascended for what seemed like a very long time until finally the car jolted gently to a stop. The door slid open, and Barbara peeked out to make sure it was Zoltan's floor. The younger man watched her, tapping his foot impatiently. She glanced at the framed photograph in the foyer of the beautiful woman in the white dress – Rebecca, Barbara now knew – and slipped by the man into the hallway. She started down the hall from the landing. Behind her the elevator door slid shut. She stopped and turned back down the hall until she reached the storage closet beside the elevator. She pulled her black card from her jeans pocket and slid it down a groove in the door frame. There was a sharp click, and she pulled the closet door open.

In such an extraordinary building, Barbara had expected some sort of exotic devices, a robotic vacuum perhaps, or maybe a secret dusting potion, but instead the small closet was filled with very conventional brooms, mops, and an old Electrolux. The shelf at the rear held bottles of Windex and cleaning solutions.

She returned the card to her pocket and took out her cell phone, turning on the flashlight function. She checked to make sure the brass knob on the inside of the door turned, retracting the latch, and pulled the door closed.

She checked the time on her phone – 4:47 — and shut off the flashlight. She was in complete darkness, the closet silent and black as a cave.

The next five minutes crawled by, each seeming longer than the next. She stood by the door, straining to hear any sound from the hallway. Once, she caught her breath as she heard the elevator approach, but it continued upward, sliding by her floor, leaving only silence behind. She checked the time on her phone, half hoping she would hear the car groan to a stop and the footsteps of people hurrying toward Zoltan's apartment before the five minutes were up so she could notify Zoltan and let the security police take over. But the foyer remained empty and quiet.

She glanced at her phone again – 4:54. She waited another minute, then turned the handle and opened the door a few inches. She listened for any noise, a creak of a floorboard under the burgundy carpeting, the brush of a coat against the wainscoting, any indication Paulson, or whoever, might have accessed the floor by some alternate route. She pushed the door ajar and looked out. There was nothing between her and the heavy wooden door at the end of the corridor.

Barbara hurried past the pictures of Rebecca, only glancing at one she hadn't noticed the first time she had so fearfully ventured down the hall. Rebecca was walking away from the photographer down a trail into the woods. Her head was turned over her shoulder, smiling at the person behind her. Her dark hair was tied back in a white ribbon, and her eyes sparkled with merriment – and love.

She reached the end of the hallway and studied the carvings on the door. She quickly found the griffin in the middle of the shield and pushed it upward, exposing the keypad behind. She palmed the pad and waited until the zero appeared at the bottom then punched in the code. The door slid upward, and she reached into the narrow space behind the panel with her fingers. She drew out a three-inch brass skeleton key. The bow had been cast as an elaborate heart that tapered into a round shaft, which ended in a heart-shaped bit carved with intricate wards.

Barbara pushed the key into the wooden keyhole underneath the doorknob, took a deep breath, and turned it to her left. Left again then right, then left once more.

She had expected to hear a snap or some sort of mechanical click, but instead a gentle whirring came from behind the brass plate that held the ivory doorknob. After several seconds, the whirring stopped and the knob turned all the way around to the left, where it stopped for a moment, and then moved halfway to the right. Then there was silence. Barbara put her hand on the knob and pushed, and the door sighed inward.

Once inside, she quickly shut the door. Behind her, the door mechanism whirred as it reset itself.

Barbara flipped on the wall switch by the door, lighting the grand chandelier in the center of the sprawling living room. She glanced around the familiar space, astonished once more as she recalled all that had occurred since she was last there. She took her phone out of her pocket, switched on the flashlight, and turned off the overhead light. No reason to draw attention.

She padded across the deep woven rugs and the gleaming wood floor toward the back of the living room where the desk sat beside the bookcase with its ladder climbing up into the gloom of the high ceiling. She reached the desk and crouched down. She grasped the brass handle of the bottom drawer and pulled it hard. It didn't budge. *Damn*, she thought. She stood up and studied the face of the desk. She reached down and tugged on the brass pull again. It was as if the drawer was cemented into the desk.

Time, time. How much time do I have before they get here? She examined the drawer more closely and found a small keyhole underneath the handle. Maybe the drawer was locked. Maybe Zoltan had forgotten. Then what? A fire ax?

Barbara pulled on the main drawer that ran across the middle of the great desk. It slid open easily, and she rummaged frantically inside for a key. There were neat ledgers and rows of sharpened pencils. A rubber eraser, a plastic tray of paper clips. In desperation she pulled the entire drawer out and dumped the contents on the floor. She dropped to her knees and sorted through the papers and scattered staples and ballpoints. There was no key. She kicked the lower drawer in frustration. It gave an inch, and then glided outward silently.

Shit. What a moron. All she had to do was open the main drawer.

She pulled the lower drawer open and quickly scanned the contents. There was a metal cash box, and this time, thankfully, the key was still in the lock. She yanked the box out and opened the lid. The top cash till was empty. She pulled it out and tossed it aside. Underneath was a leather jewel bag. She untied the strings and shook out the contents. A silver metal rectangle, about three inches by two and perhaps an inch thick, tumbled onto her palm. She examined it and pulled the two halves apart. A connector like none she'd ever seen, round and about an inch long, extended from one end. She snapped the halves together again and shoved the drive into her pocket.

She turned back to the desk to throw the empty cash box back into the drawer. As she did, she saw an album at the bottom. What would Zoltan have valued enough to keep with the flash drive? She drew out an old leather-bound photo album, the dark green cover faded and worn. Barbara opened it.

Barbara gasped. She had seen many pictures of Rebecca, but never nude. The black and white photographs were stunning; the relationship between the photographer and his model charged, adoring. She was his, and he hers. Each photo was a record of their love, each such an intense glimpse into the ferocity of their intimacy that Barbara felt like a voyeur.

She flipped to the back of the album and looked at the final picture. It had apparently been taken with a timer. Zoltan, also unclothed, lay beneath Rebecca on a patterned sofa. Rebecca leaned on one elbow, her perfect breasts open to the camera, Zoltan's right arm around her. But the erotic power of the picture came less from the sensual entwining of the two flawless bodies than from the eyes. Neither Zoltan nor Rebecca looked at the camera; they looked tenderly into each other's face. Even in the old photograph, Barbara saw Zoltan's luminous black eyes locked with Rebecca's in a connection of love and passion that crackled like an electric current.

A clatter at the door refocused her attention, causing her heart to jolt. The noise subsided, and Barbara wondered if she had imagined the noise, or maybe it was a rat in the walls. Then came the explosion.

When Zoltan had talked about "blowing the door," Barbara had recalled the dynamiting of the wall into the *Mester's* office. If it happened, she had expected the door to hurl inward in a cloud of dust and a deafening blast. But this was a muffled, concentrated bang, like the thump of a distant artillery gun. She looked toward the door in panic. Even after the blast the sturdy door held, but Barbara knew it would just be a matter of minutes. She looked around desperately. Could she make it across the wide living room to the hallway and to the bedrooms beyond?

Heavy, echoing blows to the door reverberated through her. She sensed it beginning to give and looked around for someplace to hide.

The ladder. Maybe there was space to hide at the top of the bookcase.

She threw a glance over her shoulder as the door finally crashed inward. She leapt onto the first rung and scrambled upward. She wondered if she would be frozen at the top of the ladder, treed like a raccoon.

She reached the final rung as the men clambered through the ruin of the door. One switched on a flashlight, cursing.

"Goddamn it, Hickey. Every Building security son of a bitch will be here in minutes. I told you the plastic was a last resort!

"I didn't see you making much progress," a deeper voice snarled. "We coulda been out there all night."

Barbara's heart jumped with relief as she slid onto the top of the bookcase and rolled silently out of sight. The alcove was deeper than she had guessed – there were at least two feet between the edge of the case and the row of stained-glass windows that ran the full length of the bookcase. She pressed against the cold glass and tried to calm her breathing.

"Jesus," the man swore again. "Do something useful and find a fuckin' light."

The room leapt into ghostly light as the chandelier, uncomfortably close, glowed softly. "He said it would be in the desk. You see a desk?" the first man asked.

"Can't see nothin' in this rat hole," the second man grunted. "You told me this was a piece of cake, Paulson. We'd just get the prick to let us in. Grab the drive, whack the guy, split."

"I didn't know he'd head for sanctuary. He could have been there for days. And it still might have gone that way if you hadn't decided to play with explosives, you stupid yegg. Now shut the fuck up and find the desk."

Barbara shrank against the glass, desperately hoping that the angle of the bookshelf protected her from being seen from below, hoping her black hoodie and jeans would blend into the shadows.

"Over here!" the deeper voice called just below her. "You dumb fuck, Paulson," the man roared. "The desk is smashed. Shit is all over. He got here before us."

Barbara heard Paulson run toward the man, his heavy shoes thumping hollowly on the maple floor.

"God damn it!" Paulson cursed. "But he couldn't have gotten here before us. I followed him into the Market."

"Well sure as shit someone beat us to it."

"Fuck," Paulson spit. "There was a ratty little guy hanging around the elevator. Had a ball cap on. I knew there was something funny about him. He took the elevator up about 10 minutes before you figured out DeAngelo had headed for sanctuary." Paulson looked around the dimly lit living room. "Maybe he's still here. Check out every room. Move!"

"And maybe someone else was here a week ago. Screw you, Paulson. I ain't goin' down for some bullshit flash drive and a few Gs. I'm outta here. I work here, remember? That's why you hired me. These Building guys don't fuck around."

Barbara heard the man head toward the door, and then a low hum filled the hallways. "Damn it," Hickey called out. "You follow me now or we are both in deep shit."

Barbara heard Paulson hesitate for a moment then run across the floor. They brushed through the broken door and sprinted down the hallway. Would they use the elevator? Wouldn't security seal it off? Or did they have some other escape route? Did Zoltan say there was another way down? An emergency stairway somewhere?

Now the hum had turned into a loud ululating wail. Barbara pushed herself to the edge of the bookshelf and looked over the living room. The door hung from a single heavy brass hinge, but otherwise the room was empty. Did she want to chance trying to explain what she was doing in an apartment with the front door blasted open to a bunch of armed Building security officers? What she was doing with a stolen flash drive in her pocket? And somehow, she didn't think this would be the average security force. She wondered idly how Market justice worked.

To her surprise she realized she still held the photo album in her hand. She pushed it into a dusty corner of the alcove and swung her legs over the side of the case. She found the ladder and quickly climbed down to the floor. The emergency staircase. Zoltan had said access was through the kitchen, Though the chandelier was still on, it provided only dim light, and she dodged furniture as she ran toward the kitchen entrance. She pushed through the swinging doors and scanned the darkened kitchen, not even knowing what she was looking for. The wail increased to a deafening crescendo.

She had made an omelet here a thousand years ago. What did she remember? Where could a flight of stairs be hidden? She raked the floor with her eyes, searching for a trap door, but the black and white tile seemed solid, unbroken. Her eyes travelled to the far wall and the bank of cupboards, the ones she hadn't bothered opening because she assumed they would be as empty as the shelves.

She raced to the end of the kitchen and threw open the first cupboard door. Inside there were only rows of empty shelves. *Just as I suspected*, she thought. She flung open the other door. A narrow stairway led down into the darkness. Barbara pulled the cupboard door closed behind her and began descending the steps.

Chapter 34

THE STEPS SEEMED TO GO on forever. Barbara stopped counting at 100, and still they spiraled downward. There was not a shred of light in the narrow cylinder that encased the stairway, so she couldn't see the next step, much less the bottom of the staircase. If there was a bottom.

She checked the screen on her phone, and her heart skipped. Four percent charge. She clicked off the light and groped her way in darkness, gripping the metal handrail and stumbling downward, triangular stair after stair, hoping that they did not stop suddenly, that her next step not find only an empty abyss.

As she descended the wailing siren softened and then abated altogether. All she heard was her breathing, labored and shallow, and the soft clatter of her runners on the triangular metal stairs.

Five minutes later, the gloom below her lightened slightly. Was she imagining it? She had heard that in utter darkness eyes could create the illusion of light.

No, as she continued her spiral downward, the dim smudge grew brighter.

Another few minutes and Far below a faint glow lit a cement floor. As she got closer, she realized the light came from underneath a door, a sliver of grey that glowed in the pitch dark. She increased the pace of her descent, surer of her footing, until her runners touched the hard surface of the cement.

Her legs collapsed underneath her in exhaustion. She held onto the handrail, kneeling on the hard floor, trying to get her breath.

After a few minutes, she stood up, her legs still shaky, and walked slowly toward the metal door a few feet away. Did she really want to know if it was open? Nothing else in the insane building was. She pulled the phone from her pocket and took a deep breath. She switched on the light.

The door had once been painted dark green, but now the surface was flaking, pocked with rusty patches. The round brass doorknob was green with tarnish. Even if it was unlocked, it would almost certainly be corroded shut. She stared at the mottled door, afraid to try and open it.

Without the slightest flicker, the light on her phone went dead. She stood at the bottom of a dark, dank shaft in front of the dim outline of a door she knew would not open. But she had to try. She reached out and grasped the knob. As expected, it refused to turn. She pulled inward with a hard jerk, but the door didn't budge. She slammed her shoulder into it, but it was like running into a slab of granite. She fell back, panting, and began to feel panic rising insider her again. She could never climb back up the steps. She was trapped.

Her left hand strayed to her chest and grasped her gem. A gentle warmth radiated across her chest. She pulled the chain of her necklace upward until the gem emerged from inside her shirt, glowing deep red in the darkness, like the eye of a wolf. It gleamed brighter and brighter until the small room she stood in shone deep pink. She held the gem in her hand, feeling it pulse in her palm. She took it between her thumb and forefinger and looked through it at the door. *Let's see how it works as a blowtorch*, she thought.

A broad beam of red light illuminated the door and then narrowed until it was a scarlet laser. Smoke began to curl from a small hole that appeared in the metal surface where the beam was concentrated. Barbara shifted the deep red light to the doorknob; it crackled and spit as it burned its way through the steel. She moved the beam around the knob in a circle. As the ends of the beam met, the handle fell inward with a dull clunk. She put her hand tentatively on the rusty surface and pushed. The door swung outward and soft light rushed through the open doorway.

Barbara stepped through the door onto a long unused extension of the City Hall subway station. Above her a final arch tapered into the darkness of a tunnel. Dusty cables and a stack of wooden pallets cluttered the landing. Ahead of her along the curve of the platform she saw the skylight 100 yards away.

As her eyes became accustomed to the light, faint as it was, she could see people milling about far down the platform by the elevator and could hear the faint wail of the security alarm.

Barbara slid her jewel back under her blouse and walked alertly up the platform toward the crowd. Soon she could see the faces of the people clearly and hear the babble of excited conversation. Three or four people in red and black uniforms stood by the elevator. As she got closer, she could see they were wearing red helmets fitted with black face masks that left only their eyes uncovered. They held curved scimitars across their chests.

Barbara stayed in the shadows of the old station's arched walls as she approached the small crowd. Soon she mingled with a few outliers and quietly made her way toward the elevator entrance. As she neared, the alarm blared louder.

"Hasn't happened in years," a woman in a white muslin dress muttered.

"What's that?" Barbara asked.

"Security breach in the Building." She nodded toward the uniformed figures. "Haven't seen the security forces up here for ages, and I don't like it."

"No," Barbara agreed. "I don't either."

The woman shook her head. "This used to happen all the time, but I thought those days were over." She looked darkly at the security officers. "They can keep their damned scimitars in their lockers where they belong."

"Do you know what happened?"

The woman shook her head again. "Heard the sirens. We were ordered out of our apartments to the evacuation level." She glanced around the tiled station. "Haven't been here in years either." She looked at Barbara. "Where were you?"

"Uh, visiting a friend. I heard the sirens," Barbara said quickly, "but I didn't really know what they meant at first."

The woman looked at Barbara curiously. "Visiting a friend?"

Barbara glanced nervously toward the elevator. "Listen, the man I was seeing, he left before the alarm. I was supposed to meet him in the Market. Is the elevator working?"

The woman shifted her eyes toward the security guards. "Yeah, as long as you only want to go down. The breach was somewhere upstairs in the apartments." She shook her head disgustedly. "Which, of course, is where I want to go. Who knows how long the up elevator will be out of service? Pisses me right off."

Barbara edged away from the woman. "Nice talking." She said, slipping into the crowd. "Hope you get back OK."

Barbara made her way through the murmuring crowd until she reached the elevator entrance. The tallest of the guards, the only one not carrying a scimitar, approached her. Barbara looked into the guard's face and felt her pulse race. The black mask was molded with high cheekbones and a wide nose. The narrow slit for the eyes was covered with a clear material. The guard's breathing rasped loudly through some apparatus she could not see.

"Destination," the guard demanded in a mechanical, uninflected voice. "The, uh, Market," Barbara stammered.

"Identification." The guard held out a gloved hand.

What could he want? "Jeez, with all this going on, I must have left it in the apartment."

The guard lowered his hand. "You cannot enter the Market without your identity card."

Card. "Well, let me see," she muttered. She reached into her back pocket and pulled out the black business card Zoltan had given her so long ago and presented it to the guard. She hoped to hell that was what he was looking for.

He took a thin metal rod, about six inches long, from a pocket in his tunic and ran it over the card.

Seconds passed. Then a green light at the end of the rod blinked green. "You have clearance to the Market."

He stood aside and allowed Barbara to pass. She walked through the open elevator door. "Down," she said.

Chapter 35

BARBARA WAS ALONE IN THE elevator car as it began its descent to the Market. She unzipped her hoodie and pulled it off, along with the baseball cap. Underneath the sweatshirt, she wore a fashionable cream- colored silk blouse, tailored and flattering. She looked at herself in the old mirror in the car and undid her top button. She shook her red curls loose enjoying the feel of them brushing her face.

The car creaked to a stop. She scooped up her shirt and hat and bundled them in her hand as the door slid open.

For the second time she stopped at the entrance to the Market, her eyes sweeping upward in awe at the mammoth tiled roof that loomed overhead. For a moment, she felt as if she were caught like a fly under a giant teacup.

She looked around quickly and wondered if Paulson and Hickey had somehow made their way to the Market and were looking for the ratty little guy Paulson had seen at the elevator entrance. A young man walked toward her, his red tunic open to his tooled leather belt, his long black hair tied in a ponytail. He raised his eyebrows at her as he walked by. After a few steps, she saw him turn his head and eye her approvingly. She smiled. Apparently, she didn't look like a ratty little guy any longer.

Several large wooden rubbish barrels flanked the arched entranceway. Barbara walked to the nearest one and casually tossed her cap and bundled shirt inside. She felt a pang of loss. She had bought the black hoodie for the trek through the subway maze. It had served her well.

Inside the entrance, it seemed like business as usual. Storefront doors opened onto the great courtyard in the center of the Market, and men and women milled around the enormous, tiled commonage as they had during her first visit. But Barbara sensed that something was different. There was unease in the air. Conversations were tense, faces strained. People looked up as she went by, their eyes narrowing suspiciously.

She stood to one side and assessed the situation. Knots of red and black-clad workers stood talking and gesticulating. One group on the other side of the entrance was talking loudly to a guard, his scimitar blade raised in protection. As she scanned the giant room, she saw several other guards, their red helmets gleaming in the overhead sun.

There was no reason to draw attention to herself. She looked across the crowd and could just make out Mrs. Harlow's shop perhaps 200 yards away. Her impulse was to run across the cavernous room to the sanctuary of the shop, the sanctuary of Zoltan's arms. Instead, she circulated clockwise around the perimeter of the giant circle, glancing at wares spread on tables outside shops, nodding amiably at tradespeople, blending into the crowd. She passed the entrance to the bank, wondering how long her unlimited credit would last, and then by the front of Madame Jeanine's Travel agency with the words "We Specialize In Where No One Else Goes" written across the front window. For a moment she considered going inside, maybe sharing that Primitivo Madame Jeanine had offered Zoltan what seemed like years ago and assuring her that they had made it back. But somehow, she knew Madame Jeanine would know that already.

She finished her slow circuit, staying clear of guards, who walked ominously about the floor, their covered eyes raking the crowds, their breathing rasping gently, unnervingly, in and out.

Then she was at the door of the shop. She wanted to rush in, slamming the door behind her, but instead, she glanced at the red and gold letters in the window as if reading them for the first time: "Necklaces/Settings." She turned the knob on the door and walked inside, almost collapsing in relief when she heard the bell tinkle.

"My, god, Barbara!" Zoltan shot up from a chair by the window, joy flooding his face. He ran to her and hugged her so hard she could hardly breathe. She wrapped her arms around his neck and held on, her face against his cheek.

"Zoltan," she managed at last. "I can't breathe!"

Zoltan loosened his grip and held her by the shoulders, his black eyes bright. "I thought you were gone, that I would never see you again," he stammered. "It has been so long, and then the siren and the guards." He dropped his hands to his sides. "Please, what has happened? Are you all right?"

"I'm fine. I'll tell you about it." She dug into her jeans pocket and pulled out the small leather bag with the flash drive and handed it to Zoltan. "Here," she said.

Zoltan took the bag and slipped it into his jacket pocket. "I should never have let you go," he said softly.

"Zoltan," Mrs. Harlow said softly. She had emerged from behind the curtains and stood watching. "Give the poor woman a chance to sit down."

"Of course," Zoltan said, taking Barbara by the arm and leading her to the chair. "You must sit."

Barbara looked nervously out the window. "Is your shop sanctuary, Mrs. Harlow?"

Mrs. Harlow's face turned grim. "Theoretically. But I do not like the feel of this." She drew the curtains aside and nodded toward the rear of the workshop. "Please. You will be safer in the back rooms."

Barbara followed Mrs. Harlow through the curtains and past the red velvet-covered workbenches. Workers bent over microscopes and computer screens looked at them as they passed, nodding and whispering. Mrs. Harlow opened the door at the rear of the workshop and saw them into the hallway.

"I believe you can find your way from here?"

Zoltan nodded formally to Mrs. Harlow. "We are indebted."

Mrs. Harlow brushed his comment aside with her hand. "Nonsense. What you have brought us is a professional challenge. And, perhaps, part of a danger we have only heard tales about." She gestured with her head toward the front of the shop. "It has been many years since we had armed troopers in the Market. And perhaps even longer since we had a major security breach in the Building. I don't believe that these events are unrelated to the stones you have brought us."

"You are very kind," Zoltan said. "I am sorry if we have caused distress."

"You misunderstand me, Mr. DeAngelo. I feel the threat you have brought to us is one we have ignored. Maybe even profited from. It is time for us to support those who take action against it." She nodded down the hall toward the round sitting area at the end of the hall. "I believe you have much to talk about. And we have a great deal of work to do."

Zoltan nodded again. "Indeed. But I have one more favor to ask."

Mrs. Harlow cocked her head slightly. "Of course."

Zoltan pulled the leather bag from his pocket. "May I give you this?"

Mrs. Harlow put out her hand and closed it tightly as Zoltan placed the bag in her open palm. She placed the bag in a small pocket of her leather apron and sealed it with a finger. "It will be safe."

"Thank you," Zoltan said. "It is a…"

Mrs. Harlow cut him off with a wave of her hand. "I do not need to know what is in the bag, Mr. DeAngelo. Nor do I wish to."

"Of course. But it is of great importance."

Mrs. Harlow looked slightly insulted. "I assumed as much."

"Yes, yes," Zoltan nodded. "But for your safety, let no one know you have it." He paused. "And if Barbara and I are killed or disappear, I would ask you to turn it over to the Syndicate Board, yes?"

Mrs. Harlow looked at Zoltan gravely. "You have my word."

Zoltan stood tall and gave a short, sharp nod, his arms at this side.

Mrs. Harlow motioned through the doorway. "Please." They entered, and as the door closed, Barbara heard a soft whir and then a click.

The two of them entered the sitting area; soft light from the ceiling bloomed, illuminating the round room. Barbara settled into a large sack chair that enveloped her in soft burgundy suede. Her head sank back into the leather. She breathed deeply.

"Zoltan?"

He had pulled up a stuffed chair and sat in front of her. "Yes, madam?"

"Can I keep my eyes closed while I tell you what happened?"

There was a moment of silence. "Yes, madam. You most certainly may."

Chapter 36

"PAULSON CALLED THE MAN WITH him Hickey?"

Barbara nodded as best she could without raising her head from the comforting softness of the chair. "Do you know him?"

"No, I do not. But then I really had little to do with the Market. I rarely left the Building except for work. But I do know there has been an underground of criminals for nearly as long as the Market has been open. As I said, where there is money, there are thieves. But many years ago they formed into an organized force. There was a very violent confrontation."

"Yes, I keep hearing about that. What went on?"

"As I say, it did not affect me that much personally, so I did not pay too much attention at the time." He paused. "Perhaps that is part of the problem, yes? We only get involved when it touches us. And then it is often too late."

Barbara listened quietly, her eyes still closed.

"Banking here is fairly new. Before the Syndicate initiated our current system, tradespeople kept their money in their shops or homes. In the early days, most did not even lock their doors. Then the robberies began. At first it was just one or two shops that did not lock up at night. But then it got worse."

"Break-ins?"

"Yes. Windows were smashed. Doors kicked in. People became fearful. Distrustful of each other. They could not understand why this was happening. It was not a large community. Could people inside be stealing from each other? It was a very difficult time. Then, tradespeople taking their goods outside for sale were assaulted on the train by armed robbers in black masks. The market traders had their money and products stolen. Finally, a book merchant was killed." Zoltan nodded toward the entrance to the Market. "Just a few feet from the elevator."

"Oh, no."

"Yes. It was the first murder in the history of the Market. New members were elected to the Syndicate. They were determined to stop the crime. Reestablish peace, yes? But of course, that is not always easy. And they used an old strategy. They created the Security Force."

She recalled the sentry at the elevator, intimidating and cold. "The guards in the red helmets."

"Yes. They patrolled the Market, and for a while people felt safe. But then, the Security guards became more aggressive. They began questioning innocent people, interrogating them. We were not used to that, yes? We had lived in our bubble, you see, for a very long time. People became angry, refused to cooperate. Some of the guards beat those who resisted. Several were put in a jail underneath the Market. And despite the heavy-handed tactics, the robberies continued."

Barbara sat up and cupped her chin in her palms. "So who were the criminals then?"

"Yes, who indeed? It turned out it was not people from the Market. Though a few collaborated. No. For the most part it was the Gagna. From the tunnels."

"Gagna?"

"It was a name they took for themselves. They lived all through the subway system, in abandoned stations, old lines. Normally they ran in small bands. But they heard about the Market and all of its wealth. Later we learned from some of them that a person had come from above and organized them into a small army. They would infiltrate as outside buyers or even dress in Market uniforms. They would carry out a theft, sometimes at gunpoint, and then disappear into the maze of tunnels, which they knew very well. The outsider took the goods they stole and paid them, sometimes in food and weapons. Then it came to a head."

"There was more violence?"

"Yes. One day, the Gagna stormed the Market. I was not here. I had travelled on business, but those who were say there were 100 or more."

Barbara leaned forward. "Did the guards stop them?"

"No. That is the irony. When the security perimeter was breached, the guards mobilized. There was a pitched battle in the tunnels – the Gagna raided from both ends of the platform, and many on both sides were killed. But the Gagna overran the Security Forces. They forced their way into the Market carrying guns and knives. Howling."

Barbara tried to imagine a screaming mob invading the Market through its only exit. "It sounds terrifying."

"Yes. But this is where it gets interesting. Once the alarm was raised, the people of the Market left their shops. They took up axes, poles, chairs. They formed a phalanx in the center of the Market. In the front, a small group of men and women carried trash container lids as shields."

"The tops of garbage cans?"

"Yes. But they were treated steel, designed to be resistant to wear. They proved quite as resistant to bullets. With the Gagna pouring through the entrance, the Market column counter charged. When the Gagna saw the people not rushing away or hiding but charging at them, they panicked. They were pushed back into the tunnels. There, the remaining guards killed and captured many of them."

"But I never heard anything about this," Barbara exclaimed. "How could all of this occurred, and it not be on the news?"

"Ah, yes. As you have seen, we operate somewhat, how should I put it, independent of the outside world. There are people here able to *regulate* what is known about what takes place here, yes?"

"Yes." She glanced around the round room, glowing pink. "That much I appreciate. So what was the outcome?"

"The people then charged to the Syndicate quarters and pulled the officials out of their offices. They took them back to the Circle – you know the black tiled star at the center of the Market?"

"Yes. I remember it."

"It was placed there to commemorate the resistance. It was there the people confronted the Syndicate leaders. But of course, some people defended their actions. They said the Security Force had been necessary. But the majority said they did more harm than good. The people released all the prisoners and then brought the guards to trial. The guards responsible for violence against Market folk were banished forever. The old Syndicate board was removed. Several left the Market, but others are still here. The Security Force was reduced to a few guards who were limited to patrolling the outer tunnels. Unless there was a major security breach."

"Like today."

"Yes. They returned from their posts and re-entered the Building and Market in uniform for the first time in years."

"I see. And the Gagna?"

"As I mentioned, several had been captured. They were really a pathetic lot. Some were mentally ill. Some had lived below ground for many years. They had been reduced to living on rats and what they could steal in furtive forays above ground at night. The Market folk took pity on them. They asked for a meeting. Where the black star is now. Many came. Some were apprenticed." Zoltan nodded vaguely toward the Market. "Some became great craftsmen and women. They are here now. Others could not live in a society. But they were given food. In fact, one of the guard's functions even today is to make weekly food drops at points north and south of the station."

"And Hickey. He could have been one of the Gagna?"

"Possibly. Or one of the Market collaborators, perhaps."

Barbara stared thoughtfully toward the ceiling. "That is when the Syndicate began sanctuary?"

"Yes. People were still frightened. What if another gang invaded? What if hit men wanted to kill a Market folk? Or extort at gunpoint? The new Syndicate board brought technicians to the problem, even a select few from outside. They created the sanctuary system with its cameras, its ability to neutralize violent men or women before they could do harm, though they could not cover the entire Market zone."

"Yes. Including the Building, it would appear. Neither Paulson nor his buddy seemed much concerned."

"No, they would not be. Now, if you please, you will finish your story, yes? There is much afoot we do not understand.”

“As you keep pointing out,” Barbara said. “But first, the stones. Mrs. Harlow has begun analyzing them?”

“Yes.” Zoltan studied his hands clasped in his lap. “It is early yet. But what she is finding confirms what you suspected.”

“Some of the agents’ stones have the receptor.”

“Not exactly.” Zoltan was quiet for a moment. “They have only tested four, including mine.”

“And the dark ones have it, right?”

“Yes. That is true. The first one they examined had the receptor. What Mrs. Harlow is calling the anomaly.”

“And that jewel is dark?”

Zoltan nodded. “A very deep, dark green. Very beautiful. But then they tested three more.”

Barbara looked perplexed. “Zoltan, what are you trying to tell me?”

“It is only four, but so far all of the agents’ stones contain the receptor.”

“Oh, I see.” She said slowly. “And that means…”

“Mine as well. Yes.”

Barbara looked over Zoltan’s shoulder. “But yours is a translucent blue green, like a calm sea.” She paused. “It doesn’t make sense.”

“Perhaps others will prove not to possess the anomaly. We will know more tomorrow.”

“Why would he insert the receptor into jewels he kept in a vault?” She looked at Zoltan. “It worries you, I can see. You fear it may give him control over you again. That some dormant evil will be activated.”

Zoltan gazed at her. “I can hide nothing from you, it seems. A week ago I would have been amazed. Now it just confirms what I have suspected.”

“What do you mean?”

Zoltan waved his hand. “Later, please. But first I need to hear the last of your story.” He sighed. “I am so sorry I let you get…”

“Zoltan,” Barbara said dangerously.

“Sorry. Do excuse me, but I was so…scared.” He leaned forward in his chair. “You cannot know how scared I was. And then the alarm. My fear turned to guilt. I do not know if I could have gone on if you had been killed.”

When had anyone expressed such concern for her? "I'm *sure* I couldn't have," Barbara joked. "But fortunately, neither of us has to worry about that. For now."

Zoltan reached out and covered her hand, which was resting on the soft suede. "Please, madam. I cannot view the matter with humor."

She looked into his eyes. They smoldered, she thought. With concern, worry, anger. And something else. Love, perhaps?

"Zoltan," she said. "Before I go on, I need to tell you something."

He cocked his head slightly. "Please."

"When I found the flash drive, there was something else in the drawer. A photo album." She closed her eyes and laid her head back on the chair, recalling the pictures. "They were very special pictures that I believe you took." She imagined the photos, each a passionate study of Rebecca, her eyes brimming with warmth and love as she posed for the gentle gaze of his camera.

"Black and white, but still you were able to capture her beauty. Each was luminous, alive." She paused. "But there was one, the last picture. You were with her. The two of you, naked. You were looking into each other's eyes." She saw the picture again in her mind, the bodies entwined in an embrace that was both chaste and erotic.

Sobs broke her musing. She opened her eyes and sat up. In front of her, Zoltan had his head back, his hand over his eyes. His body shuddered, and he wept uncontrollably.

"Zoltan," she said in alarm. "I'm sorry. I didn't mean to upset you." She took his other hand. "It was just so beautiful. I think I finally understood." She shook her head. "Please, Zoltan. I didn't mean to pry, to make you sad."

Zoltan's sobbing gradually subsided. He breathed deeply for several seconds and removed his hand, his head still against the chair back.

"No, madam. You did not pry. And you did not make me sad." He lowered his tear-streaked face and stared at her with great, dark eyes. "You made me love again."

"I... I didn't know it would affect you like that."

"No," Zoltan said, managing a small smile. "You did not. That is because you do not know your power." Zoltan wiped the tears away with the palm of his hand. "It is what I mentioned earlier. You do not understand that you have become an empath."

"I'm sorry?"

"I suspected it when I saw how you connected with Caraldo. And then when we were at the airport. I felt your panic surge through me. I wasn't sure, but I thought for certain there was a train bearing down on me. That is when you asked if I was having a heart attack."

"Zoltan, what are you talking about?"

"And then on the train. When I asked if you were thinking about me?"

Barbara withdrew her hand to her chest, flustered.

"I knew exactly how you were seeing me." He smiled. "It was very flattering."

Barbara felt herself blushing again. "But I don't see what that has to do with anything."

"And just now. You felt my concern, my worry. You have always been a person who can feel what others feel, see what they could see. You were able to reflect that back, yes?"

Barbara thought about her friends telling her how she always seemed to understand them, to hear what they said and feel what they felt. "Yes, I suppose, but…"

Zoltan raised his hand. "That is no doubt why you were targeted for a gem. Somehow, they sensed this ability and they wanted to use it. But they misjudged, yes? They knew your skill but not your integrity. They could not bend you to their will." Zoltan reached out and took her hand again. "You have developed, madam, in so many ways. But one is that you now not only feel other's emotions deeply, but you can also cause others to feel them as well, even if they do not wish to. And at its most intense, you project your own emotions onto others. And sometimes your memories and mental images."

An empath. Barbara sat in the chair, holding her free hand over her jewel, feeling it pulse almost imperceptibly. She knew he was right.

"Zoltan," she said softly. "It scares me."

"It is getting stronger, yes?"

Barbara nodded. "It's always been there, but now…Now these images, these emotions. Sometimes they just flood through me. What I feel from you now is warm, comforting. But it flows in from all over. From everyone. Sometimes…"

The memory of the *Mester's* black hatred, the menace from Zhukov returned with such power she flinched and squeezed her eyes shut.

"Barbara…"

"It's just that I don't know how to stop them, to control the thoughts, the feelings. Sometimes it's like, you know, I'm a windsock, blown one way and then another.

Zoltan covered her hand with his. "Your skill is strengthening but you have no filters, yes?"

"Yes, that's it. I have no filters."

"It will get better, I believe, as you learn. But you must practice, to protect yourself. You must develop a shield to avoid absorbing unwanted thoughts, energies." She looked up into his gentle black eyes.

"A shield."

"Yes. I am not an empath, certainly not like you, but this I learned so long ago. A way to keep out the pain without shutting off. Visualize a shield around your body that repels the negative, the hurtful. Like a protective bubble, yes? That allows you to keep your balance, not be emotionally overwhelmed. Then you can better focus, choose what you wish to hear, to feel."

"Is it my jewel? Is that what this is about?"

"Barbara, as I have said so many times, the jewel can do nothing but reveal who you truly are, to accelerate the skills you have. But your jewel will be a grounding for you, yes? It will help you strengthen your shield, to clear your mind. To help you at stressful times."

Her hand closed more firmly over the gem at her throat.

Chapter 37

MRS. HARLOW OPENED A DOOR off the workshop. "Mr. DeAngelo, Barbara. Would you please step inside?"

Zoltan stood aside as Barbara entered and then followed. Mrs. Harlow closed the heavy metal door and typed a sequence on a keypad. A soft click. She motioned to a round table in the middle of the windowless room. The table was covered with the same red velvet as the workbenches outside. Two computer monitors faced the wall at one end. In the center of the table a stainless-steel tray held all 12 of the agents' rings. Zoltan's was at the top, a shimmering, lustrous cerulean teardrop. A small metal box was pushed into a corner of the tray.

A man and woman were already seated. Both wore the red and black of the Market and the leather aprons Barbara had seen on all of the workers in Mrs. Harlow's workshop. The man stood as Barbara approached.

Mrs. Harlow gestured at the upholstered chairs around the table. "Please. Do have a seat. We have a good deal to discuss."

As Zoltan and Barbara sat, Mrs. Harlow nodded at the technicians. "I have asked Pierre and Samantha to join us. These are very complex problems you have brought us, quite beyond my realm. Pierre and Sam are my molecular physics team, two of the most brilliant in the world."

Barbara leaned forward slightly. Pierre was younger than she thought a world-class physicist should be, dark-skinned with handsome brown eyes and sculpted cheekbones. Curls of dense black hair were cropped short.

"I assure you, Ms...?" He spoke in a soft, gently accented voice.

"Barbara," she said. "Please, just call me Barbara."

He nodded. "I assure you I am older than I look."

Barbara looked at him in surprise and shot a glance at Zoltan.

"Yes, I see that now." She paused. "And you are worried. Puzzled. You are not sure about what you have found and do not think we will be able to understand."

Pierre sat back, his eyebrows raised.

"You are right, Barbara," Samantha broke in. Barbara turned toward her. She wore her black hair in two braided pigtails tied at the ends with red ribbon. Her face was narrow and pale; deep lines of concentration were etched into her forehead. Her lips were pressed into a thin line, but the sparkle of her deep brown eyes made her seem less severe.

"What we have found is deeply perplexing," she continued. "We do not have the entire context for these gems." She inclined her head toward the tray in front of her. "And that is really none of our affair. But what we have found indicates that you are involved in a venture of extraordinary dimensions."

Zoltan placed his hands on the table, his fingers interlaced. "We are deeply grateful to you and your team for your work on these stones. We know it was short notice. As you have suggested, what we have brought you is a part of a larger affair of considerable importance. The details are not necessary for you to know, and there is a need for secrecy." Zoltan leaned across the table toward the two physicists, fixing them with his black eyes. "And for your own safety, it is better you know no more than necessary. But your input is critical." He paused, his eyes shifting from one fact to the other. "Perhaps more critical than any of us fully understand."

The silence that followed was only broken by the creak of a chair as Pierre shifted in his seat and the low hum of a white noise machine.

"Very well," Mrs. Harlow began. "Let us get started. It is as we suspected." She placed her hand on the edge of the wood tray with the agents' jewels. "All 12 gems have the anomaly we have spoken of."

Barbara sensed Zoltan's unease and turned toward him.

"Yes," he said. "I see. Please, go on."

"Pierre, can you take it from here?"

Pierre nodded and leaned forward, his hands gesturing as he spoke.

"The anomaly in these stones," he nodded at the tray, "is one of two molecular clusters that do not fit the normal crystal profile we would expect." He looked around the table. "In fact, it is not consistent with any molecular architecture ever recorded. As you know, the one cluster is found in all of Mr. DeAngelo's jewels. We have seen it without exception. Because it is activated locally, it appears, it seems to act as an accelerator that agitates the atoms around it."

Pierre paused. "Based on what we have learned, it could serve to strengthen certain emanations from the bearer."

"The jewel would only accentuate what is there," Zoltan said.

Samantha nodded. "That is correct. It is a short-range receiver that is consistent with but separate from the molecular structure of the gem."

"And the second cluster, the anomaly?"

Pierre sat back heavily in his chair, rocking slightly back and forth. "Yes. The anomaly. That is quite another matter."

Samantha turned from Pierre and faced Barbara and Zoltan. "You are familiar with brain waves?"

Barbara rifled through her mental biology files from high school.

"Broadly," Zoltan replied. "Neurons use electricity to communicate with each other. The resulting electrical activity appears as waves with various frequencies. Alpha, beta, and theta, if I recall correctly."

Samantha nodded. "And delta, yes. These are not unlike radio waves, which are a form electromagnetic radiation created at a source and transmitted as waves of various frequencies. These waves can then be picked up by a receiver tuned to the transmission frequency, often through the use of a crystal oscillator that resonates at a particular frequency."

"What we have found," Pierre continued, "is that the anomalies are tiny resonators tuned to a single, highly selective wavelength and modularity."

"That means how often the wave peaks and the distance between those peaks," Samantha clarified.

Pierre nodded. "Generally electromagnetic radiations are classified into seven categories by length, from radio waves to gamma rays. The waves the receivers in the stones are tuned to receive are not on this spectrum. They are set to receive one signal. A signal so broad we have no name for it. We have labeled it an omega wave."

"We are calling the molecular cluster a receiver," Samantha said. "But in fact it is more than that. It does in fact receive, but it also acts as a transmitter, able to send the information it receives to the brain as infra-low brainwaves. These are below even delta waves, so low little is known about them. It would appear that what is received at this frequency would be unconscious."

They sat quietly for a moment. "If this receiver is tuned to only one frequency, a frequency that is not on the known spectrum," Zoltan said, "that would suggest that there is a single transmitter, yes?"

Samantha looked at Pierre. She reached into the corner of the wood tray and lifted out the metal box. It was small, only three- or four-inches square, but it was clearly heavy, and Samantha picked it up with her fingers with effort. She set the box on the red velvet in front of her and opened the lid.

Inside, the *Mester*'s ring with its black stone lay on a square of red velvet. "Yes," Samantha said. "And this is it."

"We have studied this stone with great care," Pierre continued. "It is quite remarkable. The mass of the stone is made up of a dense material we have never seen. It is on no periodical table. But what is most extraordinary is its core. We could hardly penetrate its electron haze. When we did, we discovered that its nucleus contains 150 protons. That is 20 more than any known element."

Barbara suddenly wished she had paid more attention in her physics classes. "What does that mean, exactly?"

"What you have here," Samantha answered, "is a tiny nuclear reactor. It functions to create electrons."

"I'm sorry. I still don't follow you."

"A peculiar fact of physics is that while there are no electrons in the nucleus of an atom, electrons are produced there," Samantha continued. "We have been able to detect the electrons produced. Though they are particles, they can be thought of as waves. We are learning there is little difference between matter and energy."

The physicist nodded at the stone in front of her. "Energy is introduced into the core of this stone. The nucleus then produces electrons, electro-magnetic particles that travel at a wavelength only the receptors in the stones can receive."

Barbara stared at the black stone. "What does it transmit?"

"That is the question, isn't it?" Pierre said. "The question only you can answer. But in the possession of one so inclined," Pierre nodded at the box, "a powerful message could be fed into the transmitter, received by the receptor in the stone, and then delivered directly to the brain, registering as a basal instinct, with the recipient unaware of how he or she was being programmed."

Barbara leaned forward. "OK. So the *Mester's* stone transmits to the agents' gems, which pick up the signals and send then out as waves that register in the agents' unconscious."

Sam nodded.

"But these stones were locked up in a safe in London," Barbara continued. "The agents didn't have them in their possession. So how could they have transmitted to the agents, who could be thousands of miles away?"

"A very good question," Pierre said. "We are not sure yet, but…" He looked to Samantha for help.

Sam spread her hands palm down on the table. "We are scientists," she said, staring at her hands. "We like dealing with facts, hard data. Known quantities. But physics takes us places that are often grey."

Samantha looked at Barbara's puzzled face and glanced at Pierre.

"What we believe is happening is this," Pierre began, his accent rounding his words. "Through a process we do not understand each of the stones has been attenuated to the owners, carefully synchronized to each agent's…"

"Soul?" Zoltan suggested.

Samantha smiled slightly. "Perhaps. Or perhaps that is a metaphor for some portion of the brain we do not yet recognize. In any event, this extraordinary 'personality' of each stone, we believe, bypasses the need for the gem to be in the owner's possession. The signal is transferred from the stone directly to the unconscious of the owner, regardless of his location."

Zoltan nodded. "We were always under surveillance, our whereabouts always known to the *Mester;* even our actions and thoughts, no?"

"*Bien sûr,*" Pierre agreed. "But only dimly I am guessing. The gems were designed more *to* send messages to you rather than to receive *from* you."

They sat in silence for several seconds. Zoltan stared past the physicists at the pink wall behind them.

"I see," Zoltan said at last, almost to himself. He glanced at the black stone in the heavy metal box. "And they would feed us a steady drip of sadness, helplessness, loss. A subconscious chatter reminding us that we were weak and alone, dependent on the *Mester* for our very lives.

"And each year, at our meetings in the compound, we were given our stones for the duration of our stay. He would recalibrate them. The signal would be much stronger in the *Mester's* presence, yes?"

"Most certainly," Pierre agreed.

"So he would impregnate us with the bitter sense of hopelessness, impotence. A kind of booster shot," he mused. "Afterwards he would only need the weaker signal to maintain our compliance and oscitancy."

As he spoke, Zoltan's voice changed little, his modulation seemingly calm and reflective. But Barbara watched as his dark eyes moved from dull and sad to an angry, dangerous glitter.

Zoltan nodded at the *Mester's* black stone. "Can it be destroyed?"

Pierre shook his head. "The surrounding material is beyond our molecular knowledge. We know of no means to penetrate to the core molecule. Not even an electron accelerator would have an impact."

"But surely," Barbara interjected, "without the *Mester* the stone has no power." She nodded at the stone, as dull and lifeless as a chip of coal.

"Perhaps," Samantha said, "But there is a worry. We do not know from what range input can be directed through the transmitter." She looked at Zoltan. "In fact, it is possible that the man you speak of, the *Mester*, may not have been the source of the transmissions at all, or at least not the only one."

Zoltan's eyes snapped upward to look into Samantha's face. "Repeat please."

Samantha tilted her head quizzically. "We do not know if the *Mester* was even the source of the transmissions." She paused. "You have someone in mind?"

"Perhaps," Zoltan said slowly. "In other words" he continued, "even now, even though you have the stone, the transmitter, others could theoretically still use it."

Samantha nodded.

"That is the reason for the metal box, yes?"

"Yes," Mrs. Harlow said. "And a very special metal box. It is made of an alloy that cannot be penetrated by electromagnetic waves or particles."

All five people at the table stared at the ring inside. "It seems we are very fortunate to have the stone in our possession," Zoltan said. "Now, it seems, my task is to destroy it."

Pierre and Samantha glanced at each other but said nothing.

"You don't think it can be done," Barbara said quietly, still staring at the black stone in the box. "That it is indestructible."

"And so it may prove to be," Zoltan added. "But I will not be free until the stone is shattered." He looked up. "And the masters of the stone, all of them, are crushed along with this evil black rock."

He reached over and snapped the lid shut. He stood and faced the two physicists. He pressed his arms to his thighs and bowed. "I cannot tell you how much we appreciate your work. We are deeply indebted."

Samantha looked searchingly into his face and then Barbara's. "I believe we are the ones who should be indebted to you. We don't know what you are facing, but we can see the extent of its power, its capacity for evil." She paused. "We wish you well."

Mrs. Harlow walked to door and opened it for the physicists. She glanced back at Barbara and Zoltan and followed, closing the door behind her.

Zoltan sat down and stared at the box on the table. Silence filled the room. "So," Barbara said finally. "What now?"

Zoltan looked up and smiled gently. "For me, it is clear, yes? For you, perhaps not so much."

"God, you can be frustrating," Barbara exclaimed. "What the hell does that mean?"

Zoltan returned his gaze to the box. "I have no choice. The *Mester's* gem must be destroyed."

"And you have to do it?"

He looked up and shrugged. "Who else?"

"There are other agents. You can contact them." She nodded toward the door. "Mrs. Harlow, Sam, and Pierre. And maybe the Market council."

"Madam, you know that is not possible. When I awoke from my long stupor, when you finally opened my eyes, I vowed to stop this madness. To end this evil."

"But you have! The *Mester* is probably dead. If not, he's crippled and weakened." He shook his head. "Remember Caraldo's words?"

Barbara slumped in her chair. "It's not over."

He nodded. "At least for me, madam. You on the other hand made no such vow. You could and should leave now." She saw the fierceness in his eyes. "For both of our sakes. I could not bear to see you die."

"No, no," she said angrily. "It's not that, you idiot. I signed on to this adventure because I had nothing to lose, no life to return to." She caught her breath. "Don't you see? Now I have something to live for." She paused. "Us."

His eyes softened. "Madam…"

"No, wait. We could make a new life for ourselves. Somewhere. Maybe Australia, where you worked. You are a brilliant photographer. We could start over."

"A bit late to start a new career at my age, yes? Madam, you do me a great honor. But I cannot. Not now. First, I must retake *this* life. I cannot live with regret, with the knowledge that this evil continues."

Barbara smiled wanly. "I knew you were going to say that."

"Yes, I suspect you did. Now, the question is what you will do. Truly, I urge you to think hard. My path will only lead to fear and terror. Unimaginable darkness and almost certainly death."

She knew Zoltan was right. She could not see the outline of what was to come, but she already felt the black tentacles creeping into her consciousness. He was also right – the path from here was hers to choose. For the first time, perhaps ever, her life was hers to decide. She was in charge now. She had no expectations to meet other than her own.

She remembered what she had told Zoltan so long ago in the garden: *The Aries hunter will not settle for something mundane but will push until the flame can burn the brightest.*

"Surely, you jest, sir. Would any red-blooded Aries pass on this?" She grinned. "What do we do next?"

Read on for an excerpt from the next Soul Catcher novel,

The Tunnels of Buda

Coming soon from Castle Bridge Media

Chapter 1

ZOLTAN STOPPED TYPING AND LEANED back heavily in his chair. He stared blankly at the words on the screen then peered over the tops of his round glasses at the room they were in. It was a backroom in Mrs. Harlow's specialty jewelry store, windowless and, other than the desk where he and Barbara sat, empty except for a scattering of chairs and a round table covered in deep red velvet in the middle of the room. And a simple wood tray holding eleven jewels.

The soft light from the glowing white walls played across the gem's facets, exploding in dazzling shades of blue, green, yellow, almost as if they were alive. Zolta sat a dozen feet away, and even from that distance the jewels glowed with startling intensity.

His gaze fixed on a single small box made of what looked like lead but was in fact an alloy so dense it was impenetrable. It held, he knew, a simple black stone set in a gold ring, a stone of such power and evil it was hidden, locked in a container created especially to muzzle it, to arrest its dark emanations, a stone Zoltan knew he must destroy at any cost.

It had only been a few hours since they had met with Samantha and Pierre, Mrs. Harlow's molecular physics team, who, she claimed, were two of the most brilliant physicists in the world. Zoltan had no reason to doubt it. Here in the Market, located deep below the streets of New York in a gigantic subway terminal abandoned in 1873, there were many brilliant minds and talented artisans with arcane – some would say – supernatural skills and knowledge.

Two hours. Two hours since they had learned the terrible truth about the gems in the tray. Yes, and the black stone.

"You are hesitant," Barbara said from the chair next to him.

Zoltan brought his eyes to the woman sitting next to him, who was studying his profile.

"You are imagining an avalanche, poised on a mountain side, appearing stable, a face of snow and ice that when triggered sweeps everything in front of it to oblivion."

He glanced into the deep green eyes of the woman, a small smile on his face. Barbara's empathic skills had grown to the point that, at times, it seemed as if she knew his thoughts and feelings better than he did. And in so short a time.

He thought back to the night – early morning, actually -- when Barbara knocked on his apartment door, the first person to do so in years. How, against all of his instincts, he had invited her in, touched her, divulged his true name, abandoning DeAngelo, the name given to him by the *Mester* forever.

BAHr-ba-ra, he thought. *The woman from a foreign land, the Santeria goddess of fire, lightning, and thunder.*

How long ago was that? he wondered. *When she crashed into my life, when she forced me to open my eyes? A year? Month?* No, not that long. He counted the days in his head. The first night, and then Barbara's introduction to The Market. The day Mrs. Harlow agreed to make an unbreakable chain for Barbar's blazing red gem. The same day they met Caraldo and Zoltan learned the *Mester* knew he had violated his vows. The flight to Budapest, the nights with poor old Dezso. Reading of his murder, his head and hands severed and taken. Zoltan and Barbara's capture, and the tense flight to London and the *Mester's* compound. The near fatal confrontation there, Caraldo's death, Barbara chopping off the *Mester's* finger with the black-stoned ring and jamming the bloodless finger in her jeans. Scooping the agents' gems from the safe as they fled the carnage, escaping over the roof and finally back to the Market. Barbara's recovery of the flash drive from his apartment and barely eluding the *Mester's* agents.

And now, today the truth they had learned about the gems, the terrifying specter that they were far more than just beautiful stones, that they fed their owners a stream of darkness and despair, that they were connected to a powerful web of evil they were just beginning to comprehend.

So much in such a short time. How long has it been? Zoltan wondered once more.

"Eleven days," Barbara said quietly. "Wel 12 counting today. Less than two weeks since I came knocking on your door. Can you believe it?"

Zoltan looked at the woman and sighed. Her bright red hair fell across her face as she peered at the monitor. God she could be so beautiful. And exasperating.

"Barbara, you are reading my mind."

"Sorry," she said absently, still peering at the message on the screen.

"So, Madam, are you now telepathic as well as an empath?"

Barbara glanced up from the screen. "I don't think so, but you're pretty transparent right now. By the way, you misspelled 'colleagues'. It has two 'ls'."

He shook his head and smiled slightly. "I guess that happens when you turn 110, no?"

When Zoltan had revealed his age that first night, she feared she had pursued not a man who could help her escape her empty life, not to mention her asshole of a husband, but a total lunatic. Only as she accepted the world she had walked into did she believe Zoltan's story of escaping Hungary after the First World War, of a failed academic career, and of his rapturous love for Rebecca, a love so profound, so passionate that her death in 1940 shattered him. And how his emptiness drove him into the hands of the *Mester* and gem making, which paid well and gave him extended life, but at a terrible cost.

"Probably," she agreed. "But as you say, you do pretty well for a guy your age." She looked up at him studying his angular features, his silver hair swept back at the temples. And his eyes, black as obsidian. "And you look *really* good."

"Thank you, madam. I am most flattered." He gestured at the message on the screen. "You approve?"

She nodded slowly.

"This is it, then," Zoltan said solemnly. "When I click the send icon, the game is on, yes?"

Barbara breathed deeply. "Yes. But then it has been on for some time, I guess."

"You are right," Zoltan replied. "For a very long time, it seems. But we were not paying attention, no?"

"No."

Zoltan's finger hovered over the mouse. Barbara's heart fluttered as his finger touched the mouse button. There was a slight swoosh. He took his hand off and stared at the screen. A banner at the top informed them that the message had been sent. Would they like to view it?

Barbara reached over and moved the cursor to View Message.

A solid black page appeared on the left-hand screen. Photos of the 11 jewels lying in the tray on the table appeared on the other. Barbara read the message in white letters on the black page.

I am Zoltan József, a gem maker like you. If you know me at all it will be as DeAngelo. You will be surprised to receive this message as we have been prohibited from communicating among ourselves. However, over many years I have obtained your personal contact information, which I am using to notify you about significant occurrences you should be aware of. After I learned of the Mester's intention to kill or re-educate me two weeks ago, I fled to Budapest, where I obtained important and disturbing information on the nature of the Mester's organization, of which we are all a part. Much of this evidence came from one of our colleagues, Bokor Dezső, who I regret to report was murdered and beheaded by Boris Zhukov. Victor Caraldo was sent to capture me. I was taken to the Mester's compound for interrogation and to be executed. In an attempt to save my life, Victor Caraldo died after being stabbed by Zhukov, who was himself killed by a bullet from Caraldo's gun. In the struggle, the Mester was blinded and sustained other injuries. In the chaos I retrieved 12 agent jewels he kept in his office safe. This included my own. I do not know which gems belong to which agents, so I am sending photographs of each of the gems I managed to seize. I regret that I could not save the remaining jewels, but I believe the potential for each agent to repossess his gem is a very real possibility if we collaborate. However, given the nature of the information I have uncovered, I am only asking each of the agents whose gem is pictured on the second page of this message to join me at a refuge site in the Market. You will, of course, be able to reclaim your jewels at that time. I will also share with you certain facts I have uncovered. Information on when and where to meet is attached in the "agent-only" encryption.

She turned to the second screen and studied the stones pictured. Each was stunning, even in a photograph. Tiny facets reflected shards of red and green light, hearts of yellow and orange burned in the center of shimmering blue and sparkling gold gems. Unset, they lay, brilliant, on the red velvet behind them. She sensed the tug of each through the screen and thought of her sense of loss even for the night her gem was being set. What would the agents, separated from their jewels except for short periods, feel when they viewed their stone?

"I am sorry you are removed from the account of events," Zoltan said seriously. "It is not because I do not fully appreciate…"

"Hush," Barbara said, shaking her head. "Sometimes you can be such an idiot."

Zoltan's eyes widened. "My apologies. I meant no offense, I assure you."

She turned to Zoltan, green eyes blazing. "Eleven men will be arriving in two days. We know little to nothing about them. Some may not be happy with this change of circumstances. Some may even be agents of the *Mester*." Barbara paused. "Or worse. Don't you think I know that? The last thing we need is to tip our hand."

"Tip our hand?"

Barbara waved impatiently. "Old saying. It means don't reveal more than we need to. Don't let our plans fall into the wrong hands."

Zoltan sat back in the chair, nodding slightly. "I see. You seem to understand the situation well, yes? So could I ask a question?"

"Of course."

"These plans of ours. Could you share them with me, perhaps?"

Now Barbara leaned backward, swiveling in her chair to face Zoltan. "You don't have a plan?"

Zoltan shrugged. "Do you?"

"Well, no. But I sort of thought that was your department."

"I am sorry to disappoint you."

Barbara stared into Zoltan's dark eyes, but they gave nothing away.

Zoltan folded his hands in his lap. "But perhaps we could review the situation. Something might occur to us, no?"

"That would be nice," Barbara remarked dryly.

"As you say, two days from now, this room we are sitting in will be filled with 11 of the *Mester's* agents. They will have travelled from all over the world. I will recognize most and know a few, but none well." He paused. "Indeed, none of us knows any other agent well. As you have quite perceptively pointed out, it is likely some may not approve of our recent encounters with the *Mester*. Or the outcomes."

"Approve?" Barbara cut in. "We didn't exactly beg to be kidnapped and nearly killed."

Zoltan held up his hand. "Nonetheless, our encounter has resulted in significant changes within the organization these men have been part of, many for a very long time. People do not like change. Especially when it threatens their finances, their way of life."

"But Zoltan, what sort of life has it been? They were forced to live lives of utter loneliness. You couldn't even share your name! You were little more than slaves to the *Mester*."

Zoltan's head moved from side to side slightly. "Perhaps. But we agreed to the enslavement. And were well paid for it."

"Well paid! Zoltan, are you crazy? The price you paid – happiness, love, companionship! And to keep you docile, any rebellion meant the threatened destruction of your jewels, of your very selves. And now you find out he's been manipulating you, injecting self-loathing directly into your unconscious. Compensation aside, that's hardly most people's idea of a great career and terrific working conditions."

Zoltan smiled slightly. "Indeed it is not. But you must remember, agents are not most people. Each of us was chosen because we were utterly alone. Orphans in every sense. We wished to leave the world we found ourselves in. For some, it was depression so dark we saw no spark to illuminate the deep caves we inhabited in our minds. For others, perhaps an illness that made us unable to live with others. Whatever it was, each of us stood at the brink, desperate to hit the reset button, yes? One way or another. And then, out of the blackness, The *Mester* appears, and he gives us something we never had before. He gave us power. Power we never dreamed of."

"Power?"

"Oh, yes. What could be more powerful than seizing a portion of someone's very soul? To encapsulate it in a sparkling stone that I created?" His eyes darted upwards. "To destroy it."

Barbara stared at him in silence.

"And in all the years, few, very few, ever complained."

"Yes," Barbara said. "And they are dead."

"True. But even fewer came to their aid."

Barbara gripped the arms of her chair in exasperation. "So what's your point? That you wish you still enjoyed that idyllic life? That you resent me prying you out of your cushy world filled with happiness and joy?"

Zoltan looked at her evenly. "No, madam, that is not what I am saying." He nodded formally. "I will forever be indebted. But the others arriving will not have had a green-eyed empath in their lives, at least not for a very, very long time."

Barbara's hands relaxed. "I'm sorry." She glanced down at the carpeted floor. "Sometimes, I think, I feel guilty for all of this. It was my unhappiness, not yours, that got you into this mess."

Zoltan leaned forward and covered her hand with his. His black eyes softened. "Please, do not say that. Do not even think it, for it is not true. You have given me the greatest gift one can receive, something I never thought I would experience again. You made me feel once more, to care." He sat back. "I want you to remember the gem maker that came to your home, not so very long ago. What sort of man was he?"

Her mind slipped back to their first meeting, the mild jewelry salesman at her door. And then later, the day he returned to create her jewel, the slightly stuffy, undistinguished gem maker fussing with his camera, his eyes dark and sad. His stories not of his loves or achievements, but of the customers whom he had served, and especially the tragedies of those whose arrangements had gone wrong. She remembered the timid, frightened man who opened his apartment door to her the night she had crept through the subway.

She stared into Zoltan's eyes. "You are not that man anymore."

"Perhaps," Zoltan agreed. "But who I was? That is who will be here in two days."

And others," Barbara declared. "As I said, there will be agents of the *Mester*. I can sense it."

Zoltan looked at her quizzically.

"There are two, possibly three. They have another relationship with the *Mester*. I felt it in the stones. They work for him."

"We all work for him."

"Yes, but this is different. They are in contact. They are part of the circle somehow. Their allegiance is to him." She looked at the ceiling and thought about the tall figure in the brown robes Dezso told them about, the man who had enlisted the *Mester*. "And to his overlord, it would seem."

Zoltan sighed. "I suppose that was to be expected. But let me go on. They will arrive and we will have their stones, yes?"

Barbara nodded.

"We place the stones on a velvet-covered table in Mrs. Harlow's shop. As they arrive, they will enter the shop and find their gem."

"What if one of the agents chooses the wrong stone?"

Zoltan's hand dropped to the jewel in his vest pocket. One of the dozen gems Barbara had managed to scoop from the Mester's safe as they escaped his London compound had been his. After they returned to the Market, Mrs. Harlow had set Zoltan's magnificent gem, a gleaming sky-blue teardrop that contained a piece of his soul, in a simple gold hoop attached to a fine unbreakable chain. An unfamiliar warmth spread through his hand. "They will not, I assure you. They will select their gem. And then they will need time. It is quite overwhelming, to feel whole again."

Her hand pressed her stone between her breasts. "Yes. I think I understand."

"After all the agents have arrived and paired with their jewel, we will convene here." He nodded to the circular table in front of them. He stared silently at the empty chairs around the table.

"And then?"

"I will explain the events of the last few weeks. And then I will try to convince them to give up everything they have known for years and join me in a revolt against some mysterious *uberMester* who, it seems, is headquartered in a yet to be identified castle presumably in one of two dozen or so countries that can be reached from London by a jet helicopter in one night." Zoltan shrugged. "What could possibly go wrong?"

Aries are exciting, mercurial, daring, she thought. *We push until our flame can burn its brightest.* She snickered. *Of course, that works best if you don't die in the process.*

CASTLE BRIDGE MEDIA RECOMMENDS...

If you liked this book, you might also enjoy reading the following titles from Castle Bridge Media available on Amazon or by order at your favorite book store:

Animal Charmer
By Rain Nox

Austinites
By In Churl Yo

Bloodsucker City
By Jim Towns

The Burning Gem
By Don Sawyer

THE CASTLE OF HORROR ANTHOLOGY SERIES
Volume 1
Volume 2: Holiday Horrors
Volume 3: Scary Summer Stories
Volume 4: Women Running From Houses
Volume 5: Thinly Veiled: The 70s
Volume 6: Femme Fatales*
Volume 7: Love Gone Wrong
Volume 8: Thinly Veiled: The 80s
Volume 9: Young Adult
Volume 10: Thinly Veiled: Saturday Mournings
Edited By Jason Henderson and In Churl Yo
*Edited By P.J. Hoover

Castle of Horror Podcast Book of Great Horror: Our Favorites, Top Tens and Bizarre Pleasures
Edited By Jason Henderson

Cherry Dark
By R.L. Wilburn

Dream State
By Martin Ott

Dominic
By Lee Guzman

FRENCH DECEPTION
A Forgery in Paris
By Janice Nagourney
A Forgery in Lyon
By Janice Nagourney

FuturePast Sci-Fi Anthology
Edited by In Churl Yo

GLAZIER'S GAP
Ghosts of the Forbidden
By Leanna Renee Hieber

Hellfall
By Jay Gould

Isonation
By In Churl Yo

JAYU CITY CHRONICLES
The Hermes Protocol
By Chris M. Arnone
Necropolis Alpha
By Chris M. Arnone

Junk Film: Why Bad Movies Matter
By Katharine Coldiron

MID-LIFE CRISIS THRILLERS
18 Miles From Town
By Jason Henderson
Lost Angel
By Sam Knight
Ties That Kill
By Deven Greene

Nightwalkers: Gothic Horror Movies
By Bruce Lanier Wright

THE PATH
The Blue-Spangled Blue
By David Bowles
The Deepest Green
By David Bowles

SURF MYSTIC
Night of the Book Man
By Peyton Douglas
Dark of the Curl
By Peyton Douglas

Yesterday's Tomorrows: The Golden Age of Science Fiction Movies
By Bruce Lanier Wright

Please remember to leave us your reviews on Amazon and Goodreads!

THANK YOU FOR SUPPORTING INDEPENDENT PUBLISHERS AND AUTHORS!
castlebridgemedia.com